THE PETTICOAT LETTERS

KELLY LYMAN

Blue Tulip Publishing INC.

Photo Credit- Rachel Givler,

www.rachelizphotographer.com

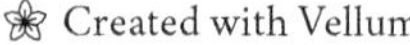

To my parents: Thank you for believing in me since my very first breath. For teaching me to never, ever give up and for dragging me to all the historic sites on the east coast when I was young. Words cannot express how thankful I am for you both. Love you.

CHAPTER 1

September 1776, Manhattan, New York

THE CLOCK CHIMED SEVEN. Any minute, the butler would usher us in to dinner, praise the Lord. But for now, he stood by the door looking as uncomfortable as I felt.

Uncle Edward and our dinner guest, Captain William Roth, stood next to the mantel deep in conversation. I could not hear what they were speaking about. From the rigid stance of both men, it was most likely about the war. The captain had looked as tense as a violin string since the moment he arrived. Did the man ever relax?

Aunt Lucinda sat on her French armchair, fanning herself nonstop with one hand while she sipped on a sherry in the other. Surely at any moment, her wig would cause a heat-stroke, for it was at least half a stone in height and likely weighed as much as a newborn baby.

"Nora, do look less miserable, please," she said then took a sip of her drink and fanned herself.

"My apologies, Aunt Lucinda. I suppose I'm just deep in thought again," I replied.

"Stop thinking so much. Nothing good comes from a lady thinking," Uncle Edward barked from across the room.

I looked up. My uncle had gone back to speaking with the captain, but the man studied me. I held his eye for only a second before looking down at my hands. The last thing I wanted was for him to suspect he made me uncomfortable, so I straightened my back and lifted my head.

Captain Roth acted very much like an English gentleman should, but a coldness hid behind his eyes that made me wary. Nothing was out of place on him. His bright, scarlet coat with long tails was exceptionally clean. It was split down the front, and his black cuffs were turned back, exactly as they should be. A gold coil braid on one shoulder glinted in the firelight, indicating he was an officer. His white powdered wig masked his black hair and was pulled back and tied with a red ribbon. A short sword hung at his side. I was positive he knew how to use it well. He was very handsome, and I was certain he most likely had an invitation to dinner every night of the week with a flock of mothers pushing their daughters in his direction — much like Aunt Lucinda was doing this very night.

My cousin, Hannah, made a disgruntled noise, barely audible to my own ears, and I held back a grin in agreement to her sentiment.

She leaned over. "Yes, we wouldn't want a female to have actual thoughts or feelings now, would we? Such a disgrace," Hannah whispered. She played the part of an obedient daughter so well she could become quite rich on the stage if she wanted.

I stifled a laugh, but no joy could be found in it.

The butler called us to dinner, somewhat easing the

tension in the room. I hoped the dinner conversation would be more congenial. By the grace of God, Hannah was seated next to the captain.

"Your uncle tells me you lost your family in a house fire a month ago, Miss Bishop. I'm sorry for your loss," Captain Roth said, though no hints of sorrow laced his voice.

My life now was vastly different from a month ago. Only four weeks prior, I'd lived at home with my parents and my siblings, John and Ruth. I had been engaged to David. And now? Now I was alone.

The pain of my parents' and sister's death from the house fire and of my beloved brother gone missing punched me in the gut. It always did when I thought about them too much. I clenched my jaw. Now was not the time to get emotional. Not when we had company. Uncle Edward would not like it.

"Tell me, were your family loyalists?" Captain Roth asked. The question lingered off his lips like bait on a hook. I flinched at the boldness of his comment and question.

I glanced at Hannah, who kept her eyes focused on her plate as though the venison was the most extraordinary thing in the world.

"They were, though I'm quite certain you know that, seeing as how you have a friendship with my uncle." Did he think he would set a trap of some sort, and I'd fall into it?

He smiled a wolfish grin, and I resisted the urge to shudder. "Mrs. Weller, I was delighted to receive your dinner invitation," he said to my aunt.

She batted her lashes and smiled.

"I did not think you would be able to come, Captain," Uncle Edward said between bites of meat, "since your troops do not plan on landing until the fifteenth—"

"Weller, I would ask that you refrain from discussing such matters with ladies present," Captain Roth said at the same time Hannah exclaimed, "Why, that's in nine days!" Hannah's eyes were wide, while the captain's had turned to slits.

"I see math is your forte, Miss Weller." Captain Roth did not bother to keep the sarcasm out of his voice.

"I meant it will be exciting! To see all the men parading in order, through the streets—"

"I don't think exciting is the word I would use, but, yes, it will be something bloody well to see. I'm sure the patriots will be simpering quite a bit once they see the British Navy coming into docks," I said, keeping my voice as light as possible, though it was far from how I felt.

How Hannah, or anyone for that matter, could be excited about more troops arriving was daunting to me. More troops meant more unrest and more battles. And more battles meant more bloodshed.

"Nora!" Uncle Edward said. He brought his fist down upon the table, and my aunt gasped. "I will not tolerate such behavior in this house! Do you wish to bring upon us a scandal? My apologies, Captain."

"Such language, Miss Bishop," the Captain said in a mocking tone.

I shrugged, my patience closely at its end. I wanted some semblance of my life back. A life that was not filled with the sound of men shouting and guns blasting. I wanted my family back. I wanted peace.

It was a relief when my part of the evening was over, and I was excused to my room. Sleep did not come easy as my thoughts stayed focused on my brother. I prayed over and over that he wasn't dead in a ditch but was found somewhere safe, even though safe these days was all a matter of opinion.

My head throbbed, so I decided to tiptoe downstairs to fix myself a cup of tea. Candlelight flickered in the front room, and the voices of my uncle and the captain filtered out into the hall.

"You are certain the troops arrive on the fifteenth?" Uncle Edward said.

"Assuming no storms at sea, then, yes, Weller." Captain Roth's voice was tight.

I knew I shouldn't listen. The tone of their voices hinted that the conversation was not meant for my ears, but I couldn't help it. All too often, men held their political discussions when the women weren't around, as though we weren't intelligent enough to take part in the dialogue.

"My house is open should any of the troops need a room."

"Seeing as how roughly four thousand men will be landing, I will keep that in mind."

"It will be a sight to behold to be sure. To see the city clothed in red. I look forward to watching the patriots' faces while they watch the fleet coming ashore!" Uncle Edward said, chuckling.

"That shan't happen as we don't plan to make the arrival known."

"Really?"

"A surprise assault is always best, Weller. Even a schoolboy recognizes a sneak attack works to his advantage while playing games," the officer said. "Those traitors won't know we're coming. It will be bloody and brilliant."

Victory laced Captain Roth's voice. I swallowed. He had clearly stated the British would launch a surprise assault on the fifteenth of the month. Hannah was right. That was only nine days away. Nine days away from more fighting. Good God. John was out there. Somewhere.

It was only a few days ago I had run into a childhood friend who had told me John was in Manhattan, though he had not been entirely certain of his exact whereabouts. I had resigned myself to never seeing him again after the death of my family since he did not come to find me. And now? *Bloody hell.* Now I had every reason in the world to make sure

I found him. Nine days. That was all I had to find my brother before the streets of Manhattan looked like London itself.

I carefully turned around on weak legs, tea forgotten, and snuck back to my room with a churning stomach.

CHAPTER 2

A WEEK LATER, I journeyed into the city, for I was to report to the apothecary where I worked. Mr. McGovern, who owned the shop, had agreed to continue the training (after much begging and pleading on my part) that my father had started with me before he died. Using the mortar and pestle gave me purpose. It was much better than sitting in my aunt's parlor doing nothing but gossiping with the local women. Once I had finished my few hours in the shop, I said my goodbyes and walked out the door.

Jeffery, my uncle's coachman, had opened the door to the coach when I saw an old childhood friend, Martin Bell, across the street. The same old friend who had told me my brother was in the city.

He had joined the cause a month before John, and I hoped beyond hope he could help me now. Without thinking or caring, I called after him.

"Martin!"

Martin stopped mid-stride and turned to look at me. He smiled, and the unease I'd been feeling since I had come to live with my uncle and aunt subsided, though only a little.

"Stay here, please. I'll be back," I said to the coachman and walked across the street.

"Nora Bishop, it is a pleasure, to be sure," Martin said, nodding. His eyes grew concerned. Everyone from my past looked at me with the same 'sorry for your loss' eyes. "How are you?"

"I'm well," I said for the sake of not wanting to hear pity in his voice. "And you? You're well?"

He nodded.

"I do not wish to delay you any further, so by chance, do you know John's whereabouts? Last we spoke, you mentioned he was in the city, but you did not know specifics."

"I do, Nora. But you're not going to go and look for trouble now, are you?"

"Now, Martin Bell, do I ever go looking for trouble?" I chuckled, but the word *trouble* made my stomach turn. The entire city of Manhattan was about to be in big trouble if what I had overheard was true.

"Ha! Should I recall all the times—"

"Trouble finds me."

"Indeed. John remains in the city. He's stationed at Kip's Bay Landing for now. Do you know where that's located?"

"Yes."

"You'll find him there," he said.

Restraining myself from hugging him, I placed my hand on his arm and squeezed it.

Not wanting to waste any time, I bade him farewell and made my way toward the water.

With it being the middle of September, the cool autumn temperature one expected came and went like the wind. The leaves, though still mainly green, were beginning to shift color. The closer I ventured to Kip's Bay Landing, the more the wind blew, rustling my hair in front of my face and wrapping my skirts around my legs. The sun was veiled by the storm clouds and the thick fogbank. The smell of rain hung in the air.

Militia stood guarding the landing, and I squinted against the sun to see them better. A swell of relief washed over me like waves lapping against the shore when I saw my brother, but I'd know him anywhere.

John rushed to greet me and wrapped me up in his arms.

The shock hit my system. For the first time since I'd witnessed my family's death, I wailed. He gripped me harder, and his own warm tears dampened my shoulder.

"Shh, Nora. I'm here. It will be all right. I promise," John said. He rubbed my back in circular motions as if I were a child.

In the moment, I felt as if I were one.

"What are you doing here? You should not be here."

"They're dead. Mama, Papa, Ruth… and… the house burned down, John. There was a fire! I've been living with Uncle Edward. He said you aren't welcome because… because you joined the Americans and—"

John tensed at the mention of our uncle, but he did not speak a word against him. "That's fine. What matters is you're safe. He'll keep you safe. You have to do what you must, Nora. We all must play our part in this war."

I clung to him, and after several minutes, he pulled back from me and wiped my eyes. I bit my lip to keep it from trembling. I had so much I needed to say to him, yet I had no idea how or where to start. I opened my mouth, but he stopped me.

"Nora, you need to leave. I don't want any redcoats seeing you with me," he said.

I flinched. "John, I have important information that you need to tell your commanding officer."

He stepped back from me and stared into my eyes. "What?"

"The British are going to invade New York. You have to run, John."

"How did you come by this information? Is it accurate?"

"I heard it from Captain William Roth. It's accurate."

His face blanched. "Nora, listen to me. You need to stay away from him. Try and persuade Uncle to stay away from him. There are stories about him. He's ruthless. He'll stop at nothing to get what he wants. Believe me."

"What exactly do you mean?" I asked, not liking the sound of it at all.

"He'll kill any who he thinks is in league with the enemy. Civilians, women, children. It doesn't matter."

I thought back to my introduction of the captain and every occasion I'd been in his presence since then. I shuddered. I didn't doubt the rumors John had heard were true.

"Did the good captain say when they were going to advance? The more information I can give Colonel Douglas the better, Nora. I'm new. I can't go with false material."

"I'd assume night. What better time to make a move if you didn't want your enemy to know you were doing so?"

"Yes. But the date." John turned around. "Michael!" He yelled.

A man ran over. He nodded to me, and John proceeded to tell him the news. As they talked, a whistling sound off the water came straight toward us.

Michael's head snapped up. "Take cover!"

The three of us turned and ran to hide behind a wagon as a cannonball flew over our heads and smashed into the hill behind us. I covered my ears and scrunched down. I peered out from behind the wagon and squinted while looking at the water. To my horror, eight to ten British ships of war were firing toward us. The vessels advanced, positioning themselves so the cannons fired on the very inexperienced militia. On John. And now, on me. The British clearly did not care to make a nighttime strike. They'd made their amphibious landing at eleven in the morning, and it worked.

The sky grew cloudy, and the wind stirred. Thunder clapped, and a huge bolt of lightning zapped across the sky. Rain pelted down; big, fat drops splattered the dirt making instant mud puddles everywhere. The mud splashed onto my gown. I shivered as the wet and wind bit into my skin, stinging it.

"Stay here, Nora," John said. "Watch for my signal. I'll wave to you, and when I do, run for the trees!"

"No! Don't leave me!"

"I have to. Now stay low and watch for me!" He loaded his gun and jumped out from our hiding spot and rushed toward the shore.

I followed him with my eyes, gasping for breath. My heart pounded in my ears. *Don't let him die. Please.* A shot rang out, and my focus landed on John.

A man to his right stopped and fell to the ground, his chest stained with blood.

I screamed.

My body trembled, yet I couldn't move, even if John hadn't ordered me not to. I watched in terror as men fell and gunshots fired, the echoes hurting my ears and the smoke all but blinding me. I buried my face in my hands, looking out through the slits between my fingers. I wanted to shut my eyes, but I could not keep from staring at John, following his every move and willing him to stay standing. I rocked back and forth.

The British ships continued to fire in our direction. When the smoke cleared, it was obvious why. They were protecting a flotilla of flat-bottomed boats ferrying British soldiers onto the shore of Manhattan. I stared at the East

River in wide-eyed horror. Thousands of redcoats were coming.

My brother shouted to me, but like the old maple tree near my family's home, my legs were rooted in place. I'd seen men die before while accompanying my father to the homes of the sick. People on their deathbed knew their time was limited, as did their loved ones. And, if they didn't, it was because they were so unconscious nothing mattered. For the most part, they were at ease. It was sad, yes, but a calmness surrounded them. However, seeing men fall on the battlefield was surreal. They'd been cheated, and they knew it. Their faces said it all.

"Nora!" John yelled, waving in my direction and sprinting toward me. "Nora! Run!"

Pushing the hysterics down, I jumped up and grabbed his hand as he ran past me. Men sprinted in every direction. I panted. My legs pushed against the upward slope of the hill as we ran from the docks toward the countryside. I flinched with each boom of cannon fire. The dirt exploded when the balls hit the surface, springing up out of the ground. Earth smacked into my body and onto my lips. By the time we reached the shelter of the trees, Kip's Bay Landing was swarming with British forces, the redcoats, chasing us out of the city and toward the woods.

CHAPTER 3

We were at the edge of the wood when I dared a glance back. I would have stayed frozen there if it hadn't been for John pulling me along. General George Washington himself sat atop a beautiful mount and rushed into the fray. He shouted and cussed at his men, while urging them to continue to fight on, only to watch them all flee to the cover of the trees. He slashed his sword back and forth in a purple rage and hit one of his men on the backside with the flat-end of his broadsword. His endeavor to rally his troops was valiant, but he failed. They ran in every direction, desperately searching for cover to escape the enemy forces. *Dear God, let him avoid capture.* The commander's aides grabbed his reins and pulled him from the field.

"Run, Nora!" John yelled at me, bringing me out of my stupor.

We were much too close to the battle. A shot fired at me, and the bullet pelted the ground at my feet. Chunks of earth flew up and hit my face. My heart thundered as sweat dripped off my brow and down my back.

"Now!" John hollered, pulling me in the opposite direction, away from the madness.

Branches sprang back, colliding with my face, and prickers scraped against my skin as my brother and I dashed between the trees. The wind and rain whipped my hair about, and my clothes clung to me. We jumped over fallen logs and rocks. I fell down, skinning and banging my knee. A musket shot zoomed over my head, biting into the bark of a nearby tree. *Damn it all to hell. We are going to die.* The soldiers were closer than I thought.

"Get down!" John said, pushing me to the ground behind a large boulder.

I winced and clutched my side. "I don't know… if I can run… anymore."

I couldn't breathe. *God, why can't I breathe? Am I shot?* My hands were shaking, but I detected no blood, only a pinch in my side from the cramp. *Focus. I need to focus.*

I shut my eyes to concentrate on my breathing, but it didn't help. The yelling and screaming of men and bullets didn't help either.

"Now what?" I said. "John! What are we going to do?" I didn't try to hide the panic in my voice. The sound of my own heartbeat thrashing around was almost too loud in my own ears.

John looked around as best he could from our position. "Do you see that opening over there?"

I nodded.

"There's a cave, hidden behind the brush. You have to run through it. And don't stop, no matter what you hear. Promise me, Nora. Even if I'm hurt."

I shook my head. "I can't leave you. I just found you again!"

"Nora. You have to go back to Uncle Edward. It isn't an option. I'm going to lead them away from here. Wait until nightfall to come out. If you're found, tell them a patriot tried to take you, and you didn't know where to go. Promise me," he said, shaking my shoulders.

"I promise," I said, though my voice was barely above a whisper.

John pulled me close and kissed me on the head. I breathed him in, making myself remember how he smelled. I feared it would be the last time I saw him. He released me and raised his head above the rock to peer out into the woods. He reached down and grabbed a handful of rocks. "Go. Now," he said, giving me a slight push.

I ran as fast as I could toward the brush he had pointed out. At the same time, he jumped up and ran in the other direction. I turned my head. John threw the rocks. A second later, shouting erupted. He'd accomplished what he set out to do. The lobsterbacks were following him, leaving me to my own devices.

By the time I reached the mouth of the small cave and found my way through all the brush, the sounds of gunshots were farther away. My chest heaved, and I clung to the stone surface of the dwelling. From the very little I could see, it wasn't a big cave. It could have been larger, but I did not possess the bravery to walk deeper into it. An anxious energy wove inside me. Was I encroaching on some animal's territory? *Dear God I hope not.*

I sunk down into the dirt, gulping for air and trying to breathe through the sobs. I grabbed my stomach as if I could find relief from my stays. *Oh, God. John.* I had found him only to lose him again. I tried to steady my breathing and get control of myself. John would be fine. He'd make it through. He had to. He was all I had left.

I squeezed my eyes shut and swiped angrily at the tears on my cheeks. Falling apart like this wouldn't do anyone any good. John was out fighting, and I was here weeping like, well, like a woman! I leaned my head back against the cave wall and laughed under my breath, still half-hysterical from everything that had happened over the past hour, thinking of all the times as a child I had gotten so furious whenever John said I couldn't join him and David in some game because I was a girl. Now John was fighting for the revolution and David... Well, once we'd been engaged. But that was before my family was slaughtered. Before David joined the redcoats. The hurt was fresh in my mind.

I had to be strong for John now. No more tears, no matter what happened next. And for whatever that might be, I needed my strength for it. I lay down on the cold earth and balled up like a baby. Shivering, I tried to rest.

* * *

ONLY A SLIGHT BREEZE blew the bushes and leaves around me when I woke and poked my head out of the cave. Gooseflesh rose on my skin. *Jesus, it is as cold as a winter's day.* My gown was damp from the rain and a bloody mess. Somewhere along the way, I had dropped my shawl, so I rubbed my arms with my hands, trying to bring some warmth into my body. I sneezed and sneezed again. I had to get warm. I had to get back to my uncle's home. I remained still and silent inside my meek shelter and listened to the outside world. All was calm. It was time to leave.

Dusk had fallen, and the sky glowed orange. The woods were eerily quiet save for the sounds of the cicadas and crickets, which were as loud as gunshots. I couldn't believe how close I had come to being caught. And John. I had to find him. Had he been captured? Dead? No. I would not think of those things. My brother was alive, and he was safe with the rest of the militia. He had to be.

My heart thrashed violently in my chest as I scrambled

over fallen tree branches and rocks through the thick forest. My hands stung from scrapes, and my feet were tired. My only thought was to get far away from the area as quick and as quiet as possible. There would be patrols wandering through, and the last thing I needed at this point was to meet one.

The plan to reenter my uncle's house, undetected, was at the forefront of my mind. How would I do that? I'd been out all day. I supposed it was something I would worry about later. For now, I had to worry about going in the right direction. My Brunswick was filthy, and the bottom was torn. I was a horrid mess. It would be a bear to mend. Would I need to burn my dress? At least it had been made for traveling.

Having no idea of the direction I walked or should go, I decided my best course of action was to follow the small creek.

After walking for another twenty minutes in the silent wood, I stopped and leaned over the creek to dip my hands into the cool water. I winced as the steady current washed away the dirt and flowed over my scratches before I shut my eyes and took a deep breath; the first one I had taken in a while, and I focused my energy on having my heartbeat return to normal. Once my hands no longer stung, I scooped up a handful of the water and did my best to take a sip before it all slipped out through my fingers.

The water dripped down my chin and the front of my dress, but I didn't care. It was wet, ice-cold, and quenched my thirst, and that was all I wanted. I slurped and was about to stick my face down into the creek when I froze. The sound of a branch snapping reached my ears. My heart, which had only returned to normal, beat frantically again. As casually as I could, I turned my head to look over my shoulder but saw nothing. I stood up and brushed my hands off on my petticoat and began walking once again, wanting to get out of danger, should it be that. *Please let it only be an animal. A squirrel. I can deal with a squirrel.*

I had taken ten paces when a man stepped out in front of me, causing me to run straight into him. A scream stuck in my throat. I couldn't move or make a noise. The man reached out and grabbed my shoulders. I jerked away and lost my balance. My body shook, and I grabbed hold of a nearby tree to steady myself.

The man looked around, and his eyes narrowed. "Who might you be, and what are you doing out in the woods, at dusk, alone?"

His dark brown hair was coming loose out of the leather strap that attempted to keep it secure. His mouth was set in a thin line, and his blue eyes pierced me in place. Goodness, he was very handsome. And, he was very intimidating, but I was not going to be terrorized by the likes of him. I had gone through too much to be bullied by a man. Especially a soldier.

"Who I am and where I'm going is none of your concern, sir," I said, lifting my chin, showing more courage than what I felt.

My heart hammered as we considered each other. He was dangerous; I wasn't ignorant to the fact, yet, a softness hid behind his gaze, giving me reason to believe he would not hurt me. Or at least I hoped so. He was, after all, still a man, and I was unnerved to find myself alone. My gaze flicked to his side, and I swallowed, but my mouth was dry. A tomahawk and small hunting knife hung on his hips, while in his hands he held a flintlock pistol. My legs shook when he raised it and pointed it at my chest.

"I asked you who you are and where you were going, madam," he said, staring at me full on, though his eyes did not hold any threatening luster.

I raised my chin and snorted, hoping to convince him he

did not have any effect on me. *God, he's handsome. And tall. He's the tallest man I've ever seen.* "And are you going to shoot me if I don't answer then?" I snapped.

He cocked his head to the side as if he was considering my question. I bit the inside of my cheek waiting for his response. *Bloody hell, what will I do if he says yes?*

"No. In truth, I don't want to harm you, nor do I have the strength at this moment." His eyes wandered over my person. He lowered his pistol. "Though you don't look very heavy, so I could manage to throw you over my good shoulder if need be," he said, shifting his weight. He winced, and his face paled.

I glanced at both his shoulders and grimaced at the amount of blood oozing down his injured left side. If I could keep him talking and standing long enough, maybe he'd faint, and I could go on my way.

"And why would you feel the need to throw me over your shoulder?"

"Because you're coming with me."

"I most certainly am not."

"You are. I can't, in good conscience, allow you to traipse all through these woods alone. Besides, I haven't quite determined if you're a spy."

"A spy?" I said, having a hard time believing my ears. "You're daft. What sort of idea is that? Do I look like a spy?"

"Nothing better than a spy with breasts. They are the least suspecting. It doesn't help that you're in the wrong place at the wrong time."

I resisted the urge to cover up and straightened my spine instead.

"I am no spy, sir. Now please step out of the way so I can continue on with my journey."

"You'll come back with me to camp. And, spy or not, it isn't safe for a lady to be out here alone."

He took a step toward me.

"I know where I'm going," I said, watching him sway. *Is he going to faint?*

"And where is that?"

"You're hurt." I gestured toward him, dismissing his question.

The corner of his mouth turned up though his face grew whiter still. "Believe me, I know."

He put his pistol inside the waist of his pants and took a few clumsy steps toward an oak tree where he leaned up against its bark. He closed his eyes for a moment and took a deep breath. When he opened them, he stared into my eyes. His look was so open and honest my heart lurched, and I could not but help take a couple of steps toward him.

He twitched a bit, then his legs gave out from under him. He slid down the bark of the tree. "What are you doing?" he said, eyeing me.

I knelt beside him and pulled back his shirt collar. My eyes grew wide. "Christ," I said. "It's a wonder you were still standing."

I ripped the edge of my petticoat, which had fortunately — or unfortunately, depending on one's opinion — already torn. I pulled hard when I thought I had enough linen, but because of the hem, it was difficult. "Bloody hell!" I said, not bothering to whisper. I didn't know what possessed me in this moment. I shouldn't be caring after a man who thought me a spy. But I couldn't leave him here to die.

The man moved, and when I looked up, he had pulled his dagger out of his belt and was handing it to me. I took it, carefully, and went back to work, slicing through the fabric. After a few pulls, the rest of the petticoat strip came off, and I laid the dagger on the ground.

"Has anyone ever told you that you have the mouth of a sailor?"

"Yes."

"It's not very ladylike to take the good Lord's name in vain, you know, or to curse." Though he rebuked me, his eyes were full of mischief.

"It also isn't very ladylike for me to rip my petticoat, but there's nothing to be done about it now, is there? Besides, right now, I don't care."

"Are you going to give my knife back to me?" the man asked, his head drooping to the side. "Or don't you trust me with it?"

I resisted the urge to lash out at him, knowing it would not help, and slid it back into its place on his belt.

It was dusk, and I knew I only had a few precious moments to secure his wound with the strip of petticoat before I would have to do it in the dark. I moved up to where he sat, shoulder to shoulder with him.

"You'll need to take your jacket off and your shirt if I'm going to dress this wound," I said.

He nodded, then sat up and sucked in air through his teeth. "I'll need some help, if you don't mind."

I took a steadying breath and helped him out of his jacket and shirt, very aware that his eyes never left my face. He only made a small sound when I pulled on the linen clinging to his shoulder as it adhered to the wound. I glanced at him then adverted my gaze, doing my best to keep my face neutral as I looked closer at his shoulder. A slice, running about the width of my hand ran vertically from the top of his shoulder coming down, stopping above his chest.

"Do you have a canteen?" I asked. "I need to wash your wound. I can't tell how deep the cut is."

"Yes, on my horse. Over there." He jerked his head to behind the oak tree where we sat.

I stood up and approached the big brown animal. It had a white streak running down the front of its face.

Not only did I find his water canteen, but I found a flask of rum or maybe whiskey, as well. He would need the burning liquid for the pain. I took the canteen and refilled it in the creek before pouring it over the man's wound. He closed his eyes and breathed deep, but never said anything.

"Bayonet?" I asked.

"How'd you guess?"

I snorted. "Not hard, seeing as how it looks like all twenty-one inches of it slashed at you."

"Not quite. But, yes almost. Luckily, I turned last second."

"Luckily, indeed, or you would be dead."

"Hmph," he said. "Have you ever met one of the Hessians?"

"No. Though I've heard the stories." And I had. These German troops were hired by the British to help them fight against the American militia. They showed no mercy and were excellent at using their bayonets, which was now evident in looking at the wound before me.

"I pray you never meet them. They're quite fond of their bayonets."

"It appears so. From the little I can see, it isn't too deep, and it is clotting up on its own. You could use a stitch or two though. I don't have the supplies needed, and I know I can't do it in the dark."

"You can stitch?"

"All ladies can stitch. You do know it is one of the pleasures we do to occupy our time," I said dryly.

Without waiting for his reply and without fair warning, I poured the rum I found on his wound. He grunted, and his body jolted, his legs digging into the leaf-clothed earth. He hissed through his teeth.

"That hurt! What the hell did you do that for?"

"Sorry. It helps clean a wound. Here, take a sip. I'm going to pour it on you one more time."

He obeyed and took a gulp. He coughed but then leaned his head back and shut his eyes.

"Ready?"

He nodded and as I poured the liquid over his bloody wound, his face contorted into a grimace. "I can't picture you sitting and enjoying needlework," he said through gritted teeth.

"You would be correct in that assumption, sir."

"Alex," he said.

I raised my eyebrows at the mention of his name, never thinking to ask because I never thought he would give it away.

"Alexander Foster," he said, meeting my eyes. "And now will you tell me your name, Sailor?" The corner of his mouth turned up.

I hesitated for a moment. "I'm Nora Bishop."

And then, Alexander Foster's eyes rolled into the back of his head, and he fainted.

CHAPTER 4

HAVING NO SMELLING SALTS on me, I could only wait. Leaving was probably the best choice, but I found I couldn't. Alex Foster's frame was intimidating. He was easily over six feet and had a very strong and natural athletic build. He had sharp, angular features, and his arms were twice the size as mine. Simply so I could say I tried, I put my arms under his and giving a very unladylike grunt, raised him up. Unable to lift him, I sat down and waited.

After what seemed like half a day, but was only a half hour or so, Alex moaned and stirred.

"Shhh," I said.

Laying my hand on his head, I checked for fever, but his skin was cool to the touch. Thankfully.

"Mr. Foster? How are you feeling?"

"It's Alex," he said.

My face warmed at the idea of using his Christian name.

"And, I feel like I've been poked like a pig and shot for Easter dinner."

"Well, that's pretty much true. Can you sit up, or do you need help?"

I put my arm under his shoulder once again, but he flinched at my touch, so I yanked my hand away.

"I can manage. Thank you," he said.

"I tried to move you earlier, but couldn't. You must weigh about twenty-five stone."

He chuckled. "I don't think I weigh that much. Twenty maybe," he said, giving me a grin.

The moon was full, casting off enough light allowing me to make out his features, but more importantly, his wounds.

"I should have a look at your shoulder," I said.

When he didn't move, I reached toward him and lifted up the linen that was now more brown and red than white. He sucked in a breath but otherwise didn't say anything. "The bleeding has stopped. That's good. Looks like you won't need a stitch after all. Unless it opens up again. Do your best not to move it."

"And how do you propose I do that?"

I shrugged. "Keep it still?"

"Hmph."

Alex stood, with only a little bit of help from me, and walked to his horse. He stroked the animal's nose and muttered in its ear. The horse snorted as if answering him. "We best get on our way, then. I would guess a patrol will be around these parts soon. We're lucky they haven't come yet."

"I told you already that I'm not going with you." I put my hands on my hips, trying to imitate my mother when she gave a command to my father and brother. The very thought of her made my heart ache, but I pushed it down. Now was not the time for those thoughts.

"And I told you I can't allow a lady to wander around the woods, especially now when it is night. There are British patrols all over the place. Your husband would kill me if I let anything happen to you. I promise I'll see you safe tomorrow."

"My husband?" I said, scrunching up my nose.

Alex gave me a questioning glance.

"I was once engaged, but believe me when I say I have no husband." I wanted to add that David was a bastard, but I refrained from doing so.

"I assumed—"

"You shouldn't assume," I snapped. I folded my arms and looked away from him. I was resolved to no longer waste any tears over David Shipman.

Alex grinned and his eyes lit up. "I'll remember that then."

In the end, he won our argument, and I ended up sitting in front of him on his horse, heading west toward the American forces' camp. More than anything, I wanted to see whether my brother was there.

Aside from the horse's footsteps through the leaves, the only sound to be heard was the cicadas and the occasional owl. The moon, being bright, helped Alex navigate his horse through the woods as if it were the middle of the day. My teeth chattered, and my body tensed, my muscles trying to warm themselves.

Alex pulled on his horse's reins, whose name I discovered was Bridger, and reached behind him into the saddle. He retrieved a wool blanket from his pack and draped it over my shoulders.

We traveled through the woods, both quiet, and after an hour, the awkwardness began to roll away, like swells in the ocean gently moving along.

"You never told me why you were tramping through this part of the woods," Alex said, dispersing the silence between us.

My back stiffened. "I wasn't tramping around in the woods for pleasure, you can be sure of that." Uncertain of how much I should tell him, but knowing there would be no way I'd find John without him, meant I had to trust someone. And Alex was obviously part of the American forces since he was taking me to their camp. "If you must know, I was with my brother. He led the redcoats away from me while I hid inside some sort of a cave," I said.

"Cave?"

"Yes. I was there at Kip's Bay when the English attacked. We ran up the hill and through the woods before my brother made me run inside. The mouth of the cave is small. Only a few people could get in the opening. I didn't walk all the way through."

"Hmph. You must have been inside Twins Cave," he said matter-of-factly.

"Twins Cave?"

"Given the name because long ago, a set of twins were found inside, dead, clinging to each other. Brother and sister, I was told. The story goes they were lost during a snowstorm and found the small opening and went inside for shelter. Unfortunately, the snow won."

"That's so sad. Is it true?"

Alex shrugged behind me. His chest moved against my back. "I'm sure there is some truth to it. Though it was well before my time. In any case, where's your brother now?"

It was my turn to shrug. Tears welled up in my eyes, but I blinked them away. I did not want to discuss the potential loss of my brother because if I talked about it, it would be true. I wasn't ready to deal with the idea that he was either dead or captured.

"What's his name?" Alex asked, his voice soft.

"John Bishop."

"I don't know him, but I'm sure we'll find something out once we get to camp."

"And where exactly is camp?"

"If I had to guess, General Putnam is gathering the forces near Harlem Heights, so we'll head there. From what I could see earlier, the British have certainly taken over New York, or at least the lower half of it anyway. I was going there when I stumbled upon you."

"You mean when you ambushed me?"

"Ah, now. Ambushed is a pretty harsh word, no?"

I snorted. "Bloody hell. You pointed a gun at me."

"I'm sorry for it," he said, his voice leaving no room for disbelief. "I'd come from a fight, you see. The battle was still raging through my veins. I'm very glad you didn't scream."

"Well, I still could you know," I said, keeping my voice light. "You did have blood dripping from you and then fainted, so I suppose I thought you weren't a threat." Though, in reality, I was quite alarmed at finding myself alone in the woods and with a strange man who I didn't know was friend or foe. I could have left him easily enough when he was unconscious, but a small, still voice from within nudged me to stay and help him. I hoped I hadn't been wrong in my actions.

He stopped Bridger, causing me to look over my shoulder and up at him.

"Rule number one, Sailor. Every man is a threat. It doesn't matter what color he wears. Until you know for certain, consider everyone your enemy until they prove it otherwise. You have to assume everyone means to do you harm."

At first, annoyance flashed through me at the use of the nickname, but his clear and steady blue eyes did not mock me. He was sincere in trying to give me advice to keep me safe, so I pushed my frustration aside.

"These are uncertain times. Do you understand?" he said.

"And what are you? My friend or my enemy?"

"If I was your enemy, we wouldn't be having this conversation. You can be sure of that."

My stomach rolled, and I cleared my throat. "Well, then, I'm quite glad I know where I stand with you." And I was. For as sure as I knew my name, I instinctively knew Alex Foster was not one to cross.

He nodded and clicked his tongue, urging Bridger to continue on.

My heart raced with his opinion. Only a few months ago, I could have walked down the road and not worried about anything. Everyone knew me, the countryside was at a relative peace. Now though, he was right. War brought out the wild nature in almost everyone. More so in men.

"Is there a rule number two?"

"If you're in trouble, try to hide where there is natural action going on — a town, a tavern. Blend in the best you can. Take to the forest if you must. If you're quiet enough, the animals will tell you when a threat is near, man or animal."

"Noted," I said, hoping there would never be reason to take cover in the woods again. Once was enough for me. "Why not hide in the forest the entire time?"

He snickered. "I could. You couldn't. You don't know enough to live off the land. Hell, I bet you didn't even know what direction to go when I found you."

I bit my tongue. He was right, and I hated it. "Any more rules I should know about?" I asked, laughing off his comment.

"Ah, well, there is the rule about thanking a person who has done you a favor," he said. "So, thank you for fixing me up when you could have left me for dead."

"You're welcome."

"I want to know why though."

"Why what?"

"Why did you help me and not leave me?"

I remained quiet for a moment as a memory of my father surfaced.

I accompanied him one day to the home of a sick man. But not any sick man. Mr. Artly was a known enemy of my father's. Father had said from the time they were boys, neither had got on well with the other. He claimed it all started when Mr. Artly spoke falsely about my father's sister. Father admitted he'd lost his cool, and so he fixed Mr. Artly's nose for him. In any case, I asked my father why we were helping the man, given their history.

"Nora. You always help someone when you can. Whether you want to or not. Whether you like them or not. If suffering can be eased and you can help it to be so, it is your obligation. You don't have to like someone to help them, but you do have to like yourself when you glance in the looking glass."

"I was taught that you should always help someone when you can," I said, not delving into any more detail.

"Who taught you that logic?"

"My father."

"He's a smart man."

"Was. *Was* a smart man." A lump formed in my throat, and I choked back tears. Not for the first time did I wonder if I would ever get to a point where I wouldn't feel like falling apart thinking about my family. Would this feeling of living in a black pit of grief ever go away?

"I'm sorry," he said.

I nodded but didn't say anything more for fear of the black pit swallowing me whole in front of him. In a matter of a month, I'd lost my father, mother, sister, my home, and now, maybe my brother. Christ, I would ring John's neck when I saw him for joining the war. If I ever saw him again. Thankfully, Alex didn't push me into further conversation.

A few moments later when I regained control of myself, I cleared my throat. "I've never had the chance to say thank you as well. For bringing me to safety now."

"Yes, well, our fathers would have gotten along, I think. It's been a tiring day, and we have many more miles to go tonight. Lay your head back and rest as you can."

I did as Alex suggested and only from pure exhaustion was I able to drift off to sleep, on top of a horse, no less, and in a stranger's arms.

CHAPTER 5

Alex shook my shoulders and put Bridger into a trot, jarring me awake. "We're here, Nora," Alex said. His mouth was close to my ear, and his warm breath brushed against my neck when he spoke.

I shivered at the sound of my real name on his lips, hoping he would assume it was from the cold air. The moon still lit the way, and I wondered what time it was. Surely, morning was not too far off.

As Alex and I rode toward the campsite, everything remained quiet, as if an invisible blanket of snow had fallen and hushed the world. It hadn't taken much intelligence to realize the troops were severely defeated physically and emotionally. While we gained further in our stride, my stomach turned to a swarm of butterflies. Was John here? Would the American militia hurt me?

A sentry stepped out in front of us, and Alex reined in Bridger, who snorted and stomped at the intrusion. He was a large man with a nose like a turnip.

"Who goes there?" he said. Even from atop the great

horse, the smell of rum wafted off the guard's breath. He stood erect enough. Clearly, the liquor had no effect on him.

"Alexander Foster, Ranger," Alex said.

"What's with the delay then?" The man strode toward us and grabbed hold of Bridger's bridle.

Bridger shook his head, but Alex patted his side. He calmed down immediately, and without realizing it, my nerves calmed as well. *How did he do that?*

"And who's this?" the man demanded, eyeing me up and down. His eyes rested on my exposed ankle.

Alex must have noticed the man's gaze because his arms tightened around me, and he moved Bridger in such a way as to make the guard step back.

"Billy, what's going on over here?" another male voice said. This man walked through the tree and stopped when he saw us. As he neared, Billy took it as his cue to leave. "My, my… Si's going to have your hide when he sees you, Alex my boy. He's been scared out of his mind. Where the hell have you been?"

"And you haven't been scared, then? Glad to know my welfare means that much to you," Alex said, grinning.

"I have more faith in you, that's all."

The man was only a few inches shorter than Alex but just as broad-shouldered with narrower hips and a strong jawline. He had reddish brown hair, which was cut short. Like Alex, his features were angular, strong. The two men looked similar, but I didn't think they were brothers. Cousins perhaps?

Alex swung down off Bridger and moved to the newcomer's outstretched hand. They shook then hugged each other. Alex winced, and the man stepped back.

The man glanced from me to Alex and raised his brow in a questioning look.

"This must be why you're late. Want to tell me now or later?"

"Later," Alex said. He turned to me, and I nodded. "And it isn't what you think. Gideon, this is Nora Bishop."

"Hmph."

"I told you I'd explain later, you old goat," Alex said, though Gideon only seemed to be ten years his senior. "I want to get her warm and get some food in her belly. She's had quite the shock."

"I'm sure she did, having to ride with you all the way here."

"Come on, Sailor," Alex said to me, smiling.

Alex walked, weaving Bridger and me through the rows of soldiers as we followed Gideon. No tents were erected, which surprised me as did finding many men awake, though the sky was still dark.

Hardly a person spoke. They sat, weary-eyed and battle-burned, huddled around small fires and each other for warmth. *God. Winter hasn't even arrived yet. What will they do then?* Some men never bothered to look up as we walked past them. The only sounds drifting in the air were of men snoring, coughing, farting, and sneezing. An occasional conversation, whispered around a fire, could be heard on the breeze, but for the most part, the camp was silent. The men were too tired, and they had nothing to celebrate. The redcoats had all but taken over New York.

The smell of sweat and blood lingered in the air as we made our way across the camp. I held tighter to Bridger's pommel as I had never been in the company of so many men before and didn't dare to allow my gaze to fall too long on any one person.

I sensed rather than saw Alex glance back at me as he led the horse through the camp. He gave me a half-hearted smile while my insides shook. Surely by now, my aunt and uncle thought me dead. Would they even bother to look for me?

"You doing all right?" Alex asked.

"I'm fine. Mr. Foster?"

"Alex, please."

"Alex. Where are their tents?" I asked, my voice hesitant.

"They won't be needing them tonight. Either they were told not to set up camp, for we're moving out early, or the commanding officers think we might be at battle again come morning. No use having a tent if you're going to be fighting."

My stomach swirled at the mention of fighting. The last twenty-four hours were taking their toll. I didn't think I could stand to see the sight of men dying again. How did these men do this? No wonder their eyes were empty.

We came to a stop right behind Gideon, who walked over and took Bridger's bridle. Alex turned and said something to him, but I didn't know what. Gideon's eyes flickered to me, and he nodded but said nothing. Alex came to my horse's side and helped me off the saddle.

"Here we are, then. Home sweet home. For the next few hours at least."

A small fire flickered in the dark. The campsite was set apart from the other soldiers. One man lay on the ground, sleeping, using his blanket as a pillow. Another pack of bedding sat next to him, and I wondered if it was Gideon's.

I had the urge to run away. Here I stood, with a man who I did not know, in an army camp, far away from home. I wrapped my arms around myself as if the motion alone would make me smaller.

Alex reached up and grabbed the wool blanket I'd been using earlier and draped it over my shoulders. Once the covering was settled over me, he turned his attention back to his saddle. "Now," he said, moving to his bags and yanking them off the horse. "Take this and eat it." He reached inside his bag then pulled out a hard biscuit along with a small parcel of dried beef and handed it to me. "It's not much, but it will fill your stomach for the moment. Gideon will stay here with you. I'll be back."

I clutched my hands together and darted a gaze between Alex, Gideon, and the man sleeping on the ground. My insides quivered. I didn't like the idea of being without Alex, though he assured me of my safety. "Where are you going?" I said, hoping he couldn't detect anxiety in my voice.

"I have to go to talk to my commanding officer. I won't be long. Don't worry," he said.

"I'm not worried. I—"

John had always told me I wore my every emotion on my face. *"I can read you like a book,"* he used to say. So could Alex, apparently.

Alex placed a reassuring hand on my shoulder and looked me in the eyes. "There's no need to be scared of anything. Understand? I promise nothing will happen to you. Gideon here will also make sure of it. Now try and rest a bit. I have a feeling we'll be moving early."

"I need to check your wound," I said out of the blue, trying my hand at anything to keep him with me longer.

He touched his shoulder and winced. "You've gone this long without looking at it. I think it can wait another half hour or so, no?"

Alex nodded and turned around, leaving me alone with Gideon and the sleeping man.

"Well, now, lass. Have a seat by the fire and rest like Alex told you," Gideon said.

The other soldier gave a snort and Gideon kicked him in the leg.

"Ouch!" he grumbled. "What the hell was that for? Leave a sleeping man lie, will you?"

"Sit up, you wee bugger. A lady is present," Gideon said, nudging him again.

The soldier on the ground mumbled something under his breath and rubbed his eyes before sitting up. He looked me once over and shook his head. "I hope you didn't buy her for me, Gideon. She's not my type. Too scrawny in the top," the man said.

Instinctively, I folded my arms over my chest so nobody else would make such an observation as Gideon smacked the man over the head.

"She's no whore, you dope. Does she look like one?" Gideon asked.

The dope of a man, who was as tall as Alex and Gideon, but not as stocky, looked me over again and raised his brows. I couldn't blame him for his reasoning. No other women were near this part of the camp, and my dress was torn and filthy. His face was scruffy and his dark hair was long and tied back, though most of it was coming undone.

"Who is she then?"

"Nora Bishop, may I introduce my arse of a brother, Josiah, or Si for short. Si, this is Nora Bishop, a, ah... friend of Alex's," Gideon said.

At the mention of Alex's name, Si stood up. "Beg your pardon, miss. A friend of Alex's is a friend of mine. Where is the lad? I'd like to wallop him over the head."

"He went to talk to the captain," Gideon said. "Now, be a gentleman and get the lady a drink, if you please."

Si picked up his canteen then walked away. I assumed he was heading toward a water source I did not see. A few moments later, he strode back, gave me his wooden canteen, and sat down next to me.

"Go on and eat. Alex will be right pissed if you don't," Si said, eyeing the food still in my hands.

I nibbled the biscuit, feeling too overwhelmed to eat.

Exhaustion weighed my body down now that I found myself sitting near a warm fire. The food was hard and dry and crumbled in my mouth, making it hard to swallow. What I wanted was a good drink. Both gentlemen watched me as I ate, no doubt wondering what the story was on how I came to be in the American forces' camp. Surprisingly, I didn't feel threatened by them and found myself at ease, though uncomfortable since they were staring at me while I chewed.

I cleared my throat. "Are you both related to Alex then?"

"What gave it away?" Si said. "The handsome face or the bulging muscles?" He flexed his arm and waggled his eyebrows. He did not have the muscles Alex did, but he was by no means puny. A round belly sat on top of his belt but with his height, he carried it well. I had no doubt he was a strong man.

"Hardly," Gideon said. "Little Alex is our cousin. Our fathers were siblings."

"Little?" I said, stifling a laugh. "I should think not."

"That's true. He's a few inches taller than both of us now. Ah, but he's younger, you see. And when he came along, we all designated him as Little Alex, not to confuse him with his father, his namesake," Si said. "We promised his sister we'd keep him safe, but the lad has a way of getting into trouble no matter where we are. He's always wandering off somewhere doing who knows what..." He waved a hand at me, indicating I was the latest who knew what.

Confirming this, he said, "Which leads me to believe that's how you came to be with him. So now I'd like to know, Miss Bishop, is how did my younger cousin end up in your company since we've come to an agreement that you are no whore."

I choked on the biscuit and coughed. "Well—"

"Leave the lady alone, would you, Si?" Alex said, behind us. He walked forward, his face grim as if he'd received a bad bit of news. "She doesn't need you interrogating her. But if you want to know, even though I told Gideon I'd tell you old fools later, she saved my life."

"Barely," I said. "I dressed your wound."

"A wound, yes, which if hadn't been taken care of, I could have bled out."

I didn't bother to correct him. A look of concern spread across both Gideon's and Si's faces. They both regarded him from head to toe, their expression returning to neutral once they were satisfied he was fine.

"Alexander. Glad to see you graced us with your presence," Si said. He met Alex halfway and looked him over the same way Gideon first had upon seeing him. Once convinced he'd not been injured, he did, in fact, wallop him on the head.

"What was that for?" Alex said, rubbing the spot Si hit.

"That, wee Alex, was for making me worry that I'd have to send word to your sister explaining something had befallen you."

"Well, praise the Lord for small miracles, or you would be meeting me at the pearly gate as well."

"Hmph," Si said. "You speak the truth in that. Are you going to tell us what happened to you? One second you were there with us fighting, and the next you were off. And what's this business about this girl here saving your life?"

Alex's eyes narrowed, then he glanced at me. "Something came up I had to take care of. As for her, I found her alone in the wood. She dressed my wound and stayed with me after I passed out," Alex said, pulling down the collar of his shirt and showing them the self-made bandage I'd put together.

"And do you care to explain what that *something* was that came up?" Si said.

"Not at the moment, no."

Alex walked over to where I sat and knelt beside me, looking at the half-eaten biscuit and dried beef in my hand.

"You didn't eat everything I gave you," Alex said.

"I'm not that hungry," I said, meaning it. Even though it had been a full twenty-four hours since I'd last eaten. *Was it that long ago I first found John and then lost him?* I found I had little appetite. How could I eat when John could be starving?

"Be that as it may, you need to eat. It might be a while until you can fill your belly again," he said, nodding toward the food. "And you need your strength."

I raised the beef and took another bite to satisfy him. My stomach churned. *Bloody hell. I hope I don't throw up.*

"And what do you plan on eating then?" Si said, crossing his arms, glaring at his younger cousin.

Alex had given me his portion of rations. I lowered the food from my lips. I held it out for him to take the rest, but he only shook his head and reached inside his coat pocket and pulled out half an apple. He handed it to me.

"I already ate," he said. When I didn't take the apple, he plopped it into my lap.

Gideon sat silent, watching the scene before him, digging dirt out from under his nails with his small hunting knife.

Alex stood up, signaling the conversation was over. "Miss Bishop, when you're finished, I found a more comfortable spot for you to sleep. It's a bit farther away from all the men," he said.

Wanting to find something else to do other than sit and make idle conversation with men who I'd only just met, I rose and brushed off my skirts. "I'm ready now. I'll finish the food over there. Thank you." I turned toward Si and Gideon, bid them goodnight, and followed Alex away from his campsite and the rest of the army.

"Alex? Why are there two campsites?" I asked. Alex and his cousins, along with another one hundred men or so, were camped away from the main army.

"Ah, well. We're Rangers. Unruly, if you ask the rest of the men and most of the officers. The majority of the Rangers don't take too kindly to orders and discipline, so they keep us out here. Far enough away so the real Continentals don't take on our bad habits, but close enough to help if need be," he said.

"You don't seem too unruly to me."

He chuckled and ran his hand through his hair. "I try not to be," he said, his face reddening. "I'm not truly a Ranger. Well, we don't get paid like they do at least. My cousins and I help them out. That's why I can come and go as I please."

"Let me guess. You don't like to take orders either?"

"Ha! I'm used to taking orders, Sailor. I had four older sisters and have lived with Gideon and Si. No, truthfully, I never wanted to fight, but there's a debt I mean to collect, and it will be easier to do it knowing I can go where and when I want."

"Had?"

"Two of them died. One when I younger and the other a few years back. My second and third sisters, Molly and Jane, and I are all that's left."

He didn't say more on the subject, so I didn't push it. We walked in silence to the small campsite he'd made for me. Once settled, only a few yards away, but far enough to offer me some privacy, I relaxed and sighed. My legs and back burned as if I'd been doing chores all day, and I was weary. Incredibly weary. I'd been doing my best to keep it together since I'd found Alex, but the events of the past day were catching up to me. The tiny bit of seclusion Alex had provided for me was enough to make me fall apart.

I pulled my knees up to my chest and laid my head in between them. I shook and bit my lip, trying not to cry. I was far away from the safety of my uncle's house, my brother was lost, and I was in the American camp among too many men. My entire body ached, and I didn't know if it was from being in the saddle all day or from the stress of everything. Probably both.

At the sound of sticks banging together, I looked up. Alex had built a small fire. He blew on the flame, and it rose higher in the air, casting a soft glow on his features. I studied him while he did this. Why would he go to so much trouble to rescue and help me?

After a beat of awkward silence between us, Alex spoke. "I'll bid you goodnight then," he said. "You should be able to get at least a few hours rest before the camp stirs and the sun rises. I'll be right over there." He indicated a tree close by. "Don't worry. I can see you should anyone try to disturb you. Gideon and Si will keep an eye out too."

"They seem awfully protective of you."

A sheepish smile spread over his face. "Ah well, we're family." He shrugged as if that explained it all. "We help each other."

"What will happen to me in the morning?" I asked, thinking of my Aunt Lucinda and Uncle Edward. It saddened me that they were not as protective of me as Alex's family was of him. It was so very hard for me to know I wasn't wanted.

"Lieutenant David Knowlton would like to see you, so I'll take you to him. Sleep well, Sailor," he said.

Alex left me alone. His tall, sturdy frame distanced itself from me, and anxiety settled in the pit of my stomach. My senses tuned in to the world around me. The crackling fire. The insects chirping. An owl hooting in the distance. I squeezed my eyes tight, wanting to focus on the sounds around me and drown out my thoughts, but it was hard to do. *I have to see a lieutenant? Whatever for? Did Alex tell him I'm a spy and is he only being kind for the time being?*

I lay down on the wet grass, thankful for the large wool blanket Alex had given me and shook my head to clear it.

Don't worry about tomorrow. It will take care of itself. Exhausted, I fell asleep wondering what Alex would use to keep warm.

Sometime later, I woke to yelling and the stomping of feet, both horses' and men's.

"Nora!" Alex's voice summoned to me through the morning fog. "Wake up. We have to go. It's starting." He pulled the warm blanket off me.

I sat up, my eyes wide at the commotion around me. How could I have slept through such a thing? "What's starting? What's happening?" I looked around, frantic. My own heart-beat was loud in my ears.

"I just came back. Myself and the rest of the Rangers," he said, his voice urgent. "I rushed back as fast as I could. You have to get to safety. Now. The British are almost upon us. Washington ordered all one thousand brigades to advance directly toward them. I can't protect you here."

Bile rose in my throat. "What? I don't understand." My eyes darted all around me. Men ran all over the place, shouting orders. It was a frenzy.

"Battle, Nora. We are about to engage in battle. Hurry up!"

"What are you going to do?" I said, standing up. My heart raced as fast as some of the horses I spied.

"I'm going to head south with the rest of the Rangers and three other companies of the Virginia Continentals. We're going to flank the British on the right."

"I don't give a damn about battle tactics! You mean you're going to fight." Hysteria rose in my voice, and I wrung my hands in front of me. Perspiration dotted my forehead. The only person I felt safe with in the camp was leaving me. What happened if he died? What would I do? How would I get home?

"It's war, Nora. Of course I'm going to fight."

CHAPTER 6

In the distance, a horn blew. The melody was "Gone Away," a fox-hunting tune. It was played when the fox had been caught and killed, and the hunt over. Alex's head snapped toward the sound and within mere moments, the men around me cussed and raised their arms and guns while shouting. They threw rocks and sticks, their faces turned red. Their sharp cries and yells rose up in the air, their attitude infuriated by the song.

"I don't understand. What's happening?" I asked, as Alex marched me away from the camp. Men were rallying behind a new face of courage. Courage I did not feel.

"The British are ignorant. Either they mean to mock our retreating army, or they mean it as an insult to General Washington. It appears it is having the opposite effect of what they were hoping," Alex said.

Groups of men, whose eyes now resembled a bull's intent on a fight, fled back toward the enemy, sprinting, their faces determined.

"An insult?" I said, trying to keep up with Alex's long legs.

My breathing worked overtime from trying to maintain his pace and from the fear that ran through me.

"Yes. Everyone knows Washington is an avid fox hunter," he said.

Well, not everyone because I don't.

Gunshots and cannon fire rang out in the distance. All around us, men ran, their muskets in hand, heading straight toward the enemy, their eyes full of resolve yet fearful, apparently knowing today could be their last day on earth.

"Who will win?" I asked, wringing my hands together.

"Hard to say," Alex said, glancing over his shoulder as we hurried along toward the woods. He moved with determination, and I went with him. "We have around eighteen hundred troops total here. The British have close to five thousand from what I could see when I rode out at first light."

"That's not good odds," I said under my breath.

"Thank you for the encouragement, Sailor. Come now. I need to get you somewhere safe and out of harm's way."

I continued to follow Alex through the disarray of men sprinting toward their stations, grabbing various weapons as they went. He strode with a clear purpose and site in mind, and I had to jog to keep up with him.

A loud crack echoed behind us, and Alex stopped. I flinched. Smoke billowed in the sky then floated downward, resting on the ground like a gigantic cloud. Gunpowder wafted through the air. I coughed and choked. The sounds of screaming men came next, shattering the silence of the smoky explosion.

Alex grabbed me by the shoulders and turned me so I faced away from him and looked at the woods in the distance. "Do you see the opening over there?" he asked.

I nodded, looking to where he pointed.

"Go there now and don't look back. And when you get there, stay put. Don't move until I come and get you. There's a small cluster of evergreen trees. You won't be able to miss them. Shimmy in between them as best you can and pull the blanket up over you to help conceal your clothes and blend in. Take this," he said, springing out his small hunting knife from his belt.

"What about you? Won't you need it?" I said, my voice starting to fill with hysteria.

"Nora, I need you stay calm. You have to focus. And breathe."

Damn it! How in the bloody hell is this happening again? First with John and now with Alex. Panic rose inside me, and I bit my lip. My hands clutched the fabric of my dress so they wouldn't shake. I took a deep breath as Alex had instructed. The last thing he needed to deal with was a frantic female. I would not be one of those.

"I have another knife. Now go. Don't look back!"

Alex stared into my eyes for one second longer and nodded before running off in the other direction.

Though tempted, I didn't look back. I kept my eyes forward and sprinted for the woods like Alex told me to. I stopped at the sound of a loud groan. To my right, two soldiers were hobbling along. One of the men clutched his side, and blood seeped through his fingers. The other limped but did his best to help his friend. Glancing back at the tree line and then back at the men, I made my decision.

"Let me help!" I shouted to the soldiers.

"Thank ye, miss. I can hardly walk, an' he's badly hurt," the man with the limp said. "Musket ball shot him."

"Is there a safer place we can put him?" I asked.

The soldier with the wounded leg nodded, and the one with the bloody side who I helped, moaned. "The medical tent. This way."

We walked, or rather, I walked, and the men limped to the

surgical area. The surgical area was roughly three-thousand to five-thousand yards in the rear of the battlefield. Five white tents were set up, and men lay around the area on hay bales, wagon beds, and the ground alike. Bandages were soaked and caked through with blood.

As we approached one of the tents, a loud shriek reached my ears as a voice yelled, "Hold him down! Bite the bullet, man!"

For the first time, I understood the difference between hearing something second-hand and seeing it. I had heard the stories of men being hurt on the battlefield, and the course of action a surgeon must take to save a life, such as amputate a limb, but seeing it was something else altogether.

By the time the two men and I reached the surgeon's camp, the man who I helped carry sagged as if he were a piece of ribbon. Blood continued to seep through his fingers and now ran down my gown. "Help!" I yelled.

A man, appearing in his mid-forties, looked my way when I bellowed. He ran over. "Lay him down over here," he said, helping to bear some of the patient's weight.

"What happened?" he asked.

"Musket ball shot him," I said, regurgitating what I'd been told.

"Let's hope it is a clean shot. Now, get out of my way, woman. This is no place for you. I want you out of my surgical area."

"I can help," I said, straightening my spine.

The man, who I now realized was the regimental surgeon, looked me up and down. "Doubt it. You'll faint in a second, and the last thing I need is a passed-out female on the ground who I have to help. Get back to the women and the laundry."

"I have strong hands and a stronger stomach. Women

have been tending to their men for ages. Besides, I have experience. I work in an apothecary shop," I said.

"An apothecary shop is different from a battlefield."

A man pushing a wheelbarrow rushed over to the surgeon. "Got another one, sir. His leg was hit," the soldier said. Blood was splattered across his face, and he wiped it away.

"Damn it. Don't be a fool. You need my help. There are too many wounded," I said. Why did men think women could not handle such things? We birthed babies, for heaven's sake.

The wounded man on the table writhed in pain, almost falling off the surface.

"I need someone to hold him down," the surgeon said.

I nodded and leaned all my weight onto the man's shoulders.

"The blood is red, but not bright," the surgeon said.

"I can see that," I spit out.

He looked up. "This means the ball didn't hit any vital organs."

"I know."

He dashed across the camp and picked up a metal instrument before coming back over to where I stood. A pair of bloody forceps were in his hand. "Ready?" he asked.

"Yes."

"Hold him as hard as you can. Put all your weight onto his shoulders in case he jerks about."

I did as he told me while he cut away the man's shirt. A bullet hole showed itself in the man's side, and when the doctor turned him, he frowned. "I feared this. It didn't go through. I'm going to have to search for it," he said. "Ready?"

My hands trembled with fear. My father's voice spoke quietly to me. *"Always help when you can, Nora. No matter how small the task, no matter if you're frightened. Always help."*

Taking a deep breath, I summoned what courage I had left and pressed on the man's shoulders with all my resolve. I was not going to faint in front of this man, no matter what.

The surgeon stuck the forceps inside the bullet hole. He twisted them, and the man beneath me screamed.

While still putting my weight on him, I shifted around so I faced him from in front, rather than behind. His eyes opened and stared into mine.

"It's all right. You're almost finished. I know it hurts, but hold on," I whispered, doing my best to imitate my mother's voice she used when we were sick as children. "You're doing well. Look at me, man. Look in my eyes. Good. Breathe. In and out. Slowly. Follow me," I said. I inhaled through my nose to the count of three and let the breath out through my mouth to the same number, all the while keeping my eyes locked on the soldier's.

"Got it," the surgeon said.

I looked over at him, and he held up a musket ball, smiling.

"I now have to put in sutures. Three should work, I think," he said, more to himself than me. He threaded a thick needle and stuck it into the man's skin. The soldier squirmed, and the physician looked up. "Keep holding him. If we're lucky, he'll faint."

The young soldier did, in fact, faint, and I suspected as long as infection or fever didn't set in, he'd make a full recovery. He would have the wound to prove his story for the rest of his life, however long that would be.

I wiped my hands on my skirt then brushed the stray hair that had come undone off my sweaty face. The surgeon looked me once over and nodded. "Good job, Miss—?"

"Bishop. Nora," I said.

"Matthew Aster, regimental surgeon," he said. "You don't

seem to shy away from wounded or sick. You've done this before?"

I shook my head. "My father was an apothecary, so I worked alongside him. This though," I said, looking around at all the bloody and sick-ridden men. "You're correct, sir. A battlefield is different. I've never been in this environment, no."

"Hopefully, none of your kinsmen will enter through this tent." Dr. Aster wiped his instrument on his bloodied apron.

I remained quiet, not bothering to correct him on the fact no family of mine resided in camp. I understood why he came to the conclusion, of course. Quite a few soldiers who were married had wives and family follow the army. Apparently, he thought that of me.

Another boom of cannon fire echoed and I swore. The earth shook. Smoke puffed into the sky shielding my sight. Alex was out there, and I worried I'd never see him again.

I could only hope that if he did get injured, it wouldn't be fatal. I needed him to take me home to Manhattan undetected.

Dr. Aster considered me for a moment longer. "I can't believe I'm about to say this, but if you're not needed back at your kinsmen camp, I would welcome your help here."

"Is having a woman working with you that bad?"

"No cooing or awwing over anyone. And no crying either. Men don't need that."

Alex had given me specific instructions to hide in the woods, and deep down, I knew I should follow what he said. He would be angry when he discovered I hadn't listened. But I didn't care. I couldn't go. These men needed me. What sort of person would I be if I ran away and didn't help those suffering when I could provide the tiniest bit of comfort?

I squared my shoulders. "Where can I help?"

"This way." Dr. Aster led me to a group of sick men, ten in total. They all lay on their sickbed, looking close to death.

"What's wrong with them?" I asked. The stench of vomit and sewage invaded my sense of smell, and I controlled the urge to put my hand over my nose.

"Scurvy mostly. These lads can hardly sit up to expel the vomit coming out of their mouths and shit where they are. And I won't beg your pardon. If you're going to help around here, get used to it," he said.

I waved it away. "So you need me to help them when sick and clean them?"

He nodded and seemed about to continue on saying something when a yell from another assistant caught his attention. "I'll leave you to it then," he said, turning away and running across the area to another man being carried in with his arm hanging on by a thin strip of muscle. I looked upward and prayed I, as well as Alex, would live through the rest of the day.

CHAPTER 7

THE EVENTS OF THE last thirty-six hours had left me exhausted. After a full day of nursing sick men, two of whom died while I cared for them, I wanted to lie down, curl into a ball, and fall asleep.

All day long, soldiers had come and gone; some men stayed because of injuries, and Dr. Aster handled it in stride. It was chaotic as the bloody soldiers came to the sick area for aide as all around us gunshots and yelling circled. Could a stray bullet hit us this far back? If the British wanted to destroy their enemy, surely they wouldn't stop when they came upon those of us helping to heal.

I entertained the idea of taking a short five-minute break to shut my eyes when a loud rejoicing echoed through the air, and a soldier ran to our area of the camp.

"We won! We won! The British fled!" he said, running back the way he'd come. A whoop and holler from the surgical mates erupted, as did from those well enough to do so.

For the next two hours, I wrapped sprained ankles, wrists, and fingers. I applied bandages to the men who had minor wounds. Surprisingly, I found the work gratifying, though tiring. Throughout the afternoon, my eyes rested on the opening of the tent, waiting for my brother or Alex to walk through. Or for one of Alex's cousins to come and let me know he was fine, but no news of him came. And that worried me. The soldiers quietly retold their stories of the battle, but my mind lingered on Alex even while I hugged men who had lost their brother or best friend on the field.

It was impossible to miss the passion in their voices while they spoke of the reasons they fought. One man had spoken of how he'd had to give away most of his money to the royal governor, leaving scarcely anything for him and his family. Men had talked about their family members and friends, sacrificing their lives during the French and Indian War, and yet, England didn't seem to care. They upped the taxes. My father had complained, and also John had said there should be no taxation without representation. Of course, everyone talked about the Sugar Act and the Stamp Act.

With each story, I agreed more and more with these men who willingly put their lives on the battlefield for liberty. For freedom. Even now, the British regulars were supposed to keep the civilians safe, but day after day, reports of them robbing homes and taking advantage of numerous pleasures surfaced. The passion within me shifted upon hearing these accounts, and my heart softened to the revolutionaries' cause. Uncle Edward had been adamant that the house fire was purely an accident made by our cook. But the more I relived that horrific day, the more I wondered if it had been, in fact, the redcoats who had burned my home to the ground. Were they the reason I had lost everything? How could I possibly be loyal to the king when he gave them the right to harm us in such a way?

A hand settled down on my shoulder. "You did a fine job

today, Miss Bishop. I can manage from here. The battle is over. For now. Go."

Dr. Aster walked away then, saying nothing more, leaving me alone to look at the soldier on the surgeon's bed. The two men who had been holding his shoulders picked him up with careful hands and laid him down elsewhere. The man never moved. I followed to where he lay and watched his chest. It rose up and down. Steady. That was a good thing, right?

I walked out of the tent, quite in a shock myself, and found a secluded tree to lean upon. I stared at nothing and everything at the same time. The wind picked up causing a flutter of leaves to float past me. My mind drifted again to Alex. By now, several hours had passed since the fighting stopped, and still I hadn't seen him. *Is he dead? Is he too injured to be carried back to the safety of the tents?* I choked on a sob, lifting the back of my hand to my mouth.

"I've been looking all over for you."

I turned around and stared into Alex's face. His blue eyes blazed, and a look of anger mixed with relief flashed behind them when he regarded me. His face was splattered with blood. My eyes drifted over his body, and when I convinced myself he wasn't mortally injured and wasn't going to fall over, I yelled at him. "And where the bloody hell have you been?"

His eyebrow rose, and his mouth tightened. "Fighting in a bloody battle, as you well know," he said through gritted teeth.

Deep down, I knew this was not what he needed, but I couldn't help it. My every emotion hung on a single thread, weaving in and out on the covering I'd constructed over myself since my family's death. What the hell did he want me to do? Didn't he understand what I had already lost? My hands shook, and I balled them into fists for fear I would hit him.

"Do you not realize that every single time a man came limping in here or was carried in on the wagon with a limb hanging off, I had to strain my neck to see if it was you or not? The fighting has been over for hours, and you've only now returned to find me? For Christ's sake! Do you have any idea what's been going on in my head?"

"No, but it seems you have it on your mind to tell me anyway. So go on, Sailor. Get it out of your system, but if you don't mind, I'm going to sit here while you do it because my legs can hardly keep me standing any longer as tired as I am." He walked over to the tree and leaned up against it.

And as quick as my anger greeted him, my tears pushed in, interrupting. I let them fall for a few seconds before wiping them away. "I'm sorry. I don't know… what's come… over me," I said between hiccups.

Without saying a word, he came to me and wrapped me in his arms while the drops streamed down my face and onto his chest.

"Shh," he said.

His body, though worn, beaten and tired, was solid and while he stroked my back, the tension, anger, and worry that had been lingering inside me started to subside. I trembled slightly, and his arms tightened around me. "Everything will be fine, Nora. You'll see. You're safe."

Embarrassed, I pulled away and peered up into his face. We held each other's eyes for a heartbeat. My face warmed, and I stepped back, wiping my eyes and nose with the apron Dr. Aster had given me at some point during the day.

He reached forward and wiped another tear off my face. "There's no need to apologize. It's been a trying few days for you. Never apologize for crying, not to me," he said. His eyes softened, and a fresh wave of tears dared to pour out again, but I held them back. "I'm glad to see you safe. As soon as the fighting ended, I rushed to the trees, but you weren't there.

I've been looking all over for you, afraid someone took you or...but then I overheard one of the men saying some lady helped out with an amputation—"

The tears I had held at bay came in full force then, like a tidal wave, and then I began to laugh. I didn't know why. Goodness, this was anything but funny, but I couldn't help it. In one month, my life had completely turned upside down in every way possible.

After another minute of me half-laughing and half-sobbing into Alex's arms, I took a deep breath, finding my composure. Christ, here I was falling apart when Alex was likely injured. He had been the one out fighting, risking his life, and he was the one bringing me comfort.

"Are you hurt?" I asked, wanting to take the attention off me. Alex's gaze alone stirred something inside of me, and I didn't want to think about it. "There's quite a bit of blood on your clothes. And mud," I said as an afterthought.

"When you fight in a sloppy wheat field, mud tends to be there. As for the blood, not much is mine. But I did manage a scrape or two." Alex flexed his hand. His knuckles were bloody and bruised.

"Now is as good as time as ever for me to tend to your old wound then while I look for others. Off with your shirt," I said, finding the authoritative voice I'd figured out how to use from my day in the surgical tent.

My entire body ached, but if I was going to help one last patient, it was going to be Alex. It was late in the day, and the sun would be setting soon. At least this time while I fixed him up it was still daylight.

"Yes, ma'am," Alex said, smirking. He carefully took off his hunting shirt, his grin replaced by wincing when his arms rose above his head.

The bandage I had applied the day before was stained brown from dried blood, new blood from it reopening, dirt, and sweat. An old wound had healed nicely on his forearm, though it was still pink. He would probably have a scar. Aside from being smothered in filth and some small scrapes and bruises on his body, he was otherwise unscathed.

"How you managed to escape unhurt I'll never know," I said, taking in his muscled form.

"Only by the grace of our good Lord am I still on this side of the roses."

I took a step toward him for closer inspection.

"Sailor, I need to sit down, if you don't mind, before we begin. I'd like to get off my feet and rest," Alex said.

My face reddened. Why didn't I think of that? "Of course. There's clean linen over in the medical tent. I'll go fetch it with some other supplies. I'll be back."

A few short minutes later, I found Alex sitting with his back up against the tree where I left him. His eyes were shut, but when I approached, he opened them and smiled.

"That was fast," he said.

"Well, thankfully, you don't need much from me." I thrust a bottle of rum into his hand.

"What's this for?"

"You look like you need a drink."

"That I do, Sailor. That I do." He raised the bottle to his lips and took a big gulp. His cheeks puffed out as he let his breath go.

I knelt next to him, reminiscent of the day before when I helped him, and peeled off his old bandage. It clung to his skin.

He kept his eyes fixed on his feet.

"It reopened a bit," I said, examining the slice. Fresh blood swelled to the surface of his skin. I dipped a piece of linen into a bowl of water and wiped the wound and all around it clean. He was amazingly dirty, and I couldn't help but wash off the dirt and grime from his other shoulder as well.

"I haven't had a woman feel the need to bathe me since I was a lad," Alex said, looking at me. The corner of his mouth lifted, and light danced in his eyes.

"Sorry. It's that you're—"

"Dirty? I know."

"I didn't mean to offend you. Since I was cleaning your one shoulder, I thought I'd clean the rest of your body—"

His eyebrows shot up.

"I mean—" Warmth seeped onto my cheeks. I couldn't look at him.

"If you want to wash the rest of my body, I'm fine with that. Though, I'd say the rest of the men wouldn't want to see it here in the open," he said. "Granted, they might ask for the same treatment."

My blush deepened and spread onto my neck. I stared at his skin, still not able to meet his eyes, and took one more swipe across his shoulder with the linen. His eyes were closed the entire time I worked, and I remained silent as to not disturb him. After a few minutes, Alex started to snore. The linen was totally black by the time I finished. I rebandaged his shoulder, discarded the old bandages, then sat with him for a few minutes while he rested. After a half hour, I nudged him, and together we walked back to find his cousins.

Gideon and Si already had a fire lit when we found them. They had set up their tent near the trees where Alex had wanted me to run earlier in the day. The sun was now beginning to set, yet the camp was anything but quiet. The American victory over the British had boosted the confidence and the attitudes of the troops and the men meant to celebrate. Rum was passed out and an extra portion of cornmeal as well.

Si's singing rang out as we approached the tent. His pure, clear tenor's voice floated through the air, leaving me dumbfounded. It didn't seem to match his looks, as he was a big, burly man. A few other men sat around, listening to him, transfixed on the song.

Gideon came up to us and nodded. "General Washington wants to see you," he said to Alex. "Both of you. Now."

"Me?" I said. "Why?"

"Seems he's heard of a lady who gave us information right before the invasion of Kip's Bay, and that same lady assisted with the wounded and sick men today," Gideon said.

I swallowed down my nervousness and tried not to fidget. Did this mean John had survived? How else would the general know about the information I'd given to him?

"At least let me get a clean shirt on before we go. Have a seat and rest yourself by the fire. You worked hard today and deserve it," he said. He touched my shoulder and gave it a slight squeeze before walking off to change.

My eyes were heavy as Si sang. His voice was soothing, and it did not surprise me men stopped to listen to him. The threat of battle was over, and though the men throughout the camp were relaxed, the taste of the fight and celebration continued to linger in their veins. This was very obvious to me since some of the men eyed me in such as way as to leave little to the imagination. Gideon must have sensed it too for he sat down next to me, not saying a word, but his presence alone made me more comfortable.

The sky was dark. A half-crescent moon shone silver in the sky, making it more difficult to see. I wondered for a moment if I would ever see clearly again, or if the path in front of me would always be dark, like night. Two months ago, my life was clearly lit. I would marry David, help my father, and become an apothecary like him, have children. I'd looked forward to it. Now most of my family was dead, my brother missing, and David wore the color red. I was in the

American camp, nursing the wounded and sick. I still didn't know if I was a friend or foe.

The brush rustled next to me, and my head snapped in the direction of the noise. Alex stepped out of the wood. Because of the fire, I detected his grin while he strolled toward me.

"Did you wash?" Gideon said, looking at him.

His hair was wet, and it dripped water down the front of his shirt.

"I did."

"Why?" Gideon said.

"I was told I was dirty, so I figured I probably smelled too. Are you ready?" Alex reached out his hand and helped me to stand. Si grunted then smelled himself.

"Ready as I'll ever be."

"We'll be back then."

"You know where to find us," Gideon said.

My palms were clammy, so I wiped them into the fabric of my gown. I bit my lip and swallowed. What could General Washington want with me, a young woman from Long Island? I had no connections, save for my brother, and I didn't know where he was. But maybe Washington did? My Uncle Edward was a loyal Tory, but that was about all I knew about him and his connections. Did the commander think me a spy? I tasted blood on my lip as Alex and I made our way to General Washington's tent, wondering what was going to happen to me now.

CHAPTER 8

A BREEZE STIRRED THE trees, and an owl hooted somewhere close by. The cicadas were deafening to the point that I wondered how I would possibly sleep later that night outside. Then again, my exhaustion helped me not to care about the bugs and animals, though the small critters gave me something else to think about as we approached General Washington's shelter.

Alex and I stopped outside the flap of a large tent. Two men stood guard, not at full attention, but alert enough to anticipate our arrival. When they saw me, their faces turned to one of confusion, no doubt wondering what a lady was doing outside the general's bivouac.

"Alexander Foster and Miss Nora Bishop," Alex said to the men. "General Washington is expecting us."

The shorter and plumper man's eyes widened a little. "I've heard of you. They say you're something to watch in a fight, and every man should want you on their side," the guard said, his face in awe. "They say you're like a god."

Alex's face reddened.

"Men shouldn't be focusing on me. They should be watching the enemy. As for a god, there's only one, and I'm not Him. Now, if you could let the general know we're here, I'd appreciate it."

"Yes, sir. Right away, sir," the guard said. He disappeared behind the flap.

I stole a quick glance at Alex. He stood as rigid as the wooden stick soldiers used to bite down on during surgery.

A moment later, the guard returned. "They're ready to see you," he said.

"They're?" I whispered to Alex. "I thought it was only General Washington?"

Alex shrugged and looked at me. "Ready?"

I very well couldn't tell him no, yet, I couldn't admit I was ready. My legs shook underneath my skirts. I took a steadying breath. Was the reason they wanted to see me because they suspected something?

Resisting the urge to clutch Alex's hand, I nodded and stepped inside the officer's tent.

Several candles flickered against the wind when we walked beyond the flaps. A medium-size table stood in the center, with a large map spread out on top. Four men seemed to be waiting for us, their expressions serious and strained. Cups and plates with scraps of food were scattered across another table, off to the side.

It was easy to pick out General Washington, as I'd seen him before. Standing before me, he didn't look as different as he had when I saw him last atop his horse, advancing into battle at Kip's Bay Landing. Yet, seeing him off his horse was startling. He was very tall. As tall as Alex but not as broad. He had auburn hair, and his eyes were serious, sharp. Lines were etched into his face, and he held himself with an authority that would rival my great-grandfather, who scared me to death, God rest his soul. However, a softness lingered in his features, and I found myself thinking that in any other situation, it would have been nice to sit down and converse with the man.

"Alex, it is nice to see you again," a young man, about Alex's age, said. He walked over, and the men clasped hands.

"I'm glad for it as well," Alex said. "Major Benjamin Tallmadge, this is Miss Nora Bishop."

"How do you do?" I said, curtseying.

Major Tallmadge and the rest of the men bowed.

Alex's eyes scanned the other men in the tent, and we waited for introductions.

"General Washington, General Putnam, and Captain Nathan Hale, this is the man I was telling you about. May I introduce Alexander Foster. We've been friends since childhood. Grew up together in Setauket, Long Island," Major Tallmadge said.

My ears perked up at hearing this. I had family in Setauket — my father's cousin, Caroline. She operated a boardinghouse. Would Alex and Major Tallmadge know her?

"Mr. Foster, Miss Bishop, on behalf of myself and the Continental Army, we thank you for your service," General Washington said. He turned toward the men again. "Thank you, General," he said to the older of the men in the room. "I bid you goodnight. We will talk on the morrow."

General Putnam nodded to the room and left.

Alex remained quiet, so I did the same. More times than I'd like to admit, I'd gotten in trouble as a girl for speaking when I ought not to, and today I did not want to make that mistake in front of several men who could order my death or imprisonment with one word.

Alex must have sensed my uneasiness for he shifted his weight, which moved him closer to me.

"Miss Bishop, Dr. Aster relayed to me your help today in the surgery. That was quite a task, and we won't forget it. I've also been told of your assistance the other day at Kip's Bay Landing, though we were a bit late in taking it into consideration, I'm afraid," General Washington said.

"My assistance, sir?" I said, not knowing if I should admit to anything or not.

"Yes. I've been told you gave important information to one Michael Drover about the British attack, though little did we know they were already in position." He clasped his hands behind his back and stood erect. "What I'm interested in knowing, Miss Bishop, is how you came about this information."

Resigned that the men knew everything, I decided to be truthful. "I told my brother the information, sir. John Bishop. He's the one who told Michael Drover," I said.

"And where is your brother so we may thank him?"

"I don't know, sir. He was either captured or killed after the skirmish. I was hoping someone could tell me where he is."

General Washington glanced over his shoulder.

I followed him with my eyes and, for the first time, saw another man sitting in the corner. He sat, taking notes. His clerk.

"Mr. Johnson, please find out what has happened to Mr. John Bishop," General Washington said. "My apologies, madam, but we are still sorting through the soldiers who have not returned to us and collecting what data we can. Someone will let you know as soon as we have the information. Now, how did you come about collecting the information you did? Please," he said.

I cleared my throat. "Captain William Roth of the British army dined with us one evening. At my uncle's home. The men were having their brandy later in the evening when I overheard them speaking of the plans. I only spoke out because my brother joined the cause."

"Would you speak out again?" General Washington inquired.

"I'm not certain I understand your meaning, sir." Did he mean what I thought he did? Was the Commander of the American Forces asking me to spy on the British?

"Miss Bishop," Major Tallmadge said, stepping forward. "You have every right to be wary of the choice we are asking you to take. You have every reason to say no. If caught, you would go to prison or suffer a worse fate. Men have been flogged, executed. It would be only fair for you to consider this. However, you have every reason to say yes as well. The British have taken everything from you, and now there is the matter of your brother—"

"Taken everything from me?" I said. A sinking feeling swelled in me like waves on the ocean and my stomach right along with the waves. I knew what he was going to say, but I didn't want to hear it.

"Why, your family's house, my lady. Your parents and sister and—"

"Stop! Please." I choked back the tears. "I don't want to hear it. It can't be true. Y-you're lying," I stammered. The fire had been an accident. Cook had started it in the kitchen. That was what my uncle had said. I wrapped my arms around myself, but deep down, I knew the truth. I'd seen it with my own eyes, but I had desperately wanted it to be false, so I had pushed the idea aside. I had made myself believe it wasn't true. How could the people who were supposed to be protecting me and my own do this? My chest grew tight, and I gripped the chair in front of me.

"Nora," Alex whispered, turning me to face him.

"Did you know?"

Alex nodded. "I was there."

My mouth opened to speak, but I couldn't make a noise. I closed my mouth and shut my eyes tight, gaining composure. I opened my eyes and stared at Alex. "What do you mean that you were there?"

"It was the first time I saw you. Then when we met in the woods, I recognized you."

"Tell me."

"I was scouting the area, on orders, when I smelled smoke burning. I rushed to the location and saw the flames licking the sky. I witnessed an officer ordering the men around. One soldier came my way, and we fought. I killed him and took his coat, hurrying to the house to see if I could help. The bastard of an officer had left by then—"

"You," I said, though I barely heard my own words. My eyes welled with tears, and the room turned cloudy as the image of a man in a scarlet coat stood near a tree watching my home burn.

"I'm sorry I couldn't save your family, Nora. The British burned your home, murdered your family because—"

"Because John joined your cause for freedom," I said. Why did Uncle Edward lie to me? I'd asked him the same question, and he'd denied it. I had believed him. Maybe he didn't know the truth? "Why didn't you tell me?"

"I didn't want to tell you in front of Si and Gideon, and then when you were settled, I thought it best for you to rest. I knew it had been a trying day for you, and I suppose I was waiting for the right moment and—"

"The right moment?" I asked, my voice shaking. "Is there ever a right moment to tell someone her family was murdered by the very people who are supposed to protect them and govern them?" My voice rose, and the men stared wide-eyed at me. I turned away from them, my body trembling.

Alex walked around and looked me in the eyes. "I'm sorry. You're right. I didn't know how to tell you, so I took the coward's way out by not saying anything. But can you understand why I did it? You'd lost your brother from the skirmish, and then you found yourself with me, in the camp, no less."

"Who?"

"Excuse me?" Alex said.

"Who? You said the British are the ones responsible, but I want to know who gave the order. Certainly, not all five thousand troops killed my family and burned my home to the ground. Who was the officer who gave the order?"

"If our information is correct, and I'm positive it is, it was Captain William Roth who gave the order," Major Tallmadge said behind me.

"Bloody hell," I said. I opened my mouth to speak again but then saw something flash in Alex's eyes at the mention of the captain's name.

His hands balled into fists, and his mouth set into a grimace. "Are you certain, Ben?"

"Yes. Alex, I know what—"

Alex put his hand out to stop him and shook his head, but his eyes never left mine. "This isn't about me tonight. You know as well as anyone I'll deal with my own matter later. This is about Miss Bishop," Alex said.

My nails bit into my palms. Captain William Roth. The snake who was in the good graces of my uncle. My jaw clenched. Hell. I knew he was a bastard from the first time I'd met him. A new battle blazed inside me as anger rushed to the forefront of my emotions at the mention of Captain Roth's name. He had said my name sounded familiar. Surely, he knew what he'd done when he had dined with me at my uncle's table. I understood why Alex hadn't told me, though I didn't know why he felt the need to protect me as it were. I hardly had any options. Taking a breath, I spun around and faced the officers.

"What is it you would have me do?" I said, finding my resolve. I would make the son of a bitch pay.

"Be our eyes and ears for the time being," Major Tallmadge said. "It is our understanding your Uncle Edward is a loyalist and friendly with British officers. Let us know if you find anything out of importance."

"You'll have to be more specific as I don't think any of the British are going to discuss their battle plans with me," I said, not bothering to keep the anger out of my voice.

"Not directly, no. At dinner parties, perhaps they'll talk about how many guns they have, food storage, number of troops, where they're marching," General Washington said. He was sitting down now and offered me a seat.

I declined.

"Pay close attention to what is going on around you. Any information you can give us will be most helpful. Rest assured in that."

I lifted my chin and straightened my shoulders. "And how am I to get this information to you?"

"Through me," Alex said. "I'm free to roam as I will. I'll be scouting and will be able to collect any messages you might have."

"And me," Captain Hale said. "I'll be in Manhattan gathering what news I can. I will find you, and we can exchange information. You in return, will provide Alex the information, who will get it to General Washington."

"And who will you be pretending to be?" I asked Captain Hale.

"I've already set up the disguise as a school teacher. I've been in Manhattan since the twelfth of the month."

My eyebrows rose at his comment. "A soldier disguised as a teacher? I'd love to see that."

Captain Hale had the decency to laugh and not take offense. "I taught before the war, madam. I assure you, I'm capable of commanding a classroom of children, but in truth, I don't enjoy it. Will there be a way for you to come into town at least once a week while at your uncle's home?"

"Yes. I work for the apothecary, Mr. McGovern," I said.

"Then I'll arrange to see you when you are there."

I turned to Alex. His eyes were narrowed, focused. "And how will I give you the information?"

"We'll do a dead drop," Alex said as if it was something he did every day.

"What in the world is that?"

"After Nathan gives you information or any information you're able to gather, you'll write it down. I'll show you a place behind your uncle's house to leave the letter, and we'll designate a sign between us so I know when to retrieve it."

"And why can't Captain Hale simply give the information to you?" I asked Alex.

"It would be too suspicious if anyone saw us talking on a regular basis. I only come into Manhattan when I must, and Nathan will not be venturing to camp. Overall, there will be less suspicion on you since you're a woman. They will never suspect you are using the information you hear to go against them."

Questions ran rampant through my mind. *What exactly is Alex's position in the army besides that of a Ranger? What will happen to me and my family if I'm caught? Am I ready to change my allegiance?* I gazed into Alex's eyes and then at the eyes of the men in front of me. I remembered all too clearly the eyes of the men who I had helped on the battlefield and their talk of liberty and freedom. I remembered the look and sinister smile of Captain Roth.

I took a deep breath. "I'll do it."

Alex touched my arm and gave it a slight squeeze and nodded. "Don't worry. It will be easy."

He used the word *easy* like he was taking a stroll after Sunday morning church. And though the plan sounded simple, I had the feeling there would be nothing simple about what I had agreed to.

CHAPTER 9

It was odd, feeling better protected with a man I'd only known for a few days — camping under the stars no less — than in my family's home.

Granted, Uncle Edward's home was a luxury I missed, especially the bed. I found it a bit more comfortable than dead leaves and a rock for a pillow, but the company of Alex and his cousins I much preferred.

Alex and I entered the back field. My uncle's house looked like an ant farm from such a distance, but I still saw it clearly. Smoke swirled into the sky, the smell of the kitchen was carried in the breeze. *Bread.* My mouth watered, and my stomach grumbled.

I shifted in my seat, unable to find a comfortable position. My legs were restless as I regarded the house that was supposed to be my home. A nervous energy ran through my veins at the thought of my mission. Uncle Edward didn't want me to associate with my brother for fear of the disgrace it would cause the family, and now I would be spying for the rebels. I gripped the pommel tighter and took a big, deep breath. Life was about to become interesting.

"Let's walk for a bit, Sailor," Alex said.

He jumped off Bridger then helped me down after him. His hand lingered on my waist for a second. His touch left a trail of warmth in its wake even through all the fabric I wore.

He cleared his throat and took Bridger by the reins, leading him on. "Are you able to venture into this outer field and the surrounding wood?"

"Yes," I said, not having the courage to look at him for fear he'd see the blush on my cheeks.

"How often?"

I shrugged. "Whenever I want, I suppose. Why?"

"This is where you'll do the dead drop," he said. "Out in these woods."

Alex walked between the various maples, oaks, and hemlocks, his eyes scanning the bottom of trees. At one point, he stooped down and looked at a hole but stood again and continued on with his search, tripping over a gray, warty-rooted branch. Alex grunted when he fell and rubbed his knee. "Ouch. My knee hit a rock," he said, biting his lower lip.

"You whimper over that, yet hardly moan when sliced open with a bayonet?" I chuckled, shaking my head.

"Believe me, Sailor. I did more than moan when that happened." He lifted the branch to look at it better.

"It's called Witch Hobble. Some say witches grow it on purpose to snag their prize. You see, the rooted branches form an obstacle of sorts to trip the unfortunate wanderer."

"Hmph."

"May I ask what you're doing anyway?" I said. He stood and walked in circles. I reached out and pulled a honeysuckle bloom off the stem, wishing it was still summer to taste the sweet nectar.

"I'm looking for a hole. Should be about this big." He held up his hands, indicating the size he was looking for.

After another three minutes and traveling a bit farther away from my uncle's house, but not far enough where I could no longer see it, Alex stopped. "This tree, right here," Alex said, running his hand over the bark of an old black walnut tree. "This is where you'll do the dead drop."

He knelt and moved a few dead leaves out of the way.

"Right. And where will I place the letter?" I strode over and stood next to him, hoping he was teasing about the hole. *Any animal could pop out and strike me.*

"You're an intelligent woman," he said, smirking. "Where do you suppose?"

"The hole? You weren't teasing then."

"I said you were intelligent. That's why the general chose you." Alex stood and wiped the sweat off his brow.

The hole was as big as both my hands combined and wide enough to hold multiple letters if needed.

"Will any animals crawl in and decide to live here?" I asked.

"I shouldn't think so. Squirrels and chipmunks don't live this close to the ground. Neither do birds. You might see a snake, but I doubt it."

I shivered. "I hope not. How will you know when I place a letter inside the tree?"

He looked me up and down. "I'll stop here every few days or so. We'll also have a signal. Perhaps the laundry? Maybe your clothes—"

"What? Hang my petticoat out, and that would be the signal?"

"That's a half-decent idea."

I shook my head. "It wouldn't work. I don't think I could manage to wash my own clothes without raising suspicion."

"Ah. Your aunt and uncle have a laundress then?"

"Yes, though I'm perfectly capable of washing my own garments," I said, not wanting him to think I was spoiled.

Though why I cared what he thought, I could not say. Perhaps it was because I'd tended to his wounds, giving us an intimacy only found between physician and patient.

"Sailor, I have the opinion that you're quite capable of many different talents." His statement caused me to blush. Again. "I'm sure washing clothes is among them. Tell me about your day. What do you do throughout? The signal needs to be something that won't cause speculation, as you mentioned."

After a few minutes of explaining what I did during the day and realizing my hours consisted of absolutely nothing but boring activities since I had come to live with my uncle, I paused. "There is nothing," I said. "I don't even tend my own fire. The only thing I do myself is light my own candle, and that's because it is in my bedchamber. Goodness, I'm bored with my own life. Unless, of course, I'm working at the apothecary."

"Better to be bored than running from the army here in the woods," Alex said. He scuffed his foot against a large rock, and it flipped over. He bent down and picked it up, running his hand back and forth over the surface of the gray stone before turning it over to examine the back of it. He was clearly thinking something over in his mind. But what?

"What—"

His head jerked up and turned toward the right. He raised his finger to his mouth silently telling me to be quiet. He grabbed hold of Bridger and led him into a thicket, motioning me to follow.

Twigs snapped, and leaves crunched underneath horse hooves while we waited in the thicket. The sound grew nearer with each heartbeat. I stole a glance at Alex who stared over my shoulder. His eyes never once fell on me. They remained out into the woods. His body was strung tight like a hunter's bow ready for the kill.

I glanced over my shoulder. Someone in red approach. Then and there, I prayed Bridger would remain quiet as Captain William Roth rode into view. My breath all but stopped, and my heart pounded in my ears. John had warned me to stay away from him, and it had been made perfectly clear bad blood boiled between him and Alex. The new information I had learned about Captain Roth giving the order to burn my home flared inside my mind and heart. My muscles quivered, and my eyes became tight at seeing him sitting erect on his gray mount. His black hair, covered by a white wig, gave him a greater image of authority and disdain. I did not know what had happened between the two men who I found myself between, but it was something so horrible that looking at Captain Roth had given cause for Alex to hold his knife in his hand.

I touched Alex's arm, and he lurched, bumping into the bush in front of us. The swish of the leaves brushed against Bridger, and he moved, causing the branches to rustle. Captain Roth's head turned in our direction, and he halted, his eyes scanning the thicket, his body rigid and waiting for an assault. He jumped off his horse, drew his broadsword, then walked toward our hiding spot. Not wanting him to discover Alex or me, I turned to go, but Alex caught my wrist. He shook his head and mouthed the word *"No."*

From the corner of my eye, I watched Captain Roth continue on with his pursuit. A certainty took over me and with a glance at each man I knew if they were to face each other, only one of them would remain standing, and today was not the day for more bloodshed.

I yanked my arm out of Alex's grasp and looked him in the eye. I nodded only once, and before I lost all sense of courage, I stumbled out onto the path, leaving my sense of security behind.

Captain Roth swung his sword in my direction and

jumped. "M'lady, this is certainly a surprise meeting." He lowered his broadsword, and I released the breath I'd been holding. "I thought I'd heard something, but never did I think I would witness you emerging from the woods," he said. He glanced around. "Are you alone, Miss Bishop?"

"Oh, Captain Roth!" I said. I bit my lip hard, making my eyes water. I put my hand to my heart and gave a soft shudder in an attempt to stifle a cry. "I'm alone, yes," I said, keeping my eyes trained on him. I refrained from turning around, fearful if I did, he would go and investigate, finding Alex. "I'm so happy to find someone I know."

I stumbled toward him and put my hand out against a tree as if I needed its support for balance.

"What has happened?" His eyes looked me over. "Your gown is filthy. And, is that blood? Search parties have been out scouring the fields. Your Uncle Edward has been extremely worried for you, Miss Bishop. We've had no idea what befell you," he said. "Tell me, what happened?"

A snapping branch behind me seemed to thunder in the otherwise silent wood. A worm of fear inched its way up my back, and my stomach overflowed with dread like a cup with too much liquid in it. Captain Roth's eyes turned into slits, and his hand tightened on the hilt of his sword. He stepped forward, and I swooned, clutching my breast, forcing him to catch me in his arms.

As best I could, I relaxed my body hoping to convince Captain Roth I had indeed fainted.

"Miss Bishop?" Captain Roth said.

I counted to thirty before I fluttered my eyes, opening them to see him only inches from my face. Tobacco and rose water lingered on him, which was so different from the smell of leather and forest that accompanied Alex. Captain Roth helped me right myself, his hands remaining on my body a little longer than what I was comfortable with. But I kept silent, wanting to get away from the thicket.

"Better?" he said.

"Yes. Thank you so much for your help, sir." Somehow, I managed to make myself cry. "I just… just need to get home."

"I would like to know, madam, how you came to be here, in the woods, all alone, after being missing for several days." Without trying to hide anything, his eyes roamed all over my body. For a moment, they settled on my breasts before rising to my face. "Your body looks unscathed, which leads me to believe you didn't run into the enemy," he said. "And yet, you have blood on you, and your gown is torn." He walked around me then, circling like a wolf does his prey. "Or, you did find them but join their ranks?"

I lifted my chin. *Damn.* He wasn't buying my act. "Are you threatening me, sir?"

He snickered. "Do you need to be threatened, m'lady? I simply find your situation curious is all."

"Well…" I began, halting only slightly and figured I would try and keep to the truth as much as possible only so I would have less chance of getting caught in a full-blown lie. "I was out walking and fighting started, so I ran into the woods. I met a man who was bleeding. That's why I have blood on me. I helped bind his wound. And then I got lost, and then night came, and I didn't know how to get home and… and… I want to go home. Take me home now," I said, pointing to my uncle's house.

I took a step in the direction of the back field leading to my uncle's house, but the captain stuck out his hand and grasped my arm. "Careful, Miss Bishop. Do I need to remind you that you're speaking to an officer of His Majesty's army?"

Fear rattled inside me, but I held myself steady and looked him in the eye. "And do I have to remind you my uncle is one of the wealthiest men in Manhattan?" I said, having no idea if that fact held any weight at all.

Captain Roth grinned then. "I'll escort you. Seeing as though I am a British officer and a gentleman, I find it my duty to be of service to you," he said. "Come."

A gentleman indeed. It was easy to see Captain Roth owned a dangerous temper, and I did not want to be on the receiving end of it. For now, thanks to my wonderful acting abilities, I'd held off his inquiries about the last couple of days. I hadn't altogether come up with my story but hoped the couple of minutes it would take to travel back through the field to my uncle's house, I would think of something. Granted, the truth wasn't horribly bad. I was captured, more or less, and forced to stay in the American camp, but did I want them to know all of that?

I nodded and allowed him to lead me away. I dared not look back at the thicket where Alex remained hidden. A small quiver brushed over my skin, and I knew Alex huddled under the cover of leaves and trees, watching me go with his enemy.

Twilight had settled in by the time we reached the front door of my uncle's home. Captain Roth pulled on the reins of his mount, and the horse jerked to a stop. He jumped down and raised his hand to help me off. His hand wrapped around my own, and he squeezed it.

My heartbeat pulsed in my fingertips.

Still holding onto me, he leaned in close, his mouth touching my hair in such an intimate way that should anyone approach us, my reputation would be ruined. "I suspect, m'lady, that you are not revealing the entire truth. And I intend to discover what it is," he said. His breath brushed against my hair, and the little worm of fear I had stamped out inched its way back into me.

The sound of the front door opening saved me then.

"Nora!" Hannah said.

Captain Roth dropped my hand and took one step away.

"Father! Come quick. Nora has returned!" she yelled into the house. Hannah fled down the stairs and wrapped me in an embrace. "I've been ever so worried. Are you all right?"

"I'm fine. Thank you," I said, not meeting Captain Roth's eyes.

"Nora," my uncle said from the porch, not hiding his disgust of my appearance. "I'm glad to see you are safely returned to us, child. And by Captain Roth, no less. What happened?"

"It is a most adventurous tale, I can assure you, Mr. Weller," Captain Roth said.

"Is it now?"

"It is. I'm sure Miss Bishop is looking forward to telling you her story. Am I correct, Miss Bishop?" Captain Roth asked. His mouth held a thin line, and his eyes narrowed.

I nodded, having found I had no voice.

"But first, I think you need to freshen up. Look at you, Nora. You must feel horrible. And your new dress!" Hannah said. "Father, Nora can tell you all about it after she washes up. What gentleman would put her through disclosing her ordeal without proper rest first?"

"Quite right, Hannah. Go. I look forward to hearing this story of yours when you have finished," Uncle Edward said.

Never in my life had I wanted to hug someone as much as I did my cousin then. "Thank you, Uncle Edward."

Without glancing at him, I allowed Hannah to usher me to the front porch, all the while sensing Captain Roth glaring at my retreating back. What was more worrying, however, was that Alex and I had never settled on a signal.

CHAPTER 10

UNCLE EDWARD HAD INSISTED on discussing the last three days as soon as the captain left, though Captain Roth stayed for a quite a bit conversing with him. Their voices drifted to my room even with my door closed. A bath be damned. It was no concern to him if I was tired, hungry, and dirty. He paced in my bedchamber as I sat on my bed, making me retell the story numerous times. As before, I stuck as close to the truth as possible but omitted certain facts. I admitted to venturing out in search of John, but I did not admit to finding him. I also let him know how I had run away from thc fighting, then found myself alone and hiding in the woods. I made sure not to mention Alex by name or the militia. Where was the harm in that? I knew he would be angry, but it was better than the truth. Uncle Edward would have to admit it was only by the grace of God I had not been hurt.

When he left, my head ached as if someone had taken an axe to it.

I stood in front of the looking glass, cleaned and dressed in one of the new gowns, and stared at my reflection. I'd only been gone from my uncle's house for a mere three days, but it felt like years to me. And my eyes reflected it.

If only the majority of the civilians in the area could witness what I had; the blood, the cannon fire and gunshots, the men shrieking in pain and wailing in grief over a friend on the field, perhaps this war would end sooner.

Of course, everyone knew war was bloody. Everyone knew men died. But to see the vital red fluid of the body spraying and limbs hanging off a man, to hear screams, to smell the salt of sweat, fear, and to taste the tang of blood was different. It changed a person. It changed me.

The clock on the mantel chimed seven as I made my way down the darkened hallway and stairs to the sitting room. The conversation stopped when I entered the room. Aunt Lucinda and Hannah sat on the blue settee, backs straight as always. Uncle Edward and Lieutenant Bates stood near the fireplace deep in conversation. Lieutenant Bates's eyes kept flicking toward my cousin, his gaze hungry as it rested on her décolletage. *Disgusting.*

My aunt stood up when I walked into the room, and everyone turned to look at me. I hated the attention, and my stomach rolled about as my eyes drifted over the room. It settled when I did not find Captain Roth in attendance.

"Now that you are rested, shall we all go in to dine? I'm famished," Uncle Edward said. "I would say you are as well, Nora, seeing as how you spent three whole days alone. Were you able to eat anything?"

"Well," I said, nodding to the servant who pulled out the chair for me to sit, "No. I found some herbs to chew on," I lied, when in my mind I remembered the hard, salty meat and the way my jaw ached while I tried to chew it. More than that though, I remembered how it had been Alex's meal, and he'd insisted I eat. My eyes focused on the large pheasant in the middle of the table, garnished with orange sauce and sprigs of rosemary while my mind drifted to the men in the militia and what their dinner would consist of tonight.

"We are so pleased you have been returned safely to us, Nora," Uncle Edward said, raising his glass of Madeira. "Thankfully, it was the good Captain Roth who found you and saw you home. There is no telling what would have happened if you stumbled upon a filthy militiaman. I daresay the only reason you came back to us unharmed was because of your wits and the good captain. To Nora," Uncle Edward said.

"To Nora," the rest of the dinner party echoed.

I smiled, but it wasn't real. It was a lie on my face much like a few of the lies I'd told to my uncle earlier in my bedchamber, much like the lies he had told me. I didn't want to look at him much less converse with the man. And now he wanted to continue to talk about my unfortunate experience in the woods.

"Are you sure you did not see any militia?" Uncle Edward asked as he cut his meat.

"I saw a few, but they ran through the woods. I crouched down as small as I could make myself, uncle. I feared I would be found out, and I didn't know what would happen to me if they saw me," I said, maintaining a neutral face as I had learned as a child whenever I stole a cookie before dinner.

"Poor girl," my aunt said.

"Poor girl?" My uncle huffed. "This is the reason I told you to not seek out John. You're fortunate you did not land in their hands."

"Edward. We have heard all this already. Please, let us have a nice conversation over our meal," Aunt Lucinda said. She raised her glass and took a sip, ending the interrogation.

He let the topic drop. My opinion of my aunt raised a bit higher after that. Thankfully, she had at least some sympathy and knew I had endured enough.

I ate the rest of my meal in silence, thinking about the events of the past few days and hoping Uncle Edward would question me no further. Only so many lies could be told before I knew I would falter and be found out.

"Nora?" Aunt Lucinda said, bringing my attention back to the present. "You look awfully tired. Shall we go and let the men discuss what they need to?"

"Yes," I said. I took one more sip of my Madeira, relishing the spice settling on my tongue and the warmth it spread through my body, relaxing me.

I had set my crystal goblet down when the butler entered the room. "Excuse me, Mr. Weller. Captain Roth is here," he said.

"See him in, Jeffery," Uncle Edward said.

I turned to my aunt, who straightened her back and lifted her hand to touch her wig, which hadn't moved an inch.

"Uncle? Why is Captain Roth here? Surely it is too late for callers." My hands twisted the napkin in my lap.

"He asked if he could stop over later to see how you were faring. Quite the gentleman, he is."

"Quite," I said.

My heart pounded like Captain Roth's boots on the wood floor as he walked toward us, and it abruptly halted the same moment his face came out of the shadows of the hall. His red coat was pristine; not a speck of dirt or dust anywhere. His black leather boots shone in the candlelight, as did his black hair. He forced a smile toward my aunt and cousin. I suspected he had plenty of calling cards at his home from available ladies. Admittedly, he was very handsome and pleasing to look at, but the pleasantness stopped there.

Captain Roth bowed. "Lieutenant Bates, Mr. Weller, Mrs. Weller, Miss Weller, Miss Bishop," he said. He stared at me, and his mouth formed a thin line. "I'm pleased to see you have recovered from your ordeal."

"Thank you, sir. I have. It was thoughtful of you to stop and inquire about my well-being. If you'll excuse me, I was about to retire," I said, standing up to make my exit from the room. I walked behind my chair and pushed it in toward the table. I smiled and looked at Hannah and Aunt Lucinda who stood up as well. *Praise the Lord.*

"Yes, well, if you don't mind, Miss Bishop, Mr. Weller, I should like to discuss your niece's extended stay in the woods."

My eyes flickered to my uncle.

"Thank you, Weller, for the information you provided me earlier, but I'd like to talk with her one on one. I've made a few general notes, of course, from our initial meeting, but General Howe would like to give His Majesty a full, detailed report. You understand? It would be unforgivable of me, as a British officer and as a gentleman, if I did not find out the whole story to make sure a fine lady like Miss Bishop was not hurt or used in some awful way."

I clutched the back of my chair, turning my knuckles white. What general report was he talking about? And, what information had my uncle told him while I was upstairs bathing and resting?

"Please, Miss Bishop. Do be seated. Lieutenant Bates, you may go. Ladies," Captain Roth said, addressing my aunt and cousin, "there is no need to stay if you planned on retiring. This will only take but a minute, and I'm sure you are tired from your day. I bid you goodnight." Captain Roth left no room for either of them to object.

Aunt Lucinda and Hannah retired with a quiet "Goodnight."

A sense of foreboding hung over me like a rain cloud while I continued to stand in the dining room.

"Mr. Weller, you may go as well," Captain Roth said.

"Sir, I do not think it proper to leave my niece alone,

unchaperoned with an eligible bachelor such as yourself," Uncle Edward said, taking another sip of his Madeira.

Thank goodness for small mercies.

"I can assure you, Mr. Weller, she will be taken care of." Captain Roth's eyes locked on mine for a moment. The corner of his mouth quirked.

I bit the inside of my cheek and tasted blood.

The captain then turned his eyes to my uncle. "Unless of course you are implying that an officer of the Crown is not a gentleman. I do not think His Majesty would approve of this sentiment, if that is, in fact, what you're saying," he said, his voice tight.

Uncle Edward cleared his throat. "Not at all. No. I'm loyal to the Crown and have the utmost respect for his soldiers. I'll be in the parlor."

Dread beat down on me while my uncle retreated from the room, leaving me alone with the man before me.

We stood there, the captain and I, staring at each other, each daring the other with our eyes to speak first. Silently, I stood my ground. Since I would rather be anywhere else, I would not begin. Why make it easy for him? He smirked and walked around the table, stirring my nerves to full alert with his closeness. When he reached me, he pulled out the chair I was standing near.

"Sit. Please. I would hate for you to be uncomfortable while I interview you. Would you like another glass of… Madeira, is it?" he asked, helping me to push in the chair while I sat down.

I shook my head to the invitation to more wine, but he refilled my drink anyway. He poured himself a full measure and raised it to me in a toast. "To safely returning home," he said.

I smiled and put the glass to my lips while the captain watched me. His dark eyes grew blacker in the candlelight, making him resemble a wild animal about to pounce on his prey.

"Shall we start at the beginning?" Captain Roth said. He set his crystal goblet down on the table but kept hold of the stem. His finger tapped it with a controlled and steady rhythm. I had no doubt this man had control over everything in his life. His eyes burned with a feral characteristic I'd never seen before.

"What exactly would you like to know, captain?"

"How did you come to be with the American militia?"

I swallowed. How did he know about that?

"I'm sorry to say I don't know what you're talking about. No doubt you could speak to my uncle? I've already given him my account, and I am still recovering from the ordeal. I would very much like to go to bed."

"Do not play coy. This won't take long. Tell me the story and off you go. Quick and painless."

"I was in town, on my way to the apothecary, Mr. McGovern—"

"You lie. I've talked to your uncle."

"No, I'm not lying. I'm starting at the beginning as you asked."

He stared then waved me on. "Why the apothecary then?"

"I work there."

"You expect me to believe this?"

I shrugged. "Ask my uncle. Are you going to tell him I left something out of my story? For if so, I do not care. I've done nothing wrong."

"You work for him? A young woman like yourself? Perhaps it is really a love affair?"

"How dare you!" I said. My brow furrowed, and my hands scrunched up the fabric of my skirt.

"A job? Why would you feel the need to have a job? Surely

your uncle has provided for you in luxury and has seen to your every need and whim."

"Yes, he has, and I am most grateful. However, I'm not used to sitting around all day long. I prefer to be busy. My father was an apothecary, and I was learning the trade before he died. I want to help where I can."

"How noble. Go on," he said, raising his glass and taking another sip.

"Well, after I finished my visit with Mr. McGovern, I decided to walk to the water's edge, by Kip's Bay Landing."

"That is quite a walk, Miss Bishop, to see the water."

"I'd overheard it was the most excellent place to view the East River," I lied. I forced myself to look at him and lifted my own glass to my lips, taking a small sip. The ruby liquid was dry on my tongue, the spices that I had at first found pleasant hard to swallow.

"Hmm. I suppose I should speak to your uncle about allowing you to travel into town unaccompanied. I'm quite surprised he permitted you to do such a thing. Moving on," he said, waving his hand in a gesture as if I didn't understand what he meant. "I'm told you spoke to one of the militia while viewing the water from this so-called perfect spot. Was it your brother? Your uncle said you had gone searching for him."

I gulped the remainder of my wine in hopes of forcing down the lump in my throat. It did not help. Before I could stop myself, another lie came out of my mouth. "I did go searching for him but did not find him. The man I did speak to, well, we simply made polite conversation about the weather. I did not realize it was a crime to talk to a member of the American army."

"A crime, no. Then again, it depends on what you were discussing."

"As I said, the weather. I was merely being polite."

"I'm sure. Let me guess, you stood in the rain and discussed it? I daresay, your memory must be so rattled from your horrible misfortune that you must have forgotten," Captain Roth said, smiling. He thought he'd caught me in a lie. This time he hadn't, but surely he would sooner or later.

"You are correct, sir. It did storm. But the storm had not yet approached when I first reached the area," I said. Needing something to do with my hands for fear they would shake, I played with the skirt of my gown. "The storm began when the fighting started. I could hardly see and was terrified of the guns, as most would be in that situation, so I ran into the woods and hid inside a cave for safety."

This was the truth or parts of a truth. I wasn't lying in the least. I'd only left out who the man was. For some reason, I feared to divulge it was John would make the situation worse, and if my brother was being held captive, he would pay for my time with the militia. Of course, I never had any doubts about not telling him I'd stayed with the American army and helped the wounded.

"What I would like to know, Miss Bishop, is how you managed to return back to your uncle unscathed. Do you think I'm foolish enough to believe you managed to spend three whole days, alone in a cave and journey back to your uncle's house through the woods, without getting lost or having anything else happen to you?"

My chest tightened as I considered my options. "Well, I did find one gentleman, a civilian, who guided me in the right direction, but aside from him, I was alone," I said.

"And let me take an educated guess. It was he who was hurt and who you helped? His blood?"

"Yes," I said. My voice came out in a hushed tone.

Captain Roth kept talking as if he'd never heard me. "I'm mystified in regard to your civilian specifically. Surely you are aware of how beautiful you are? A man might not be able to control himself around you," he said, his eyes resting on my breasts, "since he would be thinking with a different part of his anatomy."

He took a sip of the wine then licked his lips.

I refrained from shuddering. "You compliment me, sir, though if any man tried to touch me without consent, I can assure you I'd make certain that part of his anatomy would no longer exist."

The captain barked with laughter, his shoulders moving up and down with his inhale. "Well played, Miss Bishop. I pity the man who might try it. Though, rest assured, if that did happen, I would personally see to it that he was severely punished. I'd hate to see you have to get your hands dirty."

"I appreciate it, captain," I said.

"I find it odd that no one discovered you in this cave, as I know firsthand the woods were crawling with soldiers, on both sides. Or, as you wandered aimlessly around in the trees, that yet again, you never once stumbled upon anyone to help you until days later."

The clock chimed nine-thirty, and I stifled a yawn behind my hand. "Are we finished? As much as I enjoy talking, I would like to retire."

"Almost. You have yet to explain how I came to find you wandering alone through the woods."

"I've already told you, captain. The man who I helped simply pointed me in the right direction, and I left. Simple, really."

His eyebrows rose with his question. He took another sip of the wine, keeping his gaze on mine. "Really?"

"Yes." I lifted my chin. "Why is that so hard to believe?"

He snorted. "Then I need to give you credit on your navigating skills. There are lots of dogs scurrying around, Miss Bishop," he said, the metaphor not being lost on me. "Dirty hounds who need to be put down. They don't fight fair, in the least. Popping out from behind trees and bushes—"

"Fair? I did not know war was fair at all, sir. Why, how could burning a civilian's house be fair? For all I know, it could have been the British who are at fault for what happened to my family home," I said, standing up in a rush. The chair scooted back and almost fell down.

Captain Roth's hand jerked forward and caught the frame in his hand.

Damn it all to hell. Why did I say that?

He cocked his head to the side, and for a moment, it seemed as if he would crack a smile. "My lady, you seem sensitive toward the rebels. By your emotions at present, it seems you hold the mutts in high esteem."

The rage I'd been controlling escaped me in one full outburst. It couldn't be helped though the man terrified me. "I'm sensitive toward the war. And, I know there lay dogs on both sides. If you have nothing further to ask me, captain, I'm going to bed. Goodnight."

Captain Roth didn't bother to stand but watched me leave. I had reached the doorway when he called my name. "Miss Bishop?"

I stopped but didn't turn around.

"We'll speak some more on this. You can be certain of that. Goodnight."

CHAPTER 11

After a restless night of sleep, the dawn peeked through the window, casting a warm, orange glow onto the oak floor. The light filtered through a blue glass vase on the table, breaking the rays into shards, like my life. What had I gotten myself in to? Was I prepared to carry secret messages to Alex, knowing if caught, I could be put to death? Or, if they decided to show me mercy, spend time on a prison ship? According to stories, death would be better. At least autumn was upon us now as the trees in the distance resembled the quilt on my bed; an array of colors decorated the leaves in brilliant shades of orange, red, and yellow..

After getting dressed, I stepped outside into the crisp, early fall, sunlit air and took a deep breath. Shielding my eyes from the glare, I looked around me in all directions. Each way I faced brought with it a different choice, and for a moment, I wasn't sure what to do. My legs were locked in place.

If I traveled left, my path lay unknown before me. I would have no idea who I'd meet or where I would go. And, in some small way, I found freedom in that.

If I traveled right, the direction of Manhattan, it would be a perilous path. The streets were filled with redcoats, which meant information. I would need courage. Too many things lay at the end of this road, I knew to be sure. Treason. Betrayal. Lies. Sadness. Possibly death if caught. John could be this way. But there could also be change. Did I have it in me to turn my back on everything I knew for the chance of something different? Was freedom worth it, and if so, could I make much of a difference?

Before I could stop myself, I took a few steps, then a few more. I walked down the hill, heading east, toward Manhattan.

Mud caked the streets and clung to the bottom of my gown while I weaved between people, carts, horses, and vendors on my way to Mr. McGovern's apothecary shop. I held my breath twenty seconds at a time since the stench accosted my nose with manure, rotten food, and whatever else seeped into the air.

For the next two weeks, Mr. McGovern and I worked in a comfortable silence. The routine of each day calmed my ever-prickly nerves. The only sounds were of my crushing herbs at the bottom of the pewter pestle then scraping them into a dish, and the sounds of Mr. McGovern scratching away in his log, taking note of his stock. I swept the floor, tended the fire, and organized the shelves. Proudly, I could rattle off any number of remedies to middle-aged wives who complained of their husbands' intestinal irritations; Glauber's Salts, Plummer's Pills, ipecac, jalap, calomel, saline, rhubarb, and castor oil usually did the trick.

Throughout the next two weeks, I paid close attention to every single person who came into the shop in the hopes of discovering any useful information I could pass along to Alex. I also ventured to the market stall as often as I could. But I discovered nothing useful. In the evening during dinner, my uncle was oddly quiet on the subject of the revolution. I started to get frustrated at not being able to provide Alex with any information when Aunt Lucinda made a comment about a ball they had recently attended. She was aghast at what one of the women had decided to wear. But, that simple statement was all it took.

"Aunt Lucinda? May I ask a favor? I know it truly isn't my place, but what if you held a ball? It would be grand, I'm certain, since you are a most gracious hostess. And Hannah could introduce me to—"

"What a marvelous idea! Oh, we could invite everyone. And perhaps find you a husband," my aunt said, grinning.

I knew Aunt Lucinda would relish the idea of a gala and, as thus, be consumed with finding me a suitor. But, my hope was to uncover more information about the war and what the British were planning. It pleased me to hear my aunt would invite everyone. For by bringing all the important people together for the evening, I'd be able to find something to pass along to Alex.

For the next several days, preparations for the upcoming celebration preoccupied Aunt Lucinda's focus. From the way she talked, she really was inviting most the British army. As for me, my thoughts stayed concentrated on extracting any and all information from the redcoats. I needed to learn more about their plans.

The evening of the ball, I sat in my room and stared at my reflection. I had changed. I looked older somehow. Shadows marked my skin under my eyes that had never been there before. My spirits were low as I had heard nothing about John, nor had I had the chance to inquire about him. I missed my parents and sister terribly. Oh, how my mother and sister and I would have had so much fun dressing for the festivities. Our bedroom would have been full of giggles. A small tear escaped from my eye and I wiped it away. Tear stained cheeks would do me no good tonight. I needed to be cheery.

I arched my spine, hoping to crack it and find some small sort of release. My back and legs hurt, and the last thing I wanted to do was wear a pair of silk slippers. But, I had to go. I had to find out information on the enemy and pass it along. The British had taken everything from me, and now I was going to do everything in my control to make them fall.

I studied my hands and sighed. My nails were now short, and callouses rose up on my palms as if they were mountains. I had always loathed wearing gloves, but tonight I was ever so thankful that a lady was supposed to wear them during social events.

"Miss Nora? Here is your dress," Suzy, one of the house servants, said. She walked into the room without knocking, a pale blue dress that verged on the color of gray with inlays of flowers woven throughout draped over her arm. It had a lower neckline, with bell sleeves and a cream-colored petticoat. "This is freshly pressed," she said. "You'll be the talk of the evening wearing this, no doubt."

"That is the plan," I said, not hiding the contempt in my voice.

"Not to speak out of turn, miss, but that is no manner to find a husband."

She turned my shoulders so I sat straight and began to work on my hair. The pins pricked my scalp, and I twitched.

"Hold still, now. I'm makin' this extra tight so it doesn't come loose," she said, placing another pin in my hair. "There. Let's get you on downstairs."

Aunt Lucinda had outdone herself according to the lips of most of the women in attendance. The food and drink dripped with decadence, as did the decorations. Never in my life had I seen so many bouquets of flowers in one place. Candlelight danced right along with the couples. Jewels which adorned fingers, necks, wrists, and attire shimmered in the soft glow of light, and the crystal sparkled like diamonds. The soldiers' brass buttons and black leather boots gleamed as they sauntered through the crowd. With the number of men dressed in uniform, it did seem as if my aunt had invited the entire British army.

I took a deep breath and did my best to settle my stomach. It was all a flutter, and not in a good way. I wiped my hands on my gown and decided my only course of action was to just start conversing with people. The problem was bringing up the topics without seeming as though I was fishing for information. *Bloody hell.* Would the men know I was spying simply by asking questions? God, I hoped not.

Two hours had passed when Hannah found me in the corner of the main room.

"Isn't this grand?" Hannah exclaimed.

"Very much so," I said in a dry voice.

"Oh, Nora. Cheer up."

"I am cheerful. Or was cheerful. My face hurts from smiling, and my voice is tired from all the talking," I said. I tried not to sound too grumpy, but I was. I'd been putting on a show all night. Dancing, flirting, laughing at jokes that were non-amusing, all for the sake of finding out some bit of information. However, the soldiers this night were not in the mood to discuss the war.

"I have one last person for you to meet. See that man over there?" Hannah asked. She pointed to a man of medium build, average height and looks. However, when he laughed, his smile was huge.

"Yes."

"That is Private Joseph Boynton. I'm going to introduce you. He and Brandon are good friends."

"Brandon? I did not realize you were so close to be using Private Harding's Christian name."

Hannah blushed and pulled me across the room to where Private Boynton stood talking to her Private Harding.

"Oh, Miss Weller," Private Harding said. His face exploded into a wide grin upon seeing her, and his eyes lit up. "You look lovely tonight."

"Thank you," Hannah said. "Private Boynton, it is nice to see you as well."

Private Boynton looked at Hannah and bowed then looked to his friend.

I resisted the urge to sigh and introduce myself.

"Private Joseph Boynton, may I introduce you to Miss Weller's cousin, Miss Nora Bishop. She is formerly from Long Island, now living here with the Wellers."

"Miss Bishop," he said, bowing.

I curtseyed. "Hello."

"How long have you been living in Manhattan?"

"Since the end of August." I hoped he wouldn't ask why. The last thing I needed tonight was to delve into why I had to leave my home. "Where is your family from?"

It was in the middle of him explaining about his family's estate in England when I sensed a pair of eyes staring at me. I glanced over Private Boynton's shoulder. My breath caught.

Alex stood with his back against the wall next to a candelabra. The light from the flames flickered off his dark hair. His eyes locked with mine, and the corner of his mouth turned up in a knowing smile. He gave a small jerk of his head in the direction of the garden then slipped through the crowd.

"Miss Bishop? Are you all right?" Private Boynton asked. His eyes narrowed, and his face grew full of concern.

"Yes. I'm sorry. I… um, need some air. I will be back shortly," I said.

I turned to leave, but he interrupted me.

"My mother would box my ears if I did not escort you

outside. Allow me," he said. He took my hand and placed it inside the crook of his elbow and led me through the throngs of people toward the double doors that led to the balcony.

Social propriety be damned! I hid my annoyance behind a smile. Why did every man think a woman could not go anywhere alone? The contents in my stomach turned to mush. How was I supposed to talk to Alex now?

The sky was clear, allowing the stars and the moon to shine brilliantly. A soft wind blew, carrying the scent of apples and hay to my nose. The light from the moon along with the candles from inside the house cast shadows along the balcony. I squinted as I looked both right and left, but did not see Alex. He had walked out these doors. Hadn't he? Perhaps I was wrong?

"My lady, may I be of assistance?" Private Boynton said. "It appears as if you are searching for something."

"I do beg your pardon. I thought I heard a noise. Would you be so kind as to retrieve me a drink? My throat is rather parched."

"It would be my pleasure." Private Boynton spun on his heel and walked back inside. I exhaled and whipped my head around at the sound of a cough.

"Your throat is parched? I'd say so after all the flirting you've been doing in there," Alex said behind me.

He stepped out of the darkness, his eyes filled with amusement.

"Flirting? And how would you know?"

"Because I've been lingering in the shadows long enough."

"Dressed as you are, I'm shocked you did not cross the room and ask me to dance. You could have saved me from the other men and some of their roving hands. How did you manage to acquire a British uniform anyway?"

"I took it the day your family home..." Alex cleared his throat, and my own grew tight. "Show me the men, and I'll cut their hands off for you if you'd like," he said. His eyes twinkled with humor then, and my heart danced a jig.

The loud bark of laughter made me spin around. Three men, deep in conversation, stood near the double doors. Alex stepped back into the darkness near the railing. Not wanting them to think I was talking to myself since Alex was hidden from their eyes, I strolled over to where he stood and placed my hands upon the wrought-iron railing, facing the back gardens. Alex stood next to me, our shoulders nearly touching. He set his hands on the black rail so close to mine that I could feel the heat radiating off his body.

"What are you doing here?" I said, my voice barely above a whisper.

"I'm here for several reasons. First, I'm here to seek information, but so far, I haven't heard anything. The men are in no mood to discuss politics this evening. I'll be leaving after we talk. I've had a few folks stare at me a little too long for my liking."

"Men or woman?" I asked, knowing all too well women probably looked at him as if he were a delectable dessert ready to taste.

"Both," he said, casting a side glance at me. "I'm worried I might have been noticed."

"Well, it doesn't surprise me. You do seem to be the tallest man in any room, and those blue eyes are quite… um… blue." I blushed. I had never been so glad to be in the dark with a man.

He didn't say anything for several moments, and when I looked at him, he stared back.

Although we stood in the dark, I could envision the way his eyes would look. Sharp, piercing, and intent, as if he were searching through my very soul. I swallowed and looked back to the garden.

"Are you enjoying yourself tonight?" Alex asked, changing the topic quite suddenly.

"No. My cousin insists on introducing me to every eligible soldier in New York, when the only reason I have not pretended to have a headache is for the same reason you are here. I hoped to glean some useful information. However, most of the soldiers are only interested in gazing at my bosom."

"Well, it is a rather nice one."

I jerked my head toward him. "You—"

Alex laughed and shrugged. "I'll always be honest with you, Sailor. You look very beautiful in that dress tonight. Every single man in that room has noticed you, which leads me to the other reason I came here." His hands tightened around the railing.

My whole body was heated through. I glanced at the balcony entrance. Where was Private Boynton?

"You best hurry and spit it out because Private Boynton should be back any second with my drink," I said in a rushed voice.

"I only wanted to check in on you. Are you all right?"

"Oh," I said. Needing something to do with my hands, I touched my hair. "Thank you. I'm fine. Yes."

"I know it may seem as if I have left you alone, but rest assured, I've been keeping track of the house. You are in no danger. I wanted to see you to make sure—"

"Miss Bishop?" Private Boynton said from the double doors.

I jumped and put my hand to my heart. With the softest thud, something dropped to the ground. I gripped the railing and peered over the edge. As fast as a cat pounced upon a mouse, Alex was gone. But where?

My heart beat fast. I squinted into the night but saw nothing or no one.

"Miss Bishop?"

"Here. I'm over here," I said, stepping away from the railing and out of the shadows, my heart barely returning to normal. I walked across the balcony to where Private Boynton stood, holding two crystal glasses filled with wine.

"I apologize it took me longer than anticipated to bring you a drink. Regrettably, I got caught up in a discussion about the troops."

He handed me the glass of wine, and I took a rather large sip. This was my chance, and I was not about to let it slip through my fingers.

I raised my eyebrow. "What about the troops, Private?"

"I doubt a lady wants to hear about the comings and goings of the regulars."

I took a small step forward and placed my hand on his arm. "I'm not a typical lady, Private Boynton. I find it most fascinating." I tilted my head to the side and smiled. Alex did say most men were noticing me all night. Perhaps I could use this to my best interests. "I'd also like to know how much longer Manhattan will have gentlemen, such as yourself, around. Parties would be rather dull without you. And, if you do need to leave the city, I would very much like to pray for your safety."

"Is that so?"

I batted my eyes. "Yes."

"I think you are pulling the wool over my eyes, Miss Bishop, but I'll entertain what you're trying to do. No doubt you do find it fascinating as female talk is rather dull."

"You have discovered the truth," I said. "Forgive me."

"Nothing to forgive. Stories of war and soldiers are much more interesting, I agree. But, truth be told, there isn't anything to say. General Howe has decided to keep us firmly planted here in Manhattan for the time being to rest and recover after the latest battle. A shipment of gunpowder and cannon fire will hopefully be arriving within the week, and the hospitals are overrun with soldiers. Oddly, most of the men are sick from illness and infection, not necessarily battle wounds. I'm ready to leave. I'm getting restless, as are most of the others. I want to be in my own bed. In my own house. Not sleeping in Mr. Pichard's spare bedroom above his cabinetry shop."

"I'm sorry you are so far away from home," I said, meaning it. I was starting to like Private Boynton. So far tonight, he had looked me in the eyes when we spoke, which was more than I could say for half the other men I had conversed with. He didn't shy away from discussing politics with a woman, and he listened quite intently when I spoke.

"I have heard that Miss Pichard is quite happy to have a few regulars living in her house," I said.

He laughed. "Yes. Wherever I turn, she happens to be in the room forgetting something. She's a nice girl, but Miss Bishop, I must be honest, I have a lady at home waiting for me whom I cannot wait to marry. I do hope you do not think—"

I touched his arm. "I am glad to hear it, and I apologize if my cousin Hannah has given you any trouble. She is intent on finding me a match come what may," I said.

Private Boynton's face turned to astonishment. "You aren't like any other ladies here. Miss Bishop, if I were not taken already, I do believe I would be courting you."

I could not help the warmth that spread across my cheeks.

"Would you care to dance?" Private Boynton asked. "We can give everyone something to talk about, if we haven't already, being outside here on the balcony," he said.

"I'd love to." I put my hand on his arm.

We walked into the room and stood in the doorway, waiting for the best opportunity to join in the dance, when my eyes landed on Captain Roth. It was as if I had been punched in the gut when I saw his face. He looked every bit the gentleman in the room, but I knew that was far from true. The faces of my family surfaced immediately upon looking at him, and I found it hard to breathe for a moment. But, work needed to be done, so I pushed all my emotions away and focused on my anger and what I had to do. I had to finish this for them. As much as I hated to be near the man, he was the one I needed to talk to. He would most definitely have information.

"Private Boynton, I hope you do not mind, but I need to speak with Captain Roth for a moment. Would you be so kind as to wait here for me? I shall only be a few moments, and then we can have our dance?"

Surprise flashed behind the private's eyes, and his arm tensed under my hand when I mentioned the captain's name, but he was only polite. "Of course, Miss Bishop. I will wait here for your return."

I sauntered over to where the captain stood. "Good evening, Captain Roth," I said, keeping my hands clasped in front of me. I squeezed them trying to calm my nerves.

"Miss Bishop, lovely to see you again." A gleam hid behind his eyes. What was he up to?

"Is it? I'm so glad. You've been well?"

The captain squinted. "Indeed. How may I be of service, Miss Bishop?"

I let my gaze fall to the dance floor and raised my eyebrow. He was a smart man and caught on easily.

"Miss Bishop, I do not presume you truly want to dance with me, but I'll play along," he said.

He gripped my arm and escorted me to the dance floor. Fear snaked its way through my body, coiling in my stomach. I had to do this. I had to. His hands were rough, and his fingers dug into the satin of my gown. I tried not to flinch when he touched me. "Tell me, Miss Bishop, what news have you discovered tonight?"

"News?"

"Yes. Surely that is why you've been talking to almost every gentleman in this room."

He pressed his hand against my back, forcing me to come closer to him. My breasts were crushed against him. He smirked. His breath reeked of wine. "Or perhaps you are simply a whore and looking for someone to warm your bed tonight?"

"How dare you! I was coming over to make pleasantries since you are a guest in my uncle's house and to see how you and your troops fare, and you insult me in such a way!"

"Is that so? Well, since you are so inclined to know, I am wonderful. I had the honor of flogging a man today and met a sweet girl named Milly. Thankfully, she was pretty silent. And, now I find myself here, dancing with the most beautiful woman I have ever laid eyes on. As for my troops, as you can see, they are in good spirits, rested and ready to move."

"Move? Where? It seems as though the troops just arrived," I said.

"North. But enough about that. I'd like to know, Miss Bishop," he said, pulling me in tighter. My stomached swirled as his fingers dug into my back. "Are you as sweet as Milly?"

"I think we've finished our dance, sir. I find I have a headache." I cursed under my breath. I should have known it would be much too hard to gain information out of him. At least I had the news of the troops moving north. I just didn't know when.

"Nonsense," Captain Roth said.

"Let go of me," I said through clenched teeth.

"Only after you tell me what you are about, Miss Bishop. I don't trust you. I don't believe anything you have to say."

"You don't know me, and I owe you nothing. Not even an

explanation. Now let go of me, or by God, I will cause a scene." My anger flared.

We stared at each other then. Our eyes locked, neither of us budging. The captain tilted his head back and let out a hearty laugh, causing those around us to look in our direction. "I do believe that. Well, until the next time," Captain Roth said.

He released me, and without a word, I walked through the crowd and made my way toward the stairs. My mind was too rattled for another dance or trite conversation that I didn't even bother to make an excuse to Private Boynton who waited for my return. My legs shook, and my knees trembled while I climbed the steps, and it took everything I had in me not to turn around to see if the captain watched me. Sweat dripped down my back and chest, and I found it hard to breathe. More than anything I wanted to rip my stays off as soon as I entered my room. But I couldn't. I had a letter to write.

I nearly fell into the chair in my room. I took a deep breath and waited for my nerves to settle. I was safe here. He would have to have some audacity to come after me in my own room, in the middle of a ball. Or would he?

With shaking hands, I dipped my quill into ink and wrote a quick letter to Alex. Although there wasn't any important information to give him about the troops, I could at least inform him what Private Boynton had said. Perhaps knowing General Howe wanted to rest his regulars was information worth noting. Of course, the fact a shipment of gunpowder and other supplies was due later in the week was useful, though I wasn't sure if anything could or would be done about that.

After I sealed the letter with red wax, I tucked it inside my stays, not having any other place to conceal it. I grabbed my cloak and fastened it around my shoulders then carefully opened the door where Suzy stood ready to knock.

"Miss? Why, whatever are you doing?" Suzy said.

"Um, I—"

"Miss Hannah said you retired because of a headache. I brought you some tea. From the looks of it, I'd say something else is going on?"

Did I dare tell her? I had no idea what to do as I stood staring at her. If I told Suzy the truth, she could help me. But, if caught, it would surely mean her death. No. I couldn't do that to her. So I lied as I was becoming accustomed to doing.

"I'm meeting someone. In the garden," I said.

Her eyebrows rose.

"Please don't say anything. I don't want anyone to know, for obvious reasons. Especially Captain Roth."

"I saw you dancing with that man. You best be careful with him, miss. There's something not right about him," Suzy said, as if talking to herself. "Oh, forgive me. I know it isn't my place—"

"It is all right. I'll always want the truth from you. No matter what."

"And I'd like to think you'd tell me the truth too, Miss Nora. For now, I'll go along with this story. What do you need me to do?"

I squeezed her arm. "I do need to sneak out to the garden. Don't let anyone follow me. That's all. I'll explain when I can."

Suzy nodded but said no more. "Go through the servants' door. Come on," she said.

Given that the help were all rushing about attending to the needs of the ball, the hallway was free of people coming and going. Suzy and I walked quickly and quietly through the hall, and she pushed me through the door.

"You best hurry, Miss Nora before someone sees you. I'll

stay right here and wait for you," Suzy said. She cocked her head and put her finger to her lips. "Go. I hear footsteps. Someone is comin'."

Without so much as a nod, Suzy closed the door as I heard her say, "Sir."

"What are you doing, wench?"

It was Captain Roth's voice. I dashed into the shadows of the night, undetected, and as fast as I could, ran toward the edge of the wood, praying no harm would come to Suzy. I'd never forgive myself if he touched her.

The playing of strings drifted on the wind as I weaved my way through Aunt Lucinda's garden, keeping myself behind the taller bushes so no one would see me. My heart beat to the fast tempo, and my blood rushing in my ears was loud. My palms were sweaty, and the small letter inside my stays itched my skin. A small chortle of laughter caused me to stop in my tracks and caused my heart to jump up in my throat. It was a woman's voice followed by a man's. A few seconds later, nothing but silence and some heavy breathing reached my ears. Taking one careful step at a time, I snuck my way around the lovers. By the time I reached the back fence and hopped over it, only the music of chirping crickets filled the air.

The breath I'd been holding escaped my lungs when I reached the woods. I stopped and took in my surroundings, letting my eyes adjust to the darkness and my ears to the sound of the forest. I listened for footsteps and the clomping of horse hoofs, but all was quiet. I had contemplated holding off until morning, but making a dead drop in the daylight made me nervous. Though plenty of British regulars attended the ball, I betted on the fact they were mostly deep in their cups tonight and, therefore, not wandering around in the trees in the dead of night.

It was darker of course in the woods, without the candles

from the house and the lanterns, but the moon burst through the canopy of trees, casting a soft glow of light. Summoning courage, I turned and made my way to the left, toward the black walnut tree where Alex had designated I make the drop.

More leaves lay on the ground than on the branches of the trees, and with every step, they crunched underneath my feet. With each snap and break, my nerves jumped. The tree loomed up ahead. I put my head down and strode over to it, watching each footstep I took. Once I reached the tree, I paused to look around, making sure I had not been followed. I reached inside my gown and retrieved the letter then placed it inside the hole at the bottom of the trunk.

Not wanting to get caught, I hurried back the way I had traveled, my feet running through the woods and then the grass when I reached the field. My satin slippers were wet from dew, and my toes were numb. My body shook with nervousness, and my dress clung to me from perspiration. As the house came into view, I envisioned sitting in front of the warm fire with a nice cup of hot tea in my hands. I opened the gate, hearing the music once again filling the air and snuck around the garden.

When I reached the servants' door, I straightened my dress and took a deep breath for the first time since I'd left. I'd done it. I'd made a successful dead drop for Alex to retrieve, and if I should happen to be caught by someone now, I'd say I needed a breath of fresh air. Certainly there would be no evidence against me to prove otherwise.

I straightened my shoulders and pulled open the door, then screamed.

Suzy was lying still on the cold wooden floor. Her lip was split, and blood trickled out of her nose. Her eyes were closed, and when I crouched to her, finger marks were upon her neck.

"No! No... no, no! Suzy? Suzy!"

I picked up her head and cradled it in my lap. Though her face was still warm, her arms were not. I placed my fingers on the side of her neck anyway but knew what I would find. No beat. She was dead.

"Help," I squeaked out. "Someone. Please."

The tears fell down my face, wetting Suzy's hair.

"Miss Bishop?" someone said in the hallway. "Whatever is the matter?"

I looked up. A young maid, Leah, I thought, stood at the end of the hall. Her eyes widened, and she ran down to where I sat with Suzy's limp body. "Suzy? How? Who?"

"Get Uncle Edward, please. Do not draw any attention to yourself."

"Yes, miss."

A moment later, my uncle's heavy footsteps bounced down the hall. He stopped short when he saw me. "What the devil? I want answers!"

He glared at me, taking in my disheveled appearance, my tear-stained face, and my cloak. Before I could stop myself, I lied. "I was outside. Near the gardens. I needed some air as my head hurt and thought it would do me some good. When I came back in... When I opened the door—"

Damn it all to hell! I couldn't get the words out. Shock and grief froze me solid. Suzy was dead. Murdered. And it was my fault.

Uncle Edward turned and looked at Leah. "Get Isaac and Jeb from the stables. They'll take care of her."

"May I offer my assistance?" Captain Roth said from behind my uncle. I had not seen him there.

My body stiffened, and I pulled Suzy's dead body closer to me.

"No. Thank you, captain. Let's return to the festivities.

Nora, you have my leave to go to bed. I, ah, am certain this has been a shock."

Uncle Edward left, his back stiff, and walked back toward the music and his guests.

Captain Roth made no movement. His face was neutral with no form of shock anywhere within his features. He pulled out a handkerchief from his pocket and blotted the corner of his mouth. "Pity," he said. With a sadistic grin on his face, he turned and walked away, leaving me alone with Suzy's body and my guilt.

CHAPTER 12

My uncle didn't bother to attend Suzy's funeral, if one could call it that. A small group of us buried her among the wildflowers near an old oak tree. It was all surreal. I watched Jeb, one of my uncle's black slaves, throw the last bit of dirt over her, and a tear slid down my cheek.

My thoughts drifted to the black walnut tree and the missive I had placed underneath its branches as I walked back from the small funeral to the laundry line. God, I hoped the information I had secured would aid the Americans. Seeing as how Alex hadn't told me what the signal should be to let him know something waited for him, I took it upon myself and hung my black petticoat on the line I had worn for my mourning period. It was something we had joked about, after all. *Bloody hell.* Women would be wearing black for years at the rate this war was going.

The deep hole that had formed in my heart from the deaths of my family and John being missing grew deeper with Suzy's death. I was alone and scared. I knew Captain Roth had killed Suzy, but I also knew I had no way to prove it. It was only a matter of time before he came after me. I had to get out of my uncle's house, and the only way I could see to do it was to take Hannah's advice and find a husband.

I concentrated on my work in the apothecary shop, shutting out all feelings and memories as best I could and made a mental list of possible men I could approach. I could only think of two men, as I was not about to marry anyone who wore a scarlet coat. However, if I could find John and get him back, there would be no need to marry. But, I had to find him first.

I finished labeling the last of the glass bottles when my stomach growled. Without looking at the clock on the mantel, I knew it had to be well past noon. I wiped my brow and brushed a flyaway hair off my forehead before rotating my shoulders back and forth. They ached terribly from standing over the table and grinding the plants into powder. Mr. McGovern continued to scribble away in his book.

"Excuse me, Mr. McGovern?" I said, wiping my hands on my apron.

"Yes," he said, never looking up.

When my stomach growled again, he glanced at me. I shrugged my shoulders and wrapped my arms around myself. "It is past noon, sir. Would you mind if I take a few minutes to eat?"

He looked at the clock and set down his quill. "Not at all. Did you bring something?"

"I'm afraid not. I left the house in quite a rush to get here. I have a few coins on me and will go down the street to a market stall," I said, sure there would be troops lingering near the market. I had left my lunch at home on purpose. My plan was to strike up conversation and glean what I could from the troops to pass along to Alex.

"I will accompany you, as I have promised my services to Dr. Frank, who is in charge of the British infirmary. He stopped over yesterday asking for a few supplies. We'll take a bit of nourishment and then go over. You'll come with me."

I could barely believe my good fortune. Without knowing what he was doing, Mr. McGovern was giving me a way to look for my brother, or at least discover his whereabouts and discover more information on the British. I certainly hoped John wasn't in a mass grave out on the battlefield but in the infirmary we were going to visit. Surely the British army would take care of wounds on an injured enemy soldier. Perhaps he was in prison, wherever that was. At least now, I would be able to discover this information without looking suspicious. It would be perfectly natural to bring it up in conversation. At least I hoped it would be.

The sun was high in the sky when Mr. McGovern and I left the shop. The stench of town hit me the second I stepped outside. Three soldiers atop horses rode past us, nodding at me as they trotted by. One of the men whispered something, and the other two laughed. I instinctively pulled my cloak closer around my shoulders, gathering it close to my body, and found myself thankful Mr. McGovern was with me. I'd never been fearful of men, but with so many now roaming the town as if they themselves owned it, my senses took over, whispering to be more careful. I was no longer on Long Island. I was in a big town where no one knew who I was.

"Pay them no mind, Miss Bishop," Mr. McGovern said, clearly understanding the looks the men had given me. "You're a beautiful young lady, and young men have no sense of mind on how to act around someone with your charms. Accept my apology on their behalf," he said.

"Thank you. I appreciate your manners."

"Thank my wife. Let's find something to eat, shall we?"

"Do you think it wise for us to dine together and for me to go into the tavern? I do not want to be the cause of any unwarranted speculation."

"I think it very wise since we are both famished." He extended his arm.

I took it, and we began our trek down the muddy road toward Wooster Street and The Corbie Tavern.

"Where do you think those men are going?" I asked, spying another group of soldiers moving in the same direction as the first three. The man in the middle turned his head to the left to look at his fellow soldier, and I faltered in my step. David, my former fiancé. He laughed and took his hat off, running his hands through his golden hair.

Mr. McGovern stopped so I could right myself, never knowing the real reason for my misstep, while I kept my eyes on David's back. "Probably their next post, or taking a meal. They are in uniform, so they remain on duty. They could be going to the prison or to check on a friend who has been hurt. Any number of places."

"The prison? I thought prisoners were held on ships?" I said, fishing for information.

Mr. McGovern glanced at me from the corner of his eye. "Some, yes. But the British are also using the Sugar House to hold Americans these days as well."

Could the Sugar House be where David was headed? Did he know John's whereabouts, and was he watching over him? I prayed so. Certainly, David would look out for his best friend, different sides be damned. One did not hurt another because they disagreed on ideas. Or did they?

"Is it safe, do you think?"

"Safe? What do you mean?"

"To have the prison be so near to us, to town, I mean. The prisoners must be awful and—"

"Why ever wouldn't it be safe? The British have many guards stationed not only inside the prison but scattered around the outside. I'm positive nobody can get access without permission," he said. "Watch your step now." He helped me over a hole in the ground that led to the front entrance of the tavern. Wooden planks laid over the ditch, but they were covered in mud.

The tavern was filled with scarlet coats everywhere, laughing, playing dice, and all around being loud as if it were their typical nighttime sport.

I coughed in the smoky room and nodded in thanks to the serving woman who set down a mug of ale. "Not much to offer today, Mr. McGovern. The men ate me out of everything, I fear. Stew won't be ready 'till this evening's sup. Alls I have is bread, cheese, and some apple."

"Thank you, Mrs. Osborne. We'll take two plates if you please," Mr. McGovern said.

Mrs. Osborne nodded. "I'll be back in a moment."

The emotion throughout the tavern was jovial. The men all seemed to be relaxed, downing pints, smoking pipes and the like. Their hats were off, jackets unbuttoned, and if it weren't for the sun shining through the windows, I would have sworn it was late at night. I wished everyone could be as carefree but knew that couldn't be the case. Alex and his men would not be laughing like these men for a long time.

"They have reason to celebrate," Mr. McGovern said, watching me.

"Really? I heard the rebels won the Battle of Harlem Heights, or am I incorrect?"

"You're correct. However, it is only the first victory for General Washington. The redcoats still have control of the town. Washington won't get it back easily. For now, these boys are relishing in that fact."

Remaining silent, I raised my cup and took a sip. The door opened, letting in a blast of wind and a big shaft of light, blinding everyone in the darkened room. I stiffened when I realized who entered the tavern. I'd know David's silhouette anywhere.

CHAPTER 13

I WRAPPED MY HANDS around my cup to keep them from trembling. David had been walking in the other direction. What was he doing here now? He had looked directly at me and stomped across the tavern to the table where Mr. McGovern and I sat.

"A friend of yours?" Mr. McGovern asked, not looking up from his plate of food Mrs. Osborne had set down only seconds before.

"He's a childhood friend, yes," I said, not giving any more details than necessary.

I wasn't sure if I should acknowledge the fact David approached my table or not, but he had certainly known I'd seen him. He marched toward me, and I gripped my cup harder.

"Miss Bishop," David said, bowing to me.

"Mr. Shipman," I said, keeping everything formal.

"I thought I saw you walk in here, with... someone." He glanced at Mr. McGovern.

"You have good eyesight. What can I do for you?"

"I wanted to know how you're doing."

I shrugged. "Fine. Thank you for asking." I straightened in my chair and lifted my chin. I hadn't seen him since we called things off over a month ago. Back when he decided to join the British regulars, making it clear the war was more important to him than our future.

David glared at Mr. McGovern. His thoughts reflected dimly on his face. He looked back to me. "Pardon my saying, but do you think this is socially acceptable to be out with—"

Mr. McGovern coughed. "Me? I can assure you, sir," he said, standing, "it is not what you might think. I'm six-and-sixty years on this earth and have no need for a young maiden. My wife would not appreciate your ideas, sir."

"Most men your age would love to grab hold of a young—"

"David!" I said. "That is enough."

"It is at that. I will be back, Miss Bishop, once you have disposed of this... person," Mr. McGovern said. He stood up, smoothed his waistcoat, and walked to the other side of the room to a table of older gentlemen.

"What are you doing here with him? Do you have any idea what this looks like? Your reputation—"

"Bloody hell, David. I am employed by Mr. McGovern at the apothecary. He's teaching me, and yes," I said, raising my hand stopping him before he could say anything, "Uncle Edward knows. And, I don't give a damn about my reputation. I don't plan on staying in Manhattan for the rest of my life. Gracious, you not only insulted me, but you insulted him. Besides, my reputation is no longer your concern."

"I'm sorry," he said, sitting down. "And that's not true. I'm tired. And I hate seeing you with another man. Even if he is old enough to be your father. I still want to marry, Nora." His eyes softened, and he looked at me sheepishly. "I should be the one treating you to a meal."

My throat tightened, and my heart all but stopped beating. Part of me was still very angry at him, but I could surely forgive him. Couldn't I? We had a past. Perhaps we could still have a future together. With hope, the resentment I had been feeling toward him faded away.

I reached out and touched his hand. "You still can. We can still have the life we always planned, David. You hate being a soldier. I can tell. It is written on your face. Let's run away. We can go to Pennsylvania where nobody would know us and start over. In the country. We could leave and never come back."

I held my breath in anticipation. I cared for David. Truly. Though the idea of being free from Captain Roth wasn't lost on me either.

"Become a deserter, you mean? Nay, I could never do that. If I were to be found, I'd be killed, and where would that leave you? What about my family? You're right, I don't enjoy being a soldier, but my job is important."

"And what is that exactly?" I sat back and crossed my arms. I knew he was right, but his explanation still hurt. If he never would have joined the army, we wouldn't be in this situation to begin with. *Christ.* So many things would have been different. Resigning myself to the fact we were over and therefore would not be going away together, I decided to use him for whatever information I could gather. The idea of using David didn't settle well in my stomach, but my anger over what the British had done to my family gave me my resolve. It had to be done. I knew I could get him talking, and I'd use the information to my advantage.

He waved his hand. "I don't want to bore you."

"I've sat and listened to you talk about grinding wheat. I think you talking about the war and your job will be much livelier," I said, maintaining the sarcasm in my voice.

"If you must know, I'm to give updates on our gunpowder, number of cannons, and the like. They have me riding all over the place at all hours of the night. Why, I haven't slept in the last sixteen hours."

My ears pricked up at the words gunpowder and cannons. This was the intelligence Alex would be wanting from me. I had to get David to divulge more information without seeming suspicious.

"I don't see why you would need to know the facts about such things," I said.

"I personally don't, but I have to give those in charge up-to-date information on our supplies and whatnot, which is vitally important, Nora. You're a smart girl. Think about it. I now have to report to Captain Roth that General William Howe is planning on landing more troops near Westchester County."

"Why so north?" I fished.

"Because of Washington's location, silly girl. This is why women have no place in the army. The more we know about the enemy, the better we can prepare ourselves and thus, limit the causalities."

Letting David's snide remark pass, I tucked the new information he had provided away in my memory. This bit of intelligence was important. I took hold of the word causalities. "David? Have you heard anything about John? He was either captured or killed after Kip's Bay Landing. I haven't heard anything, and I would dearly love to know what has happened to him."

David's face grew somber and I feared the worst. "I'm sorry, Nora. I haven't heard anything, but if I do, I will get word to you straight away."

The hope that had first started to fill my heart when I saw David, thinking he would have some information for me about my brother faded as fast as the dying sun.

I nodded. "Now, where are you off to?"

"The Sugar House. Captain Roth is expecting me. Once I deliver the information he needs, I'll begin my post. I'm on guard duty for the next forty-eight hours."

"Have you been there before?"

"Yes. Forty-eight hours ago. Such is the life."

A shadow fell across us, and I looked up. Mr. McGovern had returned, a mug of ale in hand. David turned to him. "My apologies, sir. I meant no disrespect."

Mr. McGovern narrowed his eyes and huffed. "I suppose I can't blame you. Miss Bishop is a beautiful young lady, and if I were a suitor, I would arrive jealous as well, seeing her dining with someone else, no matter how old he was."

A blush spread across my cheeks. Thankfully, the room had dim lighting. David cleared his throat but said nothing about him being a suitor or not for that matter. "Well, I bid you both a good day," he said.

Keeping my eyes on David's back, my attention was diverted when a man reached out and touched David's arm as he walked by. David stopped, and they exchanged a quick, friendly conversation. My heart spurred on, and the air suddenly became thick. It was hard to breathe.

Nathan Hale. He looked at me after David had left the tavern and winked before returning to his conversation with the man he sat with.

While Mr. McGovern and I finished our meal in companionable silence, I couldn't help glancing over to Captain Hale every so often. However, to his credit, Captain Hale never once looked at me again. Not even when I walked past him, making my way out the door.

The sun heated my skin while we walked down Barclay Street toward King's College, which was now being used as a military hospital. The lace kerchief around my neck itched, and I wished I were home where I would leave my neck completely bare and thus, cool. But Hannah had told me all proper ladies wore the kerchiefs in town, and so I did.

Not for the first time did I wonder if Captain Hale had information to give me, and that was his reason for being in The Corbie while I was there. I also couldn't help but wonder what he thought of me talking to David in what would be perceived as a private conversation.

Mr. McGovern and I stepped up to the main doors of the now hospital. Its three-story stone building was quite the view to behold as it sat on three acres at Park Place overlooking the Hudson River.

"It is a shame the boys are no longer studying and that commencement has been delayed. But, I suppose this is the best place for a hospital. It is large enough I suspect," Mr. McGovern said.

"Did the British take it over?" I leaned over to peek inside one of the windows.

"Yes. Though I doubt the faculty and students had much say in the matter. Ready?"

I nodded.

Mr. McGovern grabbed hold of the wrought-iron handle and pushed. The door swung open, and I started to follow him inside but halted in the doorway.

The smell of rotting, putrid flesh blew through the large building, smacking me in the nose. My eyes watered, and I reached inside my pocket to find the handkerchief I carried.

Mr. McGovern looked my way. "I can understand your reaction. However, Miss Bishop, the last thing these men need is to see you act as if you can't stand to be in the same room as them. They are physically hurt. Do not make it harder for them."

Reluctantly, I stuffed the handkerchief back in my pocket and took a hesitant step inside the room. Men were lined all along the main hall and in rooms I suspected had once been used as classrooms. Nurses fluttered back and forth between them and up and down the great staircase.

"Ah! Mr. McGovern, sir," a robust lady said, scurrying over to where we stood. Her bosom heaved with each breath she took, and her face was red. For a moment, I wondered if she would need a bed of her own. "The doctor has been expectin' ye. He's right on up the stairs, he is. Third door on the left you'll find 'im. He'll be right 'appy to see ye. Ye did brin' the remedies, I take it?"

"Good day to you, Madam Morris. I did bring them, yes. I'll go straight away. This is Miss Bishop. She can assist you until I return," Mr. McGovern said. He bowed to us and walked directly up the stairs.

"Right then. 'Ave you any notion on how to dress wounds?" Madam Morris asked, taking off. She never beckoned me to follow and, after a quick run-down on what needed to be done, she picked up a handful of cloth and scurried away, leaving me alone.

Seeing no way around it and fully realizing this was what I had signed up for, I gathered the bandages and made my way down the hall. The moans and cries of men penetrated my ears, and I did my best to tune them out as best I could, but it was hard. A large part of me wondered if any of the men were involved in the burning of my home, or if they were the ones who had caused John harm. And if so, I was glad they were hurting. However, the small voice of my father spoke to me again as if he were standing next to me. As I approached my first patient and looked at his red face, my heart broke for them, for every man in the room, though they were the enemy.

A groan from the red-faced man drew me out of my thoughts. He trembled and then violently thrashed around. I rushed over to him to try and still his body. His eyes popped open, and he looked at me, his eyes glassy. He tried to sit up, all the while, moaning. I forced him to lie back down, and his head rolled to the side with his eyes shut once more. His body was as hot as fire, and the smell wafting off him made me gag. I turned my head looking around for assistance, but I was still alone. *No use being idle.* I pushed back my sleeves and went to work.

CHAPTER 14

I WORKED FOR TWO straight hours until Mr. McGovern was finally finished. The sun shone as we walked back through the city streets toward his shop. We had spent more time away than we had planned. Plenty of people milled about the city, though most were making their way home to prepare for their evening. I knew I only had a few hours or so left before I, too, would need to go home.

"The back room needs to be swept," Mr. McGovern said when we walked inside.

I picked up the broom and proceeded to work as the bell rang over the door. Someone had entered the shop. Mr. McGovern walked out to the front room to see who it was while I shut the cabinet, frustrated.

"Miss Bishop, you have a visitor!" Mr. McGovern hollered.

I paused. *Who is here?* "May I help you?" I said when I stepped into the front room.

"Miss," said Captain Nathan Hale, bowing over a bouquet of wild flowers. He rose, and when his eyes met mine, a hint of anxiousness hid behind them.

My legs wobbled and I shifted my weight from one foot to another. "Sir, I believe we have not met," I said, for the benefit of Mr. McGovern. I did not want him to be mixed up in anything I was part of.

"Mr. Nathan Hale at your service, my lady," Captain Hale said, looking every bit the school teacher.

He took a step forward, and I accepted the bouquet and brought the flowers up to my nose to hide my surprise. While I knew at some point Captain Hale would have come to see me at the apothecary, I did not think he would do so in this way.

"Thank you. These are lovely. I'm Miss Bishop. How may I help you, Mr. Hale?" I said, not knowing what else to say and hoping I remembered not to declare his rank.

He cleared his throat, and his eyes flickered over to where Mr. McGovern stood staring at him. His face reddened, as if embarrassed for bringing a lady flowers in front of another gentleman. "I saw you in the tavern earlier today, Miss Bishop, and I wanted to come and pay you a visit."

Mr. McGovern snorted. "This is a place of business, Mr. Hale, not a place to come courting. I'll give you five minutes," he said. He turned on his heel and walked into the back room.

"What is this about?" I said, my voice barely above a whisper.

"Well, I didn't want to pretend to be sick and have to spend money I don't have on medicine I don't need. I figured this was safe enough," he said, pointing to the flowers. He grinned, and I blushed.

"Do you have any news?" I asked. I walked over to one of the shelves and stood on my tiptoes to reach a glass vase.

He nodded and strode across the room. He raised his hand and grabbed hold of the vase easily. He leaned in closer to me and lowered his voice as if he were speaking to me as a lover. "I'm procuring sketches of the fortifications and have some information on the number of men at their disposal and positions. I will give you all of this information by the end of the week for you to take to the dead drop location."

"Why not now?"

"I think it is best to wait until I have the information in its entirety."

I blew out a short breath and took a step back. "Thank you," I said, turning away and walking to the table in the room where I set down the vase. "I've already put information in the spot Alex designated, but I have no idea if he has gotten to it yet. I will put your sketches there as soon as you give them to me. I've news for you as well. It seems General Howe is considering taking troops into Westchester County, but that isn't confirmed."

Captain Hale nodded. "I'll continue to search out information on that lead. As for the dead drop, he received the information. In the meantime, perhaps you could write a correspondence about the possibility of the British moving and let them know that I shall have plans for them later."

"All right. Anything else I can do for you?"

"I have discovered a John Bishop is being held in the Sugar House."

"Prison," I said as if someone had punched me in the gut. My lungs were tight. Prison was not better. In prison, he could die as easily as on the battlefield.

He nodded. "I'm sorry. From what I could discover, they do not plan on releasing him anytime soon."

"How do I get him out?"

"You can't."

"Why not?"

"Why not? Miss Bishop, the Sugar House is heavily

guarded for one thing. Not to mention every cell is full, and we have no way of knowing where he is inside."

"Couldn't you sneak in and find him? He looks like me. It would be easy." I knew what I'd said was false, but I had to hope. I started to pace the floor, wringing my hands together. I now knew where John was; all I needed was a plan to get him out. I smoothed the front of my gown. I wasn't a fool. Getting him out was going to be as hard as finding berries in the middle of winter.

"Please, Captain. He is the only family I have left. I have to find him and, God willing, get him out," I pleaded.

Captain Hale ran his hand through his hair. He turned toward the window and stared at the street. "I have a brother as well," he said, turning back to me. "Did you know?"

"No."

"He's two years my senior. Gracious, I miss Enoch. I wish I could speak with him now. There are times I fear I'm in over my head." His voice grew quiet, but it was strong. "Do not misunderstand me, Miss Bishop. You can be sure I will not waver in my position. I believe in this cause fiercely, but there are times, I pray I am not making a muck of it. I am not scared of death. Death meets everyone at some point. The details are all different, of course, but it comes to everyone the same. On the contrary, I fear being the cause of someone else's death."

I didn't speak for a moment as I did not want to ruin the intimacy of truth between us. "Then you can understand, sir, why I ask this of you?" I said, finding my voice.

He hesitated. "Yes. I will do what I can."

The floor in the back of the shop squeaked, and Mr. McGovern's feet stomped out of the room.

Captain Hale took a step toward me. He grabbed my hand and kissed it, keeping his charade in place. "It has been a pleasure, Miss Bishop. I hope you will remember the sentiments I spoke today. Perhaps write them down and keep them close to your heart?"

The corner of his mouth lifted at our secret. He squeezed my shaking hand. "I will. Thank you," I said.

Captain Hale bowed. "Good day, Miss Bishop. Good day, Mr. McGovern," he said, over my shoulder.

"Hmph," Mr. McGovern muttered behind me.

Captain Hale turned and left the shop, looking back over his shoulder one last time.

Mr. McGovern cleared his throat. "You have a few suitors, it seems," he said, grinning.

I waved his comment away and began to straighten the glass jars.

"You're finished for the day. Will you be fine walking back home by yourself, or would you like me to accompany you?"

"Thank you for the offer, but it is still light. I will be fine," I said, grateful for his concern.

He nodded. "I will see you in the morning then."

"Yes, sir. Thank you. Good day."

I left the shop and hurried down the street, keeping my eyes trained on the ground. The sun remained in the sky but it was dipping lower and soon would disappear. I hadn't realized the hour when I'd left the apothecary's shop but, it was later than I intended it to be.

I had only ventured a block when I accidentally tripped. I landed on both knees in the mud. "Bloody hell," I said, brushing my hands off on the skirt of my gown and rubbing my aching kneecaps.

"Still a foul mouth on you, Miss Bishop. Your uncle has not silenced you yet?"

I had no need to look up and see who spoke. His voice

chilled my bones, and I closed my eyes for a moment to settle myself, taking a breath. He made no move to help me to my feet.

Once I regained my footing, I looked at him. "Captain. I do not care what my uncle thinks of my language."

He smirked. "If you were part of my family, I think I would consider beating you for such an unladylike manner."

"Thankfully for me, we are not related, then," I said, stepping around him. I was not fast enough, and he caught me by the elbow while he laughed.

"You sure have a fiery spirit, don't you," he said. His eyes roamed freely all over my body. "Clearly, no one has been able to tame you. I wonder what it would take to do that?" he said, stepping closer to me.

I stared over his shoulder, afraid to look into his eyes.

"For someone to break you in and become your master."

I yanked my arm out of his grasp. A fear I had never known surged through my veins at his veiled implication. "Good day, sir," I said through my clenched teeth.

His laugh haunted me the entire way home, echoing in the recesses of my mind with every step I took. My thoughts were so inundated with Captain Roth I would have missed my uncle on the front porch if he hadn't spoken to me.

"I see you've returned home," Uncle Edward said.

I stopped at the door and spun to look at him. He leaned against the railing, his feet crossed, smoking a pipe. The smoke swirled around his head, drifting off into the sky. His blue waistcoat was stretched tight across his stomach, making me think perhaps I should mention to Hannah he be made a new one.

"Well? Are you going to answer me, girl?"

"Oh, Uncle Edward," I said, bringing my hand to my heart. "I was woolgathering and did not see you."

"That is obvious. Working awfully late, don't you agree?"

The railing groaned under his weight as he pushed himself off. We stared at each other for a few minutes. His eyes flickered to my gown. For a long moment he didn't say anything, and I found myself fooling with the hem of my sleeve out of nervousness.

"I didn't particularly care for your father, as I'm sure you know. Your mother was supposed to marry someone else, did you know that?" He turned back to look at me.

"No," I said. My voice sounded hoarse to my ears, and I cleared my throat.

"Yes, Edith was supposed to marry Jonathan Worthington, my best friend. May he rest in peace. But, one day, your father came around, and that was it. They married in secret. Edith's best friend, Susan, was there. She's the one who told us about the handfasting ceremony," he said, shaking his head. "I called your father out, of course. I wanted to duel. The only reason that didn't happen was because Edith was with child, and she begged me."

"Why are you telling me this?"

"Because I want you to know that, although I did not like your father, I did respect his ability to put aside his opinion on things and help those who needed it, no matter what. And it is only because of this fact that, yes, I will allow you to continue to train as an apothecary with Mr. McGovern. He is a respectable man and loyal to the crown. I fear you'll have to use the knowledge on our troops, though I hope it won't come to that. However, from now on, get home earlier."

"Thank you, Uncle Edward," I said, doing my best to contain my smile.

"Yes, well." He waved me away. "Get ready for dinner. We'll be eating soon."

I turned to leave, but he stopped me with his voice.

"Oh, and Nora?"

"Yes?"

"Wear something… nice," he said, his eyes glancing again at my ruined dress. The corners of his mouth turned down. "We will be having guests for dinner." He faced the road once more, deep in thoughts of his past.

CHAPTER 15

PER THE USUAL SEQUENCE of events, my aunt, uncle, and cousin waited for me in the dining room. Hannah looked lovely, as she always did. Tonight, she wore a beautiful silk gown of peach with a lace-trimmed silk petticoat. It matched her complexion nicely. I opted for a dark blue gown with a matching choker necklace, as my mood of late was less cheery. By the time Captain Roth arrived, the choker necklace around my throat was as tight as my stays, making it hard to breathe.

We finished the meal, and I relaxed slightly knowing I had made it through dinner without having to converse with the captain besides what was socially acceptable. Then the discussion turned.

"Is it true Captain Howe plans to stay in New York?" Uncle Edward asked. He placed his silver fork back down on the china, causing a small ding.

Captain Roth took a sip of his wine. "It is. I believe we will be here for quite some time," he said. "So, no need to worry, Weller. You will be protected." He smirked.

I glanced at my uncle, who didn't respond with words, but whose face reddened.

What does that mean?

"Will the army be staying in Manhattan, Captain, or will you move somewhere else?" I asked. Too many overgrown secrets lingered, and I needed the information.

"My, my, Miss Bishop. You are paying attention. And here I thought our dinner conversation has been boring you all evening," Captain Roth said.

I played with my silverware, arranging them so the ends matched each other in distance from the end of the table to their tips. "I suppose I tend to remain silent when the conversation is tiring."

"And what do you consider tiring conversation, madam?"

"The very thing you were discussing earlier this evening."

"Which was? We've discussed many a topic around the table this evening, Miss Bishop. Pray tell, which do you mean?"

I grinned sheepishly. "Truthfully, Captain, I haven't any idea. The talk did not stir any interest to me and, therefore, my mind wandered."

Captain Roth finished soaking up the blood from his venison with a piece of bread and popped it into his mouth. "Yet, politics stir you? That surprises me. We could discuss the man who visited you today at the apothecary shop?"

"Man?" *How the hell does he know that?*

"Yes. I believe he brought you flowers," Captain Roth said. His eyes lit up as if he had caught me in a snare.

"Do you have a caller, Nora?" Uncle Edward said, his eyebrows rising.

I shrugged a noncommittal gesture, but inside I shook. Did the captain recognize Captain Hale? *Is he spying on me?* "No, Uncle. A young man saw me and thought to brighten my day. That is all. Nothing more, I assure you. As for politics," I said, wanting to veer them off the topic of Captain Hale, "I suppose the topic does make me curious." I hoped he didn't read too much into my questions.

Captain Roth's dark eyes narrowed. He leaned back in his chair and crossed his ankle overtop his other knee. "Curiosity, is it? I should think a woman would have no reason to be curious about such things as the political agenda and movements of His Majesty's army."

"You mean to insult my sex, Captain?" I said, my back straightening.

"No. Perhaps I should clarify. I see no need for the fairer sex to have any information on the proceedings. I find they overembellish the emotions of it all."

"Overembellish?" I said through tight lips. My anger was restrained by a thin thread that I knew would take very little to snap. "It is war, sir. How do you propose us fair females react to it?"

"Nora," Uncle Edward said, the warning in his voice evident, but I ignored him.

"To make such a statement that a woman's emotions are embellished — are dramatic — is to imply—"

"Nora!" Uncle Edward said again, his voice firmer. His hand thumped down upon the table, and I looked at him. "That is enough. You forget yourself. You are not sitting at your father's table where you are free to speak your mind however you wish."

I laughed, but my voice held no humor. "No need to remind me of that. I'm well aware I'm not sitting at my father's table. If you'll excuse me, I'm exhausted and will retire. Good evening."

Their mumbled voices carried as I walked toward the stairs. My uncle apologized on my behalf, and the captain's voice was as clear as if I'd stood next to him.

"Her outburst is a prime example of what I was talking

about. It is no bother, Weller. Now, how about a glass of port and a smoke?"

After I shut the door harder than necessary, I paced my room. How could a man take something as horrible as war and treat it so flippantly? Did he lack a conscience for it to be so? Yes.

The fire had already been stoked in my room, and for the time being, it was too warm. The walls closed in on me, forcing me to open the window. The wind blew in, fluttering my hair and whipping the flames of the fire, but I remained at the windowsill, looking out into the crystal night toward the upper field. Somewhere in the distance, the black walnut tree stood solid, waiting for me to deposit a single letter.

I took a breath and shut my eyes, finding it helped me to regain clarity of my mind and emotions. I moved my body in such a way to ease the tightness of my stays. My feet were cold on the wooden floor, but I didn't mind it. The chill would help me stay awake for what I needed to do next. Write to Alex.

The mere thought of him stirred something inside me that I wasn't sure what to do with. His easy smile and sharp, blue eyes came to my mind and put my nerves at ease. It had been too long since I saw him last, and I hoped I'd see him again. Soon.

The wooden chair squeaked when I sat down at the small table. The flame from the candle and fire gave off enough light for me to see. The room had cooled down enough that I now needed my shawl, so I took it off the back of the chair and wrapped it around myself, although the task I was set to do was what hung heavy on my shoulders. I shifted to find a comfortable position while I arranged my writing tools. The quill trembled in my hand as I dipped the point into the ink. For a moment, my hand hovered over the parchment while I contemplated how to begin the note.

I had managed to write the salutation when a small knock sounded on the door. My stomach all but leapt into my throat at the intrusion, and I hastily slid the parchment to the bottom of the pile.

Securing my shawl around my frame, I crossed the room and put my mouth closer to the door.

"Who is it?" I said.

"It is Leah, Miss Bishop."

I eased the door open, and Leah, another servant of the home, entered the room. My uncle's and Captain Roth's voices reached the stairwell. From the sounds of it, they had retired to the drawing room and were, no doubt, sipping on brandy or port and smoking. The words I clearly heard were "Brown Bess," the most popular rifle used. They were either still discussing the war or had moved on to hunting. I glanced at the clock. It would be hours before the captain left.

"I'm sorry to come in so late, Miss Bishop. I'm here to help you untie your stays. I can leave if you want, miss," Leah said. Her eyes remained downcast and I wondered if she ever looked anyone in the eye.

"Leah? Does my uncle mistreat you?" I asked. I didn't know what made me speak the question out loud, but there it was. I wanted to know. I hoped she'd tell me the truth.

"I'm treated fairly, Miss Bishop." Her eyes glanced at me, but she said nothing more on the topic. "If you'll turn around, miss, I'll untie your stays for you an' help you ready for bed."

She worked swiftly and quietly, and my breath came easier after the laces were undone, my breasts released from the constriction of the whalebone garment. I took a deep inhale and rubbed my sides to ease the ache the binding occasionally caused.

"Do you know how long Captain Roth plans on staying

tonight?" I asked. The clock on the mantel now said midnight. Surely, he had overstayed his welcome.

"The captain is stayin' over, miss. A room has already been prepared for him."

"A room? In what section of the house?" I asked, my heart taking a few extra beats at this new revelation.

"At the end of the hall. Is there anythin' else I can do for you, Miss Bishop?" Leah asked.

"No. Thank you," I said, doing my best to cover up the trembling in my voice. I did not trust the man. He had threatened me on several occasions, and I never wanted to find myself alone with him again.

Leah walked to the door and opened it. She had set one foot into the hall before she turned around. "I don't mean to speak out of turn, miss, but I think it would be best if you locked your door tonight," she said.

The men's laughter filled the hall, and her eyes flickered in the direction of the sound. I understood her hidden meaning.

"Thank you for the advice," I said. The fear in her eyes clenched my heart. "Where are you sleeping?" I asked before I could stop myself.

Her mouth twitched. "Tonight, I'm sleepin' in the stable. Up in the loft. Underneath all the hay."

Wind swept through the room, and I shivered. It was a cold night as autumn had arrived, replacing the warm nights of summer. I turned around and opened the closet door and grabbed the extra wool blanket. "Here," I said. "Take this."

Leah's eyes widen, and she seemed about to shake her head no, when I pushed the blanket into her hands.

"I insist. I would invite you to stay in here, but I know you would never do that. Consider it a gift for your warning," I said, though I had every intention of locking my bedroom door, regardless. I did appreciate knowing my idea had been validated.

"Thank you, Miss Bishop. Goodnight."

I locked the door promptly after Leah left and took a breath. There would be no sneaking out to the upper field tonight as I had thought I would do. I would not take that risk knowing Captain Roth was downstairs and probably in his cups already. First light would be better when he and the rest of my family were sure to be sleeping. With this in mind, I sat back down, pulled out the parchment, and continued my letter of information to Alex.

* * *

THE SUN WAS A distance speck on the horizon, casting a faint glow of orange when I exited the house. I had rewritten my correspondence to Alex four times before I settled on what to include and, more importantly, what not to include. The other pages I had tossed into the fireplace. I watched the flames eat the parchment to make certain I left no evidence behind.

On tiptoes, I crept down the stairs and out of the kitchen door. Once outside, I breathed deep, thankful I made it outdoors without disturbing anyone. I stood on the dew-covered grass and looked upward. The sky directly above my head was dark gray and cloudy, but the faint blue sky in the distance told me morning was minutes away. It wouldn't take long for the sun to completely rise. I turned my head, looking to the upper field, and watched the trees and their dancing leaves, their trunks appearing as black statues against the backdrop of dawn. Much like men these days, their allegiances drifting and skipping this way and that. I swallowed, knowing I used to fit into the same category, but no longer. For the second time, I was about to commit treason against my king and country. It was my own choice. Freedom to make my own decisions, and the liberty from tyrants like Captain Roth was worth it.

I trudged through the wet grass, the leaves soaking into my wool stockings and the hem of my gown. The birds were starting to wake, and I swung the basket I carried in my hands, singing to myself, pretending I didn't have a care in the world.

There I sat on Buttermilk Hill.
Who could blame me, cry my fill?
And ev'ry tear would turn a mill;
Johnny has gone for a soldier.

The song stuck in my throat at one point, and I continued the tune, but with no words. Humming was all I could muster. I still was no closer to getting my brother out of the Sugar House, but my determination had not waned in the least. I would get John out of that bloody prison.

The edge of the wood was in sight when the hair on the back of my neck rose. The sinking feeling of being followed gnawed at me. Not wanting to let my pursuer know I had my guard in place, I stopped and sat down in the long, wet grass, putting on an act of fixing my shoe. I stopped my tune and listened to the world around me, but heard nothing. I risked a glance up and saw no one. It must have been a figment of my imagination.

Keeping still for a few seconds more, I searched the surrounding area. All was clear. Maybe it was a deer that scampered off thinking I was a threat. I stood and smoothed my gown then started off again toward the black walnut tree.

The birds were wide awake now, chirping their morning

song, their singing providing comfort and calmness to my soul. The sun had fully risen, shining bright, replacing the gray dawn with the blue cloudless sky. A small bite clung to the air, and in another few weeks, the dew on the grass would be replaced by a light frost. The wind rushed through the long grass and the leaves on the trees, blowing them each and every way, making them sound like an army invading.

On any other day, I would have breathed deep and taken in the tranquility of the wood, but today that was not to be so. The letter inside my gown weighed me down with a burden I felt eager to pass on.

I crossed over the patch of path where I had run into Captain Roth earlier. It seemed like it had been a year ago, rather than only a few weeks. My eyes glanced at the thicket where Alex had hidden and then settled on the black walnut tree where I was supposed to make the dead drop.

With my eyes focused on the tree, I didn't pay heed to anything else going on around me — not the wind carrying the scents of smoke and day-old brandy, nor the birds who had become startling silent, as much as birds could be. In fact, I hadn't noticed any of the warnings until the blade of a sword struck out in front of me, sliding underneath my chin.

"My, my," Captain Roth said. "Miss Bishop? Out and about so early? Curious. Perhaps you are meeting someone?"

Without moving an inch, my eyes slid over to where he stood, a sadistic smile plastered on his face.

An overwhelming sense of alarm burst throughout my body, and I found myself gripping hold of the basket tighter. How had he seen me? I had been sure no one spied me as I left the house that morning.

"I could ask you the same thing, Captain," I said, doing my best to mask the fear. "What sort of gentleman sneaks up on a woman, especially one who is walking alone?"

Captain Roth moved his wrist. The sun glinted off the

steel, and I swallowed. Perspiration dripped down my bodice, the chill in the air notwithstanding.

"Answer my question, Miss Bishop. You have been playing games since the minute I met you emerging from the woods. What are you hiding?"

"I'm hiding nothing, sir."

His eyes locked on mine but then drifted downward, his look hungry and feral. With a small growl escaping his throat, he pushed me until my back was up against the trunk of the nearest tree, an elm. The bark was rough and scraped my skin through the striped fabric of my gown.

"You say so, but I'm under the impression, madam," he said, spit flying out of his mouth, "that you are full of secrets. And I intend to discover them. There is nothing I like better than a game of hide and seek."

Fast and swift, like a snake striking a tiny mouse, Captain Roth's hand assaulted my person, his fingers clamped my breasts and squeezed hard. I flinched and flailed beneath his touch. His face was inches from mine, the smell of day-old brandy and smoke still potent on his breath.

"Get off of me! Let me go!" I said, knowing it was no use. I was alone in the woods with him.

Captain Roth pushed harder against me, his body now planked against mine. "No one commands me, madam. Especially a woman." With his body closer to mine, I could feel through my gown how much he was planning on commanding me. His resolve on that issue strained against his white uniform breeches. Little did he know, I didn't take kindly to being told what to do.

Moving my knee, I tried to kick him where it would hurt most, but he anticipated my move and blocked himself. Then he laughed a harsh laugh. "You don't fool me, Miss Bishop. Now, what secrets are you hiding for me to discover?"

His eye rested on my breasts once more and before I

could stop him, he lifted his sword and sliced through the ribbons holding my stomacher to my shift, then pulled it out and flung it to the ground. My breasts sprang forward as did the piece of parchment that had been concealed inside my stays.

"Ah, the secret has been revealed," he said, pinching my left breast.

I grunted at the assault, but he only laughed.

Captain Roth picked up the parchment and opened it while I did my best to cover myself up, though it was no use. My shawl had fallen to the ground. I didn't move. Fear paralyzed me. The best I could do was attempt to hold the pieces of fabric together over myself.

My throat and chest were tight, and I could scarcely breathe. Fear, anger, frustration, anxiety, all crowded inside me, each vying to burst forth. Tears brewed behind my eyes, but I would not let them fall. I had to hold it together

I watched his eyes as he read through the note. He looked up at me, and his dark eyes turned blacker. "What is the meaning of this?" His voice was too controlled, though I could see the anger rolling inside him.

"It is exactly as it appears. A list of ingredients," I said, keeping my voice as calm as I could, though it still shook.

"What for? What do they mean?"

"Well, the peppermint leaves help settle the stomach, and the wintergreen leaves we use for urinary irritants. The jewelweed, of course, is for poison ivy—"

He sprang at me, slapping my face then pinning me once more against the elm tree. His forearm pressed into my neck making it hard to respire. "What game are you playing?" he asked, his voice menacing. A small amount of spittle bubbled at the corner of his mouth.

"I'm collecting different flowers and herbs for the apothecary," I said with strangled breath.

"Then why was it hidden inside your bodice? Why not carry it in your basket?"

"Because I left early and at first feared it would rain. I didn't want the parchment to get wet, thus making it unreadable," I lied.

His eyes narrowed.

Captain Roth was breathing hard and continued to trap me against the tree. His entire frame was strung tight; spasms of his anger flowed through his body, ricocheting off mine. I knew it was only a matter of seconds to when he would release his full wrath upon me; mainly springing it from his breeches. However, a rider galloped toward us, saving me. My eye glanced to the man. Another soldier, wearing a red coat. Would Captain Roth allow the man to take part in my suffering and humiliation?

"Captain Roth, sir," the man said as he rode up to where we stood. It was Private Harding.

Private Harding managed to keep his face neutral, but anxiousness circled itself in his eyes as they darted between me and the captain. To his credit, he did not glance at my breasts, and resentment toward his superior then flashed in his eyes as he seemed to observe the way the captain pinned me to the tree. He looked away from the spectacle, his face all but saying, *"I'm sorry I can't help. He'll kill me if I try."*

"I'm busy, Private," Captain Roth spat. "Please do come back. This won't take me long," he said, his eyes never leaving my face.

I swallowed, his arm still on top of my throat making it difficult.

"I'm sorry sir, to... ah, intrude. I was at the house, but Mr. Webber said you had left and journeyed this way. It is of great importance, and I was sent to fetch you immediately. General Howe wishes to see you at once," Private Harding said. His horse began to sidestep, as if he himself knew what was happening wasn't right, and he wanted to flee.

Captain Roth's jaw clenched in anger. Without withdrawing pressure off my body, he looked over at Private Harding. "And what does he want?"

"We are moving north into Westchester County, sir. It is definite. A chance to trap Washington—"

"Stop!" Captain Roth said. "Say no more, you imbecile. I don't want her to hear anything."

"Yes, sir. Sorry, sir."

"I'm coming, Private," he said, then he spat on the parchment. "I'll be right there." He pushed into me, his body once more hard up against mine. "This isn't over, my pet. And, if you tell anyone, I'll kill your brother. I know where he is."

CHAPTER 16

I SAT ON THE ground for a long time without moving. It could have been minutes or perhaps longer, stretching into hours. I had no recollection of time, but I was acutely aware of my surroundings: the breeze fiercely blowing, trying to knock everything over in its path, the smell of damp wood and dirt with the faint scent of baking bread, my skin warming to the sun then turning cold when the yellow circle became covered by clouds. I paid attention to every detail, to every buzz of noise, to every blade of grass tickling my skin when it moved. I didn't want to focus on what had happened because I would lose control. *Oh God.* I gasped and wrapped my arms around my stomach.

I shook and shivered even though my inner being was numb. What the hell had happened? Logically, I knew. Captain Roth had threatened me on so many levels. I had heard stories of women who had been raped, beaten, but never met one who confessed her plight.

Shock, followed by hysteria on what had occurred, and what, by the grace of God, did not, jolted my numbness. With shaking hands, I reached for my stomacher. I looked down at my bare breasts before trying to fix my gown. Captain Roth had pinched me so hard a purple bruise was starting to form over my nipple. It throbbed and ached, and I shut my eyes for a moment and took a deep breath.

Feeling a bit more settled, I shoved the stomacher back inside my gown. It would need to be repaired. I grabbed my shawl that lay near my feet and wrapped it around my shoulders, clutching it tightly to my chest. At least the shawl would protect the front of my gown from wandering eyes should anyone see me on my return to the house. Hopefully, I could slip inside and upstairs without anyone being any wiser to what they saw.

Never in my life had I been so terrified of a man. Even when I found myself in the middle of battle did I not cower so as I had when pinned under Captain Roth. I shuddered, mad at myself for not putting up a greater fight. But how could I fight against someone as strong as he?

"Damn it all to hell!" I said, hitting my fist on the ground while tears slinked down my cheeks. "Get yourself together. You're not helping anyone sitting in the dirt."

I stood up, grabbing hold of the tree trunk to help me balance. My legs trembled, and my chest grew tight. If it hadn't been for Private Harding, I knew very well I would have been hurting worse than I was at the moment. I smoothed down my gown and grabbed my discarded basket, and turned to make my way to the black walnut tree.

I stumbled a few times over the large thick roots on the forest floor, teetering this way and that, as if I had come on dry land after being away at sea. My entirety shook. How long until it stopped, or would it never? Would I ever feel comfortable being alone again?

Stopping in front of the black walnut tree, I scanned the area. Confident no one else was near, I lifted my skirts and withdrew my letter from a small, secret pocket I had stitched on the inside of my petticoat. Thankfully, Captain Roth never thought to lift my skirts and invade that part of me, for if he had, he might have discovered it. As I had sat at the table the night before writing out all the information I discovered, it had dawned on me I should have two different letters in case someone happened to be out. At first, I hadn't thought it necessary, but then remembered something my father had always said, *"You must be prepared for anything and everything, Nora."* Once again, Father knew best. I shuddered, knowing Captain Roth had been close to finding the real letter.

I took a breath and pushed the thought aside, concentrating on my job at hand. I knelt and pulled the bark and moss-covered stone away and peered into the hole. Lying there inside was a small piece of parchment, no bigger than the palm of my hand. I opened it up, and my heart leapt.

Sailor,

Thank you for your first missive. It was invaluable information. I will see you soon, make no mistake.

No signature was attached to the missive, but one was not needed. I clutched Alex's letter to my chest, feeling comforted for the first time since I had left him. Its message was nothing of a personal nature and strictly business, but after what had happened to me, it helped me feel stronger.

As quick as I could, I deposited the information I had for him inside the hole and replaced the wood and bark, knowing I would have to venture back with the new details I'd just gleaned. At least, in the current correspondence, I'd let them know that the British advancing into Westchester County was a possibility, so the fact it was now definite would not be as much as a shock. I stood up and took a few steps back to make sure the area looked natural. It did. I stuffed his correspondence back into the secret pocket in my petticoat and, clutching my shawl to my bosom, I made my way back toward the house and entered through the kitchen. The servants were all wide awake and busily going about their tasks as usual. I greeted them in my normal manner but did not stop to talk as I was prone to do on occasion.

Somehow, I made it to my bedchamber without anyone seeming to take notice. Orange embers glowed in the fireplace, and once again I found the walls stifling. I crossed the room immediately and opened the window to breathe in the autumn air.

Standing away from the view and in the comfort of my own space, I released my grip on the shawl and took off my clothes until I stood only in my shift. As my clothing fell to the ground, tears traveled down my cheeks. I clutched the white fabric of my undergarments in my hands as my mind relived every bad thing that had happened to me since August. The tears that fell from my eyes had less to do with being afraid and more to do with anger. And guilt. God, the guilt. Why couldn't I have done more for my family, or Susie, or the American cause? Why could I have not stopped Captain Roth?

If John never would have signed up to join the patriots, the fire would never had started to begin with. David and I could have been married and perhaps have a baby on the way. I wouldn't be stuck in Manhattan with an aunt and uncle who only considered me an obligation rather than family, and a sinister captain who threatened me at every turn.

What the bloody hell was I supposed to do? My father was dead, John was in prison, my uncle was unfeeling toward my plight, and the man who I thought I was to marry was indifferent. I lacked help and protection. I was a young woman of marrying age with no husband and no real home.

Thinking through my choices, I wondered if Nathan Hale would be a viable option. He was attractive and only a few years older than I. I did not know if he was attached at the moment, but certainly one could not find fault in me for asking. Finding a husband was the only idea I could come up with, and I was not ashamed to ask him so.

With a new resolve in mind, I turned from the window, wiping my eyes. A knock sounded on the door, and I shoved my torn clothing underneath the bed. I would repair it later. I did not want Leah to know about it. I didn't want anyone to know.

"Come in," I said, rushing over to the table to the bowl and ewer. I poured some water into the bowl and splashed it onto my face to help conceal the fact I'd been crying.

The door pushed open, and Leah walked inside. It took everything I had not to run into her arms and cry. I leaned over the bowl once more and tossed water onto my face. I did not want to look her in the eye because I knew the second I did, she would know something had happened. Fortunately, she was too busy flitting around to seemingly take notice.

"I've cleaned these two gowns for you, Miss Bishop," she said.

"Leah?"

"Yes, Miss Bishop?"

"Please call me Miss Nora." I smiled and watched as my request challenged everything she'd been taught. "I insist."

She curtsied and went about her business. "Now do try an' stay out of the mud," she said, laying the garments across the bed.

"You realize that is like asking for the moon?"

She shot me an exasperated look, and I promptly ignored it.

"Let's get you dressed," she said, picking up one of the freshly clean gowns and holding it out for me.

* * *

MR. MCGOVERN WAS BUSY in the back room, crushing something into a powder, when I arrived. The grinding of the pestle and mortar eased my mind.

"You're late, Miss Bishop," he said, not bothering to look up when I walked back to see him.

I hung my bonnet and cloak on the wooden peg and set my basket on the table. "I'm sorry. I was delayed at home." My throat constricted as I fought back the tears that threatened to pour down my cheeks once more. Not only had the ordeal with the captain rattled me to my inner most core, but after Leah had finished helping me dress, I had to write out another missive to Alex about the new information I had discovered while pinned underneath the captain's weight. That missive was now hidden inside another secret pocket I had sewed into my clean gown.

He must have sensed something in my voice, for he looked up, but I made my face as blank as I could.

"I plucked some jewelweed. I thought I could extract the juice from inside," I said.

"Later. I have a different job for you first," he said, going back to his task.

"And what shall that be?"

"I need you to take inventory of the items listed over there." He jerked his head toward a piece of parchment on the worktable. "Place them all in the basket when you are finished."

I reached for the parchment and skimmed the list. Several

salts were listed, as well as sulphur, opium, myrrh and guaiac gum, chamomile, aloe and gentian, rhubarb, licorice, and jalap roots.

"Do you have all these in stock?" I asked.

"I believe so, but that's why I want you to do inventory."

We worked in silence, as Mr. McGovern I discovered preferred, for the morning. I usually found the work therapeutic and calming. But today it was the opposite. My mind would not stop thinking about my encounter with Captain Roth in the forest.

The way his eyes excited and his body thrilled when I cried out in pain would never leave my mind. His threat on my brother's life should I tell anyone had rattled me as much as what he physically had done to me. Now, more than ever, I had to find a way to get John out of prison. He wasn't safe at all.

Mr. McGovern's footsteps brought me out of my own thoughts. "I'll be back," he said.

Pins and needles stabbed my foot as I rose from where I sat on the floor, assembling the vials and packages of the medicine he requested. "May I inquire where you are going?" I said.

"The hospital. I'll be taking the supplies over." He reached for his overcoat and pulled it on. He grabbed his tri-cornered hat and set it upon his head before bending over and picking up the basket.

"May I accompany you?" I asked.

"No. Not today. Please stay here and work on the jewelweed you brought in."

"But—"

"I'm sorry, Miss Bishop. But I have a few other stops to make as well, of a more personal nature. And I do not want to close the shop to make the errand. There is some bread, fruit, and cheese in the back room for your lunch. Tea is in the container on the back shelf."

"What if someone comes in, and I can't help them?" I asked, fear forming inside of me. I didn't want to be alone.

"You will be fine. My book is on the worktable. You can look through that if need be. I have every confidence in you. I will not be long," he said.

He opened the door and left without another word, leaving me standing in the middle of the shop. I glanced around, my hands bunching into the fabric of my gown. My eyes focused on the lock, and for one small moment, I considered turning it.

"You're in no danger, Nora," I said to the silent room. I shook my head and breathed deeply, praying that the next person who walked through the door would be Mr. McGovern back from the hospital and his personal errands.

However, Hannah walked through the door fifteen minutes later. At first, I worried she knew what had happened to me in the upper field, but she never once mentioned it or gave the slightest hint to the situation. The only speech she gave me was a complaint of itching skin.

Hannah clawed herself everywhere. Red splotches covered her chest, arms, the back of her neck and, upon further exploration, all over her bottom and back.

"I itch everywhere!" she said, continuing to scratch.

"Dare I ask how you managed to get poison ivy all over you?" I said, arching my brows at her. "Let's get your clothes off so I can see the full extent of it. Follow me. We'll go into the back room."

Her face, which did not have the poison on it, flushed. Out of sight, we shut the door, and I helped her remove her clothes.

"If you must know, I happened to meet Private Harding for lunch yesterday," she said.

My stomach rolled at the mention of his name. I was certain he was the only reason Captain Roth had stopped his advances on me. "Hmm," I said, walking around her.

"Are you all right?"

"Never better," I lied. "Let me see the rest of you now."

She lifted her shift up to expose her thighs. She was correct. The poison was everywhere.

"It must have been some lunch," I said, trying to make light of everything and eyeing the basket of fresh jewelweed.

Hannah was covered with jewelweed and smelling like a field when the bell above the door jingled, and we both looked up, alarmed.

"Hello?" a male voice said.

"Quick, let me dress you. You can leave through the back door. As you journey home, rub the rest of this on your neck and arms. If you can, sneak inside the barn to put the rest on your legs. Has it started to work yet?"

"Yes, it has actually. Thank you."

"Hello?" the male voice said again.

I opened the door a crack. "I'll be with you in a moment, sir!" I hollered.

Together, Hannah and I finished redressing her before she snuck out the back door.

She stopped, turned, and threw her arms around me. "Thank you, Nora. I wasn't sure if you would help me or not. I have eyes. I know you are not happy with my family, but I do appreciate you. If there is anything I can do, you only need to ask."

For the first time in over a month, hope welled in my chest. "Thank you. Now go!"

I shut the door and walked toward the front of the shop, smoothing my dress and tucking a stray piece of hair behind my ear.

"Good afternoon, Miss Bishop. I was hoping you'd be here," Captain Nathan Hale said.

I crossed the room and peered out the window. Across the street, a British soldier leaned against a building, seemingly at ease, but his eyes were trained on the shop. The hair on the back of my neck stood on end. I did not think this was going to end well.

CHAPTER 17

"Captain Hale," I said, curtseying. "It is nice to see you again."

"And you." He bowed, keeping things formal. His breeches and waistcoat were a color somewhere between light brown and gold, reminding me of the autumn leaves. It brought out the golden flecks in his eyes. He lowered his voice. "Are we alone, or is Mr. McGovern in the back?"

"We are alone. But first, I have news for you. The British will be moving north toward Westchester County. I discovered this earlier today."

"And have you let Alex know?"

"I've written him, yes. I plan on dropping the missive off later today, on my way home. I thought perhaps you would like to know as well, assuming you did not already."

"Thank you. I had heard rumors, but nothing official."

"Now, do you have information on my brother?" I asked, anticipation rising in me.

Captain Hale took off his hat and ran his hand through his hair. "I do. I met a man late last night who might be able to help you get your brother out of prison."

A small spring of hope swelled within me at his news.

I took a step forward, closing the distance between us. "What do you mean? Who?"

Captain Hale took a breath. His eyes flickered left and then right. "You're sure we are alone?"

I nodded.

"He's a deserter. The fact he is showing his face in town takes quite a bit of gumption, in my opinion. In any case, we got to talking, and I found out he used to be a guard in the Sugar House. That is, up until a week ago."

"Why in God's name would I trust a deserter? And how has he not been caught?" I asked, nothing but doubt filling me. "The man has bullocks the size of—"

Captain Hale's eyes grew wide at my outburst, and he coughed. "Miss Bishop, do you always speak like a—" He paused, apparently searching for the correct description, so I helped him.

"Sailor?"

At the mention of the word, I found myself wanting to see Alex. He had been easy to talk to, and it had been comfortable between us though I hardly knew the man.

Captain Hale grinned. "Alex warned me about your tongue, but I confess I didn't believe him," he said, chuckling. "I understand what he meant now."

"Meant?" I said, putting my hands on my hips. "Why were two gentlemen, such as you and Mr. Foster, discussing me?"

"I'm sure we are not the only men discussing you, Miss Bishop, for your beauty astounds. However, rest assured, we were not conversing over your charms, though we could." He bowed while placing his hand over his heart. "Alex only stated you were one to speak your mind, and it was a breath of fresh air."

I turned my head and glanced at one of the shelves so Captain Hale would not see the blush upon my cheeks before looking back to him. "Back to John and this... this deserter. Do you think I should meet with him?"

"No. I will be the one to meet with him, and I'll provide you with the information he has given me. We will go from there."

"But I want to be there. John is my brother," I said, growing frustrated. Why did men always think women couldn't attend certain things? "You said you don't know if he can be trusted, so I can go and help determine if he is telling the truth. It would be a good idea to have two people there to observe him."

"You're right. I'm not sure if he can be trusted, which is why you will stay far away. As for the information he'll provide, it is the only lead we have on where John is located inside the prison, if, in fact, he still is. As for why the man continues to be in Manhattan, it is because his other arrangements are still being made. He plans to leave tomorrow, early morning."

"Where shall this meeting take place and at what hour?"

"The Fighting Cocks Tavern at four in the morning, which is the most important reason why you shouldn't attend. He plans on leaving Manhattan at five. Please let me handle it. I know what I'm doing."

I sighed. "Very well. But you'll tell me everything he says?"

"Yes. You can count on me. I will visit you tomorrow afternoon. Here."

I watched him through the window as he walked down the street, a British soldier following him. Captain Hale turned, stopped, and engaged the soldier in conversation. He laughed, and I wished I stood outside, listening to the conversation. I knew Captain Hale's cover story, but seeing him act it out made me uneasy.

With much haste, I wrote out a missive to Alex explaining what was going to happen tonight. I didn't know if he'd be able to help Captain Hale or not, but at least if I told him, he would have the opportunity. Assuming he received the message in time. *God, I hope so.* He had said he'd help me find John. Hadn't he?

Once finished, I lifted my gown and stuffed the note inside the secret pocket along with the other letter. It was only a half hour past noon, which meant I still had quite a few more hours to spend in the shop before I could retire for the evening. And I had to stop at the black walnut tree first before entering my uncle's house.

Knowing I couldn't leave just yet, I stayed and worked mindlessly. My irritation grew out of not being able to do anything while I rearranged the shelves and refolded the strips of linen in the back room. I swept the floor, dusted the shelves, and stoked the fire. I stood at the counter reading the fiftieth page of Mr. McGovern's notebook full of medicines and the applications when the dear old man apparently decided to show up.

"Miss Bishop? I'm back. How did everything go?" Mr. McGovern asked.

I glanced up and shut the book.

"Fine. No one came in, so I took it upon myself to rearrange the shelves by condition and not by letter. I also swept and dusted, and now I have been teaching myself from your notebook. I presume that is sufficient?"

He chuckled as he hung his hat on the peg and took off his cloak. "You've been busy." He looked around the shop and nodded his approval. His eyes settled on my basket that no longer contained the jewelweed.

"And did you preserve all the juice from the stems then?" he asked, picking the basket up as if I needed a visual to what he was talking about.

"No. A young lady came in needing itch relief," I said, inwardly laughing at my cousin.

"So, someone did enter the shop."

"Well, yes. I suppose I meant nobody came in who I needed to help and didn't know what to do."

"Ah. Very different indeed. I visited the hospital today. I thought you'd like to know the man who you nursed is alive. His fever broke in the middle of the night. Madam Morris sends her thanks."

Relief spread through me at the news of the young man who I had helped. Though he fought for the British, I didn't wish him to die. I wouldn't wish the agonizing death on anyone. Well, perhaps maybe Captain Roth. I trembled thinking of the last thing that man had said to me and of John lying in a cold, dark cell surrounded by the filth and stench of human urine and feces and probably rats. *Dear, Jesus!* Thinking of the rats gnawing away at him made me want to vomit.

My hands clenched, and I swallowed. He could possibly be wounded and hurt like the man who I had healed. He could be in agony or worse, dead, and would anyone know? From what little I knew about the prisons, they loaded men into cells like cattle. They trampled on each other and pissed where they stood.

The letter in my petticoat weighed me down, and I knew I had to leave. I had to see Alex and convince him to help Captain Hale get my brother out and get him to safety.

"Mr. McGovern? Would you mind if I left a bit early today? I have a terrible headache coming on and would like to get home and get to bed," I lied.

"Of course, of course," he said. His eyes and nose scrunched up with worry while he looked me over as a grandfather might assess his grandchild. "Your face is rather pale today. Will you be okay walking home, or should I send for a wagon?"

"I can walk. It isn't far, and perhaps the fresh air might do me some good."

"Do you need anything? Lavender or peppermint perhaps? Basil works as well, but I'm certain you know this."

"Thank you, but I believe we have those stocked in the kitchen already. I'm sure my ailment will be gone by tomorrow morning."

"Very well. Safe journey home, Miss Bishop. If you remain unwell, do send a note around, so I do not worry about your whereabouts," he said.

I nodded, bid him good day, and left, my path taking me directly to the woods behind the upper field and to the black walnut tree.

* * *

FOR MID-SEPTEMBER, THE air was hot and baked my skin as if it were the month of July. Mistakenly, I'd left my bonnet behind and cursed myself knowing a group of freckles would spring up to cover my nose because of my folly. Wisps of hair had come loose from my pins, and I pushed them off my face in a huff. I took off my lace neckerchief and wrung it in my hands, feeling much better with the skin exposed and not confined.

The dull ache I had lied about to Mr. McGovern did, in fact, reside in my head by the time I reached the tree. I rubbed my temples and took a breath, thinking of the peppermint tea I would prepare once I was settled indoors. Every muscle in my body ached, and my eyes burned from the exhaustion of the last twenty-four hours. All I wanted was to burrow myself deep under the quilts in my bed and hide away from the world. Everywhere I turned, men were killing each other and, I suspected, paying each other off. I didn't know what the relationship between my uncle and Captain Roth was, but I assumed it was nothing of honor.

Was there any honor in the world anymore? The war had begun over taxes, but now it was fought over independence. How honorable was it of our king to not allow people this basic human right? He was free to do as he wished. *Shouldn't we all be?*

"Has your day been that awful?" a man's voice said from behind me.

I jumped, my hands flying to my chest to my rapidly beating heart.

"Bloody hell! You scared me! Didn't your father teach you it isn't nice to sneak up on people, especially unsuspecting ladies?" I asked, putting my hands on my hips once my heart had returned to a semi-normal speed.

Alex shrugged. He leaned up against a nearby tree, his arms folded across his chest. His blue jacket stretched across his shoulders, and his one leg was bent back with his foot propped up on the bark of the trunk. He pushed himself off the tree and walked toward me. "My father died before he had a chance to teach me that lesson, but I thank you for the education. I will do my utmost to try and remember, but I can't promise you. The look on your face alone was worth it."

"Gah!" I said, shaking my head while Alex grinned. "Were you young when he died?"

"It was ten years ago. I was fourteen. Not a boy but not a man yet. It gets easier, Sailor. You still miss them each and every day, but each and every day, the pain isn't quite so bad."

Not wanting to talk about my dead parents or sister, I didn't say anything in relation to his comment. "Well, your mother then. Did she not teach you?"

He smiled. "As for my mother, she'd be displeased at my manners and would box my ears. You have my apologies," he said, bowing, though obviously not sincere.

"You are trying to save your ears should your mother find out," I said, teasing.

"Have you ever had your ears boxed?"

"No."

"I suspected as much. If you had, you would understand my sentiment. Alas, my mother is also gone. And no need to apologize, Sailor."

A half-hearted smile spread across my face. Though he lifted my spirits, being back in this spot unnerved me. For a few seconds, we stared at each other. The stubble on his face indicated he hadn't had a chance to shave today, and he had dark circles under his eyes. His thick, dark brown hair was pulled back as was the fashion, and when he turned his head slightly, the sun glinted off the subtle streaks of red. I found myself wanting to run my fingers through his rich locks to see if they were as silky as they looked.

I tore my eyes away from his beautiful blue ones, afraid I would get lost in their depths, as if I were drowning in the ocean, and worried he would guess what I was thinking. A slight breeze blew, giving me relief from the burning sun. Instead of languishing in the pleasure, it stirred gooseflesh to form on my arms, and I found myself quite cold. I turned away from Alex, not knowing what to do with the confusion that had come over me.

"Nora?" Alex said. His voice was low, scratchy and serious. "What's wrong?"

The leaves crunched underneath his footsteps as he approached me, and though I faced away from him, I knew he stood directly behind me. The warmth of his body was close to mine. Gently, he touched my arm, turning me around so I had to look at him. "Tell me."

His eyes, which typically were sharp, softened, and I bit my tongue to keep from crying. "Oh, it's nothing," I said, though certain he could be trusted, I hardly knew the man.

Our friendship, if that was what I could call it, was incredibly new. I couldn't tell him about what I had gone through. I didn't want his opinion of me to alter in any way. I didn't want him to think me unchaste.

"I don't believe you," he said, searching my face. His eyes lingered on my neck for a second too long. "What's this?"

He reached forward, and his fingers lightly touched my skin, trailing along my neck, leaving a path of warmth.

I swallowed. "What?"

His arm fell back to his side. "You've a bruise on your neck. Want to tell me who did it?"

Leah hadn't mentioned anything earlier when she'd dressed me, and I hadn't bothered to look at my reflection in the looking glass. My neck had hurt, but I hadn't thought Captain Roth had left a bruise. I knew an underlying tension lingered between the men, one that was as taut as a ship's sail. I knew as soon as Alex found out about the ordeal, he would head straight to the offender and kill him. I could read in his eyes that was his intention as soon as he pulled the name out of me. However, all of the information I had obtained so far had come from the captain. Was I willing to risk the information that I could easily come by for what he had done to me? For the time being, yes. Retribution would come later.

"Nora? I want the name of the bastard who touched you, for I can tell it was not by consent."

My throat went dry. I wanted to tell him, but I could not. All ideas escaped me of what I could possibly tell him, but I had to say something.

"Oh, that. It was an accident," I said, touching my neck where his fingers had been. "I was helping in the hospital yesterday, and one of the men was tossing and turning about. Thrashing on the bed, moaning. Fever. As I was trying to clean his wound, his arm reached up and wrapped around my throat. It was only for a few seconds. I'm sure he was dreaming of the battlefield."

He eyed me skeptically and grunted. "This war will haunt men's dreams for the rest of their lives. There is no doubt about that."

"I'm sure. I'm surprised to see you here this time of day," I said, wanting to change the topic of conversation to something safer.

"Yes, well, I was here earlier and received your correspondence. I rode without stopping and delivered it, then came straight back here to drop off another note to you. But, since you are here, there's no need for the missive. I'd rather speak to you anyway."

"I have more news for you as well, which I think you'll want to tell General Washington immediately."

His eyebrow rose. "What?"

"The British army is on the move or will be. They are possibly going to move north, or... ah... Turn around. I wrote you a note with the information. It would be easier to give it to you."

"Turn around?"

Giving him an exasperated sigh, I faced the opposite direction so my back was toward him and lifted up my skirts. "Us meeting here like this defeats the entire purpose of the dead drop idea, does it not?"

"Hmph. I dare say I have no idea what in heaven's name you are doing, Sailor, but I would be remiss if I didn't ask you if you needed any help."

Laughter and mischief laced his voice, and I blushed. Thankfully, he couldn't see my face. When I turned around, I held up the letter I had written to him.

He smiled, big and wide, showcasing his straight, white teeth. If only everyone was that lucky to have teeth like that. My own father had a set of false teeth made out of ivory by the renowned silversmith Paul Revere. And though Father could eat, drink, and speak with his ornamental teeth, his mouth ached every night.

"Petticoat letters? I like it. You know, it isn't every day a woman has something she wants to give me that's up her skirts," Alex said, grinning wide again.

My face, which warmed and, therefore, undoubtedly resembled a red rose, smiled too. "I believe you are lying, Mr. Foster, for I saw how the ladies who followed the camp looked at you. Even the married ones."

He shrugged and didn't comment, but his ears turned pink.

"Here, I have it all in there," I said, unhinged with the way his eyes stared into mine.

He took the note from my hand. Our fingers skimmed over each other when the parchment passed between us. The exact sensation of warmth I had felt on my neck when his hand had touched me earlier traveled into my hand. If he noticed the same thing or not, I did not know, for his face remained blank as he opened the letter. The only thing noticeable about him was his jaw clenching.

Alex scanned the missive then looked up at me, his eyes sharp. "A deserter?"

"Out of everything in that note, you want to discuss that first?" I said, glad he cared.

"I have nothing to do with the army besides making sure General Washington receives his information. Helping Nathan, as I suspect that is why you wrote about it, is a different story."

"Captain Hale came into the apothecary shop today. He told me that he'd been in contact with a deserter who knew where John is being held inside the Sugar House. This is my only chance of freeing my brother. I need to speak to him."

"You? I don't think so," he said, folding the letter up and

stuffing it down his boot.

"You could come with me."

"I can't go with you. I have to ride back and give this other information to Washington. Did Nathan say he'd go?"

I nodded. "Yes, but John is my brother, and I—"

Alex put his hand up as if to stop me from speaking. "I know that. And, I know you want him out of prison. So does every other sister, mother, and wife of every prisoner. If Nathan said he'll handle it, let him. The last thing he will need is for you to be there getting in the way."

Anger flared inside me, and like grapeshot, I exploded. "Get in the way? How dare you!"

"Nora, calm down now. This is a man's business," he said, his voice rising.

"A man's business, is it? Then why is it that I'm the one who has obtained this information? What has Captain Hale actually given you? Why am I the one sneaking around in this field," I said, waving my arms, "delivering the messages? I am perfectly capable of finding information out and doing what is necessary to—"

His sparkling blue eyes darkened like the sky directly before a storm. "Doing what is necessary? Is that how you happen to come by the bruise on your neck?" His face was red, and his breathing was fast as if he'd recently finished running a good distance. "Do you remember what happened the last time you didn't do as I told you?"

My mouth sprang open. "Oh, yes. I remember what happened, *Mr. Foster*. I assisted Dr. Aster in the physician's tent and saved lives. That's what happened!"

We stood now, nose to nose, each of our breathing labored yet in rhythm with the other. No way in hell would I back down from him, and I could see on his face he had the same thought. So we stood, barely touching each other. *All I would have to do is extend my finger, and it would touch his hand.*

"I know you're capable. I didn't mean..." he said, stepping back from me and running his hands through the hair that had come untied. "I don't want to see you hurt. And deserters can't be trusted. I know this. Promise me you'll stay here." His voice was hoarse. "Please. You'll be no help to John when he is released if you're hurt or get in trouble in the process."

He was right, of course. If Captain Hale was able to get John out, whether tonight or sometime soon, and I had been hurt or caught doing what I shouldn't be doing, I would be no help to him. Who would nurse him back to health if he needed it? He couldn't come and live with Uncle Edward. That was certain.

"Fine," I said.

Alex nodded, satisfied.

"What information do you have for me then?" I asked, still perturbed at the outcome.

"You are to continue to pay attention, and if you hear anything of importance, or what you might suspect is important, let us know. That is all."

Remaining frustrated on the direction of our conversation, for I had thought Alex would be in favor of me joining Captain Hale, I retied my lace neckerchief around myself.

"It was nice to see you again, Mr. Foster," I said, keeping my voice cool yet polite.

"And you as well, Miss Bishop." Alex gave me a look that said he didn't like me using his formal name. "It is always a pleasure."

I curtseyed, spun on my heel, and marched away toward my uncle's house. My father had always taught me to never make promises I didn't intend on keeping, which was why I never *promised* Alex I would stay away. I had to find Hannah and ask her to cover for me, for I fully intended to meet this deserter at The Fighting Cock's Tavern.

CHAPTER 18

IT WASN'T DIFFICULT GETTING Hannah to agree to cover for me. I was going to sneak out of the house early in the morning to make my way to the tavern, and if anyone asked her, she was going to tell them I went to check on a patient who I had helped earlier the day before. If all went according to plan, my aunt and uncle would not know anything since they slept late.

Hannah believed my story for herself, so I did not correct her. In the early morning before the rooster crowed, I woke, dressed by only the light of one small beeswax candle and the moon, and made my way into the center of town.

The air was dry, and the wind blew as if a storm was brewing off the coast. A few clouds floated in the sky, and the stars shone clearly. I pushed down my fear and began my trek. No way in hell was I going to miss this opportunity to discover information about my brother or pass up the chance to obtain information to pass along to Washington.

The Fighting Cock's Tavern had a reputation. And when I walked in through the front door, I understood why. No actual roosters were fighting, but plenty of cocks were strutting around, each vying for a different serving girl's attention, or rather, affection.

One girl bent over the banister, her breasts all but spilling out of her stays for the entire crowd to gawk at. She laughed, and flicked her tongue out, letting it glide over her bottom lip. Two men dashed toward the stairway, pushing each other to try to be the first to get to her. I was fascinated, yet horrified, as she grabbed each man by the bullocks and squeezed. She then raised her eyebrows, released them, and put both of her palms up. Each man withdrew a bit of money and placed it in her hand. She patted the one's face and sent him on his way, saying after him, "Yer next love." The other man smiled and grabbed hold of her bottom as they walked up the stairs.

"Hello, darlin'," a man said next to me. He appeared to be in his late twenties. His teeth were stained brown, and his eyes were bloodshot. Waves of brandy fell off of him. "You lookin' for your next customer? I could use a good lay. It's been a long day," he said, craning his neck to see me from the backside. "And you have a nice arse I'd like to put my hands on."

My stomach rolled. *Disgusting.* He reached out a meaty hand and touched my gown. I promptly slapped his hand away. "Get off of me, sir. I do not work here," I said, taking a step away from him.

He chuckled and made it quite clear he did not believe me. His eyes, undisguised, skimmed my body. "If you're not here for the work, why are you here?" he asked.

I turned away from him and scanned the crowd. Captain Hale sat at a table at the other end of the room, and inwardly I sighed with relief. "I'm meeting someone. Excuse me." I brushed past him, setting my gaze on Captain Hale.

"I'll be here all night, my darlin', should you change your mind," he called after me.

"That won't happen," I mumbled under my breath.

I traversed the room, keeping my eyes on Captain Hale. I didn't want him to be cross, but I had to let him know he wasn't alone. I would use what I could to gather information about the troops and John. We should be working as a team. I was pretty confident I could handle the men in the room; as long as I wasn't alone with them, it would be fine.

When I stopped at his table, he looked up, obviously surprised. I only had eyes for him and did not notice the man who sat across from him until his chair scooted back a little ways, and he stood. It was Alex.

His blue eyes held a deadly glare while he looked at me. I blushed under their scrutiny. His dark hair was unbound tonight, and by the lights of the candles, flickers of a deep red flashed in the wavy thickness with the smallest of movements. He wore a dark blue waistcoat and breeches, and though the room was dim, I knew in the sunlight, the color would cause his eyes to be bluer than they already were.

My throat became dry, and I swallowed, but it didn't help.

The other men at the table looked up, a twinkle in all of their eyes, no doubt thinking I worked in the tavern as well. I glanced down at my dress. *Can't they tell I'm not a whore?* Captain Hale said nothing but stood nonetheless, offering me the respect a lady deserved, but then sat down, not bothering to formally talk to me.

Alex however, did not stay silent. He strode over to me and grasped me around the waist, bringing me in close, whispering in my ear. "Sailor, I thought I told you to stay home."

He nudged my ear with his nose, and a blaze of warmth soared through my body being so near to him. He smelled of leather, brandy, and the outdoors. On anyone else, I would not have been attracted to it, but on him, it was quite intoxicating.

For a moment, I lost all manner of speech.

"Well? Are you going to answer me? What are you doing here?" He kept his hands on my waist and pulled me closer to him. "Nora. You need to look like you are enjoying this, for that is why you are here, according to the men in this room. Understand?"

I nodded.

"Good. Now, laugh as if you are liking this and I said something witty," he said.

I did.

He planted a kiss on my neck, and the heat that had clearly been on my face cascaded down to my lower stomach.

Alex turned toward the men, keeping a strong grip on me. "Gentlemen, I shall be back. We are going to a place more… ah, private." He patted then pinched my bottom, causing me to squeak.

"I'll take her when yer finished!" one of the men said at the table.

"Ah, she'll be no use to you when I'm done, Tawny!"

"How long do you plan on taking?" another said. "We've got to finish our game."

"As long as it takes," Alex said, winking at me.

I felt my face redden more than it already had, but this time, it was not from Alex's attentions. My humiliation grew, and I wanted nothing more than to get out of the room.

"So not long then, aye?" the man said, laughing. His big belly shook, and he rested his hands on his pouch.

Alex reached inside his waistcoat and pulled out a few coins. He tossed them onto the table. "That should get me out of the game. I'll see you lads in a bit."

Without another word, he reached across the table and grabbed the bottle of brandy then ushered me outside into the cool night air and around the back of the tavern.

Alex kept his hand on my waist while we walked to the alleyway. Once there, he did not release his grip but swung me around so my back was up against the building. He put both of his arms up against the red brick, on either side of my face, and pressed himself close to me.

"You do not need to stand so close," I said, a bit breathless.

"I do. They think you are out here servicing me, so if anyone comes looking for you, wanting the same attentions, it will look as though you are otherwise engaged," he said, through gritted teeth.

I swallowed the lump that had formed in my throat. He was closer to me now than he had been earlier in the woods by the black walnut tree. His eyes pierced me and caused me to become unsettled. I glanced at the sky and tried to focus on the moon, which would be leaving in a few short hours.

"I can't believe you came here. After both Nathan and I specifically told you not to!" Alex said. He tried to rein in his anger, but he was barely able to do so. His mouth set into a tight line, and his eyes narrowed at me.

"You do not have the authority to tell me what to do. You are not my brother, my father, nor are you my husband."

Heat radiated off him. I enjoyed being stuck between the cold bricks and his body. I shook my head. I cursed silently. This was not what I was supposed to be thinking about.

"John is my brother. I have every right—"

"I know. You have made that perfectly clear on numerous occasions to both myself and Nathan. That is not the point. We are only trying to keep you safe. I saw you the second you walked into the tavern. Did you know that? And did you know that every single man's eye turned toward you and evaluated your body? I could see in their eyes what they would like to do to you, as you well know, since one gentleman approached you. Nora, why do you think the tavern is named what it is? This hour of the night, the only women in the tavern are those of loose morals. The only reason the men are there is because they want a taste of Eve's custom house."

"Is that why you're here, then?"

He breathed out. His breath made small wisps of white that floated to the sky, like ghosts.

I shivered.

He leaned in closer. "You know why I'm here. What do you think would have happened if I or Nathan hadn't been inside?"

I bit my lip and glanced down. Our stomachs were almost touching.

"Our contact hasn't shown up yet, so you made this trek for nothing," he said, his voice low and husky.

My whole body warmed, and it thrilled me. I found myself, not for the first time, wanting to reach my hands out and touch him. But not as I had before, where I was fixing his wounds, but to really *touch* him. We looked into each other's eyes. *Is he thinking the same thing?*

One second later, Alex pushed off against the wall, took several steps back, and ran his hand through his thick, wavy hair.

I shut my eyes and lowered my head. *Damn it!* Why the bloody hell hadn't the deserter shown up? I sagged against the wall. I pinned my arms against my stomach and turned away. The guilt was too much. I was supposed to try and get John out of prison, yet here I was more concerned with Alex at the moment. I sighed and pushed the anger at myself and the situation away.

"I'm sorry," I said. "I did not realize what sort of establishment this place was at this hour."

Alex nodded. "It's a tavern, Nora. They are all this sort of establishment when the sun goes down. I'm glad you didn't realize it."

A noise from the side startled us, and a figure walked out. My nerves stood on end. What if it was the man from earlier, thinking I was a whore?

Alex stayed in what appeared to be a relaxed stance, but from my viewpoint, he tensed. His shoulders became more rigid, and he curled and uncurled his hands.

"Alex?" Captain Hale said as he approached.

I let out the breath I'd been holding.

Captain Hale's face was lined with worry. "Captain? Is everything all right?" I asked.

"No. It isn't. Alex, I received word that Major Robert Rodgers knows of my whereabouts. He knows who I am. He knows I am no British loyalist. I must depart now," he said. "Might I spare you for a moment for a quick word?"

"Yes, of course." Alex turned to me. "Sailor, please do not move. I will return in a few minutes. No one should come looking for you. They most likely think Nathan has come to take his turn," he said, then followed Captain Hale out to the street and around the corner.

I wrapped my arms around myself and waited for Alex's return. Drunken laughter filled the streets. A couple of men passed nearby where I stood in the shadows, singing a bawdy song. I pressed myself up against the cold brick wall, as if that alone would make me invisible. The group stopped at the corner's edge, and one gentleman unbuttoned the flap on his breeches and relieved himself. But their song continued.

Two and two may go to bed,
Two and two together;
And if there is not room enough,
Lie one a top o'to'ther.

I HAD KNOWN the tune of course. For it was only a year earlier that most of the men in New York had sung different words, thanks to the British soldiers who had occupied Boston in the very beginning of the war.

YANKEE DOODLE'S come to town
For to buy a firelock.
We will tar and feather him,
And so we will John Hancock.

THE GROUP CONTINUED down the street, and I relaxed slightly. They stumbled into the moonlight, while I anticipated Alex's return. I focused solely on what was happening on the front side of the street that I had not contemplated any danger from behind. That is, until a hand settled on my shoulder.

I shrieked and jumped.

"Shh, Nora. It's me."

"David Shipman! What the bloody hell are you thinking?" I said, my voice raised. If I spoke any louder, it would have been shouting. I was getting extremely weary of men sneaking up on me.

"What in hell are you doing in The Fighting Cock's Tavern?"

"How did you know I was in there?"

"I saw you! I was coming down the stairs and saw you leave with that, that—"

My mouth sprung open. "You were upstairs? Oh, I see," I said, taking a huge step backward as my anger flowed out of me. I had no intention to rein it in. "You were with some whore? You can't marry me, yet you can stick your prick in women who you don't even know? Is that it? Is that why you won't marry me? You want to be free to rut with any old sow?"

David's eyes became slits, and he took a step in my direction. His one hand was balled into a fist at his side, and the other held a lantern. It shook. By the look on his face, he did not care that I had caught him with another woman. "What I do is my business, Nora. And you want to talk about whoring? I saw you with that gentleman, if he could be called that. I saw him take you in his arms and kiss your neck. The only women who come here are prostitutes. Is that what you are now?" he asked, spitting on the ground. He took another step and another toward me until my back was pressed upon a wagon full of hay. "So that's it then? You're selling yourself now to the highest bidder, or does it not matter?"

I stared at him, aghast at his words. He set a lantern down on top of the wagon and reached inside his coat. He withdrew a coin and tossed it at me. "What will that give me, Nora? A pull, a suck, or both?"

He smelled terribly of drink and reached toward me, fondling my breasts. I flinched away from him and tried to shield myself from his advances. Flashes of my earlier ordeal with Captain Roth came at me, quick. What was the British army coming to? Were there no gentlemen in its ranks? I stiffened my body and looked into David's eyes. This was not the David I had known my whole life.

A small movement caught my eye, and a second later David was thrown off me. He landed on his back on the ground. Alex stood there, breathing heavy. "Stay off of her," he said, his voice tight.

Without uttering one word, David jumped up and came straight toward Alex, ramming his shoulder into Alex's stomach. Alex grunted and was pushed backward by the force but did not fall. He wrapped his arms around David's shoulders and, using David's own force against him, thrust him out of the way. David's head hit the hay wagon.

"Stop it!" I screamed. "Both of you!"

But neither man listened, both intent on their opponent, circling each other like a hawk in the air searching for its prey.

David came at Alex again, landing a punch in his jaw. Alex's head jerked back. Blood flew out of his mouth. He spat onto the ground and touched his face.

I winced. "David, you must stop this. Please. This is not you," I said, trying to maintain an ounce of calmness.

Alex kept his eyes fixed on David, watching his every move. Every time David shifted his weight, Alex shifted his.

"Did you let this... scum defile you?" David waved his hand at Alex. "Is that why you're here whoring about?"

"How dare you!" I stomped closer to David. I wanted to punch him. Or kick him. I wanted to do something.

"Enough!" Alex roared. "Nora, step back. I will not allow this man to talk to you this way."

"I see you are intimate enough that he uses your Christian name. What other names do you call her?" Even in the dim moonlight, David's face was red from anger.

"Leave, David. You're drunk, and you have no idea what you're saying," I said through gritted teeth.

He ambled toward me, taking off his overcoat. He walked like a sailor who still hadn't found his land legs, teetering this way and that. He swung his coat up onto the hay wagon. Without meaning to do so, his coat knocked the lantern over that he'd set there earlier. A pop sounded, and I spun to look at what happened. Neither men paid the noise any attention.

"Let's go, sir. Fisticuffs will have to do," David said, giving Alex a mock bow. He rolled up the cuffs of his shirt.

Alex, for his part, turned his head slightly. "Do you smell that?"

David took his opportunity and charged toward Alex once more. However, Alex, though preoccupied, caught sight of the movement. He swung around fast. His fist collided with David's face, sending David to the ground, unconsciousness. Alex stood over David's motionless body, his breath ragged. The breaking of glass echoed in the alley before the flash of flame exploded.

Fire spread across the hay and licked up the side of the tavern. The wind, which had picked up, didn't help matters. Alex took off his coat and began to beat at the flames. I followed suit with my cloak, but the flames didn't stop. I frantically searched for water but found none. In a mere matter of minutes, the fire spread to the roof of The Fighting Cock's Tavern and to the building next door.

The heat scalded my skin. Flashes of my family's home burning to the ground screamed in my memory, and I found I couldn't move from my spot. The fire spread, like smallpox, from building to building. It was petrifying. The screams of women and children, the yelling for water, echoed through the night as did the crackling of sticks, leaves, and hay. It was amazing how fast the fire took over, the black smoke billowing in the night air.

Oh, God. What did we do?

I choked as the smoke settled in my lungs and made my eyes blurry.

"Alex?" I yelled.

"Here! Grab my hand, Nora. We need to get out of here," he said. He took my hand in his rough calloused one, and I knew I would be safe. He began to pull me along.

"Wait! What about David? We can't leave him here. Please," I begged.

The decision Alex had to make was evident on his face. David lay on the ground in his British uniform. If Alex left him to die, he would be one more British soldier not up against what we were trying to accomplish. One more soldier we wouldn't have to worry about. Yet, I knew Alex would not let a man perish like this.

Without another word, he picked David up and draped him over his shoulders. "Let's go," Alex said.

On shaky legs, I followed him out to the street.

"Stay close," Alex said.

He didn't have to tell me that. I kept my eyes trained on him, not wanting to lose him in the crowd. Hundreds of people ran through the street. Their cries of distress were accentuated by the looks of fear on their faces.

Alex found two British soldiers, standing with their mouths agape at the horror of the fire around them. "Here," he said, setting David down at their feet. "My wife and I were running out of the house, and we found him like this."

One of the men dropped to one knee on the ground. "You have our thanks, sir. Madam," he said.

Before they could question us any further, Alex grabbed my hand and strode off into the night as the west side of southern Manhattan went up in flame.

CHAPTER 19

My lungs burned. My legs shook. I clutched my side and gasped for air as Alex pulled me through the streets of Manhattan then off the main roads and into the woods. From the distance we were, three miles or so, I could still see the red and orange flames reaching up into the night sky as if they were going to pluck the moon from its position and eat it.

We slowed our pace. My heart continued beating a frantic thud against my chest. *When will breathing become easier?*

"Can we stop now, please? Only for a moment?" I asked Alex.

"No. Not yet. We're almost there."

"Where are we going?"

"To get Bridger."

"You left him all alone in the woods?"

"He's fine. He's near a small stream, and I wrapped his reins around the branch of a tree. Don't worry," he said.

He had dropped my hand a mile or so ago, and I found myself missing his skin against mine. I wasn't as cold when he held my hand. I was safe. My thoughts drifted to David.

How could he have said those things to me? My heart ached, but I pushed it aside. There would be plenty of time for me to be sad over David when Alex and I reached our destination — wherever that was. He still hadn't told me anything, and I found for the time being, I didn't care. I was too numb.

Bridger stood where Alex had apparently left him, happily munching on grass. He lifted his head when we approached. He snorted when Alex rubbed his nose.

Alex grabbed his canteen from his sack strapped onto Bridger and filled it with water. He handed it to me. "Small sips now."

I nodded and sipped the cold fluid. It hurt my throat, yet at the same time quenched it. I drank and drank, hoping the water would wash away what we had encountered. It dribbled down my chin, and I wiped the water away with the back of my hand. The next thing I knew, Alex was handing me a wet piece of linen. When I didn't automatically take it, he carefully reached forward and wiped the soot and dirt off my face. I took it from him and finished on my own. His eyes remained on me for a few moments longer. Was he watching me to see if I'd break? He must have been convinced I was fine, for he took the linen from me and put it back in his sack before walking over to Bridger's side.

"Up you go, Sailor," he said. He bent down and cupped his hand, indicating I was to place my foot inside for him to boost me into the saddle.

I did and found myself seated once more in front of Alex on his mount.

"You're shaking," Alex said. "Here."

As he had done the first time I found myself in the saddle with him, he twisted around and pulled a wool blanket out of his sack and draped it over my shoulders without saying a word. His steady breathing and warm body calmed me. He urged Bridger forward, and we began our journey.

"I'll take you back to your uncle's house," Alex said.

"No. Please," I said.

Alex looked down at me, a question lingering on his lips and in his eyes.

"I'm a mess, Alex. I can't go back there like this. Uncle will know I was out and… not yet. I can't go back there yet," I said. Images of Captain Roth filled my mind. Maybe this was my chance to get away.

Alex nodded.

We rode for a few minutes without speaking until I found my voice again.

"Where are we going?" I asked, my throat and lungs feeling cleaner.

"Somewhere safe and out of the way."

We traveled for the next hour in silence. Though we didn't talk, anger and frustration rolled off Alex. His posture never once relaxed the entire time we traveled, and I was about to tell him to yell it out when the silhouette of a small house showed itself in the distance. The sky was now not as dark, and hints of the morning sun could be seen in the gray sky as we approached the building.

Smoke swirled from the chimney of the lonely log house, and a candle was lit in each of the two windows on the bottom floor. The scent of fire wafted on the wind, and my stomach clenched at remembering the destruction Alex and I had left behind. The idea struck me as how something so useful, and dare I say fascinatingly beautiful, could cause so much damage.

A small fence enclosed one side of the two-story small cabin. How odd that no animals roamed about the place, especially for a house so removed. Did whoever live here travel all the way to Manhattan whenever they needed something? Even eggs?

The sun had risen by the time we reached the yard,

waking the birds that chirped endlessly in the treetops. Two horses were tied to a tree near the house. From the looks of the place, I wondered if it was a permanent residence for the person inside. The cabin was not run-down by any means, yet it wasn't well-kept either. It was ordinary.

The two horses stomped their feet and twitched about, snorting, steam blowing out of their nostrils as we trotted closer to the cabin. Alex reined Bridger in and cupped his mouth with his hands. "Hooo. Hooo." He mimicked the calling of an owl perfectly.

He waited for a span of five heartbeats before calling out again. This time, he was answered, and he grinned. He urged Bridger forward until he stood next to the other horses then dismounted, helping me off next.

For a moment, all I was capable of doing was standing next to the horse. My arms folded across my chest. What was I going to do now? No way could I go back to Uncle Edward after what had happened. Perhaps, if he wasn't friendly with the captain I could, but not now. I didn't feel safe there. And as for David, any future prospects with him had been burned up along with the fire. My father's cousin lived in Setauket. Perhaps I could convince Alex to accompany me so I could live with her. I wiped my face with my neckerchief. It turned black.

"Are you going to tell me who lives here?" I asked him as we walked up to the front door.

It swung open. "About time. I've been sitting here twiddling my thumbs for thirty minutes now. Hello, Miss Bishop. Nice to see you again," Si said, his face one of surprise, apparently at seeing me.

Gideon peered around the door. "Step away, Si, and let them in. Welcome, Miss Bishop, to my home."

I nodded. Consolation spread through me to see it was Alex's two cousins. The men embraced each other, and I could easily see relief etched on their faces that they were all safe.

"I did not realize you lived in such close proximity to Manhattan," I said, allowing my eyes to wander through the room. "I'm confused though. Why aren't you with the regiments?"

"We are volunteers and therefore are not required to sleep with the troops. Since neither army is on the move, currently, we're here. Why sleep outside in a tent when you don't have to?" Gideon said.

The house was sparsely decorated with no womanly touch to be seen. The inside contained two rooms downstairs, one of which acted as kitchen and main living area, where the other was smaller in size. A tiny bed and dresser sat in the other room. A set of stairs led up to the second floor where I estimated another two bedrooms could be found.

Gideon must have taken in my survey, for he spread his arms and gave me a sad grin. "This was supposed to be a house for my wife and me when we married. I began building it but stopped after she died. Smallpox. Now it sits here unused for the greater part of the year. Si has been kind enough to allow me to stay with him for the time being," he said. "We now use this place as a meeting house."

"Oh. I'm sorry."

"And it's about time you moved out for good. I've been living with you for my whole life," Si growled, though by the loving expression on his face, one could easily tell he didn't mean a word.

Gideon promptly pulled away and escorted me to a chair near the fire. He walked to the back of the small home with Alex and Si close on his heels. The men began talking, keeping their voices low so I could not hear what they said. Usually this would have bothered me, but not today. I yawned. I wanted to sleep off the whole affair and deal with the fact the fault was mine. *Good Lord.* I had helped burn Manhattan to the ground. I would never be able to make amends for it.

Three pairs of heavy footsteps entered the sitting room, but I did not look up. My eyes were fixed on the dancing flames before me.

"I'll be right back, Nora," Alex said. "I must see to Bridger."

I nodded, not bothering to turn and watch him leave. Gideon set a pewter plate in my lap containing nuts and fruit. I wasn't hungry but picked up a slice of apple and nibbled on it anyway.

The silence in the room was only disturbed by the sound of my own chewing until I couldn't take it anymore. "Do either of you gentlemen want to tell me what you were discussing?"

I watched Si and Gideon as their eyes flickered to each other.

"Will you be all right, Miss Bishop? Alex might have mentioned what took place," Si said.

I shrugged. The way they looked at me led me to believe they were not speaking of the fire, or at least not solely about that.

"Please, call me Nora. And I'm fine. A little shaken up, under the circumstances, but I'll recover. Once the smoke clears from my lungs and I can wash the smell off of me."

"Begging your pardon, Nora," Gideon said. "I think what Si meant—"

"I know what he meant," I snapped. I shut my eyes and focused on calming myself down. "I'm sorry. I know you're concerned, and I thank you for it, but I'm fine. I'm fine," I said, not sure whether I was trying to convince them or myself.

"Glad to hear it. Alex said that bastard laid his hands on you. If he hadn't come back, Alex said he was certain he would have raped you," Si said, his face grim and serious.

"No, that wouldn't have happened. David was too deep in his cups. He wouldn't have done that," I said. Would he?

Si shrugged. "Other men have committed the same offense. Sober no less."

I looked at him, knowing a hidden story lay behind his words. He glanced at Gideon then looked back to me. "It isn't my story to tell. Alex has some personal connection with a victim of that sort of attack, and he does not take such a thing lightly. Neither do we."

"Who?" Alex had attacked David because he had a history with it. But this time, it was on account of me, a woman he hardly had any connection with.

"His wife," Si said.

I choked. "His wife," I said, part question, part statement.

The food I swallowed lodged in my throat at the word. Alex was married? I hadn't known it, and he had never said anything. After all we'd been through, he'd never once mentioned anything at all about having a wife. A stab of disappointment hitched in my heart though I didn't understand why. I promptly snuffed it out.

"His wife? Excuse my surprise, but I did not know he was married."

"*Was* married. He's a widower now," Si said, his eye reflective.

"He never mentioned anything. Why would he?" I added hastily.

"Listen, Nora, I'm only telling you this because rape — or even attempted rape—" Si said, watching me as I opened my mouth to interrupt him, "Alex would protect any woman from it. Even one who typically made her money on her back. He's a man of honor above all else. That offense, well…"

"Was the rape what caused her death?" I asked tentatively.

"I'll let him tell you the details. I'm only saying this now because if you need help in this area, he'll do what he can," Si said.

"All of us will," Gideon chimed in.

The mood in the room had grown quite serious, and the three of us apparently found we had nothing to talk about after their revelation.

Alex barged in through the door blowing warm air onto his hands and stopped after stepping in the room. He looked around, and his eyes narrowed. His mouth tightened into a thin line, and he raised an inquiring brow.

But before he could ask any questions, I stood up and smoothed my dirty gown. "I suspect we will be staying here?"

"Yes, you'll stay here, and I'm going to ride back to see if I can help—"

"Are you daft, man?" Si said. "What's gotten into you? Part of the reason the fire started is because of a fight you got caught up in. If anyone saw you, you'll be swinging from a branch tomorrow. No. You'll both stay here until Gideon and I ascertain the extent of the damage. We'll depart now and lend our assistance, while we try to discover if anyone saw either of you. The fire could very well still be blazing if it is as bad as you say," Si said, looking at Alex.

Alex stood with his arms crossed against his chest, his face grim. He was obviously considering everything Si had said, and behind his eyes, I sensed him weighing his options.

He nodded.

Gideon began collecting items and loading them into a bag. The three men lowered their voices once more in deep conversation. I turned away to give them some privacy, but could not help glancing at them.

Alex had looked at me in turn, and our eyes locked for a brief moment before he gave his cousins his undivided attention once more.

Si and Gideon each bid me farewell and strode out the door, leaving Alex and me entirely alone. I kept my hands clasped in front of me, not knowing what else to do with them or how to act. I'd never been this alone with a man before. Granted, this was not the first time I had found myself in his company unchaperoned; however, this time he was perfectly healthy with no wounds needing tending, except for the few scrapes he'd received from David.

With no active battle going on around us, I found myself wishing for such a distraction. For if gunshots zipped about, it would give me something else to focus on instead of the handsome, strong man with the dark hair and clear blue eyes standing in front me.

Deep down, I knew Alex would never harm me, but I'd never thought David or a captain of the British army would either.

Alex must have sensed my hesitation because he took a step away from me. "Nora, you do know I would never lay a hand on you," he said with reservation.

"Yes. I know."

He sighed. "How about we sleep? Follow me," he said. He turned and made his way toward the small staircase. He took two steps at a time and waited for me at the top.

The upstairs was as I thought it would be: two bedrooms, and only one contained a bed, along with a dresser, table, and chair. The other was vacant. I sneezed from the stale smell. Certainly, Gideon had not been in the room for a long time. Alex started a fire, then he walked to the other room and came back with another quilt.

"Here," he said, handing me the covering, though one

already lay on the bed. "Would you like the window open as well? It is a bit stuffy in here."

"I can manage."

He shrugged, crossed the room and opened the window anyway. Then he took a deep breath. "I'm not trying to be forward, Nora, but I know the smell of smoke still lingers on your gown. If you take it off and toss it to me, I'll go down by the creek and rinse it out for you. Gideon left us some soap downstairs."

His face reddened as did mine, for I had no idea how to respond. I would be left in nothing but my shift and stays. However, he was right. I would continue to smell like a fire if something wasn't done, and better for him to wash it than for me to be down by the stream in my undergarments.

"I'll need you to help with the laces," I said.

His Adam's apple moved up and down when he swallowed. He took a hesitant step toward me, his face serious and intent.

Without any grace, he unknotted my laces in the back of my dress. I could feel the ties slipping through each hole, and though I remained covered, I felt completely naked. I kept my hands on my bodice, to keep the dress in place after he finished the loosening. His hands stopped moving, and I turned around. His eyes never once moved away from my face, though my gown sagged in front, clearly giving a better view of what hid underneath.

Alex cleared his throat. "I'll step out into the hall. Toss me your gown, and I'll take care of it."

"Right," I said, not finding any other word.

Alex walked out of the room, shutting the door, leaving me standing alone. I took a deep breath. Though he had not touched any part me, my whole body burned and this was one flame I did not know how to extinguish.

I opened the door a crack and dropped the gown onto the floor.

"I'll be down at the stream if you need anything. Try and get some sleep," Alex said. He didn't look at me but kept his back turned and walked down the stairs. I stood there frozen, and only after I heard the front door shut did I manage to breathe.

The last thing I could do was sleep. Too many emotions darted through my head like a hummingbird flitting from flower to flower. Now, more than ever, I desperately needed protection. David had spoken to me and touched me in ways I didn't think he was capable of, and if he could do that to me, what else could happen? Once again, my ordeal with the captain resurfaced, and I knew it was something that would haunt me forever. If I went back to my uncle's house, and the captain found me again, he might succeed in his attempt to ruin me. Though I was a virgin still and did not know the ways of men, I did know enough that to be taken against one's will would ruin any woman, even one who was not ignorant in such acts.

After enduring David, no way in hell would I ever marry him, if it were possible. This war had destroyed him, and deep down, I knew David was not and would never be the David I had fallen in love with. Why wasn't I more emotional about it? Maybe I'd been moving on all along and was only now realizing it.

I had nowhere to turn at present. The conversation I'd had with Si and Gideon came back to me. They'd said Alex would do anything to help protect me. He would do the same for any woman. Would he go as far to marry me if I begged him? Certainly, he'd felt a little bit of attraction on his part. I knew I was attracted to him, so that would help things, wouldn't it? Many marriages had been arranged, and those couples lived well together. Maybe the same could be said for us if he agreed.

I trusted him, and I hoped he trusted me. I'd helped to heal him on several occasions after all, and he'd relied upon me for the dead drop. He was no longer married, but maybe he was attached to someone else, or possibly he still longed for his dead wife. His cousins never mentioned children, but surely he would want some to carry on his line.

As my list of reasons continued to roll through my mind, I paced the floor, speaking aloud to myself. It made perfect sense to me. All I needed was to summon the courage to ask Alex about it. How hard could it be? I had encountered way more difficult tasks.

While I paced the room, preparing my speech, a knock sounded. My thoughts consumed me so much that, without thinking, I crossed the room and pulled open the door. It was only after I watched Alex's mouth pop open in surprise and his eyes rake over me standing in nothing but my shift and stays did I become embarrassed. I slammed the door.

I grabbed the quilt I had thrown on the bed and wrapped it around me like a shawl and reopened the access. Alex stood there, a bemused expression on his face. My eyes went to his lips and the split David had given him.

"You're injured. Again," I said, stepping aside, not knowing what else to say to him.

He followed me in.

I grabbed hold of his chin, inspecting him. I didn't want him to know I was nervous. "I should have seen to your lip as soon as we came here. I'm sorry," I said. I turned his face left and right.

He stood still with his hands at his side and let me.

"Are you hurt anywhere else?" I asked, pleased it was only a small scrape. I silently chastised myself for not noticing or asking about him earlier.

"No." Alex continued to stare at me, and my face warmed. In fact, my whole body heated.

I took a step back. "You're sure? Don't try to be a hero. There are plenty around here nowadays," I said. Instinctively, I put my hands on my hips, and the quilt that had kept me covered fell from my shoulders. I snatched it up and threw it on the bed. I would not be intimated by him. I remained partially clothed. Though the fabric was lightweight, it was not transparent.

Alex grinned. "I'm certain you can inspect every last inch of me if you'd like. If you don't believe me, that is."

I shook my head and turned away from him, releasing my breath, not knowing what else to do or how to behave. Maybe the fact I only had my shift with me could work in my favor. Did I have it in me to try and seduce him into marrying me? What did that say about me though if I was willing to do it? It said I was desperate, but I knew it.

"Do you have any rum? Whiskey perhaps?" I said.

"Yes, actually. Want some?"

I faced him, and he handed me the flask, but I shook my head. "You drink it. It will help heal your lip," I said.

"But it will burn something horrible."

"Good. That'll teach you to think twice before you go off punching someone," I said, feeling frustrated.

"Speaking of, I think it's time you and I talked about what happened since it is obvious you don't intend on sleeping." He took a step toward me, but I stood my ground. "So we are clear, I punched him because of what he was doing to you." His cheerful expression turned dark.

"I could have handled it," I said tightly.

"Right. It didn't look that way to me. You're lucky I was there."

"Lucky? If you wouldn't have left, it wouldn't have happened," I said. My emotions were spinning out of control like one of the toy tops I used to play with as a child. I would spin it and watch as it cycloned around the floor, twisting and turning before falling down on its side. How had our conversation turned to this?

"Me?" Alex's voice was loud. "I warned you to stay away. I told you not to come to the tavern, and that it would have been taken care of! None of it would have happened if you would have listened! God, woman! You're lucky I've been here — several times, I might add — to protect you. And believe me, you need it. One of these days, you're going to find yourself in a position you can't get out of," he said.

His chest heaved, and his face turned scarlet with anger. The veins on the side of his neck were visible. He ran both his hands through his hair and then settled them over his eyes and nose, taking a deep breath before lowering them.

We stood there staring at each other. He was able to keep his face guarded, but his eyes told a different story. They were angry at me, yet discernible passion flared behind them. We'd been playing flirtation games, but could there be a realness behind them? He was no longer a stranger to me. He was a friend. I liked him and found him very attractive. I enjoyed his company. We would get along. Could I ask him?

The image of the young men dying on the battlefield sprung to my memory. My own situation was not much different. The possibility I would die in the war, or a stray bullet would hit me was a very real danger, not to mention frostbite, fever, or smallpox. But the greater threat was the captain. If Captain Roth ever got hold of me again, I knew a part of me would die.

Did I want that to happen without ever feeling the arms of a man around me? Holding me?

I trusted Alex. I trusted him with my life and with my body.

"Marry me," I said, my voice coming out hoarse and low.

It didn't come out as I intended, but I could not take it back. I could only forge forward.

"What?" He didn't bother to hide his surprise.

Lifting my chin, I met his eyes. Then, slowly and with trembling fingers, I began to untie the lace of my shift.

Alex's eyes grew wide.

"You're right — on all accounts. And I need someone to protect me. Marry me," I said.

Alex reached out and caught the white linen in his hands as it fell off my shoulders. The air around us grew thick, and for a moment, all was silent. He glanced at the exposed skin and then my lips.

"Nora, what are you doing?" he said, his voice husky.

"Offering myself to you, in exchange for your name. I have no one else. We could be handfasted. Now."

"What makes you think this," he said, his finger touching my collarbone, "is what I want?"

"It isn't?" I said, his question stinging.

He raised his eyebrows.

"I assumed an invitation like this would entice any man."

"And it would. But what in God's name would make you think I'm a man who would take a woman unwillingly? I already told you I'd never hurt you, and I meant it. I've done many things in my life that I'm not proud of, but never have I laid a hand on a woman who doesn't want me to," he said. "And this… this is not how you want it to be, Nora. Not offering yourself like this. You know it, and I know it, though I understand your position and am honored by your proposal. I will protect you regardless, Nora. I promise you that. I will find a way to keep you safe."

A mixture of relief, frustration, and rejection swelled through me at Alex's words. Was it something about me that made him hesitant? My shoulders sagged, the tension inching out of them until Alex's fingers moved to the neck of my shift and began retying the laces.

He watched his own fingers, and they lingered near my neck long after he finished the task. "Nora, I told you once I'd always be truthful with you," he said.

Heat spread through my body at the mention of my name on his lips. I didn't know why it had such an effect on me now, since he had used my Christian name plenty of times before, but it did. Perhaps it was because I stood in a small room, only in my shift, and we were completely alone.

"And in truth, seeing you standing here, before me, undressed as you are, offering yourself to me like you have, well, it's requiring all the self-control I have not to take you to that bed over there," he said.

I swallowed and willed myself not to look at the bed he'd mentioned. "I want you to hear me now, Nora, and understand what I'm about to say to you. If I ever take you to bed, it's because you want me to. Not because you think you can gain something from it or because you think it is expected of you. It will be honorable and lawful. And I'll be the one to untie your laces and loosen your shift, taking my time as I want to savor the gift you're giving me. Do you understand?"

The tension lingering between us could have been pierced by his knife.

"Yes," I said, my voice coming out small.

"Good."

Alex leaned forward and kissed me on my cheek. "Sleep tight, Sailor."

CHAPTER 20

THE SOUND OF GALLOPING horses and men's voices woke me only because I had kept the bedroom window open after Alex left the room. I slept. And, somehow, I slept peacefully. Too peacefully. Had Gideon or Si put something in my drink earlier?

After sitting up and scooting to the edge of the bed, I yawned and stretched. It was still daylight, though the sun was fading, bringing the day close to evening. The fire had dwindled down considerably and now a slight chill filled the room. I crossed to the window. Two horses stood tethered to the tree. The men were back.

My gown was draped over the chair. A cup and plate sat on the table. Alex must have crept inside while I slept and delivered the items. My face reddened thinking about him and our last conversation. I had thrown myself at him, practically begged him to marry me, only to be met with rejection.

I was no closer to getting John out of prison, and now that I found myself in this small cabin in the woods, I could not figure out how to continue my task of discovering information for General Washington. Hopefully Gideon and Si had news for us, ensuring I could go back to Manhattan without worry of being discovered at having been at the fire.

Stepping into my gown rather fast and doing the best I could to tie the laces myself, I walked down stairs. At first, the men did not notice I had entered the room. They sat around the table eating and talking over each other.

"You're sure?" Alex said.

"Positive. I dug around when we first heard the news because I didn't believe it myself, but it's right true. He was captured in Queens. Talk has it that Major Robert Rodgers found him."

Alex winced at the name. I had heard stories of the man but never seen him. It had been said he was ruthless and never missed his target. He apparently knew the wilderness like he did his own home.

"He's been tried for treason. He'll hang tomorrow," Si said.

"Who'll hang?" I said, stepping farther into the room.

The sun dipped lower in the sky now, and the few candles lit cast shadows over the room. Gideon rose and offered me his seat.

I shook my head, too anxious to sit.

Gideon went over to the fireplace to lay a new log on the flame.

I knew Alex sat looking at me, and though I wanted nothing more than to avoid his eyes, I couldn't. I could not — nor would not — be a coward. I lifted my chin and met his stare.

The corner of his mouth turned up as if he read my thoughts. But as quick as his mouth lifted, it turned down. "Nathan Hale."

I gasped. "What? No. How?" I was unable to come to terms with the news.

"After he left us, he apparently went to Queens. He stayed in a tavern there, and someone saw him, reported his whereabouts."

"This is my fault," I said, my voice low and tight. My throat constricted as guilt swam through me. Nathan Hale would hang because of me. How many more lives would I put in jeopardy? "If I hadn't gone to the tavern, the fire wouldn't have started, and if the fire wouldn't have started, he would not have needed to run. I'm so sorry," I said as tears brimmed up in my eyes. My knees buckled beneath me, and I sat down before I ended up in a heap on the floor.

"Nora, this is not your fault. Someone saw him at The Fighting Cock's Tavern before you arrived. He would have had to leave the place anyway," Alex said.

"Hale went to the tavern for me. I asked him to look into John's situation." I wiped my eyes and looked down at my hands resting in my lap.

Alex shook his head. He leaned forward and put his finger under my chin, making me look directly into his eyes. "He spent almost every night in one tavern or another, trying to find out information. It was bound to happen sooner or later. He should have stayed put after he left Manhattan, but he didn't. This is not your fault. Understand?"

I nodded and bit my lip. "We have to try and rescue him. We have to help him."

"Nora, we can't. It is too late now. If we would have found him on the run, perhaps, but not now. It is out of our hands and in God's," Alex said.

"So you are going to let your friend die. You're going to watch him hang?"

"Yes," Si said. "I know it sounds harsh, but this rescue would end with each of our necks on a branch next to him. Nathan knew what he signed up for. We all do. I wish it weren't so, but it has to be this way. The best we can do for him is to go and watch. To keep our eyes locked on his as the only reassurance we can offer that we'll meet him one day soon." His jaw clenched. He blinked back tears which threatened to drip down his face. His features were nothing but resolute.

Not knowing what else to say, I pushed back from the table and stood up then swiftly walked out the front door. I marched toward the tree where Bridger stood munching on grass. He snorted when I approached, and when I reached out to rub his nose, he nudged me with it. A moment later, footsteps approached. I didn't need to turn around. I recognized the walk, the way his feet fell and his weight shifted. Leather and his natural scent came to me on the wind. I shut my eyes and fell into Bridger's mane.

"Your feelings of passion are one of the things I like best about you, Sailor. You've been through a lot, and instead of building a wall like some, you continue to feel. You continue to love and fight. I know this situation is hard for you. I know you and Nathan had begun to form a friendship, and I'm sorry. Truly. But this has to happen. It would be a dishonor to him if we tried to rescue him and failed."

"I know," I said. And I did understand, but I hated it.

After a minute of lingering silence, Alex sighed.

I kept my eyes on the horse but could sense him wanting to say something more. I could feel his arm near mine, feel the heat of his skin. He was so close to me that if he wanted to, he could reach out and take me in his arms. My heartbeat rang as loud as church bells, and I feared he could hear it.

"I'll be leaving at first light to go back," Alex said at last. "I'll come directly here when it is finished."

I found my courage that I had lost momentarily. "I'm going with you."

"I don't think that is the best—"

"I don't care what you think. I'm going."

"You're not. It is no place for a lady. We'll have supper in a half hour, and then go to bed," Alex said. He turned on his heel and walked to the porch where he lifted up his saddle. He came back and began to get Bridger ready.

I stepped back, putting my hands on my hips. "And now where are you going?"

"To make sure General Washington knows what's going on. I won't take the chance that he may or may not know. I'll be back to break my fast with you if you'd like, and then I'll be off. Don't do anything rash," he said. He kicked Bridger, and they were off.

How one man could make me so angry all the time yet flare a passionate flame inside me, I would never know. I tromped back inside the house, fuming mad.

Si and Gideon remained quiet when I walked through the door. Their expressions told me they had heard everything, and a small part of me wondered if they knew about my proposal. It seemed to me the cousins rarely kept things to themselves.

"I'm going back to bed. I'm not hungry," I said. "Goodnight."

I knew they watched me clunk up the stairs, but I was in no mood to discuss anything. Alex had once again tried to tell me what I could and could not do, assuming he had the authority a husband would have over me; and my husband he was not. With each step I took toward my bedroom, I became more angry at life, and with more gusto than I'd intended, I slammed the door and flung myself onto the bed.

After rolling over to lie on my back, I stared at the ceiling, my eyes adjusting to the now-darkened room. No way in hell would I would remain here while Captain Hale suffered the noose. Alex had tried to convince me I was not at fault, and though a part of me believed him, deep down, guilt ate at me. I had to go, and I had to watch the horror and sadness of the hanging. I owed him even if the only thing I could do was be there for his final moments so he knew he wasn't alone. Seeing Uncle Edward, if he decided to attend, or Captain Roth be damned.

It was many hours later by the time Si and Gideon took to their beds. I didn't know what time it was, but the sky was completely dark, the stars crystal-clear. Taking my candle, I crept downstairs. A small clock sat upon the table. Time was important in my exit strategy. I needed to leave before Alex returned and the men woke. Alex was planning on returning at first light, that much I knew.

Bringing the flame and the clock closer together, I squinted. It was half past four. I didn't have much time. I found an old piece of burlap near the kitchen and stuffed it with a slice of bread, an apple, and a piece of cheese. I knew where the creek was, and decided, rather than hunt around in the house for a canteen, I'd use my hands.

I snuck out of the house and eased the front door closed. The woods were still sleeping. The only noises were that of crickets and other insects breaking through the quiet.

One of the horses sensed me because it lifted its head and gave a small neigh as if telling me I'd interrupted his sleep.

"Sorry, boy," I said, rubbing its nose. "Or are you a girl? Either way, I promise we aren't going too far. Besides, I'm lighter than Si or Gideon, for that you can be grateful."

The horse nuzzled me and snorted as if he found my comment amusing.

I patted him then bent over and picked up the saddle next to the tree and hauled it up. I placed it on his back.

"Sailor," Alex said.

I jumped and shrieked at the same time. "Damn it. Why? *Why* do you feel the need to do that to me?" I said. My heart pounded furiously, and I resisted the desire to slap him.

"Why do you feel the urge toward foolhardiness?"

He stomped over to me and reached for the saddle to remove it at the same time I placed my hands on it to keep it still. His huge hand covered mine, and my heart became frantic once again at our closeness. The tension between us seemed to travel from his body to me, but it was not entirely uncomfortable. An invisible thread pulled me to him, and I found it very hard to not walk nearer and put my arms around his waist.

"You're back awfully early," I said, keeping my hands gripped on the object we were both after.

"I knew you'd try this very thing. I'm not stupid," he said. His hand pressed down upon mine, and even in the dark, I could see light flare behind his eyes.

"Then you should know that I'll go no matter what. Even if I have to walk," I said, my voice raising.

"What the hell is going on out here?" a groggy voice said from the porch.

Both Alex and I turned. Si stood on the steps, rubbing his eyes and yawning. "What the blazes are you doing with my horse?"

"She thought she'd sneak out of the house and travel to Manhattan to watch the hanging," Alex said.

I glared at him, and he glared right back.

"By yourself? What the devil are you thinking, woman? Are you that thick-headed you don't listen? Did you not hear what we told you? Husbands have beat their wives over not listening, not to mention stealing," he said gruffly.

I lowered my hand and crossed my arms. "Well, it is a good thing I'm not married to any of you then." I deliberately looked at Alex with my chin lifted and my back straightened.

His mouth formed a thin line, but his eyes never wavered from my defiant gaze.

"Praise the Lord for that," Si said, almost chuckling. "A

headstrong lady like yourself, you need a man to rein you in. I'm going back to bed. Alex, she can't take my horse."

Si turned around and, as quietly as he had walked onto the porch, left.

In a calmer voice, I said, "I have to go. Please."

"Fine. You want to go? Go. But you'll wait for me. Understand?"

"Yes."

He nodded. "Now, get back inside and try to sleep. We have a few more hours until it is to take place. I need to rest Bridger. I'll wake you when it's time."

"Promise?"

"Yes."

* * *

ALEX KEPT HIS PROMISE, and at six in the morning, the four of us set off for Manhattan. The city, though swarming with people, was subdued. The smell of smoke and burnt houses was heavy in the air, like a quilt on a bed.

At first, Alex was going to take us in through the east side of town, but I insisted on seeing the damage for myself. Twenty-five percent of the southern end of Manhattan had been burned to the ground. Family homes, places of business all alike. Nothing had been spared. In the middle of the disarray, those buildings that had not been touched by the fire had been plundered by soldier and citizen. Ladies and children cried in the streets; men walked around angry with total despair. Their faces would be forever etched in my mind, knowing I had played a part in what happened.

The tragedy of the fire hit me deep in the stomach. I knew all too well what these people were going through. How many had been killed?

If the fire were not enough, we discovered that Major

General James Robertson had confiscated surviving uninhabited homes of known patriot supporters and assigned these dwellings to British officers. Churches were in the process of being converted to prisons, infirmaries, or barracks. As we passed by several houses, we saw common soldiers entering and leaving civilian family homes as now they were living with them.

"My hope of Manhattan getting out from under British occupation has now been doused out," Alex said. He sat behind me once more on top of Bridger. "The redcoats are everywhere. We will have to leave Manhattan soon. I know it."

Alex urged the horse on, and we soon came to the lower part of the island. He swung from Bridger and helped me off before securing his reins around a branch of a nearby tree. A medium-sized audience had gathered near the gallows, waiting. A hush fell over the crowd as the provost marshal made the adjustments and prepared for the hanging.

The crowd was quiet in a respectful way, but an excited tension rolled throughout the air. It was a good thing I had come with Alex and not made the journey myself. My stomach fluttered with terrified anticipation while my bottom lip quivered.

We stood there side by side and watched as Captain Hale was pulled to the gallows. His hands were tied, and a solemn yet dignified look rested on his face. The provost marshal placed the rope around his neck, and the reverend read a few verses from the scriptures. My eyes and ears were only focused on Captain Hale.

He looked out into the crowd, his gaze wandering over the heads of everyone there, until they rested on Alex and me. I wanted to call out to him, but Alex, who now had his arm around my waist, squeezed me. A tear slipped down my cheek. Captain Hale nodded, and I sensed Alex nodding back.

"Any last word, Captain Hale?" the provost marshal said.

Captain Hale took a deep breath, and staring at the British officers who were there, said in a loud voice, "I only regret that I have but one life to lose for my country."

And without another word, on the twenty-second of September, twenty-one-year old Captain Nathan Hale of the 19th Regiment of the Continental Army was hung to death for treason.

His body swung slightly from the light breeze as he lost consciousness before he started convulsing. His face became distorted and livid while his beautiful soft eyes were suddenly prominent on his face. As the body, though insentient, started to struggle against the enviable death, I turned away and buried my head in Alex's shoulder.

Alex wrapped his arm around me but stayed facing his friend. "It's almost over," he whispered.

And after fifteen minutes of silence, it was. Unable to watch the gallows or the crowd, I kept my head down. People murmured around me as they departed. Waves of grief, loss, and sadness spread over everyone in attendance, no matter their side.

"He's gone," Alex said, his voice low.

I raised my head. Nathan had already been taken away. The branch from where his body swayed, lifeless, was now bare.

"Will you be all right?" Alex asked. He reached forward and wiped my cheek with gentle fingers.

"Yes."

"I'll be back. I want to find out where they are taking the body. Wait here. Please."

"I will," I said, not taking my attention off the empty gallows.

I closed my eyes for a moment, and when I opened them, I stared into the blackest, deadliest ones of all. Captain William Roth glared at me from behind the gallows and stalked toward me. His eyes remained on mine, and though every fiber of my being wanted to run, wanted to flee, I could not.

My blood turned cold, and my heart seemed to stop beating altogether. Sweat trickled down the back of my neck, and I found it hard to breathe. What did he want? Did he know I'd caused the fire?

"My, my, my… look who we have here," Captain Roth said. He walked a circle around me. His hands remained behind his back, but I knew one false move, and he would not hesitate to grab me.

I swallowed. "Captain. I would say it is a pleasure, but we both know I'd be lying."

He chuckled. "Your father should have beat you more as a young girl. Perhaps if he would have done so, you wouldn't be so insolent. Pity he's dead." He sighed, his breath touching my neck and causing me to shiver. "Perhaps I should take on the role. I'm fairly certain your uncle would allow it, especially if I offered for your hand."

He stopped in front of me. A foul, dark, smile displayed on his lips.

My mouth popped open. "You wouldn't," I said.

"I would, to teach you a few lessons. You've been giving me nothing but a headache from the moment I first saw you. Your way of speech, manner of actions. They are horrible, madam. Not to be tolerated. But, I suppose that is to be expected since you come from a patriot-loving family." He sneered. "But I admit I find you appealing, on some level. Yes, I think I shall do that. I'll talk to your uncle today. Someone has to keep you in line," he said, moving in close to me. "And I'm certain I possess all the tools to do that."

"I'll kindly ask you to step away from the lady," Alex said. His voice was low, strained, and I knew without looking that his eyes would be narrowed and the beautiful blue color would be replaced by a dark storm.

My heart, which had been beating erratically, pounded louder and stronger. I turned my head. Alex strode nearer, his hand balled into fists at his sides.

For his part, the captain gave no indication that he knew who Alex was, but it was clear from Alex's dark expression he was holding tightly to his temper, not wanting to unleash it in this crowd.

"Come, Nora. It is time to go," Alex said. He reached out his hand.

I took it and instantly became calmer the moment our skin touched, and he snaked his other arm around my waist. It took everything I had in me not to fall down.

"And who might you be, sir?" Captain Roth asked before we could turn away.

"Her husband."

CHAPTER 21

My mind and emotions were still foggy from watching the grotesque display of the hanging and from the chance meeting of Captain Roth as we galloped back to Gideon's small house. Alex never uttered a word. His knuckles were as white as the clouds when gripping the reins. It was a wonder Bridger wasn't annoyed.

The trees rushed past me in a blur as we rode through the woods. We were two miles from Gideon's home when Alex pulled Bridger to a halt. He jumped down and helped me off then walked over to Si and handed him the reins.

Gideon remained on his horse, his eyes narrowed but stayed silent. His horse moved in circles, as if he too sensed an urgency.

Si and Alex talked in low voices. The only indication I had of them discussing me came from the quick flick of Si's eyes to where I stood watching them. With only a nod of his head in farewell, Si and Gideon rode away to the house.

The wind stirred, blowing my gown around my legs. Gooseflesh rose on my arms but not from the chill in the air. I clutched my shawl as if it were a lifeline thrown to me while I stared at Alex and he at me. His every muscle was taut as he stood facing me. His features resembled a sheet of parchment void of words, though his eyes were resolute. I knew my face must have looked the opposite for I'd never learned the art of keeping my emotions or thoughts hidden.

Alex took a breath, his shoulders relaxing with the inhale and exhale. His hands remained at his side, and I noticed he balled them into fists and uncurled them several times. His mouth arched into a small grin. He was nervous.

"I thought we could walk for a bit," he said.

"All right." I stared straight ahead and forced my feet to move in stride with him. I didn't know what to say. Would he go through with marrying me? If he didn't, I would be ruined. Did he even think of that before he'd blurted out to Captain Roth that he was my husband?

The leather strap he'd used to tie his hair had become loose, giving way for strands of his hair to blow around his face. He reached behind him and pulled on the knot, completely untying it, then stuffed the strap inside his pocket. His dark brown hair fell to his nape in thick waves giving him a more untamed look.

I focused on my feet walking through the leaves so he would not see my thoughts reflected on my face. He was making me nervous, and if I looked at him, I knew I would fall apart.

Birdsong came from the trees and sky, and the smell of dead leaves made my nose itch. Alex's expression remained neutral. The only indication I had that we were about to partake in a serious conversation was from the way his jaw clenched.

We walked in a strained silence for a few minutes before I couldn't take it anymore. I stopped and turned to him, and put my hands on my hips "Why? Why did you say it? And why at the hanging of all places? I thought you had no desire to marry me." My throat was tight, and I did my best to keep my anger in check. "You should not have said that, especially to Captain Roth, since you have no intention of following through with it. And now, well, Uncle Edward will most likely think I'm wed, which means I'm ruined if we do not go through with it, not to mention, once again I've gone missing and—"

"Sailor, stop," he said in an authoritative voice. He took a step forward and placed both of his hands on my shoulders. His voice softened. "Take a breath."

I did. He nodded then motioned for me to sit down upon a fallen log.

"You're talking so fast I'm fearful you'll faint. We've time to talk and sort everything out. Now, let's start again." He leaned over and picked up a leaf off the ground. He twisted it between his hands and stared at it for a few moments.

I watched the stem while it rotated back and forth.

Alex let go of the leaf. It twirled to the ground and landed softly. He leaned forward, placed his elbows on his knees, and clasped his hands together. "First, we will marry. As to why… well, there are several reasons. What I will tell you is because I saw the way the good captain looked at you." He glanced at me from the corner of his eye.

My face flushed. "Lots of men look at me like that. I'm not the only woman alive who is gazed upon like something to be devoured. I want to know why it bothered you so much," I said, finding the courage to ask what I wanted.

He remained in the same position, but his shoulder tightened. He stared straight ahead. "You should know I was married before."

"I know."

He sat up and looked at me. "Hmph. I shouldn't be surprised my cousins told you."

"They mentioned it. I assumed you had someone you

loved when you turned down my proposal. I'm sorry for your loss."

He nodded. "Laura was a wonderful woman. And, yes, I did love her, but not in the way you presume. Our marriage was not a love match by any means. Laura was a childhood friend. I'd known her my whole life — tormented her my whole life actually," he said, chuckling at a distant memory. "I teased the living daylights out of her. Her older brother and I were best friends. And well, when he died, I took on the responsibility of her protector as her parents were both old. Her father couldn't do much. Anyway, her brother was killed. Shot," he said, his mouth tightening. He picked up a stick then began to hit the earth with it.

"I'm sorry to hear it."

"Her parents weren't home. They were out of town, visiting relatives in Philadelphia. James was defending her honor, and it cost him."

Alex was quiet for a few seconds before continuing with his story. I found myself watching the stick as he thumped it upon the ground.

"Laura came to me one night. It was about two months after James died. She was crying. She was with child. She hadn't told anyone, and afraid of the shame, she didn't intend to tell anyone."

"So you married her to keep her reputation intact," I said. "Did the father not come forward?"

He looked at me, his blue eyes clouded by grief. Behind the clouds simmered anger. "She was raped, Nora, so... no. The father did not come forward. I couldn't allow her to have the child alone. She didn't want anyone to know what had happened to her for fear no man would want her then."

"Didn't you have an intended?"

Alex smirked and shrugged his shoulders. "There were a

few girls I had my eye on, but nothing serious. A few stolen kisses here and there, but that's all."

"I'm sure you left a trail of broken hearts after marrying," I said, smiling.

"Well, there was nothing to be done about it. I knew instantly what I had to do. Laura and I married a few days later with her parents and my sister in attendance. Everyone thought the babe was mine."

Alex's voice grew soft then, and his face became reflective. "She and the babe died in childbirth. Before she passed, she told me who had raped her." Alex threw the stick and looked deep into my eyes.

I swallowed, and my throat went dry. I knew who he was going to say. "Captain Roth," I said. It was a statement, not a question.

"Yes, and I'll be damned if he does it to someone else if I can stop him." He jumped to his feet and locked eyes with me. His voice dropped. "I will kill him for what he did to Laura and for what he did to James. I know he's hurt you before."

He stooped down in front of me then reached over and moved my hair off my neck. My bruises were now gone, but his hands around my throat would forever be seared into my memory.

"I could see the fear in your eyes as he talked to you. I promise you, Nora, I won't ever let that man hurt you again."

A small shiver ran through me from the look of protectiveness in his eyes. No man had ever looked at me as he did in this moment.

"I don't have much to offer you at the moment. I'm committed to helping the regiments in any way I can, which means we'll be traveling with the army. I'm sure it isn't what you expected when you first mentioned this to me. But sleeping under the stars can be nice and occasionally warm," he said, smirking.

My face heated at the mere thought of his implication. I looked away and stood up.

He followed, and we walked toward the house, both consumed with our own thoughts but both obviously comfortable with the silence between us.

"All those broken hearts you left behind though, after you married, I mean. Since then, have you rekindled any friendships with those women? When I first proposed the idea of marriage to you, I admit I was only thinking of myself and my situation of being alone," I said. Shame ran through me, and I lowered my eyes. "I would hate to think you are marrying again out of honor when you could be marrying for love if given the choice."

"After Laura died, I left. I haven't been back in the two years since her passing. As for someone else, I'll admit there is one lady I fancy, but I do not know if she returns my affections, so it does not matter. I won't be swayed in my decision. What about your David?"

"David?" I said, choking on his name. My heart grew heavy thinking about him. After what had happened, I knew that wasn't the real him. I had to forgive and forget. "If David wanted to marry me, I would think it would have been a done deal by now. Most women my age are going on at least a year of marriage and are with child. No, David chose to fight for his sovereign over me. And, oddly, I am fine with his choice because my allegiance now lies elsewhere. It was a fool's dream for me to ever think I would marry for love when I know most marriages do not start that way. We are friends, which means we can make this work," I said, convincing myself of this fact.

"I agree."

"When will we marry?"

"I suppose as soon as possible, since I already told Captain Roth I had the position of being your husband," he said. His eyes narrowed. "Wednesday?"

"All right." I stared ahead at a small orange leaf and bit my lip. I took a deep breath. Two days gave me plenty of time to prepare myself, I hoped. "What of my Uncle Edward?"

"A short note of correspondence is acceptable, unless of course you want to travel there to tell him. If so, we would have to leave first thing tomorrow, and I'd rather we be married when we tell him, which would have us saying vows tonight, so—"

"I'll write him a letter. I should think he would not care as he is indifferent to me anyway," I said.

Gideon's house came into view. My insides tickled like a feather traveling up and down my skin, for inside the house was a bedroom. And, knowing in two days' time I would marry, I knew what that meant for Wednesday night.

Alex and I stopped at the front door. His head cocked to the side, and his eyes softened. "I don't even know your full name. Mine is Alexander Mathias Foster."

"Nora Elizabeth Bishop."

"Well, then," Alex said. He reached forward and grabbed my hand, then bent down on one knee. My eyes widened at the gesture, and my heart pounded. "You didn't think I'd let you tell people that you proposed to me, did you? Now, Nora Elizabeth Bishop, will you do me the honor of becoming my wife and marrying me?"

My breath all but stopped. "Yes," I said.

Alex smiled and kissed the back of my hand, his eyes never leaving mine. His lips were smooth, and my cheeks warmed at his touch.

He rose. "I guess now all we have to do is let those two know what's going on." He jerked his head toward the front door.

Alex stretched his hand forward and placed it on the knob, but I halted him. "Wait. I must tell you before we go in," I said, my face reddening. "I only want you to know, I mean... to be sure this is what you want. Me," I said, my voice small even to my own ears. "I know what you must think of David and me, especially after his display in the alley." Guilt swarmed inside me though I wasn't entirely sure why.

Alex's face darkened slightly.

"But I want you to know that I've never been with a man. I've never lost my... um, I'm still a virgin."

His face rendered surprise, but he quickly concealed it. "I would not care if you weren't, Sailor. But, since you brought it up, so am I."

Alex's face turned a bright shade of red, and before I could say anything else, he pushed open the door, took my hand, and we walked inside to tell his cousins our news.

CHAPTER 22

ALEX AND SI WERE both gone the following two days. On the second day of Alex's absence, I wandered aimlessly around the house, cleaning, and roaming through the woods, collecting various herbs and flowers. If Alex and I were going to be traveling with the army, I wanted to have a small supply of what I would use the most. Peppermint for an upset stomach, yarrow to staunch bleeding, and more jewelweed to help with skin irritants should they arise. I searched for lavender, which was used to help calm and relax but found none. It was a shame too, because I wanted it for myself.

I kicked a pile of leaves and slumped down to the ground with my back against a tree. Was I doing the correct thing? Granted, life would be easier if I had a husband, yet, plenty of women nowadays lived alone and flourished. They owned and worked taverns, storehouses, and held the positions of nurses in hospitals. A few women down south operated and managed a printing press, or so I had heard. *Baltimore! A woman in Maryland operates a press too.* But those women, though without husbands, had other family to rely on. I was completely alone.

My memory tried to summon an image of my father and mother and what their reaction would be discovering I was to wed. I could picture mother clapping her hands, stopping whatever tasks she'd been involved in and setting out to prepare my wedding dress. For the past year, she had talked about making me a new gown for the occasion. In fact, she had already bought the fabric, a light cream and blue pinstripe with cream lace for around the wrists. I had begged her one afternoon to begin to make the dress as I needed a new Sunday gown regardless, but she'd denied me. She'd been insistent the first time I would wear the dress was when my father would give me over to David.

How different life had been. How different life was going to be. Alex and I respected each other, which was more than some ladies could say about their husbands, and I believed we were friends. Would he ever learn to love me though? Certainly, an attraction lay between us, but I wanted a marriage more like what my parents had, a marriage built on mutual respect, admiration, kindness, friendship, and love.

A twig snapped off to the right, and I jerked my head up at the sound.

"There you are," Gideon said. "I've been looking all over for you. Everything all right?"

He crouched down in front of me and plucked a blade of grass then set it between his lips. His eyes crinkled around the edges while he observed me.

"I'm fine. I thought I would collect some things I typically use," I said, nodding toward my basket filled with various natural remedies.

"Collect herbs, or collect your thoughts and emotions?" he said, grinning.

"Both."

He nodded. "That makes more sense. I know it isn't my place to say anything, as you're a woman grown and… well, I'm not family to you, but I think you're making the right choice in your decision."

"I know. The war has changed so much, and I know I need the protection Alex can offer me." I fiddled with a rock, rubbing it back and forth with my thumb.

"That's true enough. But, I meant you're doing the right thing with who you're marrying. Hell, if all you needed was protection, Si could marry you," he said, laughing. "You'll make a good wife to Alex. He needs someone strong, someone who can keep up with him and challenge him. And I know he'll be a good husband."

"What about love?"

"Love? Well, that'll come in time." His eyes were reflective. "Besides, there are different ways to love. And all of them are good. Love is really more action than feeling. You'll see."

"Did you love your intended?"

A smile crossed Gideon's mouth, and when it did, I could see the family resemblance clearer than before between him and his cousin.

"Oh yes. And she loved me," he said then chuckled. "I'm sure of it because why else would a woman decide to marry a man going into the church other than for love? It wasn't as if I had money."

"You were to be a reverend?"

He nodded.

"And now?"

"And now it seems as though I'm to be a soldier. For this season of life anyway." He stood up.

"But don't those two paths contradict each other?" I asked, for how could a reverend hold a Brown Bess and kill someone?

"Ah well, to everything there is a season and a time to every purpose under the heaven. A time to kill, and a time to heal. Of course, the verse ends with a time of war, and a time of peace. So, I suppose if the good Lord declares it so, it must be. Though I pray every night for the latter."

"I should have known you would spout that verse," I said.

He reached out his hand, and I grabbed it. He helped me up, and I wiped the leaves and grass off my bottom. "Most of us reverends have a verse for everything."

"And do you believe in every verse you dish out?"

Gideon paused and considered my question. "There have been moments in my life when, no, I did not. For how can war, death, and pain be of our creator God? But it is in these moments of doubt when something good will develop, even if it is a glimpse or taste of the goodness to come. And then I remember. I remember God works for the good of all those who love him. I suppose I'd rather put my trust in that, for if I'm wrong, nothing worse can happen to me that hasn't already taken place."

He extended his arm, and I placed my hand on top of it. "Now, your groom has arrived, so I'd say it is time to freshen up and get married."

* * *

ALEX WAS TENDING TO Bridger when Gideon and I reached the house. I had no words for my future husband, so I walked straight up the stairs and headed toward the bedroom. I splashed water on my face then blotted a stain on the hem of my dress. *I wish I had a clean gown to wear!* I had put the last pin in my hair and secured my mob cap in place when a knock sounded at the door.

"Come in," I said.

Alex opened the door and stood in the doorway. He was

clean-shaven, unlike the last time I'd seen him where a few days of growth had covered his chin, and his outfit was unsoiled. He wore a deep blue waistcoat, inlaid with swirls of gold thread, an overcoat the color of cranberry with a crisp white cravat and deep blue breeches. He was incredibly handsome, and my cheeks warmed. I gasped when my eyes drifted to what was draped over his arm. It was a gown, and it was one of mine. *Praise the Lord for small miracles.*

I crossed the room and stood before him. "How did you get this?" I asked, taking it from him and turning around so he did not see the blush that had formed on my cheeks.

He cleared his throat. "Si and I rode to your uncle's house. I had every intention of sneaking into your room as I did not want to see your uncle, but I thought better of it. I'm not a coward. I talked to the man."

I blanched at what he told me. "And?"

"You were right. He was a bit in shock but was indifferent, I gather, because you have no dowry to speak of."

My face turned red. "No. When father died—"

"Sailor, I do not care about that. However, your uncle made it clear I would not get a cent from him on your behalf. I only asked him if you could have a few articles of clothing."

"And he agreed?"

"He allowed two dresses. The other is downstairs. Another traveling dress. I, ah, didn't want you to have to marry me in traveling clothes. I know I'm not your first choice of husband, and well, I want to make it as nice as I can."

My heart swelled at the act of kindness and boldness, and I clutched the gown to my chest. I remembered the day vividly when Hannah and I picked this gown out, or more specifically, she picked it out. It was a subdued blue color with inlays of flowers woven throughout with a lower neckline, bell sleeves, and a cream-colored petticoat.

"Thank you. I would hate for you to remember our wedding day and picture me in this," I said, spreading the skirt of my dirty gown wide. Though Alex had cleaned it in the river, stains continued to settle in the fabric.

"Did Hannah pick this out to give to you?"

He cleared his throat. "I asked her for it. You wore it the night of your Uncle Edward's ball. Do you remember?"

I nodded, not knowing what else to do. Memories from that night came swooping back to me: seeing Alex across the room dressed as a soldier and knowing he stirred something in me… making my first successful dead drop only to discover later that Suzy had died at the hands of Captain Roth, no doubt trying to cover for me…

"I couldn't take my eyes off you that night," Alex said. He swallowed. "I didn't want to leave you alone with all those redcoats, but I had to." His blush deepened, and he shrugged. "Are you sure about going through with this?"

"Well, you already told Captain Roth we are married. My uncle thinks we are. I don't see another way out, and I don't want to go back to my uncle's house. So, yes. Yes, I'm sure."

"There is always another way. But, Nora, I promise you. I will protect you, and I will be a good husband to you. Though, I certainly won't force you to marry me. If you are against it, it isn't too late to back out," he said.

His expression remained stoic; yet, a worry hid behind his blue eyes. Was he worried I would agree we should marry, or was he worried I would change my mind?

I lifted my chin and straightened my back. "I have not changed my mind. This is the best course of action."

Alex nodded. "Well then, we'll begin the ceremony as soon as you finish changing."

He hesitated for a second but then turned around and walked down the stairs, leaving me alone to prepare for my wedding.

It did not take long to switch gowns since I did not change my stays, and therefore, did not need help with the lacing of them. I stared at my reflection in the new gown. The gold brought out the lighter tones in my typical brown eyes, which had always reminded me of dirt, and warmed my hair I'd described as dead hay. Perhaps Hannah had known what she was talking about when she picked out this color. In only a few short minutes, I'd be married to a man who was still more stranger than friend, and I'd be wed without a single family member or loved one by my side. This bloody war had taken much from me, and now it would take my chance at love, the only thing I had left.

Marrying a man I hardly knew in haste, was not something I had ever envisioned for my life, but I knew I needed Alex. Women with husbands had an easier life than those without.

Restraining the urge to sigh, I walked out of the room, along the short hallway, and down the steps.

The three men were talking in low voices when I stepped onto the landing. Gideon's and Si's heads snapped up, and they all became quiet. Alex stood with his back to me. He straightened himself, as if he had to gather his courage to face me.

Time seemed to stop when he turned around. My heart sped up, and my stomach swirled in all manner of direction. My body turned warm — very warm. *Good Lord! I am about to be married!* Was it normal to feel anxiety over something like this? Not for the first time did I wish my mother was still with me.

Alex walked over to where I stood and gave me his hand. I took it and smiled when he offered it a gentle squeeze. The slight pressure of his hand settled me a bit.

"You look beautiful, Nora," he said, his voice low so only I could hear him.

"Thank you. You clean up nice yourself."

And he did. In fact, I scarcely could remember when I had set eyes upon anyone quite as handsome as Alex.

"Well, if you two are finished staring at each other, I'd like to get started. I'm hungry," Si said, interrupting our quiet moment.

Alex winked, helped me off the last stair, and nodded. Keeping a firm grip on my hand, he guided me to where Gideon stood in front of the mantel.

"Since it is only us, I figured you might as well say your own vows of commitment. I'll bless the marriage, and both Si and I will act as witnesses. Is that fine by you, Nora?" Gideon asked.

I nodded.

"Alex, you can go first," Gideon said.

Alex turned so we faced each other and grabbed hold of my other hand. He took a big breath, and we locked eyes. His hands grasped mine, and I was ever so thankful, for it was all that held me up.

"I, Alexander Mathias Foster, take you, Nora Elizabeth Bishop, to be my lawfully wedded wife. I promise, before God and these witnesses, to honor and respect you. To protect you and provide for you. To love, cherish and be faithful to you and only you, through health and sickness, until my very last breath on this earth."

A hesitant look eased onto his face as Gideon told me it was my turn. And I, in a hoarse voice, repeated everything Alex had said back to him.

"Do you have a symbol of these vows?" Gideon asked, clearly looking at Alex.

A broad smile spread across his mouth, then he released me and reached inside his waistcoat where he pulled out a small silver ring. With gentleness, he lifted my left hand and placed the ring on my fourth finger then kissed my knuckles.

Gideon reached out and covered both of our hands with his, bowed his head, and blessed the marriage. "You may kiss your bride," he said, his voice cheerful.

Surely Si heard my heart beating from across the room where he stood watching the simple and short ceremony. I kept my eyes on Alex as he leaned toward me. My pulse raced faster than I thought possible. He pressed his mouth against mine, and I melted. His lips were warm and soft, and I shuddered. I thought of nothing else.

Si coughed in the background, and seeming reluctant, Alex let me go.

"You're married. Let's eat," Si said.

CHAPTER 23

The wedding feast was rather delicious, all things considered. Gideon had worked hard the entire morning making the supper preparations. Not only did we dine on roasted meat, but he'd rustled up boiled potatoes, cooked carrots, and baked apples.

The conversation was sparse between the four of us. The men conversed about the war and politics. My eyes wandered over them and the room. I folded and refolded the napkin in my lap. A vase of flowers sat on the mantel that I hadn't noticed before as well as a decorative candle.

"I'm sorry I was not able to provide better wine for this occasion," Gideon said, soaking up the meat juice with a piece of bread.

"It is fine." I picked up my cup, and rather than take a dainty sip, I gulped it. I blew air out of my mouth as the tartness from the alcohol went down my throat before swallowing my saliva to rid it of the dryness.

The men watched me with open surprise on their faces.

Si chuckled, and my face reddened. "I have rum in the other room. Would you prefer that?" he asked.

Alex leaned over. "So, not only do you talk like a sailor, you drink like one too. You might want to eat some food with that. Alcohol on an empty stomach has never done anyone any favors."

I poked my fork into a potato and took a small bite. My anxiety over what was to come next was what filled my stomach at the moment.

The men ate heartily, and the meal was over as fast as it had begun. Gideon cleared the plates, with Alex eventually helping since I sat in silence. Si wandered around the downstairs packing bags. He walked over and set a bottle of rum in front me, winked, and walked away.

As usual, the men talked in hushed tones. *Whatever in the world are they talking about?* I twisted the fabric of my gown and poured myself a glass of rum then took a healthy sip of it. It burned my throat, but I welcomed the distraction. A low chuckle came from Si. I picked my head up in time to see Alex glare at him. Before too long, Gideon and Si threw their bags over their shoulders and made way for the door, while Alex stood off to the side. They slapped him on the back and wished him well.

I scooted away from the table, realizing what was happening. "Where are you going?" I asked. My hands gripped the edge of the table as I held on for fear my knees would give out.

"We, ah, thought it best to give the newly married couple some privacy," Gideon said.

"Privacy?" I said, knowing full-well what he meant. I walked around the table toward them. "Surely you don't have to leave yet? We've only eaten. Perhaps a game of Whist? Another round of drinks? I could always read—"

Si walked over to me and put both hands on my shoulder. "You're stalling for no good reason. Alex will take good care of you, no doubt about it. You have to do your next duty, or the marriage isn't legal. We all know it. No need to be embarrassed or scared. There's plenty a maid who would love to be in your position, or rather, in the position you'll be in after we leave—"

"Si!" Alex said.

Si laughed. "Congratulations, cousin." He leaned forward and gave me a peck on the cheek. "Welcome to the family. We'll return in three days' time."

I swallowed. "Three days?"

"Want to give you lovebirds some time to get, ah, acquainted. The regiment can wait. We've had news both sides are not itching for battle at the moment. Everyone needs some rest, except you two. I bid you adieu. Enjoy," he said and winked. Again. He walked out toward the horses, laughing.

Gideon shook his head. "Goodnight, Nora. I'll see you soon."

He turned to Alex, shook his hand, and followed his brother.

Alex and I watched silently as his cousins mounted their horses and galloped off. Neither of us moved until their forms blended in with the darkness. The wind blew, and I wrapped my arms around myself, keeping my eyes focused on where the men had been, too afraid to look at the man next to me.

"Shall we close the door now since there is a chill to the air? Or do you want to stand there all night?"

"Oh. Right," I said, turning and walking back into the house.

Alex eased the door shut, and I wrung my hands together.

"Thank you for cleaning up," I said, feeling the need to fill the silence.

He shrugged. "I didn't want you to have to clean dishes on your wedding day."

I wet my lips. I needed another drink. *Wine or rum?* I poured both and held one out to him, and he nodded. He took the rum. I drained the wine glass. I was going to be sick in the morning if I didn't quit now. Alex watched me the entire time.

"Are you that afraid of me?" Alex asked. He set his glass down on the table and took the cup from my hand.

"Why would you say that?" I looked over his shoulder at the door. I looked anywhere to avoid his gaze.

"Can we make one more promise to each other, Nora? Since we've already said our vows, that is?"

"What?" My eyes met his.

"I've told you before I'd never be dishonest with you. And, I ask the same thing in return. Let us promise to always be truthful with each other, no matter what we have to say. No matter if you think it will hurt me or make me mad. I want you to know that you can tell me anything. Our marriage is based on mutual respect and friendship. I don't want that ruined. The only way we can keep this respect is by always telling each other what we're thinking or feeling. Do you agree?"

I thought about it for a second before I answered. He was right, of course, but did I want to tell him everything about me? My mother had always told me that a woman had a right to keep some things buried deep inside her heart that was meant for her and her alone. Was it lying if I kept some of these things to myself? I decided that no, it wasn't.

"I agree."

"Good. Now, tell me why you're afraid of me."

"I'm not afraid of you," I said. "Why would you think that?"

"First, you've had about three glasses — or maybe four — of drink, whereas I've only had two. So, I assume you are trying to calm your fears or nerves. Second, you haven't yet looked me directly in the eye for longer than a second at a time."

"And why would that indicate I'm scared?" I said, staring at him openly.

"Because you usually do look at me. I'm not going to drag you to the bed straight away and force myself on you. Take a breath. We've time to... you know, consummate this marriage."

"Three days, apparently. Truth be known, I've already taken a ton of breaths," I said, doing just that.

"I know. I've been watching you. I wondered if you would hyperventilate from them all." He smiled. "Truth though? I'm as nervous as you."

"You don't look it," I said, relief filling me at his admission. He'd been a pillar of stone since we'd first talked earlier in the evening. His voice had never once wavered, his cheeks never once blushed, and his hands had been steady in mine the entire time.

"Well, that's only because I'm much better at hiding my feelings than you are, Sailor. But my heart is beating as fast as any bullet right now," he said.

"Why are you nervous?" I asked.

He gave me a sheepish grin.

"Truth, remember?"

"Right. Truth. It is a bit embarrassing for me to admit." He shrugged. "For starters, whenever I've been in a romantic interlude, it wasn't planned... expected. I'd wager I'm as nervous as you are, it being my first experience too."

His cheeks finally grew red.

"About that...and I hate to bring it up, but I need to know. Was your marriage to Laura not legal? For how could you have been married yet you told me you were, ah..."

"A virgin still?"

I wrung my hands together. *God, this was embarrassing.* "Yes."

"She was pregnant. And emotionally, it was hard for her because of what happened. Out of respect, we decided to wait to consummate the marriage until the babe was born. No one would know if we did or didn't. And well, we never had the chance."

"I'm sorry."

"Thank you."

"And second?" I asked, picking up the glass of rum and sipping it.

His Adam's apple bobbed as he swallowed. "As a man, I suppose I don't want to disappoint you… that I'm able to, ah, perform well, I guess you can say."

Leaving me speechless, I gulped what remained of my drink and savored the burn in my throat and the small amount of courage it provided. Realizing it was now or never, I raised my hand and placed it on his chest, keeping my eyes fixed there, too afraid to look at him. Surprisingly, his heart did beat as fast as mine, if not faster. I shut my eyes and focused on the sensation of his racing pulse and of the smell of him — leather, grass, and the faintness of sweet rum. My ears tuned in to the sound of Alex's even breath, the crackling fire, and in the far-off distance, a coyote that yipped at the night sky.

Alex had taken his overcoat off and stood in his waistcoat, which was smooth against my fingers as I skimmed my hand down the fabric. I let my hand fall, meaning to put it back to my side, but he caught it in his and intertwined our fingers.

"Now that you know I'm as nervous, probably more so, will you look at me?" he said, softly.

I raised my eyes to meet his. They were so incredibility blue, but tonight, passion flared behind them, darkening them a shade so they resembled more of a sapphire than the sky.

"I promised I would never hurt you, Nora," he said.

Swallowing, for my throat was dry, and for I could not find my voice, I nodded, but did not look away. Slowly, as if he feared I was a skittish horse, he lifted my hand and lightly kissed the inside of my wrist, where my pulse raced like a stallion. Keeping his eyes locked on mine, he released my hand and cupped my face before lowering his head and brushing my lips with his.

"If you're not ready, I'll understand," he said.

"But we—"

"No one else is here, Nora. I'll not pressure you to do anything you don't want. We have time. Three days. Or," he hesitated, "we do not have to do this at all. The only two people who will know what happened tonight is us. My first marriage was never consummated, and nobody knew. I can do it again, if that's what you want."

He wet his lips as he waited for my answer. I considered his offer for only a second. We'd said the vows, and I knew he would never hurt me.

Without thinking, I raised up on my toes to reach him better, and his hands fell from my face, tracing my arms before settling on my waist. My own arms wrapped around his neck, and he pulled me closer while deepening our kiss.

A spark ignited inside of me and flared into existence, traveling between the two of us in an unspoken language, and my body sprang to life. Never had I warmed like this when kissed. The heat that radiated through me traveled from the top of my head to the tips of my toes. It settled down deep in my stomach. A fluttering feeling began lower as it responded to Alex's attentions.

His hands remained on my waist and back as he kissed me thoroughly, not rushing in any way, but as if he was savoring the moment as one did with a fine claret. He pulled back from me, leaving only enough distance for each of us to catch our composure.

“I don’t think you need to worry about disappointing me,” I said, breathless.

Alex smirked. “I believe we already covered the fact I’ve shared a kiss or two.”

“It appears so. You’ve been well trained in the art of it,” I said, staring at his lips, for I wanted to be kissed by them again.

“As have you.”

The warmth in my body spread deeper, filling me to the core as we stared at each other.

Alex leaned his head against mine. “What are you thinking?”

Dare I tell him the truth? I did not want him to think me wanton in the least, but we had promised each other the candor in any situation. I took a deep breath.

“There you go with the deep breathing. Tell me, Nora.”

“I was thinking about how much I would like you to kiss me again.”

“I believe I can do that.” He pulled me close against him for another kiss.

I put my hand on his chest and halted him. “What are you thinking?” I asked, trying to keep the distressed tone out of my voice. It occurred to me I wanted to know everything he felt and thought.

He smiled. “Truth, right?”

“That’s what we promised,” I said, fear gripping my heart. Would he tell me that although he enjoyed kissing me, he was only doing this because he had to?

“I desperately want to take you up those stairs, untie your laces, and watch your clothes slip to the floor. Then I want to stare at your body and lay kisses on every inch of your skin until you can't stand it any longer, and you ask me to make you mine."

Having no retort, I kissed him — and kept kissing him — as he moved me near the stairs. We broke apart long enough to reach the bedchamber, where we came together again, but this time, our kisses slowed down as we both, no doubt, knew what was going to happen next.

Alex's hands came to the front of my gown. His fingers hesitated, and my chest heaved up and down at the anticipation of what was to come. With slow and precise movements, he unbuttoned the front of my gown. With each button released, the fabric loosened its hold on me and slid to the ground, leaving me in nothing but my hooped petticoat, stays, and shift. His hands returned to my waist where he untied the petticoat. It fell in a heap around my feet. I carefully stepped out of it, and he pushed it away with his foot. Keeping his eyes trained on my body, he turned me around and began to work on my laces. With each thread he pulled loose, my heart thudded against my chest. After the last lace had come undone, my stays fell to the floor in front of me. For a long moment, I remained facing away from him, too nervous to turn around. My shift was the only thing separating the feel of his skin against my own.

It was as if time slowed down in this moment, and I shut my eyes knowing I wanted to hold on to whatever memory we were creating. His right hand snaked around my waist and drew me into him as his left one traveled down my hip and rested on the outside of my thigh. He kissed my neck and the top of my shoulder.

Then I turned to him. His breath caught, and with a tentative hand, he touched the neckline of my shift, a fire radiating behind his eyes. His fingertips warmed my flesh and with another skip of my heart, he pulled the lace free of the bow, and the remaining barrier of concealment slid to the ground and pooled around my legs like a pile of down feathers.

Every last inch of me tingled as his eyes wandered over my body before resting on my face.

"You're breathtaking," he said, his voice hoarse. His hand reached forward and touched me over my left breast.

My body shook.

"Your heart is beating fast," he said.

"I would think yours would be also if you were standing in front of me naked."

"Is that your way of telling me you want me to take my clothes off?" he asked, grinning. He gathered me in his arms and kissed me again.

A shiver ran through me at his touch as his hands roamed more freely over my body. I raised my hands to his chest and unbuttoned his waistcoat then pushed it off his shoulders. With his help, we loosened his breeches, and he took them off as well as his stockings. He stood in front of me in only his hunting shirt, it being already untied. With tentative hands, I lifted it up over his muscled chest and shoulders while he did the rest, taking it over his head.

It was now my turn to stare at him. His skin was slightly tanned from being outside. The scars from old and new wounds were a mixture of white, silver, and pink. He was bare-chested except for the little bit of hair around his nipples and in the middle of his chest. I let my fingers run over him there and down his chest to the muscles that covered his stomach. Swallowing the lump in my throat, I glanced down at what made him fully male, and my insides clenched.

He put a finger under my chin and lifted my eyes to meet his. "Have you ever seen a naked man before?"

"Only a few, though they were extremely old and ill. You're nothing but healthy," I said.

"That I am."

Alex embraced me then, his strong arms encircling me and holding me tight as he kissed me. Even without looking, it was evident he was ready for what was to come by the feel of him against me. To his credit, he did not rush at all for the next step. He carefully laid me down and took his time, doing exactly what he told me he wanted to do. He kissed every last inch of my skin until, willingly, I opened myself up to him. He hovered above me, his arms braced on either side of my head, as he stared deep into my eyes.

His breath was labored and his face concerned. "You'll tell me if I'm hurting you or if you want me to stop," he said.

I traced my fingers down his back and felt him shiver at my touch. "We've gone too far now for that to happen." I gave him a reassuring smile.

He traced my cheek with his hand. "True, but if you don't want—"

I interrupted him by lifting my face to meet his and kissing him deeply.

He answered me by responding in kind.

He gently eased into me, and I gasped, but aside from what Hannah had told me to expect, it did not hurt too much, and before I knew it, we had found a slow, silent rhythm between the two of us. In a matter of minutes, Alex shuddered and fell onto me, his dead weight pinning me to the mattress. I lay there, not knowing if I should move or remain still, when he rolled off me.

Without speaking, and on our backs, we stared at the ceiling. The actual act was nothing like I'd expected after seeing the glow on Hannah's face. I risked a glance at him. Alex continued to stare at the wooden beams above us, his face contemplating. He turned his head and looked back at me. A question lingered behind his eyes.

"Dare I ask how it was?" he said, his voice shy though he

looked me in the eye.

"Seeing as I have nothing to compare it to, it was as I expected," I lied.

"I appreciate you bending the truth," he said.

"It wasn't bad," I said, which was true. "I didn't expect it to be over so… soon."

Alex chuckled at that. "And for that, I'm sorry. I, ah, couldn't help myself. I promise the next time it won't be so quick," he said, causing me to blush, knowing he wanted to do it again.

"You want to do it again?" I said.

"Sailor, this would be an example of where I appreciate the phrase 'practice makes perfect.'" He grinned and rolled onto his side. I did the same, positioning us face to face I went to pull the sheet up to cover myself, but he stopped me.

"Don't. Please. Let me look at you," he said.

As before, my heart pounded from the way he gazed at me, and I swallowed at the pure intimacy of a simple look. His hand came forward, and he lightly traced his fingers over my breasts. I shivered.

He scooted toward me as his hand left my bosom and traveled down my hip and thigh, moving back and forth. He kissed me hard, and I savored the feel of him and his caresses.

"Nora?" he said as he explored my body with urgency, while I did the same to him.

"Yes?" I gasped as his hands found my most imitate place.

"I'm ready to practice again."

And practice we did. Twice more. And both times left me breathless and my heart pounding so fierce I thought it would explode out of my chest. It was during our last joining however, which was slow, gentle, and reverent, as I lay in his strong arms, I knew I would always be safe. He would protect me, and I trusted him completely.

CHAPTER 24

I AWOKE THE NEXT day with my insides feeling like a whisked potion. I stretched, enjoying the feel of my arm and leg muscles having been pulled apart and lengthened. A tiny part of me wondered if what happened last night had been a dream, but as I moved my legs to stretch again, I knew with clarity it had not. I was slightly sore where I expected to be, yet fully satisfied as well.

I turned my head. Alex was not there. Disappointment filled me knowing he had up and left while I slept. Was the one night of shared intimacy all I had to expect from my new husband? *Husband.* The word itself stuck in my throat, and my mind had trouble coming to terms with it, though my body was happy with the new title. I sat up and rubbed my eyes, reminding myself this was a marriage of necessity, and that I should not presume to think Alex wanted to make love to his wife. From what I had heard, very few husbands did. That was why most had mistresses.

Footsteps on the stairs and a man's whistling caused me to run my hand through my hair. I rolled to my side and glanced around the room. My clothes were still in a pile from the night before, as were some of Alex's. A small smile slid into place as he pushed opened the door with his foot, wearing nothing but his breeches.

He stopped short, a cup of steaming tea in his hand. His face was one of surprise at seeing me. "You're awake," he said, a shyness taking over him. "Good morning."

"Good morning." I pulled my knees, and the sheet, up to my chest as he walked toward me with the cup.

"I brought you some hot tea to sip on while you dress. It is only peppermint leaves from the woods, as we won't buy tea for good reason. But it tastes refreshing and strong. I have breakfast started and was hoping you'd eat with me at the table when you finish dressing."

The cup was nice and warm in my hands, and the emotions that had flitted through my imagination earlier dissipated.

"Yes, thank you," I said.

He leaned over and kissed me on the cheek then turned to pick up his clothes and left the room.

I waited until I no longer heard his footsteps on the stairs before I flung off the covers and stepped onto the cold, wood floor. The intimacy of the night was over, and I did not want him to see me in only my birth suit, so I dressed as quickly as I could, thankful I had learned how to put my stays on by myself if needed.

I eyed my bridal gown, which I would now wear as my Sunday best, and the traveling gown I'd been wearing. Since Alex had washed it for me earlier, the gown did not smell as terrible, so I decided it'd be best to wear it and not ruin another gown, seeing as I only had three to my new name.

The table was set for two when I came downstairs. Alex bent over the fire, stirring something in the pot. He must have sensed me, for he spun around bumping his head.

"Ouch!" he said, standing and rubbing where he hurt.

"Are you all right?" I walked toward him.

"I'll be fine. I'm not used to doing... this," he said, waving toward the fire. "This is the third time I've bumped my head after stirring the pot. You'd think I'd learn by now not to stand up while my head is still under here." He grinned and shrugged. "You must know now that you didn't marry a cook. I promise you'll never go hungry, Sailor, but I can't promise that it will taste good if I have to cook it."

"And you must know that neither did you. I'm terrible at it, but it is edible, that I will say."

"Well, I've been cooking for myself for a while now, or one of my cousins has been doing it, and I'm fairly certain anything you make will be better than what we can do. Though, out of the three of us, Si is the best."

"Really? That's surprising. I suppose you and I will learn together then."

"I'd like that."

Our conversation over our breakfast was polite, each of us seeming to search for a tidbit of information to discuss that was worthwhile, but in the end, we stuck to the basics of the weather and the estimation of the hard winter to come. The awkwardness of the conversation never waned at the table, and when I didn't know how much more I could handle, Alex stood up and cleared our plates. It was obvious that, although we had shared the most sacred part of ourselves during the night, allowing the cover of darkness to help us lose our inhibitions, the sun and the light that came with it caused us discomfort and timidity in one another's company.

"I could use some fresh air. Would you care to take a hike?" Alex said.

"Yes," I answered rather quickly, glad for the chance of having something to do.

After Alex gathered his hunting gear, and I packed food

for later, we walked outside. The air was crisp and smelled of wet leaves and earth. I couldn't help but lift my face to meet the sunshine and smiled. After the horrid events from the last few days, it was nice to think of the happy possibilities that awaited me.

We peregrinated through the woods for a bit in silence. Each step we took seemed to bring us into a greater comfort level from when we first saw each other that morning. Alex's shoulders were relaxed and his pace easy, though his stride was much longer than mine.

He pointed out different trees and birds to me, while I showed him the different flowers and plants and what they were good for. Along the way, I stopped and filled my basket with the various flowers that could be of use.

Alex touched my shoulder while I picked a heap of peppermint leaves to use for tea. I looked up at him, glad to have some form of physical contact. He raised his finger to his lips and motioned me to follow him.

As quietly as I could, I shadowed him around a series of trees and bushes then knelt beside him.

He leaned close to me. "Straight through there, do you see them?" he asked, whispering. He didn't move right away but remained near, his breath tickling my neck.

I wanted to turn to him and kiss him as I had done last night, but shyness overtook me. What sort of marriage was this going to be? He had made it clear he was marrying me to protect me, so I understood his obligation only went so far.

Peering around the side of the tree, I saw what he pointed to. A mama deer with her fawn stood munching on grass. A twig cracked, and the mother deer's head snapped up. She remained as still as any statue would; the only indication of her senses growing was the twitch of her ears.

In a fluid and very quiet movement, Alex brought his musket forward, loading and locking it into place before raising it to his shoulder. He took a deep breath and shut his left eye, keeping the right open.

"Don't," I said, not bothering to keep quiet.

The two deer ran off, and Alex lowered the gun.

I waited, expectantly for an agitated remark, but none came, though his look was not all that happy.

"You do realize that deer could have fed us for months," he said.

"I know, but the fawn was with her. How could you kill the mother, leaving the baby to fend for itself?"

"It's nature, Sailor. The fawn would have been fine. Its spots were almost gone," he said, lowering the gun. "You can't coddle the young. The same can be said for people given the state of things. Why, a mother could walk down the street and a stray bullet hit her."

"With that sort of thinking, what is the point of having children then?"

"Well, I suppose some children need to be born otherwise life would end. However, my opinion now is such that a woman better think long and hard this day and age on whether bringing life into the world is a wise choice."

"A woman? It takes two, you know." I crossed my arms and stared at him, not bothering to hide my frown. "And how could having a baby be unwise?" My gut twisted. Was this Alex's way of telling me he didn't want children?

"One word, Sailor. Redcoats. Or is that two words?"

"That does not matter. Having children is an honor and blessing. As for relationships and coddling, well, a child always needs its mother, no matter how old she is," I said, my voice losing the edge it had only seconds before.

Alex's eyes softened, obviously understanding my unspoken words. "Do you feel as though you still need your mother?"

"Yes."

"Even as a woman, full-grown?"

"Of course, especially now. Why, if she were still alive, I could ask her for her recipes," I said, wanting to lighten the mood.

"I'm sorry I didn't think of you and what happened."

I brushed it off, not wanting him to feel sorry for me. "And why should you? A deer is a very different creature from a human," I said. "But I thank you for sparing its life."

He nodded and helped me to stand. "Since I didn't kill the deer, let's continue our hike. There is a freshwater spring up ahead," he said. "But next time—"

"I know."

The sunlight sliced through the canopy of the trees, splintering the shaded areas with its rays. We came to a steep hill, and I followed Alex up, putting my hands on my thighs as I hiked, in hopes it would help propel me upward. My legs burned, and perspiration formed on my brow and the back of my neck.

"I thought you said this spring was only up ahead," I said, out of breath.

Alex climbed easily, his breathing even. He stopped midway, waiting for me to catch up, and took my hand in his, helping me toward the top. "It is... up there," he said, pointing with his other hand.

Once we reached the crest, I leaned up against a birch tree to catch my breath.

Alex grinned, his smile broad and good-natured. He looked at me, and his eyes twinkled.

"What?" I said. "You know, I'm not used to tramping around in the woods."

"Don't I know it."

"Why are you smiling then?"

He shook his head. "I like seeing your face red with exertion is all. Reminds me of last night." He winked, and my cheeks grew hot.

Alex stood, leaned the musket up against a nearby tree, and searched the area with his eyes. "Have you ever used a Brown Bess before?"

"No, I never had need to," I said. "Why?"

"You need to learn. Not because you'll use one, but I'd rather you know how to load and shoot in case an event should arise that you'd need the knowledge. When we go back to the house, I'll find a small pistol and show you how to use that also."

He gave me his hand and hauled me to my feet. "Might as well teach you now."

"Will anyone hear?" I asked, afraid someone would come looking for us if they heard the gunshot. I had only begun to relax with my new husband, and knowing the colony of New York was filled with British soldiers, I did not prefer to see any of them.

"No. There isn't anyone around for miles. We have this part of the woods to ourselves. We can do anything we want," he said, giving me a knowing smile.

"Noted."

"Now, the first thing you'll need to do is reach in the cartridge box. See that long flap there," he asked, pointing to the leather casing.

"Yes."

"That's there to make sure the black powder inside does not get wet. The powder has to stay dry, or it won't work. Remove one of the cartridges and bite down on the tail to tear it open."

I did as he told me and spat the tail of the paper on the ground.

"See these, here? This is the hammer, the frizzen, and the pan. Now, after you tear open the cartridge, you need to half cock the musket like this," he said. Alex pushed back on the hammer with flint attached to it, then pushed the L-shaped frizzen forward so the pan opened. "Then pour in a small amount of powder from the cartridge."

He handed me the musket and helped me to half cock it. The musket was extremely heavy, and I had to sit down on the ground so my thighs could help hold its weight.

"Good. Now, pull the frizzen back so the pan shuts," he said, nodding in approval as I followed instructions. The metal lip of the frizzen was now vertical so the powder would not spill out of the pan. "The weapon is now primed."

"Now what?" I asked.

"Now, you need to hold the musket with the muzzle point up. I know it's heavy, but you can rest the butt of it on the ground if you want. Pour the rest of the powder from the cartridge into the barrel. Good," Alex said. He reached inside the cartridge box and withdrew a lead ball and handed it to me.

It was cold in my hands but not heavy.

"Insert the ball into the barrel, then wad the paper up and push that in the barrel as well. Some balls come wrapped already, and if that's the case, jam the whole thing down. It skips a step," he said.

"And how do I ram it down in to make sure it stays?" I asked, peering down inside the black barrel.

With a stern look, he carefully moved the barrel away from my face. "Are you daft? Don't do that. Use this to ram it down."

He removed a ramrod from its storage pipe beneath the barrel and handed it to me.

"Take the rod out from the channel and ram the wadding and ball down the barrel to the other end. That's where the spark will take place."

"I had no idea loading a gun took so much effort," I said, sliding the rod out of the barrel and laying it on the ground.

"Hmph," Alex grunted. "One last step. You're going to cock the weapon and pull back on the dogshead, so it is fully cocked." He helped me lift the weapon so his arms carried some of the weight, and his hands directed mine on what to do.

"The dogshead?"

"This part, right here," he said, moving his fingers. "The part where the hammer and flint are attached."

"Oh."

"Raise the weapon to firing position." He guided the musket to my shoulder. "Now, look along the barrel with your right eye. That's right. Now you would fire."

"Just fire?"

"Yes," he said, taking the musket from me. "But you won't today."

"Why not?"

"Because you'll end up with a bruised shoulder, and I don't want my wife of less than twenty-four hours to be hurt on my time," he said.

"I want to shoot it."

"Sailor, it leaves a mark on a grown man. You can barely lift it as it is. It will send you flying backward."

"I want to try. If I ever need to use this thing, as you said before, I should know how to use it and what to expect." I looked him in the eye and held my ground.

"Have it your way," he said, giving me full control of the musket. He helped me to aim at a tree no more than one hundred yards away then moved to stand behind me.

After I silently counted to three, I pulled the trigger. I grunted as the force of the lead ball sped out of the barrel, causing the butt of the musket to jam into my shoulder and propel me backward, as Alex had warned. Black smoke swirled around the front of where the barrel of the gun had been. I coughed from the smell of gunpowder.

Alex caught me under the arms before I fell down.

"Are you all right?"

I rubbed my shoulder. "If you say I told you so, I will hit you," I said, wincing when I tried to move my arm.

He raised his hands in surrender. "I wouldn't dare, though you were right in shooting it once. Now you know."

"Now I know." I stood straight and moved my arm in a circle.

"Let's rest for a bit. Come. The spring is around those rocks over there," he said.

He took the musket and shouldered it then took my hand. We walked closer to each other this time as we made our way to the cluster of rocks where the small spring gurgled.

Alex knelt and filled the canteen before handing it to me to drink. I raised it to my lips. The water was sweet and cool, quenching my thirst and wetting my parched throat. I gave it back to him, and while he drank, I took off my mobcap and wet it in the water then pressed it to my face and back of my neck.

When I looked up, Alex was watching me.

"My face can hardly be red from exertion now," I said, smiling, my inside warming at the mere idea of why he liked it so much.

"I prefer you without that cap on."

"Oh?" I reached up and patted my hair.

Alex set the canteen down then walked over to me. "In fact, I like it when you wear your hair down," he said. He took out my pins, and my hair tumbled to my shoulders. He lifted a strand between his fingers then let it slide between them.

I found it hard to speak at the sudden closeness. "I usually wear the cap because I dislike my hair."

His brow furrowed. "Why?"

"It's it so straight and dull. It looks like dried, dead grass or—"

Alex shook his head. "I disagree. It reminds me of the color of tea with streaks of golden honey spread throughout," he said, brushing the hair off my shoulders. "And your skin is as white as cream… your eyes the color of brandy…" He lightly trailed his fingers over my neck and down my arm. He intertwined our fingers together and stared at my lips. "I'm rather hungry now."

I shut my eyes with my head facing down and breathed in the unique musky scent that I had come to identify as Alex: the outdoors and leather. I swayed at his closeness as if I had taken a huge gulp of the brandy he'd mentioned.

He cupped my face with his calloused hands, and his thumb brushed my lip tenderly.

I lifted my head, only to be met with his lips.

"God, Nora. I've been aching with desire to have you again," Alex said, his voice husky and low. He pulled me tight against him.

I wrapped my arms around his waist and trailed them up the scratchy homespun linen he wore. A soft wind blew, caressing my skin along with Alex's kisses. A deep longing was overtaken by instant hunger, and before I knew it, Alex had loosened the bodice of my dress, freeing my breasts as my own hands searched for the buttons of his breeches.

He laid me down on the ground underneath a canopy of trees. His hands roamed freely over my body before they pushed my skirts out of the way.

I moaned when he stroked me between my thighs. "You're ready for me," he said.

He kissed me deeply before I could answer. A strong whirlwind grew inside my core, and when he entered me, a small, high-pitched moan escaped from my mouth in relief.

We rocked together, finding a mutual rhythm, he taking his time loving me.

He kissed my neck then lifted himself up over me. My hands, which had been on his back, flung to the sides where I grabbed handfuls of dirt. "Now, Alex, please," I whimpered. I cried out then as I teetered somewhere in a world between pleasure and pain.

"Not yet," he said, looking me directly in the eyes. "I want to enjoy watching you since I couldn't last night in the dark. You have no idea what you do to me." I raised my hips so he could move deeper inside me. He drove into me hard one more time, and I called out.

Alex let go of himself, and after his release, he stayed on top of me trembling. I wrapped my arms around his back, not wanting him to move, not wanting to feel him leave me. After a moment when we both settled our breathing, he rolled off. His arm lay across his eyes; his chest moved up and down. The lower part of my stomach boiled over in warmth, and my sensitive area thumped with pleasure. Alex gathered me into his arms, and I laid my head on his chest and listened to the beat of his heart. It raced but was steady. He kissed the top of my head.

"I hope you'll be happy with me and that you'll be satisfied with, well, with everything that goes along with our marriage," Alex said. His fingers traced a pattern on my arm.

"And I hope you will be too. Are you not?"

Oh, God. What if he wished we hadn't married already? Had he said this to hint at something?

His arms tightened around me. "I knew I'd enjoy the actual act from everything I've heard about it," he said. I gazed up at him, and he reddened. "Not that I had anything to compare it to."

I giggled. "What did you hear about it?"

"I'd rather not say. Men speech. Not proper for a lady."

"Hmm."

"I do know I never gave much thought to the wanting of you," he said, his voice turning quiet. "I mean, I know men like it, but to me, it is more than that. Even this, having you in my arms well… I mean, this morning, I had to leave the room because I wanted nothing more than to wake you up and be with you again." He smiled. "I understand now why men go to whore houses and such, and why Gideon always preached to me to wait till I was married. Because once you do it, you want to keep doing it."

I laughed, and he sat up, his brows furrowing.

"Is it not the same for you?"

I reached out and touched his face, my shyness from earlier all but forgotten.

"I hadn't thought I would want to do it. Mainly because of how we had to marry. But now, well, it is the same. Though I think I can't handle anymore until tonight. I'm a bit sore," I said.

"Sorry."

"Don't be. And for future notice, I don't think I would mind being woken by your kisses."

"Noted," he said, leaning in toward me and kissing me thoroughly, taking my breath away. He stopped and cleared his throat. "We better start walking because if I remain here, kissing you, with you still half-dressed, I may have to lay you back down again."

He stood up and helped me to my feet. After we adjusted our garments, we set back off down the hill and through the woods toward the house, holding hands. Alex stopped short when we rounded the same bend and pushed me down. I peered out from behind a tree. In front of the house were four British soldiers.

CHAPTER 25

"WHAT DO YOU THINK they want?" I asked, staring at the red uniforms and looking for Captain Roth. I didn't see him and let out an audible sigh. "I don't recognize any of them. Do you?"

Alex shook his head then searched the area with his eyes. "I have no idea."

"What do you think we should do?"

"Looks like we're going to have to talk to them. I have a feeling they will wait around if we don't. Follow my lead. Remember, we're very loyal subjects."

We stood up, and I instantly reached for his hand as we walked down the hill.

"Hello there!" Alex called. He strolled through the small yard to the lobsterbacks who all regarded him with open curiosity and hesitation.

One of the soldiers maneuvered his mount and pushed his way toward us, nodding his head at Alex's musket. "Stop."

Alex did and looked at the Brown Bess in his hand. "Sorry, I was about to teach my new bride how to use it," he said and gingerly set the musket down against the bark of a nearby tree. Visible relief spread throughout the group of young soldiers. "Can I help you gentlemen with anything?"

Judging by his uniform, I discerned the soldier who was the spokesperson for the group held the rank of lieutenant. He swung off his horse and closed the distance between himself and Alex. He didn't appear much older than twenty-two. He stood to Alex's shoulders, and his hair was the color of sweet corn. Purple coloring was shaded under his eyes, and it looked like he hadn't shaved in several days.

I clasped my hands together in front of me.

The lieutenant raised his eyebrows. "Do you think it wise teaching a woman how to fire that thing?"

Alex laughed. "Well, it can't hurt. The way I figure it, it's only the two of us, and should anything happen to me, I'd like her to at least be able to hunt for a rabbit or squirrel if she needs to, though, no doubt she'll not hit her target."

The lieutenant, seeming satisfied with his answer, moved on. "Very true. Have you seen anyone run through these parts? We are on the lookout for a deserter. The man we are searching for was last seen at The Fighting Cock's Tavern the night of the great fire."

"We haven't seen anyone around these parts. We've only arrived ourselves," Alex said. "As you can see, we don't have much. Not even one chicken yet. But, we'll do our best to keep our eyes open. Though I doubt very much we'll see anything since we're so far removed."

"Yes, you are. I've been through the woods numerous times, and this is the first time I've happened to come across your homestead. Did you have permission to build here?"

"Yes, sir. The house belongs to a member of the family and was built several years ago."

"Well, now that I know where you are, I do hope it would not be an intrusion to call upon you when His Majesty's soldiers need sustenance or shelter?"

"They would be welcome anytime, sir. Though, may I ask a favor in return?"

The lieutenant cocked his head, and his mouth formed a thin line, but Alex remained relaxed, a small grin turning his lips upward. He leaned in closer to the British soldier, but I still heard every word. "Might you stay away for at least a week? We married two days ago," he said, winking.

I blushed, my face turning as red as the men's coats.

The lieutenant half smiled and nodded. "You have my word. If I had a new bride as lovely as yours, I would have asked for a whole month. I'll make sure no one comes around for at least two weeks," he said. "On behalf of His Royal Highness, please accept my felicitations."

Alex bowed. "We thank you."

The redcoat officer mounted his horse, bid us farewell, and the soldiers rode off. I remained still until the dust settled, my eyes never leaving the last horse's rump to make certain they were not returning.

My eyes snapped to Alex, who stood in front of me, watching my face. "If they find the deserter, they could find us. Then they'll know we had a hand in the fire, and—"

Alex put his hands on my arms. "First, you had nothing to do with it. I did. Second, your friend David would have already given me away, and the lobsterbacks would have already come looking for me," he said.

"But where would they search?"

"Exactly. For now, I don't have a home. My home for the last six months has been in the woods and on the outskirts of the American camp. It will take quite the scout to discover me, if they know who I am. Which I don't think they do. So for now, take a breath and join me inside," he said, extending his arm.

Later that afternoon, after our midday meal, I sat down at the table with quill, ink, and parchment from the stash I'd found earlier in the day while rummaging through Gideon's writing table.

Alex came up behind me and brushed the hair off my shoulders. He leaned over, and his breath tickled my neck. "What are you doing?"

"First, I'm going to write to Hannah. I assume you informed my cousin we were married when you retrieved my gown. However, I thought it best to write to her myself."

"And second?"

"I thought I'd start to make a list of supplies we will need. I've looked through Gideon's storehouse, and there isn't much," I said. I tapped the end of the feathered quill on the table. "How long do you think we'll be here?"

He shrugged and sat down on the bench opposite me. "Hard to say. We'll see if we can find you another place to stay by the end of two weeks now that the soldiers know about this place. If we can't, well, we'll talk more about it later. I don't know about me."

"I don't understand."

"Gideon and Si are out scouting now, watching what the British are up to. We'll report their findings to Washington after they return. If General Howe is planning on moving his army north, I can't see how Washington will be able to stay in southern Manhattan. He'll have to move north as well so he isn't trapped. Gideon and Si are due back here tomorrow or the next day, so we'll know more then. If everything has remained the same, we'll stay here and continue to spy on the British until we are confident what is happening and then report our findings. So, make your list with the understanding it may be just you for a while."

My face turned sour.

"Don't look at me like that," Alex said. His fingers drummed on the tabletop.

"When we first discussed marriage, I was of the assumption I was going to go with you. You are the one who mentioned sleeping under the stars and whatnot. Do you mean to tell me that you now plan on leaving me here — alone, I might add — while you go off to war?"

"Yes. Or, I believe Si has a lady friend who I'm sure you could stay with."

My mouth popped open as I searched for a rebuttal. But none came to me.

"Nora, I had more time to think about it. You could be killed if we engage in another battle. You do remember what it was like the last time, no?"

"And how is me, staying here, *alone*," I said, using the word again for emphasis, "protecting me? Any man could come walking onto the property, find me by myself, and take advantage, especially if they know I have no husband coming back for a few weeks — or months!" My voice raised in exasperation. "Case in point, the soldiers who showed up today. What if it had been Captain Roth?"

"What about it? You told me he had never harmed you, that he never—" he said, his eyes glaring at me. He knew without me telling him the captain had attacked me.

"He did not rape me, if that is what you are getting at. You should know after last night that you have been the only one," I said, my cheeks reddening. "You said you would protect me. I thought that was the whole reason we married."

Alex's clenched his jaw, and his lips formed a tight, thin line.

"Well?" I said, snapping at him.

"I know what I said."

"Then I don't understand how—"

He pushed up off the bench and ran his hands through his hair. "I can't argue about this now, Nora. You will listen to what I have to say—"

My voice caught in my throat as the anger coiled around me. "How dare you."

Before I could throw at him the number of unsavory remarks I had in my mind, he stomped across the room and out the door, mumbling something about splitting wood, leaving me stewing alone.

I sat unmoving for a few minutes, my breath short. I could not believe the conversation that had taken place. Tears brewed behind my eyes, but I would not allow them to spill down my cheeks. I would not cry over this. Over him. There had been too many tears shed on behalf of my brother and family. On David. On things that mattered. Our first married squabble did not and would not get that precedence.

Squaring my shoulders, I dipped the quill into the ink and wrote out a letter to Hannah, assuring her of my happiness. I asked her to hold my dresses or at least keep one of them in hopes I could reclaim it, if my uncle would allow for me to do so. He had paid for them after all.

When my anger and frustration had dissipated to a simmer, I set to boil water for hot tea as the sun was now fully gone, and the chill in the air had picked up. With the water set over the fire, I busied myself with preparing a simple meal of oatcakes and what was left of the roasted meat from our wedding meal. I had collected walnuts earlier in the day and found some root vegetables as well, which I planned to cook. Having very little in the way of spices, I deemed the best way to make the meal was to throw everything together in the pot and boil it. At least the salt from the meat would give the meal some flavor, if only a little.

The supper was completely prepared, overdone, in fact, by the time Alex strode inside, his arms loaded with wood. His nose and cheeks were red from the cold night air, and he smelled of pine and the musky scent that was his own.

Seeing him conjured up a small amount of irritation from

our earlier argument, not to mention our food had been ready for the past hour, and yet, the desire that moved through me upon seeing him stunned me.

Without saying a word, he set the wood down by the fireplace and shrugged off his coat and hat. "Smells awfully nice in here, Sailor. Supper ready?"

"It has been ready for the last hour. It is probably ruined by now. What took you so long?" I brusquely asked.

"You're still cross?"

I folded my arms and stared at him.

He sighed and blew on his hands to warm them. "I stormed out of here with every intention of splitting wood to ease my frustration but ended up walking a few miles before I did so. That's why I'm late. I'm sorry. I needed to clear my mind," he said. He rubbed his hand over his face and stood by the fire. "You're right. I did agree to marry you for your protection, but I'm discovering I don't know how best to go about it. Is it better to leave you here to fend for yourself and not be close to battle? Do you return to your uncle knowing what we know about Captain Roth? They have a relationship that I have not figured out yet. My guess is your Uncle Edward is supplying the tories with money, which is why Captain Roth seems friendly with him. Or, is it better for you to come with me, where we could be forced into battle, where you'll sleep in a tent, in the cold, with very little to eat, surrounded by men, knowing that the enemy could break our line of defense, and then who knows what could happen. You could be arrested for treason. A stray bullet could find you—"

For the first time since our argument, I understood how much of a burden I was to him.

"I thought I was doing the right thing by having you stay behind, but if you don't think so, we'll talk about it," he said.

Dumbfounded at his comment, I appeared to be at a loss for words for a second. "You mean, I have a say in this?"

"Of course you do. Nora, you were your own person before you ever met me. I'm very aware of how independent you are, and while it scares me a bit, I don't want to be a tyrant of a husband. The only way we are going to survive this war and this marriage is if we work together. I understand why you want to come along and, after giving it much thought, I'll agree to it," he said.

I opened my mouth to speak, having found the words I wanted, when Alex held up his hand to stop me.

"But, you have to promise that you'll heed what I say. We'll be camping with the regiments, and a lot of those men haven't held a woman in months, and though you are married, well, that won't stop the monsters from either side. Do you promise? I can't protect you if you don't listen to me."

I considered him for a moment. I knew he was trying to meet me in the middle, and while I did appreciate it, a question still lingered. What if I needed to make a quick decision without consulting him first? I certainly wasn't going to be idle the entire time. "I promise on one condition," I said.

"And that would be what?"

"I want to help again with the wounded and sick. I know Dr. Aster will be able to use me. If there is any fighting, if it gets too rough, I will hide in any designated spot you have decided upon."

"Agreed," Alex said. He struck out his hand, and I shook it. He didn't let go. "Am I forgiven?" He took two steps toward me, closing the distance between us.

"Yes, I suppose you are."

"Good. Come here."

I stepped into his arms and enjoyed the warmth of his strong body while he hugged me.

His stomach grumbled. "Can I have something to eat, or is the kitchen closed for the night?"

We parted, and he walked over to the pot that I had removed from the fire and placed on the table.

"You're lucky it is still warm. Another half hour and it would most likely be cool."

Alex shrugged. "No matter. I've eaten all kinds of food at all sorts of temperatures. This will do fine," he said, scooping a spoonful out of the pot and putting it into a bowl.

"Tea?" I asked.

"Please. Will you join me?"

"I ate without you. Before it overcooked."

As Alex ate what was left of the evening meal, I walked around the front room and lit the beeswax candles. The flames gave the room a soft glow and a warm comfort from the night air. Even inside the four walls, the wind was loud as it howled through the sky, rustling the branches of trees and their leaves. A pitter-patter sounded on the roof, and a steady rain fell. I took my shawl, which I had discarded earlier onto the back of one of the chairs, and wrapped it around my shoulders.

I sat down near the fire to warm myself and picked up a book. I opened it and began reading while I waited for Alex to finish eating.

"What are you reading?" Alex asked between mouthfuls.

I put my finger on the page to hold my place and turned it back to the front. "A book with a rather long title it seems. It's called *The Life and Strange Surprizing Adventures of Robinson Crusoe, Of York, Mariner: Who lived Eight and Twenty Years, all alone in an un-inhabited Island on the Coast of America, near the Mouth of the Great River of Oroonoque; Having been cast on Shore by Shipwreck, wherein all the Men perished but himself. With an Account how he was at last as strangely deliver'd by Pyrates. Written by Himself*," I said, taking a deep breath.

"Good Lord. Why didn't the author title it Robinson Crusoe? Do you think this is all true?"

Alex chuckled and stood, crossing the room and sat down next to me. "If it is true, he's had some adventure. Quite the life if you ask me. Though, as much as I love the idea of all that he's seen, I admit for now, I'm rather fond of my new life." He gazed into my eyes.

"Are you now?"

"Yes."

"And why is that?" I asked, though I was certain I already knew where this conversation was headed.

"Because now I have a wife to cook for me and keep my bed and myself warm at night. I must say, Sailor, I did like the look of you bending over the fire tending to my meal." Alex squeezed my knee, and I slapped his hand away. He laughed.

"Is that all? I'm merely someone to cook your food and keep your bed warm each night?"

"I think that's about all I can handle at the moment since you bring your own set of adventure with you," he said, smiling. "But, for as much as I love you warming me at night, I'm glad I'm there to warm you too."

I grinned at his teasing as I knew it was exactly that. His eyes stared straight into mine, a fire lit behind them, and he leaned in closer to my face. "How about we go upstairs and warm the bed together?"

"It isn't even bedtime yet," I said. My insides turned to liquid heat at the idea of what we would do together upstairs, but I planned on making him wait as he'd done to me with dinner. It would be fun to watch him squirm.

"It's dark. That's bedtime enough. Besides, I'm sure by now, Gideon and Si know members of the army stopped by here today, as word gets around. They will be here tomorrow, and after that, I have no way of knowing when we'll get uninterrupted alone-time together."

"Hmm, you do make a point, Mr. Foster. I shall think about it," I said, picking the book back up and opening its pages.

I waited with bated breath, wondering what Alex's next move would be. And he didn't disappoint.

"Well, you continue to read and think about my proposition while I try to help you come to your decision sooner," he said. He knelt in front of me and lifted my skirts. With careful movements, he slid his hands up my leg and took off my stockings, one at a time.

Trying not to squirm and to keep my breathing controlled, I kept my eyes focused on the book and the words of Robinson Crusoe. With vigilant strokes, his fingers and lips brushed against my ankles and traveled up my legs. Still, I pretended Alex's attentions had no effect on me, though I was well aware he knew it all a ruse. Alex kissed his way up my legs and thighs, and then kissed the swell of my breasts, until his lips found my neck.

"Is Robinson Crusoe still entertaining?" he asked, his hands now roaming very freely.

"Hmm," I answered, for that was all I could manage.

"Thought so." He took my mouth in his own then broke away from me. "And this right here is why I would never want his adventures. I can die a happy man," he said, kissing me again, then continuing for the most of the night.

CHAPTER 26

THE SWEET SCENT OF tobacco woke me from dreams of a sun-filled forest and kisses. I stretched and yawned, wiggling my toes underneath the blankets, thinking about the night before. I had no real memory of how Alex and I had ended up in the bed as we had spent most of the night in front of the fire exploring each other in slow, deliberate movements, knowing it would be a very long time until we had privacy again. And, from the sound of men talking downstairs, our privacy was now officially over.

Taking my time, I readied for the day, wearing my wedding dress, knowing that now it would be deemed as my Sunday best. If we were going to leave soon, I needed time to wash my old gown so it was as clean and fresh as it could be. Men might not mind wearing the same clothes and smelling like a pigsty, but I would do no such thing if it could be prevented or helped.

Knowing Alex preferred me without a mobcap, I kept my hair down, securing two sides back with hairpins and the small amount of ribbon I had. I studied my reflection, wondering if I looked different now that I was married. Would anyone notice anything changed about me?

I walked along the hallway and down the stairs to greet the men. It was Si's gruff voice I heard first before he turned around. Behind his gray beard, his mouth curled into a small grin. When I returned the expression, he scowled, though his blue eyes still held a hint of joy.

Gideon walked over and embraced me. "It is good to see you, cousin," he said.

The use of a family term surprised me, but I didn't mind. Alex, for his part, observed with a look of satisfaction.

"We brought fresh eggs and a jar of honey if you can make oatcakes," Gideon said. "We still need to see to the horses, as we only arrived."

"How wonderful! I believe I can do that," I took the jar of honey from him.

Gideon and Alex walked outside, while Si stoked the fire.

"I see your smile, Si. It suits you. You should do it more often. Want to tell me what it's all about?" I asked.

"I only smile because I don't have to sleep outdoors tonight," he said. He stood and brushed his hands off on his breeches. "And, it does me well to see that marriage suits Alex."

"How do you know marriage suits him?" I asked.

He looked pointedly at me. "A man knows when another one is well-bedded," he said, in his matter-of-fact way that was distinctly Josiah Foster. "And we know when a lady is, too." He winked as my face heated and walked outside to help the men with the horses.

Embarrassed beyond words, I went back to the task at hand, making oatcakes — lots of them — for I had heard someone's stomach grumble on his way out the door. I looked out the small window. The wind blew leaves across the front of the house and howled. I was glad Gideon and Si would not be sleeping outdoors tonight either. Had they been this whole time? I hoped not.

While I made breakfast, I occasionally glanced out to observe the men. It was hard to not watch Alex as he worked, or did anything for that matter. The way his body moved, his muscles taut and flexing, gave me a sense of wonder every time I looked at him. In that moment, it seemed it would always be that way for me, and I wondered if he thought of me the same, though we had entered into our union out of a mutual convenience. I knew he held me in high-esteem as I did him, but would our feelings of friendship ever turn into something more? The last few days had felt more like a dream than anything else, and deep down, with the arrival of Si and Gideon, I knew that our marriage, and what it would end up being, was about to be tested.

The men came back inside, shivering, their noses colored red from the cold, and seated themselves down at the table, nodding at the hot peppermint tea I already had poured for them.

"I'm looking forward to the day we drink real tea again. No offense, Nora. I daresay, I would even drink Labrador tea right now in place of Bohea," Si said, sniffing his cup. "That's how much I miss it."

"Seeing as there was nothing stored here, least of all tea, peppermint leaves from the forest floor will have to do. However, I do agree with your opinion. I'm curious, though, how long it's been since you drank English tea?"

"Three years," Alex said.

I choked on the hot drink. "Three years?"

The men all nodded at the same time. "After the Sons of Liberty in Boston dumped all the tea into the Boston Harbor, well, we decided as a family that we wouldn't drink the filthy redcoats' tea either," Si said. His usual frown turned even sourer as he began mumbling under his breath about taxes.

Gideon cleared his throat. "Word has it the redcoats are searching for a deserter, and a small band of them journeyed this direction. Did you see them?"

"We saw them. They stopped here," Alex said, taking a bit of oatcake slathered with honey.

Gideon didn't say anything but waited patiently for his cousin to continue.

"They were looking for the same man who we talked with at The Fighting Cock's Tavern the night of the fire. Apparently, someone recognized him. Did you learn his name? I do not know it."

"Travis Platt," Si said. "Coward. That's what he is."

"What will happen to him if they do catch him?" I asked.

"If he's lucky? Shot on sight. If not, I heard rumors of some men being flogged to the point where they are begging for death."

I shivered. "Any other news? Something more appropriate for the breakfast table?"

Wiping his mouth on his sleeve before pushing back from the table, Si stood up and stretched then lit his pipe. "Actually, there is. Washington is moving north, thanks to the information Nora provided," he said. "Gideon and I checked into it, and indeed, General Howe has already made preparations to move into Westchester County. General Washington has requested our talents to help scout the surrounding areas."

"When would he like us to leave?" Alex said.

"Now. But don't worry. I told him you were newly wed and would need to make arrangements for your new bride before we headed out. He agreed."

I looked at Alex with a knowing glance, hoping he would

take it as a reminder to our earlier conversation from the day before.

His eyes flicked to mine then away. He nodded. "A few days will be good to gather everything we need. I had a feeling it would come to this, so Nora made a list for us. We'll need to ride into the city and procure another blanket and a canteen if we can, unless you have them here Gideon. I could not find any. We'll need another horse too."

Si pursed his lips then took a long inhale out of his pipe. The embers flared inside the small cup, filling the room with its aromatic scent. The smoke puffed around him in a cloud. He took another toke then asked his question. "And why do we need another blanket, canteen, and horse?" Si's eyes regarded me as if he already knew what Alex was going to say.

"Because I'm not leaving my wife behind. Nora is coming with us."

"I've said it before, and I'll say it again, Alexander," Si said, his voice tight, "The camp is no place for a woman. It is bad enough the other soldiers have their women and children following us. It messes with a man's head to have his lady there because he'll be too worried about making sure she is safe. No offense," Si said, nodding to me.

"You're right," Alex said. His stance was wide, and he crossed his arms, his dark blue coat stretching over his broad shoulders. "But, a man's lady not being present can mess with his head too. We don't know how long we'll be gone. It could be a month or more. Nora will be alone, and that doesn't sit well with me, Si. She's coming with us."

No more was said on the subject. Everyone seemed to understand without having to be told that the topic was closed and would not be opened again in the immediate future, if at all.

The next day we rode into Manhattan, and I stopped in to

see Mr. McGovern. The bell rang when I opened the door, and he took his time lifting his head, finishing whatever he was writing, before he looked up.

"Miss Bishop," Mr. McGovern said, his gaze worried. "I daresay, I never thought I would see you again. You left without one word." His eyes skimmed over me in a fatherly way. He relaxed. "You look well. Are you?"

"Yes, Mr. McGovern. I'm fine. Thank you. And, it is Mrs. Foster now."

Mr. McGovern whistled through his teeth. "Married? You don't say?"

"I do."

"And who would the lucky gentleman be then? I fear I worried for you after the hanging. I told Mrs. McGovern I'd thought the fellow was courting you, but I see I was wrong."

My chest ached thinking of Nathan Hale. If he hadn't stayed in Manhattan and hadn't gone to The Fighting Cock's Tavern to locate the deserter to find information on John, he may never have been detained.

"Captain Hale was an acquaintance," I said. "Nothing more. My husband's name is Alexander Foster."

"I do not know him."

"I don't doubt it in a place as crowded as Manhattan. He isn't originally from here and sticks to the outskirts as it is. He much prefers the quietness of the wilderness."

"He's a farmer then?"

I hesitated. Alex had never told me what he did before he joined the Rangers. I hadn't thought to ask him as too many other things pressed on my mind when we married. It flustered me to not know the answer. I tucked the question away to ask Alex later.

Not wanting to admit I had no idea, I changed the subject. "I am awfully sorry I left so abruptly and that I did not write.

Things were a bit unsettled after the fire. I'm glad to see your shop was not affected."

"As am I. There are many people who lost their businesses, not to mention houses," he said, glancing up toward the ceiling.

Footsteps could be heard on the boards above us. Mrs. McGovern must have been home.

"But, I do not think that is why you are here, and I'm certain you do not want to come back and crush herbs and pills into powder either. So, out with it."

"My husband and I are going to be leaving Manhattan for a while. I do not know when we will return, and as of now, I'm not entirely certain of our final destination. I do not have any flaxseed stored—"

"And you know that I have plenty of it in case there is ever a need? Is that it?"

"Yes. I have money. I will certainly pay you for it."

"You will do nothing of the sort. What else do you need?"

"More yarrow if you have it. I have some of my own, but fear I may need more," I said, thinking of all the possible wounds I may have to treat between Alex and his two cousins.

"Very well. Follow me to the back room, and we will get your items together."

And so for the remainder of the afternoon, I sat and worked alongside Mr. McGovern for what could have been the last time. As was usual, we didn't converse much, but each went about our own tasks of filing, writing, crushing, pounding, grinding, mixing and weighing. The work relaxed me. My fingers turned brown with dirt from the different plants, potions, and lotions. I wrote down a few recipes and stuffed the note in my pocket to keep with me. At one point, Mr. McGovern left the shop for a quick errand, returning an hour later.

The familiar sound of his boots pounding on the floor brought a smile to my face. I would miss the older man greatly, though he had only been in my life for a few short months.

"I have a present for you," he said before he hung up his hat and outer coat.

"Me? Why—"

He held up his hands in protest. "It isn't much, and it is nothing special. But every woman should have one, according to my wife, that is."

The corner of his mouth turned up, and he set down two little boxes in front of me.

"Think of the first as a gift from my wife and the second from me," he said.

I unwrapped the first parcel, and my heart warmed. He was right; it was nothing special as far as gifts go, but it meant the world to me seeing as how my own mother was no longer around. It was a small sewing kit, including a scissors clip to attach to my dress. A small tear slid down my cheek. I didn't wipe it away. I could easily picture my mother's own sewing kit that I had used countless times.

"How thoughtful of you and Mrs. McGovern. It is perfect, and very much needed," I said, speaking true. I'd been mending the men's clothing with an old needle and brown thread. I'd had to cut the thread with Alex's hunting knife as no scissors were to be found in the house. It had been horrible.

With the scissor clip attached to my gown and the sewing kit stored in my pocket, I picked up the other parcel and unwrapped it. Inside the small box lay two needles, though a bit larger than sewing needles.

"Those," Mr. McGovern said, picking one up and rotating it between his fingers, "Are for a different sort of sewing.

These will be for mending your husband, should he need you to do so."

I swallowed. How did he know?

"Don't look at me like that, Nora," Mr. McGovern said in his fatherly voice. "I put it together myself, long ago. I am very much aware, especially now, of your acquaintance, Nathan Hale. And, since you don't know your exact destination yet, nor how long you plan on being there, it leaves me to guess you'll be traveling with the regiments. I came to this conclusion since most new brides are wanting and ready to find a house of their own and make babies. I was not born yesterday, mind you."

Speechless, I sat and watched him for any sign of hostility, gifts notwithstanding. None could be found. He reached out and touched my shoulder and gave me a light squeeze. "We're on the same side, Nora. I promise, and I'll be here if you need anything. No matter what."

He looked over at the mantel to the clock. "It is getting late, and I don't want your new husband to worry for you. I'll help you pack up. Will you need a ride?"

"No, thank you. My husband will be waiting for me only a block away. And, thank you again for the gifts. It means a great deal that you thought of me."

He smiled and nodded. "Very well."

Mr. McGovern walked me to the door and hesitated for a moment before he took me by surprise and wrapped his arms around me. "You be careful now. I want to see that smiling face of yours the next time you are in town. Understand?"

"Yes. I am so grateful. For everything."

My throat was sore from holding back the tears as we said goodbye. I stepped out onto the street and took a deep breath, wishing I hadn't. The scent of manure from animals filled my lungs, and I coughed. The wind whipped me in the face as I strode toward the east end to the meeting place Alex and I had decided upon. Horses raced through the streets, the riders not caring at all who was in the way, yelling for walkers to move. A man shepherded two pigs to the alleyway, and in the distance, I heard the clucking of chickens. While the sounds were not unfamiliar to me in the least, it continued to seem strange to see such farm animals in the center of the city.

I pulled my shawl tighter around my shoulders and took quick steps down the street. Though it was still daylight, the nightlife activities were beginning to come alive in the city. New York was known as the most sinful place in the colonies, and I fully agreed. The prostitutes alone were in abundance, not to mention the liquor that flowed through the taverns every night. I had once heard that roughly five-hundred women plied their trade all throughout the city, and men, no matter whose side they were on, enjoyed what the ladies had to offer. It was no wonder pox ran amuck.

I uttered a small praise to myself when my eyes found Alex across the street. He stood with his back against a brick wall, facing my direction. Our eyes locked several yards away, and he smiled. I hurried to his side.

"Come on. Let's get home. The next few days will be busy before we leave."

"Haven't they been busy enough? It never seems to end."

"The lazy man will not plow because of winter. He will beg during harvest and have nothing."

"Hmm, thank you, Reverend Alexander," I said, not bothering to hide the mocking tone.

"Anytime." He put his arm around me and guided me to the horses, which were tied to a fence outside of the city.

"Do you know any other useful scriptures?" I asked as he helped me up on the mount Si had bought for me.

A smile played on his lips. He grasped my ankle, and his thumb made small circles on my skin above the bone.

I breathed in.

His voice was low and husky. "Your lips are like a strand of scarlet, and your mouth is lovely. Your temples behind your veil are like a piece of pomegranate. Your neck is like—"

"Alex. Someone will see my exposed ankle if you do not stop," I said, yearning clearly in my voice. The wanting him to stop and the wanting him to keep going taunted me.

His hand journeyed further up my calf muscle. "Shall we take a quick stop before going home?" he asked, his eyebrows raised in question.

"Yes, most definitely, yes," I said, breathless with anticipation.

He stilled his hand then squeezed before letting go and jumping into his own saddle. "Let's hurry. I know the perfect spot," he said.

We raced through the woods, and I laughed as the wind whipped my hair back, and the sun heated my skin. The air was cool, but heat rushed all the way through me, knowing what awaited when we arrived at Alex's perfect spot.

He slowed down, smiling at me big and broad. His eyes raked over my body, and I shivered. "I like seeing you bounce up and down on that horse, Sailor," he said, winking.

"Do you now?"

"Very much so, yes." He pulled Bridger to a stop. He swung off and looped the reins over a tree branch before coming over to me and helping me down.

As my feet touched the ground, Alex kissed me deeply. When we pulled away for a breath, his eyes were hooded. "Don't move," he said. He led my mount next to Bridger and wrapped the reins around the same branch.

After he secured the horses, he came back and kissed me again, this time with more passion than ever before. We ended up on the fallen leaves of the woods, his back against a boulder and me straddling him. We came together hungrily, each of us wanting, craving more of the other. I succumbed to him almost immediately. He, too, did not take long. It was as if we both needed a swift release, though I did not know why.

Once we finished, we sat side by side, our hands clasped. "I regret while we are at camp, all of our moments together will be like this. Under the stars, on leaves, or up against trees. Where we are going will not be comfortable at all. Ever. Are you sure you want to go?"

I looked at him. "Of course. Where you go, I go. I can handle it."

"I know you can. But I want you to be certain," Alex said.

"I'm sure."

He kissed the top of my head. "I found out something today that you'll want to know. It's about John."

I sat up straighter. "What?"

"He is no longer in the Sugar House."

My heart all but stopped. "Please don't tell me he is on one of the prison ships. Everyone dies who gets sent there," I said. My bottom lip trembled, and I bit it to keep it still.

"He is not on a prison ship. Or at least, that is what I've been told."

I shut my eyes and took a deep breath. "Where?"

"They are sending him with the army, north into Westchester County."

My eyes opened, and I leaned away from Alex to better look at him. My thoughts became scrambled. "Why would they do that? I didn't know they took prisoners with them like that."

"They don't. Or at least not typically. Special prisoners, yes. But I can't figure out why they would take your brother. Do you know?"

I shook my head. "But this is good news, right? He isn't behind the prison walls, so it should be easier to free him."

"In theory, I suppose you are correct. But why bring John along with them? He was a newly enlisted man. He has no connections or none that we know about."

"Is he the only one being transported north?"

"I don't know, but we are going to find out."

CHAPTER 27

LATER THAT DAY, THE four of us traveled twenty-eight miles from Gideon's log house to White Plains, New York. Thankfully, the trip was fairly easy and only took us roughly five hours to arrive. By the time we reached the regiment, General Washington had already established his headquarters in Mr. Elijah Miller's house.

Unwillingly, Alex left me to settle our things and set up a campsite while he and his cousins took off, searching the area for the approach of British troops. They scouted the surrounding region all evening and the following two days, while the regiment took a defensive position by fortifying two lines of entrenchments situated on raised terrain. Washington had stationed his troops in such a manner so we would be protected on the right by swampy ground near the Bronx River while keeping the steeper hills farther back to be used as a place for retreat, though everyone hoped that would not be the case.

Per Alex's instructions, I made our tiny camp of four away from the main unit, near the edge of the woods. He said even men on the same side fought for what they wanted, and he was of the opinion I would be something many would want.

That night, Gideon and Si had been called to Washington's tent, so the two of us sat around our small campfire waiting for them. It sizzled and cracked, and the smoke snaked up into the dark sky. All Hallows' Eve was only four days away. I buried my hands between the folds of fabric in my skirts as the late October winds rustled the leaves. I remembered the parties Mrs. Shipman would throw to celebrate the day. It was at one of these parties three years ago, at the age of seventeen, that I had my first kiss with David.

"What are you thinking of?" Alex asked. He sat on the ground next to me, his long legs stretched out, almost reaching the flames.

"The past," I said.

He raised his eyebrows. "Want to elaborate?"

After a pause on my part, he nudged me with his elbow. "Truth, remember?"

"I was only thinking of All Hallows' Eve. The Shipmans, David's family. It was a tradition for them to host a dance every year. It was always so fun. The singing, games, the telling of ghost stories. The dancing." The flames licked the sky, wrapping around each other as if they themselves danced.

I glanced at Alex, but he sat listening intently.

He nodded for me to continue.

"It was only three years ago. I was seventeen. David had asked me to dance. I was so nervous. I had danced with him plenty of times in the years before, but this night, something shone in his eyes. I accepted, of course." My stomach twisted in knots. *Is this a story I should be telling him?* "Later that night, David and I played a trick on John. We were running away from him when we ended up in the barn. I remember laughing so hard my side ached," I said, chuckling.

Alex took my hand and kissed the back of it then entwined our fingers together. He gave my hand a reassuring squeeze, and I continued.

"It was in the middle of laughing he kissed me. My first kiss. It took me by surprise because for most of my life, he had treated me as a little sister. But in that one moment, that relationship faded away, and we became something more. We talked of marriage a few months later, and he asked my father for my hand."

"Why did your father say no?" Alex asked.

"He didn't. He asked us to wait until I was twenty years old. This war has turned everything upside down. Nothing came out the way I thought it was going to," I said.

"And now you're twenty, and you find yourself married to me." His voice was tighter than what it had been a moment earlier.

Up until this point, I had kept my eyes on the fire, but now, I turned and looked at him. "Yes. And now I find myself married to a man who is still a stranger in a lot of ways, and yet, this feels right," I said. "The kisses I shared with David were wonderful, but, when you kiss me, it is different. It's like my soul merges with yours. You ignite a passion within. Heavens, the way you look at me now makes me think I will combust." I glanced away. My face was hot with embarrassment.

He put his finger under my chin and turned my head so I had to look at him. "Do you think it is different with me? I married you to protect you from unwanted attentions and to make sure you would always have a place to go. I never thought it would turn into something more, but my God, Nora. I can't stand to be more than one foot from you. And the want — no, the need — to have you in arms overtakes me completely sometimes." He leaned in and rested his forehead against mine before he kissed me. His kiss seemed to plead with me to know, to understand what he said was the truth, and I believed him.

"Ahem."

We parted our kiss, but the desire radiating in Alex's eyes didn't leave.

He closed them, took a deep breath, and turned to face our intruder. "Yes, Si? What is it?"

"General Washington has requested your presence."

Alex nodded. He kissed me one more time then pressed in close and whispered in my ear, "I'll be back, and maybe we can pick up where we left off. I know of a small thicket close by. No one will notice we've gone."

"I'll wait here," I said.

After Alex left I settled myself beneath the wool blanket he had given me. It made me warm all over now. Not meaning to, I fell asleep and dreamed of stolen kisses and secret touches underneath the moonlight.

* * *

MIST LAY ON THE ground when I woke the next morning. Alex and his cousins were packing their bags and whispering to each other. I sat up and rubbed my eyes.

"What's going on?" I asked, yawning.

"Morning," Alex said. "We didn't mean to rouse you. I was hoping you'd sleep a bit longer. I was planning on waking you up before we departed."

"Where are we going?"

"*We* are not going anywhere. Si, Gideon, and I are on a mission for Washington. You are staying here."

"All right. Fine. Where are *you* going then?"

I stood up and stretched. The sun was barely visible, casting an orange glow in the still mainly gray sky.

"The same place as yesterday morning. Scouting to see where the British are."

I considered my options. Camp was already set up, and so far, Dr. Aster would have nothing that needed to be accomplished, as there had been no fighting. If I went with Alex, I could possibly gain some knowledge of John's whereabouts.

"Let me go. Please. There is nothing for me to do here today. All of your socks and shirts are mended because I did them before we left. Our food will only need to be reheated, as we have leftovers."

"I don't think that would be wise. The last time we were in this position, we were fired upon. How would that be protecting you if that happened again?"

"You could ride out and see nothing though. I promise I'll do whatever you ask of me. I have a good set of eyes on me. Please?"

Alex sighed and secured the leather strap in his hair. "Only this once. And only because I don't think we'll see anything. But, you have to swear that if I tell you to ride hard back to camp, you will listen. Understood?"

"Understood."

Without bothering to keep his voice quiet, Si turned to Alex. "I don't think this is a good idea."

"It will be fine."

The four of us rode away, scoping the land for any signs of the British. We had ridden seven miles to Scarsdale, where General Howe and his British soldiers had last been seen. After securing the horses to a nearby oak, we crept toward a hidden spot among the trees to spy on their camp. However, they were already advancing toward the American lines.

My eyes were fixed on the sea of redcoats in front of me. Their black leather boots pounded the earth and kicked up dust, causing my heart to race. But it was not only the British who advanced.

"Bloody hell," I said. "The Hessians are with them as well. Over there, all on the left." I shivered, remembering the bayonet slice Alex had obtained. They took no mercy. There would be a battle today. That was certain. "What now?"

"Now we race back to camp and let the general know what is going on."

As fast as our horses would take us, we galloped back to camp. Thankfully, John, much to my mother's horror, had taught me to ride astride, for if I had ridden sidesaddle, I would never have been able to keep up. Alex jumped off Bridger outside of Washington's headquarters, leaving me and his cousins to wait. Five minutes later, he rushed back to us, and we followed him to our small campsite.

"What's the plan?" Gideon asked. He began to check his cartridge bag.

"General Washington is going to send out the Second Connecticut Regiment to slow the British advance," Alex said.

"Joseph Spencer leads them, yes?" Gideon said, now checking his Brown Bess.

"Yes. He's also sending Haslet and the First Delaware Regiment along with Alexander McDougall's brigade to reinforce Chatterton Hill."

"Where's that?" I asked.

Si pointed to the far-off distance. "See that huge hill in front of you? That's it."

I refrained from mouthing off as I knew that was not needed at the moment. "Will you fight?" I asked Alex.

He nodded.

"With whose regiment?"

"I'll go with Haslet's regiment and help reinforce the hill. Listen, Sailor, I want you to stay here," he said. He put his hands on my shoulders and locked his eyes with mine. "Promise me you'll stay here."

"I should go help Dr. Aster. I'm positive he'll need it."

"I'm positive he will too. But not yet. Wait. There will be plenty of men to tend to once the fighting is over. We are far enough away that you'll be safe here," he said.

"Alex, I will be fine. I need to do my part, too. If there are going to be men that need to be taken care of, they will need it as soon as possible. I won't sit here idle, twiddling my thumbs while everyone else is out fighting."

"I don't want you to get hurt," he said, touching my cheek.

"I don't want you to get hurt either, but you still plan on putting yourself in the line of fire."

He sighed. "Promise me you'll stay with the wounded until I can come and get you."

"I promise."

Alex gently kissed my lips then gathered me close to him. The steady pulse of his heart put me at ease, yet also terrified me. What if this was the last time I would ever feel his heartbeat?

"Promise me you'll come back," I said.

"I promise."

Alex kissed me once more then sprinted off to join the rest of the troops. I kept my eyes on his retreating body until he disappeared from my line of vision then set off to find Dr. Aster.

As I knew he would be, Dr. Aster was barking orders while ripping linen in preparation of what was to come. He looked the same as he had when I first met him several weeks ago but with large purple shadows under his eyes.

"Doctor? How can I help, or do you still prefer not to have women in your medic tent?"

"Nora Bishop. I heard you were back in camp," Dr. Aster said upon seeing me.

"I am. Though my name is Foster now. Nora Foster."

He dumped the pile of linen in front of me. "I predict we'll need lots of bandages."

I set to work immediately while Dr. Aster filled pots and bowls with water and checked his tools, laying them out on a small wooden table. I had slit my fourth piece of linen into a long strip when the sound of the fife and drums played.

Dr. Aster stilled his work. "It has begun."

The fire of muskets reverberated off the hillside, causing me to look. Clouds of smoke and the backs of our men could be seen from our vantage point. I prayed I would not see any redcoats come over the hill. But that was not to be.

Haslet's men were doing a fine job of keeping the forward progression at bay, and for a couple of hours, it seemed as though the men had stopped the advance. However, Hessian artillery opened fire on the left side of Chatterton Hill, succeeding in driving the militia into a panicked retreat. Men swarmed like thousands of bees and drove back down the hillside. It was horrifying. From out of nowhere, a British column attacked, scattering the militia on the American's right side, leaving the flank exposed.

"Who is over there?" I asked Dr. Aster, hoping neither Alex nor his cousins would be part of the unit.

Dr. Aster raised his hand as he looked into the sunlight in order to see better. "I think it is Maryland and Delaware Regiments, but I can't be certain."

For the next couple of hours, the fighting continued, and I fretted the entire time. The numbness of battle had long worn off, and now I ran only on adrenaline. Every time anxiousness slithered toward the back of my mind, I bit my lip and found a new patient to take care of. Alex would make it through this day. He had to. Throughout this time, men trickled in by wagons or between other soldiers who carried them to our tent needing care. The sight of blood wasn't as much of a shock this time as it had been the first time I helped Dr. Aster, though I was by no means desensitized by it. The blood ran red, and with the aid of Dr. Aster, I managed to set up my own station and tend to the smaller, less-threatening wounds.

A panic shout outside our tent reverberated through the flaps while I secured a bandage on a man's thigh. I turned to look as a man sprawled out on a wooden cart was carried in. A pile of linen was stretched across his abdomen, soaked red.

"Nora!" Dr. Aster called. "I'll need your hands. Now!"

I dashed over. When I reached the wounded soldier's side, Dr. Aster removed the linen. His stomach was ripped open, and his innards sprawled out like noodles. I gagged as my morning breakfast threatened to exit my mouth but swallowed it down. The man's thigh had a tourniquet tied tight around it as a bayonet blade had slit his leg open as well.

My eyes searched Dr. Aster's, hoping he would give an order on what to do first, but he didn't say anything. His face turned pale, and his eyes, which were usually sharp, turned soft. He set the linen back down over the gaping hole and shook his head while he untied the band.

"There is nothing I can do for him," he said, his voice quiet. He laid his hand on the soldier's head. "Be at peace, soldier. You fought valiantly. Be at peace and rest with our Lord and Savior."

The unconscious man's chest moved up and down while he struggled for air. A few moments later, he stopped breathing all together and passed away.

The tent grew quiet; even the wounded who had been writhing in pain seemed to know a soldier's spirit was passing through. The only sounds were that of musket and cannonball fire, and the yelling of men still in combat.

Time moved slowly from the minute the young man died to the end of the battle. I worked, but my thoughts were elsewhere as our militia made a fighting retreat.

I waited and waited for Alex to come to the tent, but he never showed. I mended broken men, reassured them, encouraged them as best I could, and wept with them. For several hours, I worked and worried about Alex. And still he didn't show up though the fighting was finished. The battle was over, the British had won, and my husband was missing.

* * *

AFTER DR. ASTER RELEASED me to rest for the remainder of the night, I ran back to the little campsite Alex and I shared with his cousins. They were already seated around the fire. Gideon next to Si, inspecting his brother's bicep, while Si strung along a line of profanity.

"Will you let my arm go, you damn fool? You don't have the slightest idea of what you're doing. I'd rather let a whore look at," he said. "At least she would have an idea of how to use a needle and thread." Si cussed some more under his breath while he shut his eyes.

"Have either of you seen Alex?" I asked, striding toward them and peering over Gideon's shoulder. "Here, I can do it." I focused on Si, though my thoughts ran rampant on Alex. I took a steadying breath.

"Thank God for that," Si said. He nodded to me as I picked up my bag and dug through it to find the needle Mr. McGovern had given me.

"Did you clean his wound?" I asked Gideon.

"With water to wash the blood away," he said.

"Do you have any rum or whiskey? Brandy will do too."

"Yes. Not a lot though."

"I'll take whatever you can give me. Bring me a cup as well."

Once Gideon had gathered the alcohol and the cup, I poured a decent amount into the cup then handed it to Si.

He raised his eyebrows at me.

"Trust me, you'll need it. Take a few sips then let me know when you're ready. In the meantime, tell me when you last saw your cousin, because I haven't seen him yet."

Si took a few sips then nodded to me. Without giving him warning, I poured the rum onto his arm. He hollered but then got himself under control.

"You could have told me first," he said through clenched teeth. "Why did you do that?"

"I could have, but where is the fun in that? According to medical books, it helps clean the wound. I'll give you a medical lecture later, but for now, talk while I fix you up."

"Gideon will. I don't think I'll be capable," Si said.

I began to stitch his arm while Si breathed in heavily through his nose, and Gideon recounted the battle for me. By the end of his report, I was no further in finding out where my husband was.

"So what you're telling me is that you have no idea where he is?" I paused in my stitching to allow Si to throw up.

Si wiped his mouth on his sleeve. "The three of us always fight alongside each other. And we were doing so when he took off, running after some British fella. But seeing as I had a huge bayonet coming at me, I didn't follow him with my eyes," Si said. He winced when I pulled the thread.

"Sorry. I'm almost finished."

"We will find him, Nora. I'll go ask around now while you finish up. For all we know, he could be in the officers' tent getting other orders. I'm sure Washington will want us to scout out the area again," Gideon said.

"Please let me know as soon as you hear anything." I made a knot in the stitch and clipped off the end then reached over and picked up the cup of rum Si had sat on the ground. One last swallow remained in the cup, and I took it.

"Trust me, Nora, we want to know where he is as much as

you do. There's nothing to be done about it at the moment, so rest while you can. I'll be back," Gideon said. He left as Si stood up and walked back into the trees to vomit once more.

The afternoon sky had turned into darkness by the time Gideon made his way back to the campsite. My eyes were fluttering shut as exhaustion was about to consume me.

"Nora?" Gideon said. He knelt next to me. "I bring news."

The anticipation of what he was about to tell me caused any exhaustion within me to leave. I rubbed my eyes. "From the way you are looking at me, I suspect it isn't good. Tell me."

"I'm afraid no one knows where he is. There are only two conclusions. He is either dead on the hill, or he's been taken prisoner."

My heart all but stopped. *No. Please God, don't let him be dead.* My hand went to my mouth to hold back the moan. He wasn't dead. He couldn't be. I would know. Deep down, I would know.

"When will we hear? Have all the deceased been accounted for yet?" I asked.

"No." He crossed his arms. Worry was etched on his face.

I bit my thumbnail. "Have you spoken to the officers?"

Gideon shook his head. "I haven't been able to see them as of yet, but I've asked around. Those who would possibly recognize him have not seen him since the fighting earlier in the day."

I buried my face in my hands. Deep down inside of me, a feeling stirred that I could not name. All I knew was that it told me Alex was not dead. "Do you think they'll kill him if he's been captured?"

"It's hard to say. They may be willing to do a prisoner exchange, depending if we've taken anyone of high enough status from them, but that I do not know," Gideon said.

"What do we do now? We can't sit here and wait." I

dropped my hands to the grass then pushed myself to a standing position and began to pace, not knowing what else to do.

"I've asked for an audience with the officers. As soon as they can see me, I'm positive they will, and we'll figure something out. Try not to worry."

"Try not to worry? That is the most ridiculous thing I've ever heard! How am I not to worry?"

"This may not help, but, the scriptures tell us 'Therefore do not worry about tomorrow, for tomorrow will worry about its own things. Sufficient for the day is its own trouble—'"

"I do not give a damn what the bloody scriptures says, Gideon! By you quoting Matthew — oh, don't look at me like that, I attend church — by you going on with what they say, it certainly doesn't bring my husband back, does it? No. So unless you have an actual plan that will bring Alex here, safely, you're right, it doesn't help," I snapped.

I turned away from him, embarrassed by my outburst. All this time, my feelings for Alex had been softening. I knew the exact moment they had started to change from mere friendship to something more: my uncle's ball when he told me I was beautiful. But, at the time, I had been too worried about my own protection that I had pushed them aside. The possibility he was gone was much too real. I stifled a laugh, for I had no idea how to respond to my own foolishness. I had actual feelings for my husband and had had them for a while now; I'd only never wanted to admit it to anyone. With the loss of my family and the loss of David, I was too scared to lose anyone else. And now I had, and he never would know how I felt.

"I'm sorry, Gideon. I didn't mean to yell at you. I know you're only trying to help," I said.

"It's fine. We'll bring him home."

"When?"

"I should have more information tomorrow. Don't go and do something foolish. Understand me? We'll take care of it. Try to sleep. It has been a long day for all of us."

Gideon woke Si, and they left together to help bring in the dead soldiers off the field. I sat alone at the fire. I picked up a dead stick and twirled it around between my hands. I tapped the ground over and over. I had to do something. Not only was my husband more than likely being held prisoner in the British camp, but my brother was as well. I couldn't wait for tomorrow. Alex could be dead by then, and I would be surprised if John was still alive. Tears welled behind my eyes. What would I do if I found them both dead?

As I sat and watched the fire, a plan started to formulate. The British camp was close to the village. I didn't have any doubt the men were taking liberties of all kinds to celebrate their victory. Confident in knowing I could sneak across the line, I decided I'd play the role of nurse, for surely, they had wounded soldiers as well. I would pretend to be a Tory supporter come to help the camp doctor.

With my mind resolute on my task, I dug around the campsite trying to locate anything I could take with me, but came up short. The men were carrying all their weapons. I'd have to cross over enemy lines with nothing but my skirts, for that was what needed to be done.

CHAPTER 28

THE NIGHT SKY WAS CLEAR, and though the moon was only a crescent, it still shone bright. It took me longer to reach the British camp than it had earlier when I rode out with Alex, but I managed to reach them without any mishaps.

I had accomplished bringing a horse with me and hoped Alex and I would be able to steal one from the redcoats as I could not control two mounts on my own. I brought the mare to a stop and tied the reins around a branch then walked one more mile until I came to the edge of the village. The street was clear. However, I waited to make sure no one was paying attention. I made my way out from the cover of the trees, pretending it was not out of the ordinary at all. I kept to the shadows as best I could until I made it to the street.

As I walked toward the British campsite, I gazed at the houses. Hardly any candles were lit in the windows, and I wondered if they'd all fled the village or if they were all huddled together, keeping the lights out on purpose in hopes no one would knock on their doors.

Firelight gleamed in the darkness, and men's laughter and drunken song echoed through the night. I adjusted my mobcap and straightened my shoulders as I approached the camp, though inside I trembled.

I had managed to make it several yards when I stopped short, my breath caught in my throat. Captain William Roth and General Howe stood in deep conversation. Neither man appeared delighted. Captain Roth's lips were drawn tight as the general spoke to him, his eye becoming slits as well. General Howe turned on his heel and strode off to the right without another word, dismissing the captain with his leaving. Captain Roth, for his part, remained still, glaring after his superior before making his own exit. He walked in my direction, but his eyes stayed focused straight ahead of him. I kept my head down and, with slow steps, made my way behind the tents, keeping to the shadows, following General Howe.

I needed to get as far away from the captain as possible. If he discovered me, my ruse as a nurse would be over. He knew who I was. But, now that I'd found where the general's tent was located, I hoped I would be able to stand close by and listen in and discover something of use. For if I was to overhear anyone's conversation, it would be from the man in charge.

General Howe stopped outside his tent and talked to the guard stationed there.

"Private, I will be meeting with my officers in one hour. Until then, make sure I am not disturbed," General Howe said.

"Yes, sir."

I doubled checked the area to make sure nobody was paying attention to me. Once I was sure I hadn't been noticed, I made my way to the back of the tent. Would I have time to wait the one hour and then look for John and Alex?

"Madam," a young man's voice said the moment I stepped next to the white tent. "Might I inquire what you are doing?"

Damn. "Hello," I said. "Um, my mother sent me down to see if I could be of any help with the wounded. But first, I have a message for the guard watching the prisoners. If you would be so kind and show me where to go and then lead me to the wounded?"

The young man couldn't have been any older than seventeen years old. He was still pimpled face with barely a whisker on him at all. "You?"

"Yes," I said and batted my eyes.

The young man shrugged. "Right. This way," he said without questioning me at all.

As we walked through the campsite, I fished around for information, hoping that it would help diffuse my nerves and give off the impression that I was supposed to be there, as I noticed many different men gazing at me.

"What is your name?" I asked politely.

"Rufus. What's yours?"

"Abigail Small," I said, the lie slipping off my tongue with ease. "Tell me, Rufus, how many prisoners are residing here? And, I can't help but ask, will I be safe?"

"Prisoners? At moment, thirty, I think. Of course you'll be safe. Why wouldn't you be?"

I smiled demurely and gave off an embarrassed look. "I suppose that is silly of me to say, with strong men like you standing guard and protecting us. In fact, I'd much rather get to the wounded men and help. Would you mind running this errand for me? I must confess, I'm a bit afraid of the prisoners anyway."

The boy's chest puffed up. "I'd be happy to. What do you need?"

"I ran into a captain on my way here. And, oh, how dreadful, I forget his name! He had dark hair. A sour-looking chap.

Anyway, he requested a prisoner by the name of John Bishop be sent over to the west side of camp, by the edge of trees."

I shivered, making it look as though I feared what might befall the prisoner. God help me. I had decided in that moment to seek John first before trying to locate Alex. My only reasoning was that I figured John was probably in a worse state and would require more help in escaping. It wasn't the best justification, but it was what I told myself. Rufus looked very scared. "Was it Captain Roth, ma'am?"

"Why, yes, I think that was his name. Thank you for providing it. Now tell me, where do you hold the rebels?"

"Any rebel we caught earlier today is over here," he said, guiding me left. "There are also a few rebels who we brought along from the city as well."

"I was under the impression most militia who are caught go on board the prison ships. Is this not so?"

"Oh, it is, madam. For certain. I'd hate to be on there. I heard most men die from rat bites. But, I don't know. The men here are being taken to the fort."

"The fort?"

He nodded but then paused. I needed him to continue. I batted my eyes again. "I'm sure you don't wish to frighten me, but I can handle it. With men like you serving, who are so brave, I know I have nothing to fear. It helps me sleep at night knowing you are keeping me safe."

He straightened his spine. "We will keep you safe. Fort Washington. News is we're headed there next after we launch another attack on the rebels."

I sighed on purpose. "Another fight? Well, I certainly hope General Howe allows you men to rest a bit before fighting again. I dare say, you all need it."

"That's awfully kind of you. Rumor has it we're staying here for two days and then attacking. Sure wish it could be longer. Truth be told, I'm ready to go home. I'm only here because my family needed the money. I don't care if these folks are part of England or not," he said.

"Shh," I said, meaning it. Even though I'd baited him for information, I certainly didn't want him arrested for treason. "If anyone hears you say that, it will be your neck on the end of a noose, not those prisoners over there."

The boy, not realizing what he had done, grew red, and his eyes glanced around. "You're right. Sorry. You won't say anything, will you?"

I shook my head. "I promise. Make sure you remember to watch your words though. Not everyone will be as kind as I."

"Thank you, ma'am. Um, the tent is right there," he said, pointing. "I'll go and retrieve this Mr. Bishop posthaste."

I forced a grin. "I'm much obliged."

The boy turned and ran toward the prisoners' jail while I inconspicuously maneuvered my way west. I walked with hurried steps to the meeting location, looking over my shoulder as I went, but saw no one. The hair on the back of my neck stood on end. This was all too easy.

Forty minutes later, as my hands twisted in the fabric of my gown, Rufus and John came into view from my hiding spot. John's hands were tied in front of him, and he limped heavily on his right leg. As they came nearer, John's posture shifted as he caught sight of me standing near a tree. His expression remained neutral, though his eyes were alert.

"Hallo, ma'am," Rufus said, his face wary. "The guard was a bit confused when I told him Captain Roth wanted him, but no matter. Everyone knows you never want to end up on the bad side of that man. Yesterday they caught a deserter, and he flogged him till the man almost died upon the pole. It was horrible."

I cringed. "Was the man Travis Platt?"

"Yes. Word travels fast, I take it. Now, I don't agree with him deserting, but the captain could have shot him on sight. I think he got pleasure out of the torture. It was as if the man's back was a piece of canvas. Captain kept walking around him, examining his back like he was deciding on where to make the next stroke."

"You are most likely right. Thank you, Rufus. I do appreciate you helping, and I do hope you will remember to mind what you say. You might find yourself tied to the pole with Captain Roth's lash upon your back if you aren't careful. And, to make sure that doesn't happen this time, please know I'm only doing this to protect you," I said, taking a deep breath.

Rufus's eyes narrowed and his face became alarmed. "Doing what?"

Before he could say anything more or I could lose my nerve, I picked up a tree branch and hit him over the head, knocking him unconscious.

"Nora?" John swayed, and I darted forward, catching him in my arms.

We hung to each other and wept. We stepped apart, and I took my time inspecting him. Heavens, he was skinnier than what I remembered, and dark shadows rested under his eyes. I touched his hair as the tears continue to fall down my face. It had grown long and was filled with knots. I suspected if I stepped closer, I'd be able to see lice crawling through it. He had a beard too.

"I'm fine, Nora. My wrists hurt though. You didn't happen to steal the key to these locks, did you?" he asked, smirking.

"No. Unfortunately, you'll have to wait till we get back to camp to take those off. It's about seven miles from here."

"I've endured them this long, seven more miles I can handle. But first, what the blazes are you doing here?"

"What does it look like? I've been trying to figure out how to get you free since you were first captured," I said.

I explained everything to him starting with the Battle of Harlem Heights and ending with the great fire.

"Christ," he said.

"It was lucky they removed you from the Sugar House and brought you here. Young Rufus told me you were destined to travel to Fort Washington with them. Any idea why?"

John shook his head.

The horse I had brought snorted when we approached. I dug into the sack tied to the saddle and helped John use the canteen. He gulped the water and it trickled down his chin.

"We best hurry, Nora, before anyone finds Rufus. I don't think it will be long until they discover someone has pulled the wool over their eyes and come looking for us," John said, raising the canteen to lips once more.

"I know. I have an unsettled feeling about it all. It was much too easy to get you out, and I don't know why," I said. Every nerve in my body screamed at me to flee. I glanced around the woods but saw nothing amiss.

"Let's go. I'll need your help mounting. It's been a while, and I'm too weak to do it on my own," John said.

I nodded. "We'll leave as soon as I get back. I promise."

"What are you talking about? Where are you going?"

"I have to go back to the camp."

"Are you daft? It was a suicide mission coming to get me! What is so important that you have to go back and risk your neck a second time?"

"My husband."

"Your husband? What the hell are you talking about?"

"I'm married, John. What else does the word *husband* imply?" I said, my frustration growing.

"To whom? David?"

"Good Lord, no. I'd never marry that bloody bastard after what he did."

John cocked his eyebrow. "What did he do?"

"To start, he joined the British army. I'll explain everything later. I promise."

"You better believe you'll be explaining everything later. I can't believe you went off and got yourself married without asking my permission first."

"Your permission? John Alan Bishop." My hands fitted themselves onto my hips, and my eyes narrowed. "I did not need your permission to marry, especially when you were in prison! I had to do something, didn't I? Father was dead, you were not around, Uncle Edward was indifferent," I said, my voice clipped. I stopped and took a deep breath. My hands were now balled into fists at my side.

"Look, I didn't know when you would be released, or even if you would be. It is a miracle you are still alive and strong enough to be standing here talking to me. I was alone, I was scared, and though I am independent to a point, I knew I needed the protection of a man's name. I did what I had to do. I'm not sorry one bit about it. In fact, it was the best decision I've ever made. You'll see. You and Alex will get along fine. I know it."

John's face fell, and tears welled in his eyes. "God, Nora. This is all my fault. The fire at the house, you being alone and being forced to marry some man—"

"This isn't your fault, John."

"But it is. If I hadn't joined the rebels—"

"If you hadn't joined the rebels, you would have found another way to play your part in all this. You did what you believed was right, and I'm proud of you. What happened to Mother and Father is not your fault. Captain Roth set fire to the house as a lesson to the locals of what happens if you go against the Crown. It was his choice. One of many that he'll pay for. Believe me. Now—"

"And exactly how do you plan to make me pay for it, Mrs. Foster?"

My blood turned cold.

CHAPTER 29

I SPUN TO THE left, instinctively putting John behind me so I faced Captain William Roth.

"Hello, Mrs. Foster. It is so very lovely to see you again. First, I offer my congratulations on your marriage. When I first met your husband at Nathan Hale's hanging, I didn't have the chance to formally introduce myself to him. Your uncle let me know your new name. I say, he was a bit put out when he discovered you'd run off and married, but he has since gotten over it," he said. He looked around and then settled his eyes on me. His hands were clasped behind his back, and he held his body in a relaxed and condescending posture.

"I wondered when you would come. I admit I'm surprised you did not try to rescue your brother while he was at the Sugar House. It takes quite a bit of gumption to cross enemy lines — alone, no less — and try to rescue someone. I do say *try,* because, well, you failed. Obviously," Captain Roth said, his arms spreading out to his sides with a sneer on his face. "I saw you in camp, Mrs. Foster. It was not hard to figure out why you came, especially since I had your brother brought with us in hopes of your attempt at a rescue. I'm pleased to know my plan worked. It was quite easy, I assure you."

I blinked. I had been set up and trapped.

"What do you want?" I said through gritted teeth.

My heart raced, and the sound of my blood rushed in my ears. Sweat dripped down my back and the front of my stays. I swallowed, but my throat remained dry and tight.

Captain Roth took a step forward, the corner of his lips staying in a wicked grin. "What I want, Mrs. Foster, is for my prisoner to be returned, and for you and me to stop playing these games. I know you are a spy."

Without turning around, I felt John move away from me. From the edge of my vision, I watched my brother reach his hand out and touch the bark of a tree. He was weaker than what he had let on.

"I'm not a spy," I said.

"Come now, Mrs. Foster. I know that you've been part of a clandestine group, partaking in dead drops, listening to private conversations when you shouldn't. You can't fool me," he said. His hand went to his belt where he pulled out a pistol. He stroked the barrel of it with care then turned it over, skimming the weapon with his eyes as if we were gazing upon a beautiful woman.

Before I understood what was happening, John moved behind me and lunged at the captain. He hit him with enough force to knock the officer to the ground. The pistol fell from his hand, but it was still too close to them for me to grab it.

It was terrifying to watch my brother and the captain rolling on the ground, each of them punching and kicking the other. I froze as the display took place, a mass of twisted limbs, each vying for the position of the victor. An audible snap reached my ears, and John let out a loud scream. His leg was bent at an odd angle.

John, feeble from the weeks of being held captive, had already used most of his strength in the initial assault, and it showed. Now the captain had broken his leg. Blood ran from his nose, and his eyes were already black from the officer's fists. His lip was split open.

The captain had John pinned to the ground and sat on top of him. Captain Roth's white wig was cocked to the side, and he laughed. He wiped his own bloody lip on the back of his hand and straightened his wig.

He turned and looked at me while John groaned in pain then set his eyes on John.

"Any last words?" Captain Roth said.

John looked at me. His face was pale, but his eyes held a fire I'd never seen before. They conveyed so much that he couldn't say, and I knew he loved me. "Run, Nora. Run!"

I took off through the trees, never once looking back, with tears streaming down my face. I had managed to run a few yards when I heard the sound of a pistol explode.

My lungs were tight, and my side hurt by the time I crossed the edge of the woods. I slowed my stride and bent over, putting my hands on my knees to catch my breath. I wiped my eyes and pushed John's death to the back of my mind. I could not grieve now. I would cry for him when I made it back to camp with my husband. My heart ached with every step though, as I reentered the British camp. I had more information to gather. I needed to destroy the captain. I needed to find Alex.

The men continued to lie about, obviously exhausted from their day of fighting. A few drunken songs and mild laughter reached my ears, but for the most part, the emotions of the camp were like a contained surprise in a box, ready to burst out when the lid opened. Much different from the rebel camp where not only were the men physically wounded, but their pride and morale had taken hits too.

I lifted scraps of linen off a table and carried them in my arms, hoping it would help me to blend in. My heart thudded with each step, and I kept my face down. I even stopped once at the request of a wounded soldier and helped him rebandage his arm.

Fear raced through me. *God! What if I can't find Alex in time?* I took a breath. The only way I could calm down was to focus on my surroundings. The ground crunched underneath my feet from the dead leaves and the frost beginning to form. Men's breath clouded around them by the fire as they spoke, looking like small ghosts floating into the heavens. The sky was clear tonight, and the stars shone brilliantly, but a chill still hung in the air. A storm was coming. It was only a matter of time.

As I continued to weave my way around the encampment, the hair on the back of my neck stood on end like it had before. I glanced over my shoulder but saw no one, though the feeling of someone following me pricked my mind. Could Captain Roth have made it back already?

I dismissed the idea. He could not have made it here before me, unless he knew a shortcut. *Bloody hell! The horse!* I shook my head. I needed to focus.

I stuck to the shadows slowly nearing General Howe's tent. The hour was almost up, and I did not want to miss the meeting. I'd failed John. I would not fail at this nor at finding Alex.

The officers entered the tent, which was the largest by far. Surely, every man inside could hear the way my heart thundered as I waited, keeping silent. With the wind rustling the trees and the voices of the soldiers around, I had to strain my ears to listen while staying alert for any signs of guards, though I stood at the back of the tent. Guilt swept in me at stopping to spy on the general when Alex could possibly be hurt, but I knew he would have wanted me to try and gather information if it could be done.

"The fact remains, sir, that he became out of hand. The deserter should have been shot on sight. Not tortured, for that is precisely what Captain Roth did. No wonder the rebels think the way they do about us. He is portraying us as if we are brutal animals. To do what he did to one of his own…" a man said.

"I agree, Captain, but we need him. Though I do not agree with all his methods, there are times when his particular way of going about things work better. We'll discuss him later. For now, let's focus on what we are going to do with the rebels who are only a mere seven miles away from us, according to our sources," another man said.

I guessed it was General Howe, for his voice, though nasal, held a distinct tone of authority to it.

"I say we sneak back tonight and finish them before they make a full retreat," a younger voice said.

I drew in a sharp breath.

"And this is why I'm general, and you are not, Traverse. They are not going anywhere tonight, and neither are we. Both sides have lost men, and both have an incredible amount of men who are wounded. We need the rest."

It was silent for a moment, and I heard things being moved around. Something thumped down upon a table.

"No. We'll wait two days. That will give both sides plenty of time to recoup," General Howe said.

"Sir?"

"I will follow the rules of war, Captain Traverse. At least this time, I shall. Perhaps, if our soldiers weren't in such dire capabilities, it would be different, but this time, I will allow it. We shall attack during the night, and after we have claimed a true victory, we will march on to Fort Washington. Bring me the map, and let's discuss strategies," the general said. "We'll use the Hessians again, and I want to double our cannon fire."

"Sir, should we send troops ahead to Fort Washington or wait?"

"Wait. I don't want to split yet. We have roughly seven thousand troops, and I think it would be most effective and impressive to march together to the fort."

My legs shook at the news. From what little I knew, the British outnumbered us by double. And Rufus had been correct about the redcoats attacking the fort. The American army would not withstand another attack. They had suffered too many causalities, and far too many men were wounded to the point where they could not hold a gun, let alone stand or run. I had to find Alex, and we had to warn Washington as soon as we could.

Before I could turn around, an arm snaked its way around my waist. A hand clamped tight over my mouth. I shrieked and kicked my legs out as my assailant hauled me up.

"Shhh. Don't scream. Sailor, it's me."

I sank to my knees, relief spreading over me like a thick, wool blanket. Alex went down with me, and I turned and buried my face in his shoulder, scratching my cheek on the red, stiff, smelly coat he wore.

"Take a breath, Nora. There, there," Alex said into my hair.

"I thought you were captured. I was told you ran after a soldier and were never seen again. How—"

"I killed him and took his uniform and made my way back here to camp. What the hell are you doing here?"

Though he whispered, by the tone I could tell that if we were alone, he would have been yelling.

"You disobeyed me! Again. You were supposed to stay at the camp. When we married, you promised to listen and to obey—"

"I never promised such a thing. Now isn't the time anyway," I said. I didn't care that he was mad. All I cared about was that he was alive and well. I sniffed and wiped my eyes. "I came looking for you and my brother."

Alex let out a breath. "You shouldn't have. Do you have any idea what will happen if you are caught? Roth is here. Did you know that? I discovered where they were keeping John, but when I went there to retrieve him, he was missing. I'm sorry, Sailor, but he isn't here."

He stood up and helped me to my feet. "I know. I found him and got him out of camp. But now's he's dead. Captain Roth found us and he… and he shot him. I ran — ran back here. Now I've found you. I have information. I have a horse—"

He reached up and wiped the tear off my cheek that escaped. "I'm sorry about John. I want the full story later. But not now. You thought of everything, did you?" he asked, shaking his head.

I sniffed. "As much as I could."

"But, Sailor, what are you doing snooping behind General Howe's tent?"

Before I could answer, footsteps tromped toward us. Without saying anything, Alex swooped me into his arms and kissed me.

A male voice coughed, and Alex jumped back, making his face appear shocked and scandalized.

"Sir," Alex said, standing at attention.

"Private," the man said. "May I ask what it is you are doing?" From the looks of his uniform, the man was a captain. The deep baritone voice indicated it was Captain Traverse who I'd heard discussing strategies with General Howe.

Out of my peripheral vision, I saw Alex glance at me. My face heated, and I looked down at my shoes, acting embarrassed at being caught in a lover's embrace though the blood was rushing in my veins out of fear.

"Sorry, sir. We were... ah, that is to say... the lady and I were—"

"I'm fairly certain, private, I know what it is you and the lady were getting ready to do. Your whispers could be detected inside the tent, though thankfully, I could not hear precisely what it was you were saying."

The captain stood with his hands clasped behind his back and stared at me, but I did not meet his gaze. "You look familiar to me, Miss—"

I cleared my throat. "Miss Wilbur," I lied. My heart pounded, and my breathing became rapid. I squeezed Alex's hand to the point where I thought I would break it.

"Do I know you from somewhere, Miss Wilbur?"

This time, I summoned the courage to look at him and gasped in surprise. It was the fevered man I had tended to in the hospital in Manhattan. If I let on that it was I who nursed him back to health, he might let Alex and me continue on with our tryst without saying anything. However, if word went around that a nurse from Manhattan was in camp, and he described me, Roth would know it was I. Nothing about my appearance was special but I still didn't want to chance it.

"I'm sorry. No. I do not believe we've ever been introduced," I said, relieved that he apparently hadn't heard my gasp.

Alex gripped my hand and wrapped his arm around my waist. My heart continued to hammer inside my chest. Lord, if we were caught, it would be hanging for sure.

"Private, only because I miss my wife, and I'm in good humor tonight, will I not say anything about this and look the other way. But only this once. You know full-well we do not approve of this sort of relations in camp. I do not care what you do while in town, but here is a different story. Am I clear?"

"Yes, captain. Thank you, captain."

The officer bowed toward me. "Miss Wilbur, I hope to meet you again, although not like this," Captain Traverse said.

I dipped into a low curtsey and watched him leave. My legs shook as Alex pulled me toward the woods, but I stopped him. "Wait. I need paper and ink. I learned some information that I need to write down."

"You're going to have to remember it, Sailor. We need to leave. Now," Alex said.

I paused. I knew he was right, but the fear of forgetting what I had overheard gave me pause.

"You're right. This way," I said.

We held hands and ran toward the woods. We passed the place where I'd hit Rufus, but he wasn't there. I didn't know how long we had until the alarm was raised.

"Sailor, are you certain John is… dead?"

My throat tightened, but I forced the words out. "Yes. Now come on," I said, not bothering to wait. I didn't want to think about it, because if I did, then he would be gone.

We didn't stop running until we were halfway to where I had left John and the captain. Alex pulled me to a stop.

"We can stop to breathe for a minute. Explain everything, Nora."

I had too much I wanted to say to him, but I didn't know how to begin. My body trembled. I had lost my brother but saved Alex. Never in my life had I felt this strongly about another person before. We stood there underneath the crescent moon, and I stared at him, lost for words.

He reached forward and tucked a stray piece of hair behind my ear. "Sailor? What's wrong?"

I lifted my hand and placed it in his. Now was not the

time for sentiment. "Captain Roth set a trap, and I was too ignorant not to know it. I was able to get John out easily, and I knew… I knew it was easy… but I kept going. He was there. He was waiting for us. He killed him, and I ran. John traded his life for mine. I can't… I don't… God, Alex. He's dead. My brother is dead," I said. The tears streamed down my face as I clung to him.

Alex held me and rubbed my back, never saying a word. He didn't need to. I pushed back from him, wiping my tears away. I could not — would not — fall apart at this moment. We were too close to the camp and too close to escape.

"You are not responsible for John's death. Captain Roth is. You did everything in your power to rescue him, Nora. He died a hero. He died for his country and for you. There is no greater love than to give your life for another," Alex said.

I shook my head. I needed to focus. I *needed* something to busy myself. Purpose. I needed purpose. "Please, I don't want to talk about it right now. Are you hurt? I want to make sure you aren't wounded and haven't told me because you think you are tough and can handle it. I need to know now if there is something I can try to fix before we ride."

"Well, Doctor Foster, aside from bruises and scrapes, I am otherwise unscathed. If you can believe it."

"I can't, actually."

"Neither can I, but it is the truth. Now, let us continue on and get as far away from here as possible."

"I don't think it's safe to go back to where I have left the horse. That is where Captain Roth was waiting for John and me. He could still be there."

Alex considered my question. "We'll have to chance it. Camp is seven miles away, and we'd be caught if we tried to walk it. Hopefully, he went back to camp to try and find you," Alex said. "Though I want to wring your neck for going back to enemy territory."

I shrugged. "I did what I needed. I'd like to retrieve John's body if possible. I can't leave him."

He stretched out his hand for me, and I led the way. When we arrived at the grove, John's body was lying cold and lifeless on the ground. The horse was still standing by the tree, munching contentedly on grass, and the pack I had brought with me was still on the saddle.

Dead leaves crunched off to the right. Alex and I looked to where the sound came from. Captain Roth strode out from behind a tree, his pistol in his hand. "Ah, Mrs. Foster, you came back. How lovely."

My heart nearly stopped beating. *Bloody hell.*

CHAPTER 30

Everything around me slowed down: the leaves that swished about in the trees… the hooting of an owl in the distance… Alex's breath, my own heart. I cursed inwardly. We should have risked walking.

I stared into Captain Roth's eyes, knowing time had never been on my side, nor would it ever be. Chaucer came to my mind in that moment. *"Time waits for no man."* And it didn't. There was never enough time. I should have woken and kissed my family goodbye on that fateful day in September. I should have taken the time to tell Captain Hale how glad I had been to be trusted by him and considered a friend, though we hadn't known each other long. I should have told Alex only five minutes earlier how much he meant to me and how much I had fallen in love with him.

"Let me guess," Captain Roth said. "You're going to play the card where you pretend your husband is part of the British army, hence the uniform," Captain Roth said. "Mr. Foster, is it? Toss your pistol on to the ground."

When Alex didn't move, Captain Roth cocked his own gun and pointed it at my heart.

"Did you not hear me? Or is your knowledge of the English language entirely too barbaric that you did not understand me?"

Without a word, and without his eyes ever leaving the captain's, Alex took his pistol and did what the officer had ordered him to do.

The captain walked toward us, and using his foot, kicked the pistol away from Alex. He circled around us, having us at a disadvantage since he had his weapon drawn and cocked. He stopped behind me and pushed me forward, away from my husband's side.

The captain gripped my arm and turned us around so we walked backward.

Alex took a step in my direction, but the captain pointed the gun at my temple. "Tsk, tsk," he said. "I wouldn't do that if I were you. Now, Mrs. Foster, I must confess, I do prefer to have you alone in the woods. First, your brother was with you and now, your husband. We had a lovely time getting to know each other, didn't we? You remember, on the edge of your uncle's property. It was so… intimate. Wouldn't you agree?"

"Don't you touch me," I said. I lifted my hand to strike him, but he caught my wrist. "Feisty little thing you are. She must be loads of fun in bed, Mr. Foster. To be honest, I'm eager to try her out."

"If you lay a hand on her, you won't live to regret it," Alex said. His eyes were trained on the captain.

"A hand, you say. How about a few fingers?"

Keeping the gun pointed at my head, Captain Roth pulled me so my back was against him. I kept my eyes on Alex while the captain's free hand groped my chest, then his fingers plunged down into the neck of my gown, between my breasts.

"Nothing there. I wonder if you are keeping anything underneath your skirts?" Captain Roth said. He lifted the hem of my gown, and his hand searched under my petticoat along the waistline. He pinched my bottom and laughed.

Alex's eyes were slits, and his lips quivered. He was going to explode.

"Nothing there either. Mrs. Foster, could it be as simple as you put it in your pocket? I must say that disappoints me if it is so. A spy should know better," he said.

"I've already told you, I'm not a spy," I said through gritted teeth. My pulse raced erratically. Thankfully, I hadn't written anything down. For if I had, he would have found it, and I would soon hang from the end of a rope.

He stuck his hand into each pocket and pulled out the note I had written earlier while at Mr. McGovern's shop. I hadn't even remembered it was there. I had written different recipes for various treatments.

Captain Roth gave it to me. "Open it."

With trembling fingers, I unfolded the piece of paper and held it flat in my hands for the captain to see.

The cold barrel of the pistol pressed over my eye. "What is this? What do these numbers mean?"

My eyes flicked to Alex, and with the barest of motions, he shook his head yes.

"Recipes," I said.

"I doubt that, Mrs. Foster. I'm in no mood to play this game again. Why would you have what appears to be vital information in your pocket? You cannot expect me to believe it is recipes? Or perhaps you hope I'll think someone else put it there? Planted it on you?"

"That's exactly it," Alex said. "The note is mine, and I put it in her pocket. She has no place in this."

"How valiant. Taking the blame. Even if I did believe you,

which I do not, she has aided that prisoner to escape," he said, his eyes flickering to John's body, "and helped you cross enemy lines to gather information."

"I forced her," Alex said.

My throat had gone dry. What was Alex doing? I would not allow him to sacrifice himself for me like this, for it was obvious the captain didn't believe me. The one time I was being truthful. *How ironic.* My brother was already dead because he tried to play the hero. I would not allow Alex the same fate. If he was going to sink, I was going down with him.

"Forced her? Come now, Mr. Foster, I may not know Mrs. Foster as well as you do, but I know her well enough to know you cannot force her to do anything, though I am sure she would be much more manageable if you did. Do you know much about equine?"

Captain Roth paused as if he was expecting someone to answer him. He shrugged. "Mrs. Foster here reminds me of an ill-tempered mare. Do you know how you tame an ill-tempered mare?" His hand settled on my neck, and he squeezed slightly while he leaned in close to me. His breath was warm against my neck. "You need to desensitize them first. I find using a rope to be the best method."

He stepped in front of me and dragged the cold metal pistol down the side of my face then across my mouth as if it were my lover's fingers. He licked his lips, and my body betrayed me by trembling.

"Yes, I would definitely use a rope on you," Captain Roth said under his breath but clear enough for me to hear. He swung around to face Alex. "You see I'm in a predicament. I have a dead prisoner who has escaped under false orders. I have a rebel dressed as a member of the British army. And I have a lady spy, for I have no doubt, madam, that is what you are, especially with this proof of intelligence you've gathered. The fact of this situation is this. Someone will have to die. Well, another person will have to die." He pointed the gun at Alex. "And it seems as though you are the sacrificing sort," he said. "However, because I am ever the gentleman, I will, of course, give Mrs. Foster a choice. Shall I shoot you or your husband? Someone has to stand trial, which is why I'll leave one of you alive," he said.

My heart all but stopped, and I found myself at a loss for words. Was the captain serious? For once, the note of recipes truly were... recipes.

"Mrs. Foster?" Captain Roth said. He pointed his pistol at Alex. "Did you hear me, madam? Whom am I to shoot?"

"Stop it. You can't do this," I blurted out. "Why not take us both to trial?"

"I can. You both have turned against your king. You've been caught and charged with treason. I do not need a jury to find you guilty in this regard for I have the proof needed. But, I'll allow one of you to try and change the jury's mind, no matter how futile I think it will be. As for killing one of you now, it is for my pleasure. Besides, I think it is more fun this way, don't you agree? I'm being considerate. I know you are a lady who prefers to make her own choices, so I'm allowing you to do so. However, we don't have all the time in the world for you to come to your decision, so please hurry up, or I shall decide for you."

"You sick, twisted, vicious, dark—"

Captain Roth put his face inches from my ear. Spittle formed on the side of his mouth when he spoke, and the sweet scent of cigar smoke permeated my nose.

I flinched.

"You think you have me figured out, don't you? You know *nothing* of the darkness I linger in. How that's where I'm meant to be. Need to be." Captain Roth paused and for a moment his eyes glassed over as if his thoughts were far away. He shook his head then and his eyes resumed their normal evil. "Have you decided?"

Tears streamed down my face while I looked at Alex. The cool metal of the pistol touched my skin again. In one fluid movement, Alex pulled out his dagger from the back of his breeches and flung it at the captain.

Captain Roth yelled, and his hand dropped, but he kept hold of the pistol. Alex sprang forward and rushed toward the captain at the same time the officer pulled the trigger.

"No!" I screamed.

The bullet found its intended mark. Alex yelped in agony. Blood seeped through the fabric, and his face turned pale. I tried to rush forward through the cloud of smoke, but the captain grabbed hold of me.

"No! No… no… no," I sobbed. My eyes were tear-soaked. "How could you?"

"I told you my plan, Mrs. Foster. This was not a shock," Captain Roth said while he stuffed the used weapon back inside his belt. He touched his arm where Alex's knife had sliced him before he pulled another loaded pistol out of his coat pocket and pointed it again at my husband.

Alex moaned and twisted on the ground. He was still alive! For now.

"Please. Let him go. I'll stay, and I'll do anything you want," I said. "I'll go and stand trial." The fear in my voice was evident, and I didn't care. My legs shook, and I wrung my hands together to keep them from trembling.

"Mrs. Foster, you do realize you should never utter that phrase to a man, for you may live to regret it," he said. His mouth turned up into a sadistic smile.

I had hoped I could at least buy Alex a few more minutes,

but I knew with every bone in my body he would kill him then kill me after I finished being his plaything.

"Captain, I'm begging you. You can do anything you want to me. I promise I won't struggle. Please release my husband."

"Nora, no. Do not… do this," Alex said between breaths, but I would not look at him.

John was gone and my parents and sister also. Their deaths would follow me everywhere. The fire in Manhattan was on my hands, too. If I could do anything to prevent Alex from dying, I would, even if that meant putting my life in the hands of someone as sick as Captain Roth.

My eyes left the captain's, and they locked with Alex's, his blue irises that were as clear as a spring day and as deep as the ocean itself. His look held so much warmth and love in it for me that I nearly lost all resolve.

"Your life is worth more, Nora. Do not do this. Do not go with him. If he kills me today, I'll die a happy man because of you."

"He'll do what he pleases with me whether you are dead or not, Alex. If I can spare your life, and if I know you are alive somewhere, I will endure it."

"Are we finished yet?" Captain Roth said.

I twisted around so I stood in front of Alex, blocking him from the captain's view. "Will you let him live if I go with you willingly?" I asked.

The captain considered me for a moment before he answered. "Only to prove I do have manners when the situation calls for it, I will not kill him with this shot," he said.

I understood his double-meaning. He might not kill him with the current bullet in the pistol, but that did not promise he wouldn't reload it.

"I want your word you will not kill him at all," I said. "With that bullet or another one," I said.

"You have my word as an officer of the Crown and an English gentleman," Captain Roth said. He flashed a brilliant smile, and once again I was struck by how handsome he could seem, if one didn't look deep into his coal, soulless eyes.

"Let me say goodbye. Please," I said.

The captain made a spectacle of his exaggerated sigh, but I went over to my husband.

Alex stretched out his hand, wincing. The captain had shot him in the thigh. Blood poured down his leg. He would not be able to stand for long. I kissed him, my tears running down my cheeks and onto our joined lips. "I love you," I whispered.

"I love you too, and I will come back for you. I swear it," Alex whispered. "He will not get far."

"I'm waiting, Mrs. Foster," Captain Roth said.

I pushed away from Alex and walked to where the officer stood. "You're evil," I said.

Captain Roth smirked. "All in the eyes of the beholder, I suppose," he said. He looked at Alex. "Do not bother to follow us, Foster, or I'll kill her on the spot."

My captor tugged on my arm, and we began walking. I looked over my shoulder at Alex. He sat on the ground, clutching his wound. His whole body was tense, and he looked like a spring ready to pop forward. Even in the moonlight, the hard lines on his face shone as he was, no doubt, plotting his course of action.

Captain Roth must have sensed the same thing as I about Alex because, before I understood what was happening, he turned and whipped the pistol forward and shot my husband. Again.

I screamed as Alex fell back to the ground. Captain Roth grabbed me around the waist and pulled me through the woods, kicking and screaming.

"You bastard! You said you wouldn't kill him!"

"And I didn't, madam. I shot him in the shoulder or possibly the arm, I couldn't tell, so he wouldn't be able to come after us. Hopefully, he'll bleed out before any help comes along or by the time he crawls to the horse. Now, I'm going to remove my arms from around your waist, but only if you promise to keep still and quiet. If you try to run back to him, I promise you will find a bullet in your back, and I will finish him off. As I told you before, I always keep my word. Do we understand each other?"

I nodded, too afraid to talk. Too afraid to do anything. Everyone I had ever loved was dead, and I could not add Alex to that list. It didn't matter what Captain Roth did to me now. And knowing this gave me a new unwavering courage. I would kill him because I had no one left to try and protect. But how?

We followed the path toward camp. The smell of fire drifted in the breeze, and in the distance, the braying of a hound pierced the air. We then turned left, moving away from camp and any detection of other people. A nervous energy bounced off the captain, making me more anxious. Blood rushed through my ears.

"Where are we going?"

"No place too far. I do have to get back to my post, but I have an hour or so before anyone will come and look for me," Captain Roth said. He glanced at me. "And I think an hour will be fine with what I have planned."

"And what is that?"

He stopped short and pushed me up against a tree. "I thought we could finish what we started in the back of your uncle's field." He leaned in and sniffed my hair before planting a hard kiss on my mouth. He bit my lip. "But first, I want to know everything, Nora. I can call you Nora, yes? I'd say we are close enough for that."

"I don't know anything," I said, sucking on my lips. I tasted iron.

"Ah, but you do. I know you do."

Captain Roth backed away and walked to a tree a few feet away. He bent over and laid his pistol next to a burlap sack. He opened it and reached inside. He brought out a rope and a whip. He held the leather switch in his hands like a small child might hold a puppy or a kitten. His fingers stroked it, and his face relaxed into an expression of softness as if he were meeting an old friend.

In one swift movement, he unleashed the whip onto my skin. It lashed out at me as quick as lightning, striking me on my side. I screamed in pain, and with the flick of his wrist, he did it again. But this time, the whip snapped me across the spine as I turned. The scissor clip I had attached to my gown swung and hit my hand.

"Oh, Nora, how I do love to hear you scream."

"Stop! Please," I said, whimpering.

My back and the side of my body burned from where the leather had struck me, but a greater burning filled the pit of my stomach.

The captain came at me, pushing me up against the bark of the tree. It scraped my back, and I cried out in pain.

"If you only knew what your cries do to me," he said, pressing himself up against me.

I kept my hands by my sides as his own roamed my body. With both of his hands fastened onto my bosom, my left hand grabbed hold of the bottom end of the scissors from my scissors clip. I counted to three and took a deep breath then plunged the point into his upper arm.

He jumped back, his face red with anger and snarled in pain.

"You bitch!"

He sprung at me, but I jumped out of the way and ran

toward the tree where his weapon lay against the burlap bag. Without hesitation, I picked up the pistol, cocked it, pointed, and fired.

I watched through a cloud of smoke as Captain Roth fell to the ground. I left everything where it lay and ran.

CHAPTER 31

Sweat dripped down my back as I ran toward Alex. My skin burned from the whip, and my feet ached with blisters. I was only a few yards away from where Alex had been shot when, out of nowhere, a soldier stepped out from behind a tree and caught me by the arm.

I curled my hand into a fist, pulled my free arm back, and tried to punch him, but he caught my hand mid-strike.

"Nora? What the devil?"

"David," I said, gasping for air. "What are you doing here?"

"I'm on patrol. There's several of us out here. You better start explaining now before any more of my unit comes through here."

"Please. You have to let me go. He killed John, and now Alex may be dead and—"

David helped me find my balance. "Who did? Why are you here in White Plains of all places?"

I looked over my shoulder. No one was there. "Captain Roth."

His face paled. "Captain Roth?"

"He killed John, and then he shot my… my husband," I

blurted out.

David opened his mouth and took a few steps away from me.

"I'm sorry to tell you like this. I had to marry. You know I did. I'll explain later when there is more time, but for now, will you help me? Please?"

"This is treason."

"Your best friend is dead, David. Dead. For once, since this bloody war started, will you please be the man I once knew you to be? The man who I—"

"Loved?"

I swallowed not finding my voice but nodded. When David didn't move or say anything, I jogged away.

John was still lying where he'd been shot, but Alex was nowhere, nor was the horse.

"Alex?" I said.

The sun was rising, and a trail of blood lay on the ground through the fog-bearded trees. I followed it. Leaves crunched behind me. I turned to look. David stood over John's dead body. He looked up and began to walk behind me, silent. A small groan came from the right, and I darted toward it. Alex sat next to the horse, holding the tip of the reins. His leg was soaked with blood. His face was pale and his lips were almost blue. The pistol that Captain Roth had made him give up was in his hands. He pointed it at me. The breath seemed to leave him the minute he realized it was me.

"Alex!" I said. I knelt next to him, tears running down my face, and kissed him. "You're alive."

"He barely is," David said behind me. "He's lost a lot of blood. Look how pale he is," he said. "You need to stop the bleeding."

I jumped up and dug inside the sack I had carried on the horse, looking for the extra linen I had brought. Once I found them, I worked as fast as I could, locating the gunshot wounds, which were in his upper thigh and his shoulder. I applied bandages to both of them and prayed they would hold until we made it back to camp. All the while, I explained everything to David.

"I think I killed him, David. I think I killed Captain Roth dead, and I'm not sorry about it either."

"I don't think anyone would be, to tell you the truth, but as a soldier of His Majesty's army, I'll have to go and make sure. I can't leave him there."

"I understand, but I would rather you come with us," I said.

He sat back on his haunches. "I'll help you get him on the saddle, and I'll bury John, but I can't go with you, Nora."

"Why?"

I tied another knot on the linen and looked down at Alex. He was unconscious. I placed my fingers on his neck to check for a pulse. It was there, steady, though faint. David helped me to stand.

"We have — had — a good life here. I see nothing wrong with pledging alliance with the king. God, Nora. What happened to us?" He reached out and stroked my face. I placed my hand over his.

"We grew up."

"As much as I want to see you again, if I do, I won't be able to help you, unless, of course, it is over a mud puddle," he said, bowing.

I bit my lip to keep from crying. One of the first times David had helped me as a lady and not as his best friend's sister was over a mud puddle. He had taken my hand, I'd lost my balance, and we'd both toppled in together.

With David's help, we managed to get Alex on top of the mount. He leaned over in the saddle, his hands hanging limply on both sides.

The pounding of horse hooves approached. I gave David

a kiss on the cheek, and then he helped me into the saddle behind Alex. My horse took a few steps forward when two men galloped into view. They stopped when they spied us. David drew his pistol, but I stuck my hand out to stop him from firing.

"Don't. Please. They are my husband's cousins. They came looking for me, I'm sure," I said as consolation washed over me. "Thank you, David."

He grasped my hand and kissed it. When he looked at me, tears stung my eyes as his own welled with tears. "Go," he said.

Without another word, I spurred the horse on until I reached Si and Gideon only a few yards away. Their faces, which had been red from riding and from the chill of the air, turned white when they saw Alex, who appeared dead, slumped over on the saddle.

Si swallowed, and Gideon closed his eyes, murmuring.

"He's not dead. But he will be if we don't hurry. One of you should jump in behind him because I don't think I can manage both him and the horse," I said, sliding down from my mount.

Si bounded off his horse then climbed up behind Alex. He reached forward and placed his hand near Alex's mouth. "The bugger is still breathing. Thank God," he said. "You have explaining to do. Do you have any idea—"

"Si!" I snapped. "What part did you not understand? We have to get him back to camp. He's lost a lot of blood. Gideon," I said, turning to the other man.

His face had regained some color.

"Do you have a quill and ink in your saddlebag? Paper?"

Both men looked at me, confused.

"Do you? Quick! I have information I need to write down," I said, not bothering to keep the panic out of my voice.

Gideon reached into his bag and pulled out what I needed. "Make it fast," he said.

And I did. I took the quill and dipped it in ink. "Jump down and turn over, let me use your back. This will only take a few moments," I said.

I wrote a series of numbers on the parchment, along with rambling sentences in case the information was confiscated or became lost. It took a few minutes longer than what I'd wanted, but I managed. Si kept looking around for signs of trouble.

"Finished," I said.

Gideon stood up and put the quill and ink back in his bag. He held out his hand, and I gave him the paper. "What does that mean?" he asked.

I took the message from him and folded it. "It means the redcoats plan to attack in two days' time, at night, then they plan on marching to Fort Washington. We have to let the general know. The numbers relate to a letter in the alphabet. I know it looks like a lot of words, but, I only wrote two, night, and general."

"Here," I said, handing it back to him. "I need you to ride as fast as you can to camp and let General Washington know that General Howe plans on ambushing tomorrow night. We have to retreat. We won't survive if we don't. The British are going to reinforce their position on Chatterton Hill. After this attack, they are headed to Fort Washington. He must be warned."

Gideon took the note and stuffed it inside a hidden pocket on the inside of his jacket then helped me get back on Si's mount.

The pounding of hooves thundered a few miles away. I jerked my head toward the sound.

"Gideon! Go! The British are coming!"

CHAPTER 32

Gideon whipped his mount around and galloped off toward the American camp.

"Si? What do we do?" I said. My heart was frantic in my chest.

"Follow me!" he shouted over his shoulder, already riding hard into the cover of trees, off the trail.

I squeezed my thighs against the saddle as we streaked through the woods. I panted along with the horse. It jumped over branches and small bushes while I clutched the pommel. Alex was still slumped over in front of Si.

The sound of muskets rang out and split the air. Both Si and I stopped. The British had followed Gideon. We watched from behind the shelter of the thicket. Five redcoats spurred their horses on after him. They were but a speck on the horizon, and I let out the breath I'd been holding. Si held out his arm to stop me from moving further.

"I don't think any of them are near us, but be quiet to make sure. We'll go slow," he said. His eyes never left the pinprick of his brother in the distance.

Another musket fired, and the dot of Gideon fell off the saddle.

"No!" I said, pushing my horse forward.

Si stopped me, his mouth wide open in horror as a redcoat jumped down from his horse and stood over what could only have been Gideon's body. He then plunged his bayonet.

Bile rose in my throat, and I turned to the side and threw up. "Gideon!" I said, my voice quivering. "He's… he's…"

I let out a strangled cry as I turned and looked at Si. His hands held tight to his cousin as if Alex's seemingly lifeless body was the only thing keeping him in the saddle. *God, no. No, no, no.*

"Why aren't you doing anything?" I said, my voice rising.

Si turned and glared at me. "What would you have me do?"

"Go out there!"

"And leave you here by yourself with Alex, who is bloody unconscious? I'd get killed, and then you'd be alone. Gideon would want me to stay with you. There is time to mourn him later."

I blanched at his words. How could he say that? Why wasn't he screaming or crying? I shut my eyes and took a steadying breath. He was right, but I didn't want him to be. He'd watched his brother die. Killed.

"Nora?" Si said, his voice gruff and gravely. "Stop. They're coming this way. It's a miracle they didn't see us before. Let's not let them find us now."

I opened my eyes and held my breath. The British were coming toward us, but Gideon was not with them. They had left him to the birds but had taken his horse. They galloped past us, several yards away. My hands shook, and it was hard to swallow.

Si and I waited for several minutes afterward in total stillness. What could I say? Nothing. I could say nothing.

Si broke the silence. "Follow me."

I did as he ordered, and we made our way until we were parallel with Gideon's body. Si turned and opened the sack that was on the horse. He brought out rope, then jumped down and secured Alex to the horse.

"Get on here with your husband. I'll be right back," he said.

I scooted off my mount, and he helped me into the saddle behind Alex. I wrapped my arms around his waist, relieved to find him still warm and to feel the rise and fall of his chest. "Where are you going?"

"To get Gideon. I don't think any British are around, but should I be ambushed, you ride straight, and you ride hard. Understand?"

I nodded, and with my chest tight and my cheeks warm with tears, I sat still as Si galloped out into the small clearing and picked up his brother.

CHAPTER 33

Because we had to move at a slower pace to keep Alex from falling off the horse while also trying to protect his wound, it took us over an hour to travel the six-mile distance from our place in the woods to the American camp. We didn't talk the entire way.

I never thought I would find solace in hundreds of white tents, but on this day, I did. With careful steps, Si maneuvered his horse through the camp toward Dr. Aster's medical area.

"Wait here with Alex. I'll go and get Dr. Aster to help. I'll have to let him know about Gideon so he has correct numbers concerning the dead," he said, his face stoic. "Keep him steady as best you can, and we'll help him off once I'm… once I'm…" Si took a breath, and his lips quivered.

"Si, it is fine to cry."

He wiped away the tears that now poured down his cheeks with an angry hand.

"With all due respect to the doctor, I want Alex with us," I said. "I'll ask another soldier to help me get him off and will tend to him at our campsite. Dr. Aster does what he can, but our space is cleaner, and that is of the utmost importance. I will not have him lying around where other men have vomited and—"

Si put his hands up in surrender. "I get it. You know where to go, and you'll be all right until I can get back?"

I nodded. "I just need to clean his wounds and bind him."

"I'll be there as soon as I'm finished," he said. "I have to take the letter you gave Gideon to General Washington. The British never found it."

I struggled to speak but couldn't find the words, so I nodded.

He turned the horse and made his way toward the surgical tent.

I stopped on the way to our tent and asked a man to fetch Major Tallmadge to help me. The young soldier glanced at Alex and dashed across the encampment. *God, I hope he comes fast.*

I reached the small campsite and swallowed. Gideon's bedroll was neatly laid out on the ground, a small cup and plate next to it. I resigned myself to waiting as I knew I would not be able to lift Alex off. I stood next to him and the horse, stroking Alex's leg. Though he wasn't awake, I hoped he knew I was there.

A cough came from behind me. It was Major Benjamin Tallmadge. He was out of breath. He must have sprinted and for that I was glad. I hadn't seen him since my first time at camp. *Christ. That seems like an eternity ago.*

"I do not plan to lose any more friends today, so let's get to it," he said. His lack of emotion rattled me, but I supposed everyone dealt with death differently.

"We need to gently get him off the horse and onto his back. I'll need plenty of water and rum. Or whiskey. Si went to see if Dr. Aster will help. One of the balls is still lodged in his thigh. The other went straight through his shoulder," I said.

He nodded. After we had Alex off the horse, he helped me find the various items I would need and then left saying he'd be back shortly.

I looked down at Alex. Normally, I would have been in a tizzy knowing he was still unconscious, but for what I was about to do, I was glad for it. I unwrapped his bandage. The blood had started to clot, and a small part of me relaxed. I poured water on a clean cloth, and as gently as I could, wiped the excess blood off his skin so I could see better.

For my sanity, I checked his pulse again. It was still there. I took the cap off the bottle of rum Si had given me and poured it over the wound. Alex thrashed as the liquid hit his thigh, and a moan escaped from his throat, but his eyes never opened.

The camp stirred. The sun was now up, the sky an orange-pink color. Frost glistened on the grass, and the breeze gently blew. My fingers were numb, and I feared I would not be able to proceed properly if they didn't warm up.

Heavy footsteps and huffing made me turn my head in time to see Dr. Aster running — or what he considered running — over to me. "Mrs. Foster, I came as quickly as I could," Dr. Aster said.

Si was with him.

"Thank you. I appreciate it."

"I brought the forceps, extra linen, and thread for sutures. Here's another needle if you need one."

I took the supplies from him so he could inspect my husband.

"The ball is still inside. Will you get it out?" I asked.

"*Will* is a much different word than *can*," Dr. Aster said. He peered down close to the wound. "You're in luck. In some situations, it is better to leave the ball. However, in this case, I believe it can be removed. If I move this flap of skin out of the way…" he said, doing exactly that. Alex stirred but did not wake. "…I can see the ball. Thankfully, the sun is up, and we do not have to perform this task at night. Go ahead." He looked at me, and I at him.

"Me?"

"Yes. I've watched you enough. You have steady hands, and it would be good to have another person who can do this. I'll be here to help guide you."

I muttered a quick prayer then poured rum over the forceps to clean them off and took a deep breath. My hand hovered over Alex for a moment before I stuck the forceps inside the wound on Alex's thigh.

His leg jerked, and his eyes popped open. He looked around in a frantic state, his eyes watery and glassed-over.

"Someone hold him steady," I said, steeling my nerve.

Si put both of his hands on Alex's shoulders while Dr. Aster held his legs. Then Si bent over him and spoke soft and low. "We have you, wee Alex. You're fine. Soon you'll be feeling better."

Alex blinked. "Nora? Captain?" His words were barely audible, but I'd heard them.

My throat restricted as I swallowed back tears. *There is no time for crying now.*

"I'm here," I said. "Give him some of the rum since we don't have any laudanum. It will help dull the pain and hopefully, will help him sleep. Deeply."

I turned the forceps to the right. Alex yelped in agony, but I found the ball. Fresh blood welled up and over Alex's skin, dripping down his exposed leg and upper thigh.

"Dr. Aster, I found it," I said.

"Good. Careful as you open the forceps, yes, like that, and

extract the ball. Go slowly. You don't want to damage any more of the tissue than there is already."

With hands as steady as I could make them, I clamped the end of the forceps around the ball. I pulled it out of Alex's body, exhaled, then dumped the metal into a wooden bowl next to me. The ball hit the bowl with a thud as if singing the end on a final note. I wiped his skin clean of the blood then poured more whiskey onto it. It was time for sutures.

After dipping the needle in oil and threading it with string, I had Si assist me in holding the wound closed. I passed the needle back and forth, making a straight line of sutures before I tied each ligature with a double knot. No one spoke as I worked. We all let out a large breath when I finished.

I stretched my neck and cracked my back. Alex had endured the easy part. Now we would sit, wait, and pray fever or infection did not creep in.

For the remainder of the day, I stayed next to Alex, holding his hand. The only assurance was in his breathing and the occasional moan. Every hour, I either checked his pulse or put my hand in front of his mouth to feel his breath. Around dawn, a fever set in, and for the next several hours, I applied cold compresses to his head. I wasn't sure if I should be thankful the weather was now constantly chilly or not. Fear of ague along with his raised temperature tapped at the back of my mind.

The camp was now in full swing, packing their belongings, stomping on fires, and filing north. The men who passed by us were battered, their faces full of weariness and defeat.

It was close to midnight when Major Tallmadge walked over to our tent. Now that I had the chance to fully focus on him, I realized he was in the same condition as most of the soldiers I had met earlier. He hadn't changed, except for the tiredness that etched around his eyes.

"Good evening, Mrs. Foster. I'm sorry to disturb you," he said.

"Major Tallmadge. It is good to see you again," I said. "I trust you are well?"

"Yes. Please forgive my intrusion and please forgive me that it took so long to come and see how Alex is faring. We've been discussing our next move," he said.

I motioned for him to follow me outside the tent so as to not disturb Alex. "I see we are retreating. Where to?"

"We plan on establishing camp near North Castle for now. Si recently came back with news that the redcoats are preparing to attack. Thanks to you, we have almost completely evacuated."

"Glad I could have been of service," I said.

"Yes, well, I know now is not the right time, but I do hope once Alex is clear, you'll consider helping us more."

"You mean spying?"

"Yes. Between you and Nathan Hale, we have avoided some major conflicts. Tonight, for example," he said.

Thunder boomed in the distance, and the wind picked up speed. My hair, which had come unbound, blew in my face. A streak of lightning flashed and crackled across the sky.

"I only provided tonight's details and the information Captain Hale gave me. I hardly did a thing. And, if you do not know, I was almost caught both times, and now Nathan Hale is dead. I'm not convinced any more lives are worth the trouble this spying brings," I said, allowing my frustration to show. I had thought arming the rebels with information would be helpful, but all that it had brought was death. How in the world had that helped?

"Nathan Hale's death is tragic. Not only was he a decent soldier, but he was my friend. I feel his loss deeply, I assure you. But because of the information he gave you, which you passed along to us, hundreds of lives were saved. Nathan knew what he was getting himself into. He believed in it," the major said. He reached into his pocket and withdrew the paper I had written about the immediate attack. "I was surprised to see your code. Tell me, how did you know to correspond in such as way?"

"Major, though I may be a woman, I will have you know my education is more than cooking and mending. I know the Romans used codes. Granted, the encryption I used could be easily broken, but it served its purpose. I knew if I was caught, I'd be hung. So, I figured I would at least prolong my chances by writing the information down this way so if found, it would take the officers a bit longer to decipher it."

"It was smart thinking on your part. In fact, I've been given the task of coming up with an encryption for such purposes because of your idea. I have already begun a code of sorts. Your name is 355."

"My name?"

"Yes. The code name for lady, which is you, is 355. That is how I'd like you to sign your name, or if you ever see that number written anywhere, you'll know the correspondence is for you."

"Major, I did not agree—"

Major Tallmadge raised his hands. "I know. We'll discuss everything with Alex when he is ready. Now, back to you spyi—"

"That decision will be up to my husband, Major," I said, "The only future I am contemplating right now is the next several hours and what that will look like."

"I understand. A wagon should be here any moment to assist you since Alex is unable to move," he said and turned on his heel.

He left, and I took a deep breath before reentering the tent.

The thunder rumbled once again in the sky followed by the lightning. I pressed my hand to Alex's head. He was still hot to the touch. Sweat beaded on his forehead, and the smell of sickness wafted off his breath. I flipped the blanket off him and untied the linen bandage. The wound was beginning to fester. Panic began to rise inside me, but I squashed it down and focused my resolve. I refused to lose Alex to a bloody fever after everything we had endured. *No way in hell.*

I took the small pot of water off the fire that I had allowed to simmer and poured it into a bowl. I would need to wash the wound first before I wrapped it again.

"So help me, Alexander Mathias Foster, if you die on me, I will kill you."

"If I'm already dead, how will you manage to do that?" Alex said. His voice was hoarse, but I nearly burst into tears at its sound.

"You're awake," I said.

"For the moment, though I want nothing more than to shut my eyes. I cannot decide if I'm cold or hot."

He shivered then. "Cold. I'm cold."

I placed the blanket back over most of him, except for his injured leg. "I'll cover this leg in a minute. Your wound is starting to fester, and I need to take care of it before it gets worse. This might hurt."

Alex's blue eyes stared into mine, and for the first time in over twenty-four hours, they were not glassy. They were sharp. "*Might,* you say? Remember that I can read you like a book, Sailor. I know it is going to hurt like hell. What do you mean to do?"

"There is a small amount of puss, so I need to clean it. I have to cut your wound back open and restitch you. I'll do it now before the wagon comes, as I can promise you, you will not want me to do it on a moving cart."

"Get to it then," he said.

I snipped the thread that held his wound together and slid them out of his skin.

Alex grimaced but never said a word.

"Ready?" I asked. I picked up the scissors and doused them with the whiskey that sat by my side.

He nodded.

I blew a few times on the water then poured it onto the wound.

Alex gripped the blanket and breathed heavily through his nose. He grunted a few times but still did not call out.

Before he lost the last bit of his nerve, I poured more hot water onto him followed by the whiskey.

A string of profanities escaped his mouth. It was the first time I had ever heard him take the Lord's name in vain.

I smiled. Alex was going to be fine.

Thankfully, the wagon had indeed showed up a few minutes after Major Tallmadge left. The soldier in charge of driving it assisted me in not only restitching Alex's leg, but he helped me load him as well.

The journey through the hilly woodside was horrible, especially given the pouring rain and the wind. The hay we lay on was soaked through, and everything clung to us. We pressed on, knowing that it was better to be miserably wet than have bullets or cannon fire blasting toward us.

Alex drifted in and out of consciousness the entire five-mile journey. Si traveled on foot next to the wagon the whole time, leading the horses. And when we came to a stop, he set up the tent and helped settle a sleeping Alex inside. Neither Si nor I had discussed when to tell Alex about Gideon. He was hurting as it was, and I didn't want to add to his pain, though I knew it couldn't be helped.

Two hours later, Alex woke. "Sailor?"

"Here," I said. I moved over to his bedroll and sat next to him. I took his hand in mine and kissed it. "Glad to see you awake. How are you feeling?"

"Like I've been shot." He tried to grin. "Where are we? Where are my cousins?"

"We are in North Castle. Si is off seeing to his duties. He's been checking in on you every hour. He's been worried. Everyone has been," I said, my voice quiet.

"You said Si, but what about Gideon? He's more of the mothering type anyway. Where is he?"

I choked back a sob and looked away from him.

Alex reached out and grabbed my hand. "Nora?"

"I'm sorry," I said, my voice shaking. "He was killed."

"How?"

"We were trying to get you back here. A small band of British found us, and Gideon rode into a small clearing. They shot him off his horse."

Alex twisted his head from me. The corner of his eye became wet before a tear fell. He wiped it away.

"Alex, I'm so sorry..." I said, my voice trailing off.

"How's Si?"

I shrugged. "He hasn't talked about it. He hasn't said much actually."

Alex nodded. "Typical Si."

He shut his eyes and took a deep breath. His head turned back around and faced me.

"You said *everybody*. Everybody has been worried. You too?"

"Goodness, Alex. How can you ask that? I haven't left your side! You have no idea what you put me through!"

He tried to sit up, but I wouldn't let him. He glared at me and then sat up again, leaning back on his elbows. He winced but did not lie back down.

"Hmph. What I put *you* through? What the hell do you think I was feeling when you made that bargain with Captain Roth and walked away with him? Did he… did he—"

"No."

"You knew what he did to Laura, and still you—"

"I did it to save you!"

"It's my job to save you. Not the other way around."

"He would have killed you as he had John. I couldn't let that happen." Tears were now streaming down my cheeks. I had held them at bay for too long.

Alex reached out and grabbed my hand. "Why did you do it, Nora? It would have killed me had he touched you," he said.

I swallowed the lump in my throat. "You're my husband. I love you, Alex," I said through the tears. "I never planned on feeling this way, and when you went missing, all I could think of was getting you back. I would travel to hell to find you," I said, surprised by my reaction.

"You love me?" he said. The side of his mouth turned up into a grin.

"I've said so before. Yes."

"I suppose I wasn't certain if you meant it," he said.

"If I didn't mean it, I wouldn't have said it. So, yes. Yes, I love you, you big, stubborn—"

"Come here." Alex reached up and put his hand behind my head and pulled me to him. He kissed me. "I love you too. I've been in love with you, and it's been killing me not knowing—"

"When?"

"Sailor, I fell in love with you the moment we met. I could hardly believe my eyes when I woke up after fainting and found you with me, cursing, no less. Then you fixed my wound with the hem of your petticoat. You are quite the woman, Nora Elizabeth Foster. And I love you. Don't you ever forget it. And please, for the love of all things holy and dear, never try a rescue mission by yourself again."

I nodded and kissed him.

A cough sounded behind us. We broke apart, neither one of us ashamed at being caught.

"I see you're feeling better?" Si said.

"No, not really. I can't decide if I'm hot or cold," Alex said. He tried to swallow, and I put the water canteen to his lips.

"You look hot to me," Si said, his eyebrows rising. He walked over and gently put his hand on his cousin's head. "Good to see you awake."

"Si—" Alex began, but his cousin stopped him.

"I know. I'm not ready to talk about it. Soon."

Alex said no more of the subject of Gideon. "What happened to Captain Roth? How did you get me out, and how did you escape?"

"Remember when you taught me to use your musket?" I said.

Alex nodded.

"Well, after I stabbed him with my sewing scissors I keep on my clip, I picked up the pistol he had laid down and shot him."

"You stabbed him with sewing scissors?"

"Yes. And then I shot him. That's the important part."

"Is he dead?"

"I can't be certain. He fell and didn't get up. I hope he is. He knows I was spying."

"The important thing is you're both safe now. Try not to worry," Si said. He reached into his pocket then walked over to Alex. He dropped the iron ball I had pulled out of his thigh into Alex's opened hand.

Alex gave him a questioning look.

"That's the ball your wife took out of your body. If the bastard isn't dead yet, you can pay him back one day."

Alex narrowed his eyes and considered the ball in his hands. "Thank you. Si? Will you please make sure nobody interrupts us? Nora and I have some things to discuss," he said.

"Hmph," Si answered. He grinned though and gave us a knowing look, before turning around and leaving.

Alex sunk onto his back and stared at the top of the tent.

"What are you thinking?" I asked. I crawled over and lay down next to him, resting my head on his chest.

He kissed the top of my head. "Only that part of me hopes the captain is six feet under, while another part of me wishes I could be the one to shoot this bullet through his heart. He put Laura through something awful, and though it was childbirth that killed her, I still blame him. And you, well..." he said. His voice caught in his throat.

"I'm fine. He didn't hurt me."

"He did too hurt you. And he killed your family. Frankly, I'm not sure how I feel. And we still don't know if he is alive. What if—"

"Alex, I'm not going to live the rest of my life thinking about what if. *If* he is alive, and we have to face him again, so be it. For now, you need to rest and gain your strength, so *if* it does happen, you'll be ready."

"Do you want to know what I am ready for?" Alex asked. His hand brushed down my side, and he twisted toward me. He grimaced in pain, but once he was settled, his face returned to normal.

"You cannot be serious."

"Ah, but I am. If I'm to regain my strength, what better way than for a bit of exercise to help."

"Won't it hurt your wound? What if someone comes in?"

Alex shrugged. "Si won't let that happen. And, I'll gladly suffer for you," he said, a smile playing on his lips.

I patted him gently on his chest. "As your nurse, I'm going to say no, as I want you healthy," I said.

"Making love to my wife is healthy."

"Noted, but not while wounded. We will have plenty of time to make you healthy," I said, smiling. "For now, would you settle for a kiss?"

"Gladly," he said.

Alex kissed me then, long and hard. We were cold, hungry, and in the middle of the American camp, no doubt on the verge of another battle, but Alex was with me, and I knew he would make a full recovery. We would take each day as it came, whether it included spying or not. All that mattered was that we were together.

ACKNOWLEDGMENTS

Goodness. Where to even begin! It takes a village for sure to bring a book to life and I'm so thankful for my small, but dear tribe who has surrounded me with encouragement, support and most importantly, prayer.

Tiana Smith, my awesome, fantastic, wonderful, smart, funny critique partner. You rock! The Petticoat Letters would be nothing without you! Thank you for the brainstorming sessions over Voxer, for your honest comments, for the countless times you kept me off the ledge and for the constant support and friendship. I've learned so much from you and I'm so glad we "met" up years ago. I can't imagine being on this writing journey without you!

Thanks to Heather Anastasiu for reading one of the early drafts of The Petticoat Letters and for all of your insight. Your edits truly helped shaped this story to what it is.

Thank you to my editors and the entire Blue Tulip Publishing team. Thank you for believing in me and The Petticoat Letters; for loving Nora and Alex as much as I do and for taking a chance on them. I am forever grateful to you guys for making this dream come true.

Suz, Jewels, Kelly and Joelle- Thank you for believing in me. Thank you for being my prayer warriors. Thank you for listening to my heart and treating my dreams with respect. Thank you for your excitement and not rolling your eyes when all I wanted to do was talk about writing. I love you ladies!

Mom, Dad, and Bobby. You made me the person I am today. You are the reason I have always dreamed big and learned to persevere even when I wanted to give up. Thank you for teaching me to pick myself up, dust myself off and start all over again.

Brian- Words can't express what your support means to me. From the day we met, you've been on board with everything I dabble in. From music, to teaching, to ministry and now, this whole writing gig. Thank you for listening to my plot ideas (and helping when I get stuck on something!), to listening to me babble on and on about my characters as if they are real people, and for being willing to do countless loads of laundry (even if you put them in the wrong drawers) and for taking on dinner duty (pizza and cereal totally counts!). I love you and can't imagine doing life with anyone else. A big shout out to my four little loves. You inspire me every single day. Being your mom is my greatest joy. I love you.

To all my readers. Thank you! Thank you for being willing to travel to 1776 and spending time with Nora and Alex. It means the world to me. Stay tuned for more as their story isn't over!

Lastly, all thanks and glory to God. He never ceases to amaze me. With Him, all things are possible.

ABOUT THE AUTHOR

Kelly Lyman writes adult historical romance and YA paranormal/fantasy. She has a degree in education from West Chester University and taught 5th grade before deciding to stay home full time. She loves, loves, loves history and can usually be found daydreaming about people who lived centuries ago...that is, when she's not taking care of her four kids. Traveling to Scotland, England, and Ireland are on her bucket list. Skydiving is not. She's mildly obsessed with mint chocolate chip ice cream, peanut butter M&MS, drinking coffee (cream only), and thinks chips and salsa is a perfectly acceptable dinner option. Her favorite color is green and if she could, she would sit on the beach and read all day long.

www.authorkellylyman.com
kellyblyman@gmail.com

CPSIA information can be obtained
at www.ICGtesting.com
Printed in the USA
BVHW031302300320
576362BV00001B/46

9 781986 903035